Waterfalls

Eugene Meskania

For Anne
all Best.
Sept. 2000

Waterfalls

EUGENE McNAMARA

COTEAU BOOKS
TWENTY-FIVE YEARS

This is a work of fiction. Names, characters, places, and incidents either are the product of the author's imagination or are used fictitiously. Any resemblance to actual persons, living or dead, is coincidental.

Edited by Dave Margoshes

Cover image "Waterfall at Yosemite National Park, California, USA" by Chigmaross/Dawson/Superstock.
Cover Design by Minal Kharkar.
Book Design by Duncan Campbell .

Printed and bound in Canada at Houghton Boston Lithographers, Saskatoon, SK, Canada.

Canadian Cataloguing in Publication Data

Eugene McNamara, 1930–
Waterfalls
ISBN 1-55050-162-3

I. Title.

PS8575. N34 W38 2000   C813'.54   C00-920037-1
PR9199.3.M3348 W38 2000

COTEAU BOOKS
401-2206 Dewdney Ave.
Regina, Saskatchewan
Canada   S4R 1H3

AVAILABLE IN THE US FROM
General Distribution Services
4500 Witmer Industrial Estates
Niagara Falls, NY, 14305-1386

The publisher gratefully acknowledges the financial assistance of the Saskatchewan Arts Board, the Canada Council for the Arts, the Government of Canada through the Book Publishing Industry Development Program (BPIDP), and the City of Regina Arts Commission, for its publishing program.

This book is for Margaret

Where there is great love there are always miracles.
One might almost say that an apparition is human vision corrected
by divine love…. The miracles of the Church seem to me to rest
not so much upon faces or voices or healing power coming suddenly
near us from afar off, but upon our perceptions being made finer, so
that for a moment our eyes can see and our ears can hear what is
there about us always.

—*Willa Cather,* DEATH COMES FOR THE ARCHBISHOP

Contents

The May Irwin-John C. Rice Kiss

CONRAD MISSED THE EARLY MORNING showing of the uncut *Greed*. He had drunk too much after the Arthur Penn panel with a bunch of the younger documentary freaks and overslept. He missed breakfast too, although this was academic; his head ballooned, his stomach felt beaten up. He wrapped his raincoat around him and stumbled down the hall towards the shower. A woman in a blue robe went in the door right in front of him. What the hell. No, she was right, the door was plainly marked Women. The other end of the hall. What she must have thought. Had she seen him. The swift way she got in there, the set of her neck, back of head, taut back, trying not to have to acknowledge him.

Paranoid. He caught a glimpse of himself passing a mirror in the hallway. The place was a girls' dorm, empty for the Spring recess and used for conferences like this one, so each hallway was doomed to have a full-length mirror in it for the girls' last minute primp, and he was forced to look into the damn things as he passed them. A well-used forty-year-old face, which he sometimes was able to live with by thinking of Jean Gabin, or Montand, the drooping Zapata moustache which every film maker of his generation wore; why shouldn't the girl in blue avoid him?

The shower room was blessedly empty. No need for the hearty jockstrap banter, or the rehashing of the panels. The shower. He opened himself to it, letting it beat against the back of his wounded head, thinking of nothing for a while. Vittorio Da Sica in the shower. He came out dripping, squinted into the mirror. Dick Powell in *Cornered*.

As he went down the hall, the figure in blue came out of the door down at the other end. She seemed to hesitate, then moved swiftly towards him. She was holding the robe closed at the neck, clutching a plastic bag in the other hand, moving fast. But there was no escape, as fast as they both moved.

"Morning," he said.

"Good morning," with a slight upward tone on the end.

Now he remembered her. She was the one on the Buñuel panel, the one he was sure was a nun from the way she kept her knees together in the dress that was about an inch out of fashion. She carried a cassette tape recorder too, a dead giveaway. And she was about a year out of date on the ideas too, quoting the McLuhan of

Understanding Media, all hot on the Theological Bergman and the obsolete Czech innovations from 1967. Difficult for nuns these days, not hidden under all those black robes, having to have their legs out there with all the other girls' for the men to see. Good idea for a film, a hand-held thing in a new convent. Voice-over and maybe Gregorian chant. But hadn't he seen her before too? Another country? She looked like Emmanuelle Riva.

He had about ten minutes to spare before the showing of the new Kurosawa and the panel on documentary. This was the one he was on. It was a great day, with the sun out, a few fat white clouds, what the hell were they called, cirrus, no, and the campus was as green and beguiling as a thirties movie about Andy Hardy at college. Red brick buildings that went back to the mid-nineteenth century and one ostentatious modern one that had been milked out of the alumni in the fat sixties.

But it would be nice, he thought, startled by two girls, students he supposed, who smiled and said hello, to live in a place like this, out of it, far from everything, no pollution, in the middle of farm country, students like those girls, a little dumb, athletic, probably rode bikes, played tennis. Back at Tecumseh College, where he taught media to grey-faced cynical children of line workers from the plants in Windsor, there was no such innocence. Conrad recognized the stage that his hangover was reaching: the yearning for youth and purity, a desire for white sailboats and blue water.

Emerson Hall was already full of the film people,

pausing to look over the distributors' flyers and cata-
logues in the hallway, peering at their programs, pondering their choices. Simultaneity was the keyword at
the conference. At least three panels were going on at
the same time in different buildings. It was all to peak
tomorrow afternoon in a grand panel discussion called
Postcinema Perspectives, after which they would all
scatter off to the places they taught, eyes smarting, liv-
ers bruised by the late-night post-film winding down.
One fellow stayed up after everybody else finally col-
lapsed, watching Japanese monster movies on a TV set
in a lounge on the third floor.

Conrad made his way down the aisle in the auditorium, nodding to people he knew, or had met, feeling a little more at peace with himself, after all here he was with
his people, men who wore the same moustaches, some
in Peter Fonda shades, the corduroy suits, the burlap
shirts, all texture, all hot, all nonverbal. There was
Peters, who had made a documentary at the age of
twenty of a sixties flower power thing in Vancouver,
shot the whole thing with the lens cap on, whole thing
a blank, had turned it in anyhow to a contest, won a
prize, it was rumored, as an example of anti-film, a soci-
ological comment on the coming end of the peace freak
phenomenon.

And there was the nun in blue, wearing a kind of
suit, wasn't blue, but a sort of white, hair pulled back
from her face, women's lib intellectual style. Skirt wasn't
as long as the one she wore, when had it been? Then he
remembered. Of course, she was the one he had the

argument with last year at the Southern Ontario conference. She had all these silly ideas about reality in cinema, and he had countered with the concept of interference by presence. He remembered the telling point he had made about Flaherty cutting an igloo in half during the making of *Nanook*. God, if that wasn't interference, the presence of art, of forming, what was? Silly broad. Damn nuns with their minds all categories.

But she looked pretty good. Must be exciting for Catholic men these days, seeing the nuns as women. Something there for Buñuel.

"Hello there," she said, smiling. "Feeling better?"

"My God," Conrad said. "Was it that obvious?"

She laughed. She had a nice laugh. Very, very blue eyes too.

"No, no. I guess it's that early morning dormitory look...."

"I should at least get a bathrobe for these conferences," Conrad said as they walked up to the stage. He pulled a chair out for her at the table. Should he? Maybe a male chauvinist thing to do... "I got in the habit of using my raincoat in Europe. Less to pack."

He dropped into the seat next to her, opened his manila folder. Notes looked a bit yellowed, frayed at the edges. He closed the folder. Hell, he knew it all by heart, could do it under water. She was half-twisted in her chair, saying something to the moderator behind the back of the man next to her. The twisted torso showed very nice healthy lungs indeed, yes sir, and the legs were crossed and, though a trifle too heavy for some tastes, suited him; they would do very well. What kind of nun was this?

"Say, this may sound strange – but you may remember the conference last year…."

"How could I forget," she smiled right into his face, a few laugh wrinkles around the eyes, fine and exciting in a kind of Simone Signoret way. "You really blistered me…."

"Sorry about that, no what I meant was I had this impression, call it intuition, or maybe somebody told me, anyhow, I thought that you were somehow connected with a kind of religious order…."

"Oh yes, I used to be a nun…."

"Used…."

"Yes, I was a Sister of Holy Innocents for fifteen years…."

"Uh."

"I'm just Laura Stevens now."

"Miss Stevens."

"Yes, it's Miss."

She was smiling that crinkle-eyed vaguely sexy smile. Convent capers. Awful revelations of Maria Monk.

"Fifteen years," he said in a think-of-that tone.

"I went in when I was very young."

"And came out young too," he said gallantly.

Now the moderator was standing up and introducing them, he heard his own name and smiled out at the audience, kept his legs stretched out and crossed at the ankle under the table, the bottoms of his desert boots exposed to the crowd, nothing to hide, vulnerable, easy, open, his smile under the moustache self-deprecating, the awards, the achievements listed, titles of films, the years of experience in industrial filmmaking, the work in the Army, now the teaching, the work in multimedia, the scholarship, other conferences like this one, all weighed lightly on his shoulders.

Conrad hunched forward when the intro ended, listened to what was said about Miss Stevens, staring down at the table where someone had carved *I will pass this course* into the wood. Taught at Nigel College, which wasn't too far away from Tecumseh. In miles that is. It was a place where second generation Italians and Irish sent their daughters to keep them from the hedonism and the dope smoking boys of the modern world. The girls were kept untouched for as long as possible, pondering St. Thomas in philosophy classes and daring into Graham Greene in English and early McLuhan in what passed for Media. Had written articles and film reviews for various journals, mostly denominational. Was engaged in writing a book about the films of the forties.

This last brought Conrad's head up. It was the area which most interested him, about which he hoped to write his own book. He felt a mixture of interest, desire, and envy. The detective ethos of *Crack-Up*, *Somewhere in the Night*, *Murder My Sweet*, the wet-street symbolism in *Dark Corner*, the whole shaping sensibility of his own youth. What did she know about it? Back then she was probably fumbling with a rosary.

"I read your piece on Chandler in *Dark Cinema*," she

whispered to him. "I thought it excellent."

Before he could reply, the moderator was talking again, introducing him and telling the crowd what they would hear from him. There was a scatter of applause and he grated his chair back, moved to the podium, buttoning his jacket. He started with an anecdote about Don Owens and the making of *A Married Couple*, went into the "Rosebud" device from Citizen Kane being used as "How-it-all-Began" in *Double Indemnity*, tied them together with the McLuhan idea of Poe's working backwards from the conclusion, the fatalism built into the device, the existential model thus created, and went on towards *Gimme Shelter*. He was able to do it all in about twelve minutes and give the impression of leaving out another month of talk. This worked very well with cinemananiacs, who liked to think in montage.

The panel went well. Nobody seemed to be out for scalps. Everybody was very nice, quoting each other, agreeing all over the place. Even the questions were sane and well-mannered, good-natured and open to lots of I'm-glad-you-asked-that extrapolation.

Lunch was right after, and Conrad walked along with Laura and the moderator, who taught TV production and media at a small community college. They compared dwindling enrollments all the way to the dining hall, trading horror stories about friends who were out of work. Laura topped it all with a friend who had left the convent a year after her, had worked in New York, taught in Montana, lost her job, couldn't find another, and finally tried to get back into the convent.

"They wouldn't take her," she said.

"That doesn't sound Christian," said the moderator, who was balding the way some young men do. He looked about thirty. Conrad pushed his fingers through his own hair, which was quite thick and long and going grey here and there.

Lunch was the usual ham and corn, but with a surprisingly good array of salads and cottage cheese. The conversation bounced along nicely, and Conrad noticed how it began to be more of a two-way thing between him and Laura, with the moderator saying less and less, though she kept bringing him back in, for the form of it Conrad supposed.

When they got up to leave, the moderator said he had to get back to the Admin building, and maybe he did, who knows, but Conrad felt gratified. Alone at last, he almost said. More clichés ran through his mind and he suppressed a desire to giggle. We can't go on like this.

They walked over to the Otis Building where a special showing of *Sunset Boulevard* was to be followed by either a discussion of the Fifties mystique or a car pool into town by the more daring who had located a beer and peanuts pub. Conrad wondered all through the movie if she would stay or go. The nun and the woman must war in her.

As William Holden floated face downward and Gloria Swanson swooped down the staircase right into the camera lens, Laura whispered, Are you going into town? and he said Yes without thinking and she said Let's go before the lights go on, and they were down the aisle and at the back door pushing past a group of people who looked, Conrad thought, disapproving, as if they knew where they were going, and out down the hall, and he felt himself grinning, the wonderful feeling of freedom, like cutting classes in high school to go to the movies. It wasn't until they were in his car and out of the campus parking lot that it struck him that it had happened so easily.

"I've always found that sequence with the key chain too intrusive," Laura said.

He was having trouble passing a pickup truck. The truck had a leaping fish decal on its door and the owner's name and his wife's name.

"Well. Uh. Of course there is so much gothicism in it, all that Von Stroheim organ playing...."

"Well, I've always felt that too much emphasis has – Well, take all the *Graduate* comment on Mrs. Robinson, the vampiric theory – when all along what she needed was simply love...."

"It's so simple."

"Yes. Exactly, just as she said...."

So that was it, he thought. A Carné romantic. No wonder she left the convent. He felt a faint rush of rising desire, threw a quick look at her profile in the neons from the shopping plaza, tried to see her legs, her face was composed and thoughtful.

There were two tables of film people in the pub, which was mostly teenagers and a rock group which seemed determined to deafen everyone in the room by closing time. They squeezed in with Peters and the moderator, who was named Frank something, and some of the National Film Board people, whom he did not fear because he kept firmly to the belief that they were all queer.

It wasn't long before group conversation was given up to the assault of the rock group, and after a few shouted remarks, they broke into two-way head-to-head discussions. Laura went on with her romantic revisionism, rewriting movies, putting happy endings on them, quoting Buber, talking about the power of Nature and the Inner Self, was she a Zen freak, what the hell had happened to Catholics? It began to dawn on him that her book on the forties would be no threat. She was turning off all those neon signs which blinked into the cheap hotel rooms where Sterling Hayden or Dane Clark lay smoking and staring at the ceiling. She was building playgrounds for the Dead End Kids and sending John Garfield to summer camp.

"More beer," Peters cried, beating a fist on the table and waving to the waitress.

"Don't you think she looks like Ella Raines?" Frank said.

The waitress looked bored, which was her role.

"Who's she?" she said. Conrad nodded, that was right too.

"Before your time dear," said one of the NFB people.

"Watch for her on the late show," Frank called after her, as she twitched her butt gracefully between the chairs, swaying the tray in disdain above the bent heads at the tables.

"The movies have been my whole damn life," Conrad said. Laura nodded in sympathetic agreement, though he wasn't sure she really understood. "I mean, I think the movies lived my life and what I do isn't really life – I mean it's a movie...."

The waitress was putting the pitchers down and Conrad made a supreme effort not to look at the buttock which swished next to his cheek; that would convince Laura of his sincerity.

"I may even have been conceived at the damn movies, I mean – my parents used to talk about nothing else, I was raised on stories about movie palaces of the twenties, and Bebe Daniels, Doug and Mary – it was like a whole nexus, a corpus of myth...."

"Last call," the waitress said, and they shouted a double order, Frank asked if they had anything to eat, she said the kitchen was closed, they ordered peanuts and the rock group made one final attempt to destroy them.

Finally they were all out on the sidewalk, talking too loud, laughing a lot and Peters said they all had to get up at three AM to see all the Tracy-Hepburn movies, and they went to their cars and Conrad wasn't too sure how to get back, but Laura remembered that right turn, no, that wasn't it and they went down some silent streets, past lilac bushes in bloom, Victorian houses in excellent condition, all the gingerbread carefully painted, he felt the after-peak peace, relishing the silence, the lights hitting the overbranching trees, a pretty woman close to him and he pulled over, the radio was playing something nostalgic from the fifties, he cut the ignition and the lights and turned to her and they kissed and her mouth opened by god, just like the shock of the teen forties, phrases like bare boob and make out flickered in his mind and she said softly, we'd better get back I think they lock the dorm at one....

It was easy now, just a right turn, and down a few blocks, he felt a funny kind of confidence, and there they were back at the campus, and he drove with one arm around her, James Dean for gods sake and Natalie Wood.

They were both giggling and shushing one another and into the dorm, Let's neck in the hallway he whispered and she doubled over laughing, and then they were in the hallway outside her room and he had his arms around her, her whole body swayed against him, he realized that she was a bit drunker than he had thought and they were kissing deep, how the hell could he make the next step, get her into the damn room, a door opened down the hall, voices, people walking, he swerved his back towards them, bent his head deeper into the kiss, her arms locked around his neck, he felt the steps coming closer, the voices stopped as they passed, would they recognize him by his back?

"We better go in," he whispered. "They can – there are people...."

She nodded, kissed his cheek near his ear and stepped back. She frowned into her purse, came up with the key, and probed at the lock, another door down the hall opened, for gods sake why aren't they all in bed, he pawed at the key, but she had it, they pushed in, he eased the door shut. She slumped down on the edge of the bed.

"I'm so tired, I don't think I can even get my shoes off," she mumbled.

"Here, let me," he bent down, then knelt, lifting one foot, then the other, she fell back, her skirt slewed around above her knees, he bent forward, kissed her slack open mouth, she mumbled Wha? and he knelt down again, pushing her skirt further up, she was wearing nylons, and a garterbelt, hadn't they heard of pantyhose in the convent? Conrad felt a quivering excitement. Legs in the moonlight, a bit too heavy for some tastes, but for him they were a ripe metaphor of Dietrich in *Blue Angel*. He pressed a reverent kiss on her bare thigh, tried to push her legs up on the bed, she groaned, rolled over on her side, he tried opening the jacket, one breast flopped into his hand, she said something he couldn't make out, he said Laura? Dear? and squeezed the breast, bent to kiss her neck, and fell off the edge of the bed.

One of her shoes was under his hip. He pulled it out. A soft snoring came from the bed above him. The moon fell across the room, lighting on the bare cork bulletin board where some coed had hung Jimi Hendrix or whoever it was these days. He pulled himself up, swayed above Laura for a moment, then lay down gently at her side. Her breath was a not unpleasant mixture of something sweet and beer.

FOR A MOMENT Conrad did not know where he was. He was on his back, a nyloned leg was across his thigh, a bare expanse of female thigh lay open to his gaze, a few dark strands of hair were pasted to his cheek, some tangled in his moustache. His head, poor thing, hurt as much as yesterday, which was like some other life, movies ago. Had he missed breakfast again?

He couldn't wake Laura up. She just kept curling deeper into a fetal ball and mumbling something he couldn't make out. So he finally left, hunching down the hall, doors kept opening, voices and footsteps coming down from the floor above, where was his damn key, he made it with not a moment to spare, he heard the voices and a door opening right behind him...someone said something that sounded like disgrace and carrying on like....

The shower wasn't as helpful as yesterday. He had passion cramps too, just as in 1946, or was it '47. He thought about all the thrashing around on Laura's bed, like Tony Curtis and Jack Lemmon in *Some Like It Hot* and snickered, he'd have to tell Laura that, put it in perspective, hell, they were both grown-up, one strike and you're not out – he remembered Kirk Douglas rising from the canvas. In his mind, William Holden stirred, began to swim to the side of the pool, pull himself up, his suit running and sodden, but he was alive.

Back in his room, fumbling through his bag for another shirt, god his suit was a wrinkled ruin, he brushed at the jacket, would it look okay with those denim trousers, then he noticed the time, shook his wrist with the watch on it, peered closer. It was only 7 AM. He had two hours before the morning showing of

Z and the discussion of political statement in cinema. He wasn't on again until the afternoon panel. Maybe they could skip Z and just stay in. Her room. And.

He hurried down the hall, knocked softly at her door. No sound at all, maybe in the washroom. He stood in the hall for a few moments, paced back, looked in the mirror, godalmighty, ran his fingers through the hair, a little better, maybe sunglasses, where the hell were they, he tugged the jacket lapels down. Someone came out of the washroom, wasn't her, went the other way. It was really too early. He went back to his room, lay down on the bed, but he was wide awake, the headache gone, shrunken into the middle of his brain, leaving his limbs galvanized, jerking a little with each outside peripheral stimulus.

He waited until eight, went back down the hall, which was full of people coming and going, doors banging, the washroom doors swinging, good mornings, hellos, sleep wells? echoing, he smiled hello a little shyly at a few people, self-consciously knocked at her door. Still no answer.

Finally he went over to breakfast. Lots of coffee and a few danish, he poked the eggs around on the plate for a while, looking up quickly as each newcomer came in. Peters came over, said something about the dark glasses, laughed about something from the previous evening, still no sign of her, maybe she had a heart attack or died of throwing up or something, could he ask some woman to go in....

She wasn't at the showing of Z and the discussion

turned into an ugly fight between convinced factions. Luncheon was chicken with peas followed by red jello. He went for a frantic and determined walk all the way back to the dorm. Still no answer.

He was almost late for the panel. There was only one place left at the table, at the end. The moderator, a wry looking grey-haired man this time whom he didn't know, was gathering his papers together and obviously about to get up. He hurried down the aisle. She was sitting at the opposite end of the table, looking through her notes. Had a blue skirt on and some kind of sweater. He went hurriedly past the back of the panel, pulled his chair out just as the moderator rose.

He half heard the introduction, which was mostly these who need no introduction, but then seemed to be about the relation of truth and the authentic in film, the integrity of the artist, the camera's refusal to compromise and the new, what the hell had he said, romanticism?

Peters was responding, and doing well, he thought, with some basic stuff on the documentary thrust, *Woodstock* and new consciousness, which came first? and somebody else down the tale went on with some stuff about Cassavetes and before he knew it, he was talking too, this time about certain obsessive metaphors in NFB documentaries, mainly the fishing village in the Maritimes variety.

"It's just this sort of thing," Laura was saying, "That I meant yesterday when I said it was destructive rather than constructive.... I mean a kind of clinical, cold un-loving manipulation – like books on sex and marriage –

which is ultimately going to emasculate cinema...."

She went on and it began to grow in Conrad like a cold fist that it was he she was talking about, that this was a kind of delayed answer to last year's argument, that she may have planned this answer for a whole year, and he had absolutely nothing to say in response, and maybe it was in revenge for last night, but for what, nothing had actually....

He realized that she had stopped on a kind of up tone, a question. The other panelists were all turned, looking at him.

"Uh. Sorry," he cleared his throat. "Would you mind repeating...."

"I simply asked if you thought cinema might finally reach a point – which you might find admirable and desirable – where cameras could be computerized, set off by timers, film spliced by machines according to formula...."

"Uh. No, no, I never said that," he began to mumble.

"Well, you certainly gave that impression," she said in a kind of cool drawl. "In your piece in *Cahiers* on Kubrick, you seem to move towards an anti-auteur position, which I for one find repellent...."

Conrad's confusion bagan to churn into a glowing anger.

"Just a minute," he said.

"I mean there seems to be a kind of denial of person – of a whole dimension of interiority...."

"What the hell does that –" he began to shout, "Person – maybe you should define that – for godssake – maybe your view of the whole damn world is different from mine – or anybody else's – anyway isn't that the whole damn point –" He pushed his fingers through his hair, frowning down at the table. He could sense a kind of shocked silence, looked down the table, she was smiling pleasantly, coolly at him, in a detached way.

"I mean," he said in a quieter voice, "that my view of film isn't the final word, I don't think any mono-theory of film can be, and I certainly never, ever want to see film become some kind of robotized thing – God no! I love it too much…."

There was a burst of applause which startled him, he looked open-mouthed at the crowd, and then it all was smoothly wrapped up by the moderator, who it turned out, taught English at the college here and had no ax to grind in cinema at all. Admirable moderator. As the panel stood up, clutching their manila folders, one of them with an old green bookbag, he tried to inch down the stage towards Laura who was talking with animation to a younger man in a green corduroy suit.

"The ultimate truth," she was saying, "will out, and he'll be discovered to be…."

"Laura, I wanted, I tried this morning…."

"Conrad," she laid a swift hand on his arm. "I want to tell you that I harbour no ill feelings about last year's Flaherty thing…." And she smiled a dazzling crinkle-eyed smile and turned away from him, still deep in conversation with the younger man in green. Well, well. Conrad moved slowly down the aisle away from the stage. Wonder if they ever show movies in here.

Outside it was still daylight. The film people were

hurrying to their cars. The weekend was over. Nuns with cassettes were going to wherever it was they played them back, the NFB boys were perhaps going to Ottawa to report on how successful they had been, perhaps that nut, whatsisname, was going home to see what Raf Vallone movies were on TV all night. Maybe they were all going to different movies. He walked easily across the pretty green campus towards the dorm. Robert Donat. All my boys.

There were always movies to go to. He smiled to himself, perhaps it looked like Alan Ladd's smile in *Blue Dahlia*, perhaps not. Movies flickered in his mind, Joseph Cotten watching Valli walk past him in the autumn Viennese cemetery, Robert Montgomery entering a restaurant with his topcoat thrown over his shoulders, Dana Andrews swiftly suppressed smile at Gene Tierney, John Garfield's self-rueful smile, half defiance, half hurt, yes that was it, Love Finds Andy Hardy, that long dead couple whose kiss arrested the world. The clouds still raced across the blue sky. He could be home before the last show at the Odeon. What was playing? It didn't matter. Whatever it was, it would do just fine.

The conference had begun with some rare old Edison kinetescopes, the man sneezing, the man tipping his hat, repeatedly, over and over, bowing to watchers over seventy years later. Funny how the past lives again, he thought, is made to live again, over and over, relentlessly. Perhaps that was why he loved movies: they were an ultimate denial of time and death. But not of love. No, never of love.

The Search for Sarah Grace

"A PIECE OF INGENUITY PURE AND SIMPLE," Lloyd quoted. "A cold artistic calculation, an amusette to catch those not easily caught."

"To catch those not easily caught," he repeated. "Surely James must have had Boticelli's model in mind when he named the child Flora. Or even if he had not, the effect is the same. In the neoplatonic system, Venus is at the centre, the power of love, the three Graces and the god Mercury and the wind Zephyrus are all to the sides, at the edges, preparing the way for the coming to flower, the coming of Flora, the coming of love."

The others in the seminar listened with increasing bewilderment. It was so plausible. It was so persuasive. Why had no one thought of it before?

"The men are absent," he went on, "yet still oppressive. Only little Miles is with the women. The little man. Perhaps a pun on the male organ. But certainly 'Miles' as name qua evokes Miles Standish, that earlier American stalwart of Puritan rectitude and repression, the love that dares not speak for itself. Examples abound of the governess' antipathy to him and her corresponding and increasing attraction to Flora. Without Miles the three women would have a Sapphic paradise. With him, there is only the stasis of unresolved desire. And that is the reason for the final turning of the screw, the final dissolution."

Dr Wellman cleared his throat, dangerously.

"Examples abound," said Lloyd. "Page three-fifty. 'The attraction of my small charges was a constant joy.' Earlier, page three-thirty-nine, 'The little girl – blah blah – appeared to me on the spot a creature so charming as to make it a great fortune to have to do with her. She was the most beautiful child I had ever seen, and I afterwards wondered that my employer had not told me more of her. I slept little that night.'"

"But surely –" Sue cut in.

"'I was too excited,'" Lloyd finished the quote.

"Page three-forty," he went on. "'It had been arranged – blah blah – that after this first occasion I would have her as a matter of course at night, her small white bed being already arranged, to that end, in my room.'"

"And her language, when she fears that Flora has been lost to her ghostly first love, Miss Jessel, is right out of the penny dreadful lexicon of abandoned lovers: '...I must have thrown myself on my face and given way to a wildness of grief. I must have lain there long and cried and sobbed....'"

There was more, and Lloyd laid it out like a winning

hand in a game, card by card, precise and cool. The others objected, Sue subsided into a thoughtful silence, Wellman shuffled his notes. Olinka, who was working on next week's seminar said that maybe he'd have to rethink his Hawthorne: maybe little Pearl was a baby prostitute, Hepzibah Pyncheon was a closet lesbian, Olinka laughed at his own wit, nobody else did, Wellman looked grave.

Lloyd waited until everybody else had gone and fell into step with Sue.

"You really take chances," she said. "Wellman won't appreciate this."

"Isn't he a scholar? Doesn't he want to advance the cause of scholarship?"

"I had the impression that *you* didn't. You once told me it was all bullshit."

"It is, Susan, it is. I don't believe a word of it."

Sue stopped, laid a hand on his arm. "You will be visited," she said, "by three spirits. Expect the first at...."

"Susan," Lloyd said with mock sincerity burning in his eyes, "All I want to do is survive and get a job and get tenure and marry you and wear rusty tweeds like Wellman."

"Three spirits," she said. "Expect the first at...."

Only one spirit arrived.

It was a female ghost.

SARAH GRACE, BORN 1901, Windsor, Ont. Called Sandwich then. After Earl of S.? Married Douglas Murray 1921. He was a veteran of War. Divorced 1927. No children. She went to Spain 1932. Lived Majorca after Civil War (Graves there? Know?) She was correspondent for Socialist paper during late thirties. (Name of paper?) Met Hemingway. Malraux. H's letters? Paris late thirties. Left before 1940. Back to Majorca during w.w. II. Back to Canada late forties. Fifties gets job college in US. Denied visa because of red past. There was lots of McCarthyism then. College in Ohio. Went to England. Came back to Canada in sixties. Now in Toronto?

To Bake Our Bread, Editions Neuve, 1938 (poems)
Brothers Keep, Thornprick, Majorca, 1947 (poems)
The Mirrored Room, Kegan Paul, 1955 (novel)
Minotaur's House, Locke Press (Regina?) 1955 (out of print)
Theatre Pieces, Icarian Folio Press, 1960 (London, Prose poems.)
Collected Poems, Quartz Press, 1968

She was a socialist. There were lots of people in thirties with social consciousness. What happened between 1901 and 1921. 1921 to 1932. Why divorce. Grounds. Why she expelled from Roedean (1912?) Under a cloud. Sent down. Like Miles in *Turn*. Maybe something there. Any pattern in works arranged chrono. And that face in ad from twenties by Leyendecker. All those men with clean firm jaws, eyes so fine, all manliness, one woman, all willow and all eyes, cupidbow lips, clothes limp with success. Supposed to be her accord to Ada Young in memoir (*Not Wanted on the Voyage*, Boni & L, 1931, pp. 119-121). But could hardly be. All her socialist ideas, posing for capitalist ads. But always this connection with artists. Patterns there? Legend that Sarah centre of art cult in 1912-13. (Same time as Roedean scandal?) Painting by Felicien Rops (or school of?) a circle of evil naked children surrounding a priapic statue. How could parents permit. Where did this rumour start. Where is this Painting. No mention of it in any standard work on Felicien Rops.

But also said that she posed for C.D. Gibson. "One saw in the child's eyes," Gibson supposed to have said (*My Life in Art. Conversations With Contemporaries*, Colin Judd, Coffin Press, 1939) "The clear innocence of the old habitant... Promise of new hope for tired old world...."

Check on this: Long naughty Poem by distinguished old respected poet just before death. She? But it was 1911. Too young?

In the androgynous style of the day, the boys looked like girls, the girls could have been pretty boys. All the hair hung in dark ringlets, daisies garlanded their soft brows and in the centre of the circle stood a child more beautiful than any. A look of radiant illumination, of sudden insight transfigured her face, which was turned slightly upwards. It was a typical work of the period, with a blend of the genteel erotic and the religio-sentimental. It was tinted with a queer ambivalence. Something was lurking in the eyes of the circling children, a hint of a lewd grin shaded the corner of this or that mouth, a muslin covered buttock rounded a bit more maturely than usual for the subject, a pink-tipped preadolescent breast peeped out of an opened and wanton blouse. Only the luminescent child in the centre escaped the aura of knowing evil and sexuality. I thought the title was *Sarah's Trial* or *Sarah's Initiation*, but now think it was simply *The Initiation*. The child was a great favourite of that smart circle. She was from someplace in Canada, and was at Roedean.

HARLAN SELF, *Lines Brief and Otherwise,*
LONDON, 1927

And in the atelier, Lloyd thought, high ceilinged, dim, dusty, shot through with golden light, stacks of canvasses against the wall, the painter in a loose smock and large felt beret, Sarah at rest on a stool for the moment just before tea and biscuits are to be served. The light on the folds in her white linen dress, in her hair, her solemn eyes dreaming, thoughtful. Hands clasped in her demure child's lap. The remarkable eyes alive in the high windowed light. The painter's hand, unaccountably shaking. Someone else, a visitor in the shadows, on a chair in a corner, morning-coated, gnaws at the silver handle of his cane. *A child*, he thinks, *only a child. And yet....*

"HARDLY GERMANE," Dr Gregory frowned at the notes. "I'm afraid that you haven't really come to grips with Sarah Grace. All this surmise – even if you were to deal specifically with early work – *Is* there anything before *To Bake Our Bread?* Wellman told me of ah, your penchant to ah rush into conjecture especially in these ah fringe areas. No no no no Edison, you just have got to ah *something* to the sticking post and leave all this biographical...."

English 660.
MINOR CANADIAN POETS BETWEEN THE WARS
Dr Gregory. Tues. 4-6
Seminar Topics:
Sarah Grace. (Lloyd Edison)
Raymond Knister. (Susan Moog)
Robert Finch. (Emily Hodgson)
L.A. MacKay. (Robert Olinka)

"I DON'T SEE HOW you can say anything about a person's life," Susan said. "I mean *really*. I mean so much is left out...."

"I do have all these facts," said Lloyd. "Listen. Born 1901. Father either a brutal tycoon or a captain of industry, depending on your political bent. Mother a social doyenne. Born in Windsor, Ont. Family moved to England 1910. Maybe 1911...."

"That's just paper. Dates and things. I mean did she have a headache on some day in 1939? What day of the week was it? OK, you might find that out. But did she enjoy dinner that day? If she said so to somebody, couldn't she have been lying? If she said so in her diary, maybe she was lying there too? Did she have lovers?

When did she fall in love with one and out of love with another? I mean the *precise* moment. The rest is crap."

LLOYD'S SEMINAR PAPER was a straightforward, workman-like explication of *To Bake Our Bread*. He received an A-. He received his degree and went looking for a job. He didn't find one. Sue moved out West. He discovered that he missed her.

"It was always raining in Windsor."
– SARAH GRACE IN CONVERSATION (1937)

LLOYD CAME IN on the afternoon train. They were distilling or whatever it was they did at Hiram Walkers and clouds of malt-smelling stuff hung over the station. The rain was steady, rough, falling in veils of fat water. The cab driver was equally morose. The brief reference in Wyndham Lewis had been enough to bring Lloyd here, and a letter to the archivist had given him grudging though lukewarm permission to search.

("...Farley, Jenney and that whole Grace crowd pompously deeding their 'papers' to the College...." Unpublished letter from W. Lewis to Noel Ryder, all rights reserved, Ryder Family Trust.)

HE WAS VERY OLD and claimed to remember all of the chief events during his reign as archivist.

"Yes yes yes yes," he looked closely at the bunch of keys. "Wyndham was here and then Marshall and the War started ah…."

He inserted a key into a door which was inconspicuous in a long hallway of innocent mundane offices.

"Watch your head," he said. "It's quite steep."

Lloyd followed him, groping for a handrail, there was none. The stairs descended at a dangerous pitch. And then they were in the tunnel. Steam pipes clanked overhead. It was very stuffy. A deleterious dankness salted the walls.

"Of course the man Grace – Colonel Grace – he married into the Le Canard family. They were beautiful girls, beautiful. Used to drive around town in one of those electric cars. Dressed like princesses."

Piled all along the walls of the tunnel, the discards of a century half blocked their progress. Ink-stained school desks, gold-framed portraits of dead bishops, a framed photo of the Rhetoric Class of 1901, the football team of 1913, burst files of deeds, flaking bundles of long-settled accounts, dusty sprung chairs were arranged along the walls in a seemingly random order. Lloyd bumped into a mouldy couch, stepped on a cracked plate.

"And then Colonel Grace came to town. From the West I think. Swept her off her feet – the younger Le Canard girl – now what was her name – watch your step there…."

The tunnel ran in the general direction of the river and seemed to descend, gently but perceptibly, as they went on. Low-watted light bulbs were set in the ceiling at fixed intervals.

"Ah and then the little girl…."

"Sarah?" Lloyd said.

"I don't think that was her name. Alicia? Alice?"

"Did they have more than one daughter? Maybe sisters?"

"No no there was just the one child. They were very generous back in the early days. That would have been the twenties…"

"No," said Lloyd. "The time I'm talking about must have been 1905 or 6. The family moved to England about 1910."

"1910?"

The old man's face in the dim light looked foolish and puzzled.

"Well. She was a beautiful girl all the same. Little princess. I was a little boy and I used to watch her in her car. All in white."

It was obvious that whatever the papers might reveal, Lloyd would gain nothing from the old man's confused memories.

"Just duck your head here…."

The low doorway led off to the right. One of the bulbs was out, leaving half the room in darkness. Bundles of newspapers, filing cabinets, papers in cardboard boxes, how could the old man remember where anything was. Archivist. What a joke. Fool's errand.

"Hmm. Locked."

The bunch of keys was produced again. More peering and fumbling in the uncertain light and then the file drawer squeaked open. The old man shuffled the files.

"This is it. It was opened in 1954. That was the terms of the gift. Not much though. Long time to wait for nothing."

Lloyd took the fat folder and held it under the lone bulb. Letters. 1897. Handwriting in school-approved feminine loops. "My dearest one –" 1900. Too early. "We returned from the lakes yesterday –" 1902. Business correspondence from a brewery. Part of a journal. Same handwriting? 1904. "Cold today. William returned from trip –" No mention of child.

Lloyd sat down on a bundle of newspapers. He kept on. No birth announcement. No steamship ticket receipts. No letter from Roedean. Nothing to prove that Sarah had even existed.

Lloyd realized that the old man had not spoken for some time. He looked up from the file to find that he was alone. The dark side of the room seemed to extend on for a yawning gulf of space.

"Hello?" he said. The word sounded dull and heavy. He set the file down and went back into the tunnel. Which way? The tunnel stretched in both directions further than he could see, light bulbs marching off to both vanishing points. There no longer seemed to be a slope to the floor. He turned right. No. They had turned right into the room. Or was it left? He kept on. The bulbs seemed to dim as he walked. He banged his shin against an old lectern. Cobwebs fell over his face.

Then suddenly there was no more tunnel. A wall of

earth filled the corridor. Possibly a cave in. The other way. He turned. Would he see a white rabbit? And a little girl all in white with long blonde hair. A princess in an electric car. He tripped over some bulky thing and fell headlong. The smell of age rose from the damp floor, as if the walls were gradually, patiently crumbling away, adding layer on layer of time past on the floor. He got up, brushed himself off. The smell remained.

Despite the evidence of mundane everydayness, the light bulbs, the steam pipes, he began to feel an increasing sense of quite irrational panic. An impending encounter with something very old – And then he was at the stairway. No one was in the hallway when he came up. The old man was nowhere. Outside, the rain had stopped. Everywhere, the sun shone on the ordinary grass.

THE POEMS IN *To Bake Our Bread* (Editions Neuve, Paris, 1938) are mainly from her Spanish period, after her divorce from Douglas Murray. After her divorce from Douglas Murray she went to Spain. She went to Spain after her divorce.

The poems in TBOB, in the Lorca style, are bitter in tone, filled with anger. Know Lorca? Check on this.

Photograph in newsmagazine of period. Looked like an aviatrix, hair a tight cap of blond ringlets. Like Maria in *For Whom the Bell*. A man's shirt, open at the neck, jodhpurs, boots. Standing between two men dressed in

Spanish khaki war outfits. Rumours linked her to Hemingway. Maybe model later for Maria. Another photograph of her, same outfit, with fellow reporter for *Canadian Socialist*.

THE WORK OF THE FORTIES shows a different thrust. Poems collected in *Our Brothers Keep* (Thornprick, London, 1947) exhibit show develop a more – employ – a more subtle range of technique as well as a bent towards liberalism, away from doctrinaire socialism, and in general exhibit show employ a quieter tone are more reflective (philosophical) and thus demonstrate again the move from protest to acceptance.

Lloyd considers Sarah in her manifestations:
Alice (1911. In Wonderland. Wonderchild.)
Semele (1913? Salambo, Salome etc.)
Amelia Earhart (1930s. Boyish activism.)
The White Goddess (1940s. Myth and all that.)
?

IN 1968, SARAH GRACE'S *Collected Poems* came out. Lloyd read it through. Yes. She did move from the early protest mode to the "period of acceptance" and on to myth and a complex use of archetypes. Things were looking up. What had begun as a "minor" poet between the Wars was shaping into a possible Major. It cried out for a definitive edition.

IF I AM AWARDED THE GRANT, I intend to go to London to study the work on deposit at the Workmen's Alliance Library, in London. These comprise not only poetry, but short fiction from various little and literary magazines of the period, manuscripts of unpublished work and other papers. I have written to Ms. Grace to ask her permission to do this and have little doubt that....

My Dear Mr Edison (Such an illuminating name!) I am somewhat surprised and flattered that anyone would want to take the time – waste I would have put, though that sounds overly harsh – to go through all that dead matter. But eheu, my young, if you must, if you will, you must....

If you are ever in Toronto, and had the time, we might have lunch.

Had the time! In Toronto! There it was, in actual blue ink. A sinuous *S*, a line to a stile of an *h*, a caracole of a G a hiss of a *c* and a blending final *e*. She existed. Tangible.

HER PARENTS HAD DIED. Mother 1926. Father 1940. She lived in England in semi-detached off Brompton Road. Roedean founded 1884. No 1885. Present building not there then. "Dean" à la "dune" after general topographical etc of area. Girls used to bathe in the sea. Play field hockey. Sarah running, showing innocent leg. Maybe not so innocent. Seashore influence?

She was denied a visa to the United States in 1952, presumably because of her 1930s political activities.

Theatre Pieces (1955) were highly complex poems,

style of Pound Eliot. Personae. Masks. Histrionic stuff. *Minotaur* (1960) likewise.

No. *Theatre Pieces* is 1960 and *Minotaur's House* 1955. Why earlier book more mythic, Jungian etc. and later one more obscurantist? Maybe earlier book is actually *later* poems, next book perhaps *older* stuff? Read novel.

LLOYD DISCOVERED A CHAPBOOK in a book-seller's catalogue.

Strange Relations, Broadside Production Company, 1970. Grace, Sarah. Limited and signed. Lloyd paid fifty dollars out of his grant money for number 201. Same signature. One long poem. Style of *Minotaur's House*. Lot of veiled significance. Double entendres. Does "mouthing the dark salt of you" mean fellatio? Any of this in Frazer? Corn god business? He rubbed his finger over the inked number 201. And the name. Her hand had done this.

In that room so walled with mirrors, the man pursues still the silver image of her. Vision within vision in the cold glass, dwindling into infinity. She seems bloodless, an icon, yet her breath which he remembers clouds the mirrors. Still her presence. Still he persists, pressing against the obdurate cool surface with his whole body until his blood cools to the temperature of the glass.

Later he sleeps and something noiseless

glides to his side. So much wine had blurred the candles at dinner. He dreams of the room full of mirrors. He sees his image, repeated, falling forward towards her. Under, far under. He moans in his sleep. Someone soothes him. A white hand encounters him. He groans deep and rises to meet the hand, fill the hand with his rising flesh, rising, rising.

FROM The Mirrored Room, P.48.

DEAR LLOYD:

It is late summer in Ontario and the tomatoes are much in and the Americans are lining up at fruit stands and searching for the home-baked bread. Do you remember the summer you were finishing the last seminar paper and you sat in your underwear and no shirt at the card table at the open balcony door and my air conditioner was broken like my heart you bastard.

What I started to say was that it was a day of high bright and no clouds and I was bothered by this vague sense of – what? I made a little list of make-work things to do. I remember your presence in my life.

A girl from California has interrupted this to leave me a late paper in a blue folder. I was remembering you....

As I write this I'm in a crowded room. Actually I'm alone but the room is small and full of books and papers and coffee cartons and a stapler. Nice lovely machine, this stapler. You press it down and it binds things together. Separate things united. Symbiosis.

Still. The girl of the blue folder from California is named Dawn. I think it is an actual name, unlike mine which is so often Suzie or something flamboyant as I am not. Names. Names like Dwayne and Elroy are south. Nathan seems New England, Bernard New York, Nigel England, Heather is Toronto. Joan is born in the thirties, Debbie the forties. Willard is a mother's boy, Jack lives in Vancouver (someplace west), Sue should be a beach baby all tanned and Help Me Rhonda etc. and Lloyd should be in London which is why I'm writing.

The California girl. Has read Joan Didion and doesn't get it on. I mean she can't cut it she says.

Our little literary magazine done by the students has the editor's baby pictures on the cover. I remember seeing one with the editor posed sitting on the john. There was another done in photo album sepia and they're dressed in ancestral clothes – derbies, calico and so on. I remember a bunch of twenties dadaists posed with their eyes closed. I'm coming to London. My flight gets into Heathrow early in the morning and it's BOAC #235 and you'd better be there. I have my eyes open in my passport picture. I still love you. Eyes

open. Arrive Aug. 15. Be there. 7 AM. We can take
a nap later. Or earlier, I'm easy.

Susan

IN THE LONDON PERIOD Sarah Grace had lived
off Beauchamp Place, near Lennox Gardens. Lloyd
walked from Sloane Square up to Cadogan, and then
over to the quiet street. Wasn't this where Oscar Wilde
was arrested? Seemed incongruous. This elegant area
and the ghosts of buggered pageboys. And Sarah herself, coming back to the city of her childhood, now a
mature woman with a civil war a marriage and several
careers left behind. Coming back in those bleak postwar days. Did she think of the long dead time past, of
the painters who had immortalized themselves and her?
There it was. The very building. Now a bed and breakfast tatty ruin, full of wogs.

IF MY GRANT IS EXTENDED, I hope to continue
collating the materials here in London with the published works as they appear in (a) little and literary
magazines and then in (b) the books of collected work.
My initial surmise, that much later work appeared in
earlier collections, seems at this stage of investigation a
feasible one. Of course, if I am correct, all critical opinion will have to be reassessed. I have done a preliminary
survey which was published ("Sarah Grace's Early
Work: Foreground and Background," *Southern Ohio*

Review, Spring, 1970) and I think that another six month's work will either establish or challenge my hypothesis. What is at stake here is the literary reputation of one of Canada's most distinguished and lamentably ignored writers.

"YOU'VE LOST WEIGHT," Susan said. She was wearing a print dress with no sleeves. It was a blue and green pattern. "You look all drawn and intense."

"You haven't," said Lloyd. "Lost weight I mean. It's all still, well, there where it should be and all...."

"I THINK I LIKED YOU BETTER when you were a flippant academic fake. Making up a gay governess in James and carrying on...."

"You know. Let me carry that damn thing."

"You haven't kissed me yet."

"On the bus. We have to catch it. The James thing. Maybe that wasn't so far-fetched at all. Worth a note somewhere or other."

There was a queue for the bus. Lloyd put the bag down. Susan's hair in the morning light.

"Your hair."

"I know. But I've been up all night...."

"I didn't mean that."

He took her arm in his hand. She moved toward him. He kicked the damn bag, they were kissing, the queue moved. More jets landed and took off over them.

THE BED WAS UNMADE. Piles of notes, three-by-five cards, typescript, perched in dangerous striations on a table in front of the window, which looked out on the back of a hospital. The sound of traffic on Fulham Road came faintly over the roofs.

"Not many amenities I'm afraid," Lloyd said.

"It's sort of, well, Russian," Susan said. "Poor Russian student's place I mean."

"I'm sorry it's not bigger. You probably want to take a nap."

"Maybe," said Susan, smiling. "Or maybe I'm not *that* tired. Yet."

"WE REALLY DON'T HAVE to keep at this you know. I have these eight whole glorious days and seven exciting nights…."

"I'm sorry. I guess it's been all this time away from you and all this work and I guess this *place*…."

"Place didn't used to matter," said Susan, sitting up. "I seem to remember…."

"Well, I am sorry."

"Some really funny places," Susan said, getting up and going over to her purse. "Never mind, darling."

She caught his eyes in the mirror over the sink. What was lost.

"We have time," she said. "Let's not make a big deal out of it."

Dear Susan:

When I wrote the following, I was trying to say I'm sorry I guess:

Susan, do you remember when I first discovered the journals? I grew up ignorant of them and then found that they were there all the time, waiting for me. Their thick weight, the solid feel of them, the square honest edges of the learned journals. Back then when I fell prey to them. What I mean in a kind of roundabout way is that what happened – or didn't happen – is somehow linked to it. I simply wanted to be in one of them. (No Freudian business here, my dear.) And when my first article on S.G. was there, the title simple but portentous the colon after the subject, two heavy words after it and my! name!

Right there on the white page with margins discreet around it.

Susan, I have loved the journals. They were more real to me than Ohio or Utah or Texas. Sometimes I even read the articles of others in them. Stern ghostly minions stand near me now in my need, stand in dignity as I invoke you....

Louis D. Rubin, Henry Nash Smith, be with me. But I wanted more. And so the definitive search began. Or the search for the definitive. What does this have to do with the recent fiasco, ie, failing you. Not making it?

Well (pompous ass tone.)

My sense of the inauthentic is perhaps merely

a momentary feeling of displacement, like a letter or a book mislaid – temporarily – not irrevocably lost I mean. Not a permanent absence. It is only when a pile up of these small gaps in transmission happen all at once that we have this overwhelming sense of alienation, etc. Or don't make it with somebody we really love.

What I meant was I couldn't get it up not because I don't care for you....

NO. There is also this funny feeling of being disconnected, as if a psychic plug ran from my foot to a socket in the wall and someone has casually pulled it out and I've run down. I feel that all my encounters are peripheral and superficial. There's no real touching or knowing. I have a feeling that I did live once, that I did love you, in another country etc. Once I enjoyed the sun, wind etc. The sight of lakes, smell of night, smell of water from a garden hose on hot sidewalks. When did I lose it all? When did I begin to lose you? It scares me. I want it all back without all the double-thinking and the self irony.... Oh Susan my Susan. My dear lost Susan.

I'll be coming back to you, I mean it. Haunted or not, I'll be back and it will be good again....

Love, tho trite,

Lloyd

The rose turned inward. He entered it, a labyrinth of painful beauty, fold within fold.

The silver music was fainter now, heard far off as if in drowned dreams, and he knew that his ordeal, whether of pain or pleasure, was beginning. Winter was coming, and the rose tightened into itself ....

FROM *The Mirrored Room*, P.112

LONDON WAS ALMOST FREE of dacron-suited tourists now. And Lloyd was getting to the bottom of the packing crate at the Alliance Library. Nothing much now but bills from estate agents, receipts from Harrod's and like that. A rented car took him to Sussex and down to the coast. No use stopping at Roedean. Letters had gotten him nothing but polite refusals. He drove past it though, looking nervously at the traffic, the green field swooping off towards the building, the sea on the other side of the road, glistening gunmetal. He drove on to Rye.

At Lamb House, he walked in the garden and in the rooms where James had worked. The "telephone room" where James communed with technology. He had also loved the automobile and the typewriter. Lloyd bowed his head and asked forgiveness for his impudence and disrespect so long ago. He went outside and took a picture. Edith Wharton used to motor up here. H.G. Wells used to bicycle down. Why *up* and *down?* There was a distinct chill in the afternoon sun. It was time, he suddenly knew, to return home. His quest was almost finished.

IT WAS ONE OF THOSE new glass and concrete buildings set down in an older neighbourhood. It would always look a little shocked and out of place. Incongruous that she would be living in it. Yet it was clear that this was the right place. He saw and rejected the minute attempt at a lobby: a few chairs and a coffee table in a Spanish style. She was waiting at the opened door of her apartment.

"You found it," she called to him as he walked down from the elevator. *Although in her seventies, Sarah Grace retains a graceful* – no, can't use that word – *elegant? lithe? lissome? carriage....*

She was tall, almost as tall as he, grey hair pulled back in a kind of Greek style. She wore a long dress of a dull metal weave. Amazing eyes. She took his hand in both of hers. Aged hands. There was where the age showed. *A simple but tasteful necklace....*

"And how was London?"

"Crowded. Uh. Ms. Grace...."

"Call me Sarah, please. Much simpler. I can't stand 'Miz.' When I hear it I think of mint juleps, which I loathe."

Lloyd tried to see it all, the room, the furniture which was a kind of Norwegian, Danish, something Scandinavian, simple and uncluttered, a glass or plastic table laid for lunch with plates and silver, single rose in a silver vase on the table, a stereo on shelves, playing some modern piece – Bloch? Paintings cool. The view was just tops of Toronto middle-class houses. No books in sight, nothing on the coffee table, no clues. *She lives a deliberately uncluttered existence....*

"I read the piece you sent me," she said. Amazing eyes. What colour were they? They seemed to get bigger as you looked at them.

"What did you think? I've been reworking the thing since I went to England...."

"And did you like England?"

She moved to the coffee table, bent for a cigarette. Certainly still a handsome figure of a woman.

"I haven't been back there for years," she smiled.

"I know. I saw your old school just before I left...."

Hell. What if it was still a sore subject.

"My God, does it still exist?"

"Well, of course, a famous place...."

"That wretched dump? I always thought it inspired St. Trinian's."

"It is lovely down there," Lloyd said. How could he get out of this. "I mean the setting and all...."

"Lovely? I remember looking out the refectory window and seeing nothing but the windows of a factory. Some of the men used to make gestures at us. It was a few years before I realized what they meant."

"Factory? Down there?"

"My dear boy, where do you think I went to school?"

"Well. Roedean?"

"Oh no," she laughed. "Father could never have afforded a school like that. I went to a drab little place near Battersea. Horrid. Can I offer you something? Scotch? I'm having a martini."

"Not Roedean? I'd like some Scotch please – Not...."

"Water? I have soda too. No dear, not Roedean."

"Uh. With water please."

"I went on to an art college for a while after I finished there. Never did finish art college though. Here you are."

She handed him the drink. He drank half of it.

"I suppose it was all those artists from the early period – time – uh – I mean what with the Royal Academy – the connections – but that would have been so much earlier…."

He stopped, confused. He finished the rest of his drink. She took it gently out of his hand and went over to the small bar set up on top of a sideboard.

"Artists," she said, handing him the new drink. "The only artist I ever met was Andy Warhol. If he is an artist…."

Lloyd stammered the names of those famous turn-of-the-century men. She looked blank.

"Of course I did meet a young man in Majorca who said he was an artist. He lived with me for a whole winter. I never saw a *sketch*, let alone a canvas."

Why would she be covering up? Why? After all this time.

The music continued. Yes, she said, it was Bloch. They sat at the small glass table. He could see their knees, precariously close, through it. Luncheon was shrimp done in garlic and a salad. Dew on the silver vase. A Chablis. Lloyd still had some of his Scotch. He alternated between the wine and the Scotch.

"This is excellent," he said. He almost knocked the

vase over, grabbed it in time. The rose shook. He asked about the socialist period.

"Oh, I was such a little prig in those days," she sighed. "I think we all lived for the future in the thirties. I don't think we realized how swiftly the future would come. And here it is. What a mistake! We should always live for today, don't you think?"

They were on the second bottle of Chablis.

"Excellent wine," he said. "Really. Ex...."

She put her hand on his, brushed his knee getting up, went to the stereo. More Bloch. That lovely Scherzo. Her hand, light and cool, trembled for a moment on the back of his neck.

"Will you pour the wine?" she said.

"Sure. You know, I visited Lamb House – where James – I mean I got into this business in a funny way." He spilled some of the wine, made a sort of swipe at it with his napkin.

"Let's sit over here," she said. He got up, knocked the vase over, this time for real, water all over the damn table.

"Don't bother with that," she said, patting the cushion next to her. "I'll get it later."

"Later," he agreed. He sat down too fast. Laughed. Wow. Here he was, sitting next to Sarah Grace. He looked at her. Really amazing, for her age. And those remarkable eyes. You could see how that painter – whatsisname – got so hung up. If he did. Or didn't.

His head was muzzy with the wine and the drinks. What was she? He found himself bending forward, to put the empty bottle carefully on the table. Then he was swaying the other way, bending far.

"Too much wine," he murmured.

"Yes," she said, close in his ear. "Poor dear…."

She was somehow under him, lying back on the couch. Over there, the simple rose and the silver vase lay on the table. Water from the vase dripped slowly over the edge of the table. Her lips moved at his ear. What saying? And at the same time her hand had found.

Yes. Busy too and. He closed his eyes but the room whirled. He opened his eyes wide and looked down. Her hand. Her old hand, corded with blue veins, circled him. The hand. The hand that wrote *To Bake Our Bread, The Mirrored Room*….

He swelled into her hand. She led him into her. Her breath soaked in wine and garlic and something else, something indefinable, ages old, faintly rank, like over-ripe fruit, was moaning in his mouth, went deep into him, as deep as he was in her.

At last he had found her, he thought, looking down again at the blue-knotted hand still guiding him, at least that much of the search was over, whatever else lay ahead. Confidant, consort, friend, lover, child, secretary, yes, even executor when that time came: his excitement mounted and communicated to her and now her withered hands were imploring at his thighs. *Sarah Grace*, he shouted in his mind, *at last I know you*….

The music ended. The rose waited to be picked up.

Fathers and Daughters

THE SUMMER AFTER KATE DIVORCED HIM and moved back to the States, that summer when Leslie turned nine, it seemed to Miles that his own life had come to a dead end. Kate sent a monthly duty letter, which was mainly about Leslie, anecdotes about new friends, a trip to the shoe store, where she had gotten and lost a balloon, and a few tantalizing off-hand allusions to her own activities, which sounded too nun-like to be real: she had taken a job with the County as a school nurse, beginning in the fall, Mother wasn't too well, the hot weather bothered her, never a word about a man.

Leslie came on the first Visitation at the end of the summer. Miles had been looking forward to it. He spent his spare time going for long drives, often over the river into Detroit, where he had the odd sensation of streets listlessly connecting to other streets, doggedly going on from one neighborhood to another, finally ending in straggled suburbs, sudden signs of arrogant wealth, expensive-looking women driving station wagons full of children and dogs, then more ugly clutters of gas stations and mean-looking bars with pickup trucks parked in back of them where he imagined assignations between hillbillies and waitresses, and on and on it went until you were almost out of the state, almost in Toledo. It was the same no matter which way he drove. Detroit was suddenly gone, and he hadn't even seen it.

Sundays he read the *New York Times*. All the pubs were closed. The *Times*. All of it. He searched for Canadian news. The girdle ads in the Magazine didn't seem to have any effect on him. Was he getting old? No more fantasy life? He read everything, even the tiny ads in the back section. Huge discounts. Get rid of unwanted, unsightly. Tree stump KILLER. Beautify your home with the new translucent. Exotic Plunge bra, deep plunge cups swoop bust inwards and upwards. Jewelled Underwater Watch.

Who would want all these things? He imagined wanting them. To become Waterproof, Shockproof, Unbreakable, Anti-magnetic. Sunday was like one long four o'clock in the afternoon.

The radio played Vivaldi's *Four Seasons*.

THE MAN IN THE SHOE STORE offered Leslie the balloon, which was blue. It was filled with lighter-than-air gas from a tank and tied to Leslie's wrist by the salesman. Outside the store, she tugged at the string and the balloon escaped, riding high above the crowd, soaring off free above her face, set in a sun-squint watching it go go go. No more. Gone off.

That same summer, Leslie saw the word *cancer* on a poster on a wall. She read the words *sudden* and *only* in a book. These became important words to her.

KATE WAS STILL very much with him. Like a tangible ghost. He kept bumping into her as he paced around the rooms, staring blankly out the window at a scrabby lawn or at a wall. Sometimes he forgot and expected to hear her in the next room, closing a drawer or opening a window. Sometimes he almost called her name, then remembered with a sour pang. Gone. No more.

HE WATCHED THE ROAD with great care. Leslie sat with her hands in her lap, staring straight ahead. He turned on the radio, tried for music, ah there were the Beatles, what did she think about the Beatles? Who? Oh, yes, well, she guessed she liked them.

Well, well, Miles said.

He took her to the Henry Ford Museum and Greenfield Village. She looked at everything he showed her. They had dinner in a place that was made to look like a stagecoach inn with electric candles flickering in lanterns. They drove back to Windsor. He took her to his office. Leslie looked at the framed pictures on his desk. Kate in a mid-1950's dress, smiling shyly, and Leslie at the age of three or four at the zoo wearing a white dotted dress, a gravel patch in back of her leading off to the lion house, his shadow on the lawn in front of her, hunched over the camera probably. Leslie looked at the pictures for a while and then they went back to his apartment.

The next morning Leslie woke up before him and fixed herself a bowl of Cornflakes. The place was much smaller than the one they had in Toronto. Back then. She turned the television on. There wasn't much on. It was too early. There was an English lesson for New Canadians.

"Aha," said a young man, pointing at a large clock.

"What is the time?"

"The time," said a young woman in a black dress, "is eleven. Are you hungry? Are you thirsty?"

"Leslie?"

Miles stumbled out of the bedroom.

"Are you up already?"

"I'm in here, Daddy."

"Yes I have hunger and I have thirst also."

"Aha," said the young woman. "It is more correct to say *I am hungry, I am thirsty.*"

Miles looked in the bathroom mirror. They had an hour to make the boat.

"This is a chair. There is a table," came the voice from the other room. "I am a man. You are a woman."

They took the boat to Bob-Lo Island. A dwarf in a sailor's outfit pressed a red balloon into Leslie's hand.

She asked if she could exchange it for a blue one. A band played on board and a group of people was attempting to do the Twist.

"Would you like to dance?"

Miles moved in a kind of stiff twisting imitation.

Leslie smiled, then giggled, said *Daddy!* in mock surprise as she always used to, he bought her a bottle of pop, they found chairs on the top deck, sat in the white glare. The boat whistle made them jump. The band played even more frantically. The deck under their feet trembled as the engines reversed. How old was this boat? Older than he was, and probably sounder....

They had hot dogs for lunch and went on every ride she wanted to. The Dodgems. The Moon Rocket. And there was one ride especially: the Flying Scooter, which was a kind of metal sailboat suspended on chains. The thing was thrown out in a wide maypole orbit, but it could be controlled by moving a kind of rudder or sail either towards the ground or away from it. Miles dipped it down until it seemed that they would hit the circle of watchers outside the surrounding fence, then swiftly turned it the other way. The car seemed to hesitate in the air for a second, then snapped at the end of its tether, went into a high arc, higher still, as if it were trying to break its chain and go on soaring up into the bright sky, carrying them off the petty earth. Leslie clung to his arm and kept up a constant delicious squealing.

They came back on the five o'clock boat. Miles felt his eyelids droop. His face was sunburned and stiff. Leslie fell asleep against his shoulder. There was a cool breeze off the river now, and Miles hung his coat over her shoulders. He was thirsty. But there was something about this moment. He didn't want to interrupt it.

She wouldn't be his little girl much longer, asleep against his shoulder. Soon her time with him would be over and she would be going away again.

Just for now, in this brief chill time before the summer afternoon ended, before the ship found its dock, before the morning, when she would leave, there was this little moment when she slept in his trust.

WHEN LESLIE WAS FIFTEEN she got into the habit of playing her radio after her roommate went to sleep. It was the only time in the whole day that she felt alone. All the other time, there were so many people, a crowd of faces like hovering balloons, but there was no being alone. At night, through a haze of static, the volume low, far-off stations came through: Chicago, St. Louis, a French voice from Quebec, once an unnamed city in Texas. The night air was crowded with voices. She liked the foreign language stations. It was wonderful to hear people speaking in Greek or Polish with great authority, earnest and intense conviction, and not to understand a thing. Words. Noise. No sense.

Joan never woke up and never discovered what she did at night. It wasn't that she'd mind, but perhaps she'd want to join in the listening. This was a pleasure all the more sweet because it was unshared.

Sometimes Leslie would fall asleep with the radio

still on, a voice from some far-off place, a distant city, muttering, and would wake up hours later to find the station gone off the air, the radio buzzing like a patient insect.

One night she had on a station in what seemed to be Boston, which played classical music all night. They played a piano concerto by Ravel. There was a long, slow section, almost hesitant at first, the piano alone, like someone trying to say something very important and reaching for the right words. Then the orchestra, what must have been a flute alone, then other instruments, reassuring, soothing, answering.

Is this what it is to love, she thought, *so that you want to die of it?*

And she got softly out of bed and began to move gravely to the music, a stately dance, turning slowly in the shadows, hardly daring to breathe so the sleeping girl would not wake up, the music growing in her like a piece of burning brightness, dancing, solemn as someone in a ceremony, then saw herself in the dim mirror, eyes dark and large, hair all wild around her startled face, and the music ended, there was a pause of silence like a drawn breath.

Then the piano lashed like a shower of icicles falling in the sun, and she rushed to put the volume down. She stood over her empty bed, thought, I must be crazy, and got back into bed, turned the radio off and listened to her own breathing.

Where am I now? If I looked out the window, as someone on a plane or train might, I could not tell where the earth around me was. I wish I could be some place not here, on a ship cleared from port. leaving the harbor at night, seeing the hills around the harbor fall back, setting out, setting out on a long journey across an ocean which has no other shore. Where am I going? Where have I been? Give me someone, something, a place....

She slept.

MILES BEGAN GOING to the local pub almost every night with a young man named Keith who was a graduate student at the University. The pub, a block from Miles' apartment, was a gathering place for the younger instructors, a few graduate students, like Keith, departmental secretaries, a few nurses, a woman who ran a small boutique called However who was divorced but whose husband took her home at closing time, and a floating population of female undergraduates.

At first Miles thought yes, yes, yes, the girls are in the marriage market and are angling for eligible instructors, or maybe for something less, perhaps grades. But then he found that most of the younger instructors were already married, to nurses, not the ones who came to the pub, but to mysterious distant presences who had, at times, to be phoned but were otherwise seldom referred to.

The crowd was in the pub most afternoons and later on until closing time, then on for Chinese food, sometimes over the river, sometimes going off with one or another of the young girls or a secretary.

The *ambiance* of the *whole thing*, thought Miles, *that* was what kept him coming back.

He kept on showing up, a baggy presence, often in a deep half-drunken, half-heard conversation with some of them, sometimes just sitting there hearing it wash around him, over and past him, people saying *scenario* and *charisma*, and finally he would stumble home to fall into a stupid sleep, to experience the Whirling Pit, the Accelerating Bed, the Falling Backwards Through the Mattress.

By noon the next day he was able to take off the dark glasses, he would tell himself that he must not go there again, it was demeaning, they were all secretly laughing at him. He would begin a regime of health, clean living, sane and sensible rigor, begin running at the Y, go mountain climbing, learn French at night school.

Then by eight or nine or sometimes as late as nine-thirty, having read the paper, attempted a kind of dinner, fingered a book or two, he would think *oh hell just one or two* or so.

He was there. Home, that place where when you go they have to take you in, or was it always have to take you in? Or was it the closest thing he had found yet in that funny pilgrimage he called a life, more an exile than a journey. He felt like a character in fiction. *Miles went into his apartment. Miles took off his jacket. What was Miles thinking now?*

The man without a country. A character with no weather. A nowhere man. Nothing. Nobody. Alone. He was so very tired. *Miles was so very tired. His bones were rot-*

ten with sleep. The whole world was crowded with Fathers and Daughters. Maybe he could cope with it tomorrow. Another day.

In the life of. Miles slept. *His dreams were bad.*

LESLIE WAS DREAMING. It was a terrible dream, almost a nightmare. A chorus of voices singing, a choir of evil children, grinning, lewd looks, knowing smiles, sly eyes. A woman advancing towards her, face furious, intent, threatening. The woman was like a statue, arms at her sides, draped robe falling like stone past her knees, one of them bent under the marble fabric, legs not moving, breasts bared and pendulant, coming closer, advancing with terrible speed, choir sang louder, louder.

She awoke with a start. Morning. Innocent light. Paul Newman smiled reassuringly from the wall. Next to him, Rodin's lovers submerged in their eternal embrace were indifferent to her. She had gotten that postcard at the Tate the summer of – when was it – she had been maybe fourteen.

The visit to Daddy had been late that year. It was the first year of the miniskirt in England and Mother had been so embarrassed by it all. Besides the nude lovers in the museum, all those thighs in the summer sun. She kept trying to divert Leslie's attention, *Ohhhh, look at this dear,* and *Isn't that a divine, look, look,* but there was simply too much to avoid.

It had been a nervous trip. Mother didn't know that she bought the postcard. The Kiss *(Le Baiser)* was made of pentelican marble (the back of the postcard told you) and stood something inches high. If she turned the postcard over, it would tell her exactly. But it wouldn't tell what a kiss meant, what those stone figures were saying silently about human love. She had never kissed like that. And neither had Mother. Of that, she was sure.

Father.

She began to brush her hair. Joan came back from the shower.

"Any mail?" Leslie asked.

Mail at the Alice Parker School was delivered to each dorm floor and left on a sideboard near the stairs. It was a method, like so many things at the school, which reflected nervous compromise: half-cheap rooming house, half-aristocratic snobbery. The Headmistress had been born in Duluth but had gone to Radcliffe. The mail was put on an old hallstand, but on a silver platter with the school crest engraved on it.

"I didn't look," said Joan. She vigorously toweled her hair. "Look, Connally, are you going to this thing with Hatch or not? I have to let whoosie know by tonight so he can get the tickets…."

Leslie stared at her image in the mirror.

"Hatch," she sighed. "You know, Hatch is really Lane Cottrell…."

"Omigod…."

"No, really, he is. All smug and self, I don't know, just so filled with himself…."

"Connally," said Joan, in a dangerous tone. "Could you please address yourself to the issue, which is…."

"I know, I know," Leslie sighed. "But all boys are Lane Cottrell to me. Look. I can let you know later today. Like I'm not sure if I'm supposed to go to Canada or not...."

"The Father scene again? So soon?"

"It's not so soon," Leslie said, staring into the mirror. "You know, I had an awful dream last night...."

"Uh huh. Well, when will you know, because they have to get the tickets...."

"Tonight, I should know by tonight."

Then after a moment Leslie said:

"You know, I sometimes wish I could cry, just cry and cry. I haven't cried in years."

"The Old Good Cry, huh?"

"Any kind of cry, Good or Bad."

Actually, Leslie knew about her plans in the next few minutes, because when she finished dressing and went down the hall she saw the letter waiting for her on the engraved plate.

There was the queen's head stamp, the airmail sticker in French and English, with the little maple leaf. From another country.

As it turned out, she didn't have to make the visitation after all. It was postponed until the end of August. How about that. Leslie thought. Now she'd go out with whoosie's friend Hatch instead. Life was so full of coming and going, hustle and bustle, hither and yon. It was more fun than a barrel of monkeys. She carefully refolded the letter and went down the stairs. She could tell Joan later.

LESLIE ROLLED OVER on her stomach, leaned out to turn the little travelling clock around. Three-fifteen. She rolled back, ran one hand down his bare side, over his buttocks, noticed the small fine tuft of hair at the base of his spine for the first time. She sat up, looking at his back as if at a map of an unfamiliar country. He turned on his side, took her in his arms and kissed her between the breasts.

"We only have a few minutes," Leslie whispered into the top of his dark head.

"That's long enough," he said, turned her body on its back and entered her again. This time was not as high and chaotic as the first time that afternoon, but much better than the really first time they had done it, over a week ago now, in the back seat of his car, with toys and magazines on the floor, a few dark finger marks on the car roof right above her head. She had stared up at them, wondering if a careless mechanic had balanced his body there, leaving his mark there, not knowing as he peered at whatever it was he was fixing, that she would be lying looking up at it as her virginity was taken.

Theo was married, of course, had three children, of course, and had been her English teacher only since the beginning of the spring term. Of course. If he had been a little older, then the old Freudian thing, the Electra or Oedipus thing, would have neatly been a casebook example. But he was only ten years older, didn't look a bit like Daddy, and she felt actually older than he.

She wasn't sure how it started, who had started it,

who had made the first move. A new teacher, a young man, darkly good looking, at the Alice Parker School was enough to cause a certain amount of prescribed commotion, fluttering hearts, giggling, gasping. Sally Harris kept crossing her legs carelessly on purpose in class, but he did not respond, or even look deliberately away.

"I can't get my skirt much higher," Sally said. "I give him a little eye of thigh, he just looks and takes it in, well, like...."

"Meat. Butcher shop meat," said Joan helpfully.

"Bitch," said Sally. "Anyhow, I'll have the damn skirt up around my neck by tomorrow at this rate...."

"Just where you'd like it to be, Harris," said Mona, all crisp disdain. Mona liked to play the decisive, aloof role, like the girl in *The Group*, the one who turned out to be queer.

Leslie wasn't sure about the whole sex thing as far as other girls went. They were very good at projecting an air of knowing experience. But how much of it was based on novels and movies and how much on actual existential encounters was a mystery to her.

They all spent a lot of time talking about Love, I-Thou encounters, some even in the old terms of saving themselves for some vague event in the future; others spoke passionately of the need to give themselves, to be open to all experience. But the talk usually stayed on a theoretical level, seldom coming near to autobiography. Leslie decided that nobody could give her any real advice. No real help. She was entirely on her own.

Talk to your clergyman, the magazines said. *Talk to your Mother.*

Ha.

When she saw Theo, Leslie knew that he was It. In a strange fatalistic way, something in her decided, and in the same calm deliberate way, she prepared herself like a priestess for the immolation. And it happened. Of course.

At the term break. Just before her spring visitation to her father. Joan took a quick trip home. Most of the girls did. All it took was a phone call to Mother, pleading that she had a late paper to finish, it was such a long trip for a few days anyhow.

Not that it was cold and calculated, or that she threw herself at him. She wasn't Sally Harris, offering herself openly. It was, it seemed to her, as if she were carrying out orders lasered into her from another planet, moving through the necessary sequence of actions as if through a programmed flow chart. Do this, then that, and then they were doing it in his car down in the lane past the lacrosse field.

And then in the dorm, dangerous as it was, sweet and naked, kisses making them both drunk and timeless, oblivious to place, their skin slightly chill in the early spring air, the bed making small noises as they thrust together.

It was to be all. When term began again, and the exams began, and after them her visit to Canada, it would be over. Leslie knew that. It was the final stage of the flow chart, the final instruction from the unseen extraterrestrial forces.

Theo didn't. He was just enough older than her to be intensely romantic, concerned for his wife, feeling deep guilt, sentimental pangs of anguish for his children, poor little innocents, torn by the ravaging sweetness aroused in him by this girl, this large-eyed sea nymph who was pulling him down in green waters.

Should he give up his family? Take Leslie off somewhere, get some job or other, he'd never get a recommendation from the Alice Parker School, that was for sure.

Start life all over again? What the hell. Only ten years difference. When he was thirty-seven, she'd be twenty-seven. It was only *now* that it seemed so ugly. The older man, married, a father of children, seducing his child student.

And she was sweet, so wild and loving. It was such ecstasy to be in her. He didn't want it to end. So he wrestled with his problem, not knowing that the end had been foreordained, that there was no problem, that it had all been clearly seen whole in Leslie's mind.

From the moment when it began to form behind her somber eyes, to the startled look of recognition in his eyes just before he kissed her, her unselfconscious pulling up of her skirt, the look of the grease mark on the car roof just near the door jamb, moment to moment, it all stepped its careful way.

But not just yet. They had another afternoon. It was the best time. The dorm was still empty. The cook came in about four-thirty to begin the meal for the few students who had stayed on. Most of them were in the library, honestly grinding away at papers. Theo's wife thought he was in the sparse office the Alice Parker School had given him, marking term essays.

One more afternoon. Then it would be too risky. The idea flashed forbidden just once across Leslie's mind that it would be delicious to have him at night, one long moonlit night of loving just before the others returned, before Joan came back to fill up that primly made-up bed across the room from their tangled white expanse.

But why spoil it? It was perfect as it was, like a piece of music. He would, she was sure, try for more. But it was not to be. It was to end tomorrow afternoon, whether or not – it was better that he not know. Otherwise the last afternoon would be all cluttered up with talk, posturing, pleading, plans, offers, threats, all sorts of stuff. Things she didn't need.

Keep it straight. Maybe they could try for three times tomorrow.

Whatever happened tomorrow, it was to be all.

It was all she had to give. And whatever it was, she knew it wasn't enough. But it was good enough. Just for now.

She lay on the bed, half-listening to the music coming from the muted radio. What was it? Some baroque composer or other. She was too deliciously tired to care. Whatever it was, it was quite good enough.

HERE COMES MILES walking out of his front door looking for all the world like a suitor of the 1940's, a double-breasted blue pinstriped suit on, smelling of shaving lotion, stepping jauntily along the street like a cartoon of a man with Somewhere to Go, a man with a Big Date. *Miles came out of his door.*

He is going to meet his daughter for Dinner. It is an occasion. He feels at peace with himself this evening. The sun has not completely set behind the bridge, the clouds are shot with summer light, a riot of chrome color. He is full of sentiment tonight, a patsy for any nostalgia pusher. He would even buy a stuffed animal for his daughter, if it were that type of restaurant. He will gallantly offer his daughter a drink. What the hell. She looks almost old enough. How daring he feels, how up to date, how progressive. A grown-up drink with his daughter. *Miles was thinking.*

His wife has married again. He has not, though there are prospects. Certainly, lots of prospects. The old crowd from the pub has been replaced, pushed further downtown by a newer, younger crowd. The girl who owned the However, who tried to make it again with her first husband, and gave it up as a bad job, has been going out with Miles here and there. It looks as if it might be more than a sometime thing.

Miles walked down the street. Miles felt in his pocket to be sure he had not left his keys behind, his wallet.

Who knows? Miles thinks. Life is full of surprises.

Miles looked both ways and rapidly crossed the street. He is on his way. The street is crowded with fathers, husbands, sons, daughters. They are all on their way someplace.

Midwinter

THERE HAD BEEN RUMOURS OF SHARKS, not only because of that movie or the popular book, but because there had been an actual attack on a tourist the week before their tour began, and it had not been hushed up. It happened on the north end of the island, and most of the hotels were on the south, where the hotel managers claimed the best beaches were and no shark had ever come there. Still, very few ventured out into the surf and the pool got more than the usual use. Ethan had a tendency to burn, so he kept as close under the palm frond umbrella as possible, finishing his second cup of coffee and wondering if it were too early for a pina fling, the hotel's specialty, based on a recipe from Aruba.

The two girls pulled themselves up out of the pool and walked swiftly towards their chairs and towels. With a quick casual preoccupied air, both simultaneously tugged their bathing suits over the rounded bottoms of their ass cheeks. A Malacca stick appeared under Ethan's chin. He leaned on it. A white Leghorn hat grew above his thoughtful eyes and his face lengthened into aristocratic and depraved lines. Snap snap, and the bathing suit bottoms were neatly, decorously in place.

"Why in hell didn't they tell us about the sharks," a man in a native hat and white trunks was saying at the next table. "We would have gone to St. Vincent instead."

"That's why they didn't tell us," a woman said in a New York accent. "Why should they cut their throats?"

"Sure," said a tall, thin man wearing bathing trunks in a beer-label design. "Look at Jamaica. Deserted. Who needs all that hassle?"

Now the girls were strolling back towards the pool, indolently sipping tall, frothy, pink drinks. One girl was petite, the other tall. Earlier, Ethan had noticed the little one at breakfast, wearing a kaftan, looking like an illustration from an Andrew Lang fairy tale. He kept glancing over at her as she ate her pineapple with dainty gusto. Here, with her kaftan off, he could see that she had a full figure, even a suggestion of baby fat about the hips. A brief hour ago she had looked thirteen. The tall friend had a cool and insolent set to her mouth. She was doing all the talking. They didn't look at each other. As they passed Ethan's table, they both broke into helpless laughter at something the tall one said. For a moment, a rich delight of girlish voices rose above the tables and the pool. Then the girls went on down the steps to the sand.

Every winter, since the children had moved out, Karen and Ethan had taken a midwinter vacation. Just a week package tour, usually at the same hotel in the Windward Islands where Karen could indulge herself at the casino. Ethan had no gambling instinct. On these trips he swam, looked for conch shells on the island, got sunburned, read trashy novels and drank much too much. So the first winter after the divorce he decided to go on his own to a different hotel and a different island.

Tropictours advertised a perfect little hideaway where the days were sunscorched and the nights pulsed to the exotic beat of Leo and the Fabulous Tradewinds, where sun on the sparkling sands waited for you after a full American breakfast, where unlimited beverages were served free on the flight. Baggage and embarkation taxes paid for, scuba diving lessons available, golf and tennis nearby, shuffleboard, manager's cocktail party, an open air lobster barbecue, free transport to the nearby casino, etc.

"What does this mean?" Ethan read. *"For your comfort there are no smoking sections on all sections on all Tropictour flights."*

The travel agent, a woman with her hair cut in a trendy capped style, looked at the line in the brochure, handed it back to him.

"Just what it says," she said.

On the plane, he sat next to a woman from Cleveland, whose name was Julie and whose husband could not get away from his business, which was something in plastic injection molding. Ethan tried to tell her about his work on the Architectural Journal. Julie was a healthy, tanned woman in her middle forties, pleasant enough, attractive enough, with a lot of blonde streaked hair that she possibly thought of as "tawny." She obviously played a lot of golf. Her eyes were a faded blue in a very leathery face. Reporters would have termed her a surburban matron. The thing was that she would not have been insulted by the term. That was the trouble with Julie.

Ethan smothered a desire to tell her about his divorce. Just last Christmas people had been announcing their divorces in the mimeoed letters folded into the cards, after all the births, the graceful growing up of children, the promotions, the move to new houses, the vacations to fascinating places, all escalating in successive Christmas messages, with the odd hint of some flaws in the picture: The children have all moved into their own places. Of course, we still see them. Dennis has a scholarship at State but he isn't going to take it. He wants to see the country. Jennie is working with disadvantaged children in the ghetto. It certainly keeps her hopping! What was left now except divorce and death?

Karen and Ethan had always felt superior to the senders of these programmed missives. So there was no medium to announce their own divorce. People would just have to find out the hard way.

A plump man wearing a white leisure suit and a broad-brimmed hat stood in the aisle, talking to Julie, waving his drink around. He ordered a second, and one for Julie. Ethan tried to wave his own empty glass at the stewardess, but she didn't see him.

ETHAN LIKED HIS ROOM. It was large and cool, with a hanging black lantern with a candle in it, which the maid lit at night. A fresh native flower floated in a bowl. The room was comforting to Ethan perhaps because it had an air of tidy impersonality. A lack of familiar home-worn edges. The drawers were hollow and waiting. The Bible waited, the stationery waited. But there would be no reading, no looking up texts fit for sorrow or loneliness. And there would be no letters. There would be little time to write, nobody stayed in these rooms that long anyhow, and besides there was nobody waiting for a letter from him.

That first morning, at the full American breakfast, a tourist in flowered shirt and white pants, an immense wallet sagging his rear pocket, walked, swaggered, strutted over to a waiter and said something in a biting-off-the-words manner, then turned abruptly and tall-walked back to his table, the wallet slung low like a peacemaker, a John Wayne macho power riding there on his hip. The waiter still leaned against the wall, indolent and uppity, not shot, hadn't bit the dust.

"I don't really like it here," said the very tanned woman of a certain age at the next table. "It goes against all my weak-kneed white liberal principles."

"Why don't you fuck a native?" someone else at the table said. A man who had stood behind Ethan at customs stood next to his table. "Is it all right if my friend and I join you?" "Uh. Certainly –" The man waved to someone still in line. "Paul," he called. "Over here." "I'm Phil Gower," the man said. He was Ethan's age, but was dressed in youthful clothing. Paul came to the table. He was a man with hair so dark and curly that it looked like wire. His skin was so tanned that his teeth and eyes seemed to blaze.

Paul wore several gold chains which lay uneasily on his chest hair.

"How is Mary Ellen?" the very tanned woman at the next table called to Phil.

"That bitch," said Phil. "That cunt. She still hasn't got a divorce...."

"Decent thing to do," said Paul.

In the bright blue morning, all the people on the tour smiled shyly at one another as they came into the eating area, which became the dance floor at night. The indolent waiter was slouching from table to table, pouring coffee. Phil glanced at the waiter's back. Paul smiled slowly.

"I don't want to screw a native," said someone at the other table. "I'm not that old yet."

"Yet," Phil said in a low voice. "Huh. I saw her with that overweight tourist last night – the one from Cleveland or someplace – drinking all that Dutch beer and sticking her leg between his when they danced...."

"I don't want the fat tourist either," said Paul.

"What do you want?" said Phil.

"I wish I knew," said Paul, turning his dazzling smile on Ethan.

Ethan excused himself, said he had some cards to write and took his coffee out to a table near the pool. As he passed the other table, the very tanned woman said good morning – he realized that it was Julie from the plane – and someone else said something in a low voice that sounded like well-hung. The sun was getting very hot. He sat as close to the palm frond umbrella as he could. Two girls dove in graceful arcs into the empty pool. He had left the postcards in the room. He watched the girls swim across the pool.

THE LATE AFTERNOON SUN slanted through the bamboo blinds on the shore side of the bar. A fresh breeze blew the blinds in sail-like billows. The bartenders were gearing up for Happy Hour. Ethan was lucky to get a seat. People were making entrances. The band began to gather on the little raised platform on the pool side of the bar.

Leo was ill. His place was taken by his very good friend, his very very good friend, Freddy, who hoped they'd all enjoy the Happy Hour and let it all hang out until seven, dancing nightly, and they'd all be back at nine until who knows when and let it hang loose and then the Tradewinds ripped into a medley beginning with Little Yellow Bird.

Phil and Paul went past him. Paul grinned hello. Phil apparently did not see him. They wore identical outfits: white trousers and black shirts open to the waist. The tanned blonde was dancing with a succession of men. When the band took a break she came to the bar and sat on a stool next to Ethan.

"I'm Julie," she said, in cute cocktail waitress style. "And I'm here for fun."

Ethan smiled and waved his glass in a what the hell gesture.

"Me too," he yelled because the band had started again with a series of fifties favourites. Julie yelled something back and was off on the dance floor again. The two girls made an entrance. There was some adjusting and crowding of chairs at a table near the band and they were sunk in the mass, gone from Ethan's sight. The little one was wearing yellow pajamas of a flowing shiny material. The tall one had on a black jumpsuit and obviously no bra. Some of the men down the bar had Spanish looking purses over their shoulders. There was a confusion of cologne on the afternoon air. Most of the men wore gold chains or silver bracelets or both. Ethan rolled his thumb over the ridge on his finger where his ring had been. Maybe he should buy a ring or a bracelet. What to buy? He signaled for another drink. He had switched to scotch and soda now. A ring. He'd never wear a bracelet or a chain around his neck back home. Look at rings tomorrow. But the shops were open now. They stayed open late. The little girl in yellow was standing next to him, trying to catch the waiter's eye. Ethan waved, trying to be of service. "Alicia," they were calling from her table, "we've got a waiter –" She and Ethan looked at each other. She shrugged her shoulders in an oh well manner and went back towards the table. What should he have said? Alicia. Perhaps he should go to the jewelry store or stay here and ask Alicia to dance, or Julie. Or have another drink.

The sun had gone all the way down now and the price of drinks had gone back up and the band played some slower songs. They played the song that was so popular on the islands that year. The Tradewinds were no substitute for the studio version one heard on all the radios: the lyric sung by an ambivalent high-voiced young man against a background of rich piano and plucked strings, a chorus of vital and urgent voices. The lyrics were trite and sententious, but Ethan felt moved almost to tears and knew that the song would wound him now whenever he heard it again.

There were several shops in the hotel. There was, besides the jewelry store, a ladies boutique, a men's shop, and a place for souvenirs and postcards, heaped high with native hats and maracas. He went into the men's shop. There were tables with denim trousers piled on them. All were in small sizes. There were racks of shirts made in Pakistan, also in small sizes. Heavy decibel rock music made his feeling of displacement more acute. A young salesman, also small, stared blankly through him. The jewelry store closed just as he got to the door. He didn't want to go back to the bar. He had missed dinner and didn't want to bother hunting for food. Perhaps a walk on the beach. After the confusion of voices at the Happy Hour, the moonstruck silence on the beach seemed a haven. The waves came on more gently than they did in the daytime. He had drunk enough to feel maudlin and overly sensitive to the sounds, or rather, the absence of them. He felt an urgent sense of anticipation. Maybe he would meet someone out here, somebody who also wished to retreat from the superficial clash of hectic selves at the bar. Perhaps Alicia. Or, indeed, anybody.

He walked down to the surf-packed firmer sand and went further away from the hotel's lights. After ten minutes, he reversed direction and went back towards the music. There was no room at the bar now. The dance floor pulsed with people. It was impossible to discern anybody he recognized.

THE NEXT MORNING, after breakfast, he went to the jewelry shop. The ring was gold, shaped like a small crown, with a dark stone set in the centre. Ethan looked at a lot of silver rings, but kept coming back to the gold one, which he didn't really think he could afford. Besides, the regal gold ring seemed somehow unsuitable for him, too, well, flashy, although to tell the truth, in an understated modest way. It was definitely not gaudy. Karen loved jewelry. Her wedding ring, the mate of his, was surrounded by other more conspicuous rings. She wore bracelets, pins, earrings, necklaces, chains, and on each of their trips and holidays, they searched for and found more gold for her. Ethan wore only his wedding ring and a rather tame watch.

After the divorce, for some time, he continued wearing the wedding ring. He had taken it off for this holiday as a gesture of hope and the end of something and the beginning of something else. The fresh start, the new life that Karen had talked about; this holiday, at the end of January, the month named after a god with two faces, looking both backwards and forwards, patron of endings and beginnings, might be that new life's opening note. And if he had not gone on this trip, the time at home would not have been bearable.

He bought the rich ring with the dark stone. Luckily the store took his bank charge card, because it would have taken most of the traveller's cheques he had left. He wore it on his right hand, because it fit more securely there. He watched its reflection flash in the shop windows as he passed them. Already, his hand seemed more important.

He sat at the bar. There was nobody there. A young couple, possibly honeymooners, were at a table having a late lunch. Where was everybody? He ordered beer. After awhile he switched to gin and tonic, which was so cold it gave him a headache. He had two of them. The wind stirred the palm fronds on the roof. The sun dazzled on the beach. Hardly anyone down there. A child called from the pool.

"Hardly anybody around," he said to the bartender, who shrugged indifferently. He ordered a native drink made with two pints of fruit juice and rum. After a while, he decided to switch back to beer. He stared at the ring, placed his hand on the bar so he could see it in various angles of light.

Life should be more than admiring the asses of young girls, he thought.

This bit of wisdom sat in his thoughts and seemed so profound that he felt urged to go back to his room to write it down. He was distracted on the way there by a display of native woodcarvings in the souvenir shop. They were, on closer inspection, not very good, but at least they were a local product. He went in and considered two of them for his children. They would not, of course, want them. Receiving these gifts might for a moment remind the children of his continuing existence.

By the time he had them back in his room, he had lost his impulse to write down his insight. The shuttered room was dark and hollow. He left it swiftly and went out to sit by the pool. He ordered a beer. Two little children paddled in the shallow end. The fat Jewess who seemed so proud of her figure was offering gobs of it to the sun. A woman pranced past him, arching her back in a coy Slavic manner.

THE SCUBA DIVING LESSON was in the hotel pool, early in the morning, before breakfast. Ethan felt clumsy and heavy. The only other pupil was a teenaged boy.

"I was into tennis and basketball before I broke my leg," the boy said to Ethan as they waited for the instructor. "Still hasn't healed right."

He slapped his thigh gently, massaged it.

"I guess swimming would be good for it," Ethan said. He didn't know what else to say. The night before, his dreams had been fearful, anxious visions of drowning. Foolish to be doing this so late in life.

"Well," a voice called. It was Captain Jack, the main

charter man on the island. He was a short, muscled and weathered man. Setting the tanks and flippers next to a poolside table, he waved them to come over. Captain Jack explained each function of the apparatus and demonstrated basic underwater signals. Then Ethan and the boy, Robbie, helped each other on with the tanks. Then they went into the pool and practised using the respirator and practised buddy breathing.

As they got out of the pool, the waiters were setting up the hot trays for breakfast and joshing the cashier in a quick singsong patois. The cashier, a young woman with splendid eyes, paid scant attention, but she smiled, something she seldom did while toting up the guest bills.

Down in a shower of bubbles, thinking breathe, breathe, at first awkward, body arching up, then down the anchor rope and over the ridges of coral. Captain Jack's face bobbed ahead of him, Robbie went under him, and off towards another outcropping of coral. A school of fish sped just ahead of him, all orange and blue.

"It's a whole different world down there, " Captain Jack said as he helped Ethan off with the tanks. "Do you realize we were down there almost thirty-five minutes?"

Ethan hadn't. Time seemed an illusion of the surface world, a fiction invented to deal with boredom. The mate took up the anchor and they moved to a different spot for snorkeling. Ethan found a sand dollar which broke apart as he picked it up. A sea urchin undulated on the bottom just ahead of it. There was a large rusty automobile engine down there. Robbie found a conch. The piece of coral Ethan had brought up was beginning to smell. The mate put it in a bucket of bleach. They headed back to the hotel pier, wing on wing. Ethan stood, hanging onto the main shroud, squinting in the noon sun. Back on the dock, trying to put his shoes on, he discovered that his feet were alarmingly burned. Then he remembered the shark stories. He had not even thought of sharks. And nobody else – Robbie, the captain – had mentioned the possibility of them.

Ethan brought the local sunburn unguent and winced as he spread it on his swollen feet. He could not get his shoes on. Or his beach sandals. Barefoot, the tops of his trousers touching his feet like the ends of electric wires, he limped to the men's boutique.

The little salesman made a moue of concern and he brought out larger-sized white shoes. In agony, Ethan got them on. They were light and soft to the touch, and strangely comforting. He paid with his bank card and walked out to the bar. Again, he saw his ring flashing in the shop windows and now the white shoes, moving casually and easily like white birds in flight.

At the final night's barbecue, Ethan watched a native boy trying to get around the floor with a large tray of hors d'oeuvres. The tourists were on him before he made even a few steps and they pressed in from all sides. Ethan caught a glimpse of the boy's face through the jumble of arms going in, under, over, and the boy seemed wide-eyed with actual fear.

"That's disgusting," he said to the person next to him.

"Gross," she agreed. It was Alicia.

The line had begun to form for the serving. Those same ones who had assailed the hors d'oeuvres turned their intent fury on the quiet beginnings of a line and Ethan found himself jostled away from Alicia.

He sat with Julie and Phil and Paul. Julie seemed tired, or quiet, or both. So did Phil. Paul did most of the talking. Plenty of wine was served with the meal, and the band began to play. After coffee, the bar was opened again. Ethan bought a round for his table. People began to dance. He saw Alicia dancing very close with one of the waiters, not the uppity one. Paul asked Julie to dance. Ethan and Phil sat close, not talking. Alicia and the waiter were on the steps leading down to the dark beach, talking intently.

An impromptu snake dance, or conga line, or Greek dance began; it was none of these but partook of all, and was really only an excuse to move all together. Ethan found himself between Paul and the taller sardonic girl. She yelled to him that her name was Debbie and he yelled his name back, but she called back What? as the music reached a higher level of frenzy. He caught a glimpse of his shoes, flashing across the floor, white and young.

Even later, dishevelled and woozy, he found himself dancing with Julie, and yes, each time they took a stumbling step, she pressed her thigh firmly between his legs. The bar was closing. Only a few stalwarts were left.

Ethan went to the washroom. When he came out everyone was gone. Julie too.

When people leave us, he thought, walking slowly back to his room, they go on elsewhere with their own existence and he stabbed the key towards the lock, once, twice. A difficult truth, we have to keep re-learning it.

He dreamed that night of scuba diving, going further down into darker and colder waters, until he was all alone in freezing heaviness. Then he dreamed of walking, alone again, down gently curving streets with those lamp posts that looked like Old English gas lights, with frosted glass and wrought iron points. Somehow, although he had never been on this street before, he knew it was where Karen and her new husband lived. Someone fair and far off was beckoning him onward.

THE LAST MORNING'S breakfast was subdued. Some of the guests didn't make it. The young waiter Alicia had been with was doing the coffee pouring. He didn't look too happy. Paul came and sat with him. Paul talked about his wife and children. There was no sign of Alicia or Debbie, or indeed, of Julie.

As they waited in the lobby for the airport bus, he began to feel very short of breath. He thought, the goddam gentleman from San Francisco, and then the lobby whirled and he fell forward. Then he was lying beside the piles of luggage and voices were saying take it easy, don't try to get up, and Debbie was bending over him, frowning in concern.

When he got to his seat he found Debbie buckling herself into the seat next to his.

"You don't smoke either, huh?" she smiled up at him. "I wish they were showing a movie. I hate to think about going back."

"Well," said Ethan, fiddling with the seat belt, "at least we get drinks. That'll help."

"Say," she put a hand on his arm, looked concerned, "how are you feeling?"

"Oh, I'm OK," he laughed. "Just too much sun I guess. I have to be so damn careful…."

She smiled and it seemed to him left her hand on his arm a little longer and then the plane's engines were revving up and then they were off and banking once over the island. The water was a bright blue and the beaches shimmered.

"It looks like a postcard," Debbie said. "Unreal."

"Too real," Ethan said. And now the drink cart was bouncing down the aisle.

"Say, wasn't your friend, uh, Alicia, sitting with you on the way down? Where is she anyhow?"

Debbie sucked on her swizzle stick, shrugged.

"I think she decided to take a side trip to Curaçao with some dude she met."

"Won't she forfeit the charter thing? I mean the fare?" Ethan said.

"I guess she doesn't give a damn," Debbie said. "I really don't know her that well. We just met on the way down."

"Oh."

"Yes. She's from Toronto or someplace."

"Well," Ethan said.

"I'm from Southgate. That's near Detroit, you know," she said.

Debbie went on to say that she was a receptionist for a team of allergists. Ethan started to tell her about the magazine he edited. More drinks arrived. Voices were rising around them. Debbie said that she was divorced. Ethan started to say that he was too and Debbie went on to say that her ex was a burned out case, on and off drugs, a heavy scene.

"Well, I had it all wrong," Ethan said. "I mean I thought you and Alicia were friends from college or something. You know it's strange to think we won't be seeing all these people after the plane lands. I mean seeing them everyday for a week, and then zip…."

The lout from Cleveland was weaving down the aisle, trying to get to the washroom, giving the stewardess with the drink cart a hard time as he squeezed past her.

"I won't miss him," Debbie said. "What a pig…."

They had yet another drink. Ethan began to talk about his divorce. It all sounded like a soap opera.

"I don't know why I keep thinking about her. Karen I mean, I mean my wife, actually ex-wife. But you know when you have a tooth pulled you feel this big space in your mouth. It feels bigger than it is, and you keep wanting to touch it with your tongue, but it's so sensitive that it'll hurt if you do, but you touch it anyway…."

"That's a beautiful analogy," she said. "Really."

After a while dinner was served, then coffee, and

then Ethan felt very sleepy. Debbie excused herself to go to the washroom. He could hardly keep his eyes open. Like a great slow folding of dark wings. The night gently took him up.

When he woke, he was aware of the engines' drone. Debbie wasn't back yet. People were quieter now. He looked at his watch. How long had he slept? The stewardess was announcing their arrival and would they please extinguish all cigarettes and put their chair backs and chair tables in an upright position. Debbie wasn't back yet. He had dreamed anxiously, Alicia had been murdered, buried out on the beach by the young waiter. Or fed to the waiting sharks. He couldn't remember.

As the plane banked and came lower down, he could see that it was snowing. It was drifting between the houses and across the frozen river. The plane made its approach and down they went. Descend, descend, the snow said. Ethan looked at his white shoes. Unsuitable. From another zone. Descend, descend. The plane was on the ground now and an audacious few were unbuckling and gathering the souvenir hats and bags and goods.

To little avail, as they waited another several minutes to disembark. The muzak played the polka. *In Heaven There is No Beer.* Ethan looked back down the aisle. No Debbie. Disgruntled remarks were made. Instead of a tunnel, there was a portable stairway, right out there on the snow-swept apron. Ethan went down it in his turn, back into his cold and usual world, his white shoes in the wet white snow. Into the airport to find his luggage and make his declaration. During his brief sleep, what had he dreamed. Someone, Alicia perhaps, or Debbie, far off beckoning him to follow. Follow to what or where? He went on alone in the cold dark, towards the lighted building.

At The Going Down Of The Sun
And In The Morning

FRED RAN EVERY MORNING. HE WAS UP and out and running in all seasons, any weather, at 6:30 a.m. The street went to the south for two blocks and then became the access to the expressway. At the street's north end, it turned into a winding road that curved along the edge of a forest preserve and ended some five miles away at a shopping centre. Fred always ran north for about half an hour, then turned and ran back home. Betty was usually up by then and had the coffee on. They had coffee together after his shower and he was on his way to work by eight.

Betty said that his running was compulsive. She said it was one of Kubler-Ross' stages of dealing with death. He forgot which one. Probably bargaining. There was, Fred thought, possibly some truth to Betty's theory. If he missed a day of running, he felt anxious and guilty about it.

On this particular morning, one of those ambiguous

days at the end of summer or beginning of autumn, he had run as usual down the border of the forest preserve to the large elm that marked his turnaround point. His mind, as usual, was rambling from one thought to another, and then the words began:

The captain and the crew were seated about the campfire. The captain arose and said, "Alphonso, tell us one of your famous stories." And Alphonso began as follows. The captain and the crew were seated about the campfire....

The silly Boy Scout jingle ran through his mind, over and over. Must have been the summer of 1945. No. Earlier. The summer of 1942. Because in 1945 he had been long past the Boy Scouts. The summer of 1945 had been the last summer of the war, although nobody knew it at the time. Fred had been waiting for the autumn, for his birthday, so he could join the Marines. He had seen *Wake Island* five times.

It was the summer he learned to drink. The drinking took place in dark malt-smelling places where there were advertisements hanging on the walls, of men in red coats blowing curved brass hunting horns, noble stags posed at the edge of a precipice or at the bank of a white-water river, fat monks raising foamy steins in rude stone cellars. Usually there were mounted fish on the walls too.

All this seemed to suggest Wisconsin, resorts, lakes, outdoors, manly friendship, and sports. Wisconsin was that mysterious place to the north where they often drove on a summer night, hoping to find the willing girls and the dim indulgent taverns. No fuss about how old you were. Hell, they'd all be in the service soon anyway. Ah yes. Alphonso, tell us.

And 1945 was also the summer of polio. Everybody knew somebody – a friend, a cousin, an acquaintance from school, someone from the next block or next door – who had it. Some cases ended in death. Swimming pools were closed.

Fred was running back home and was almost at the end of the forest preserve road. A young girl stood at the intersection where his block began, thumb out. Usually he encountered nobody on his run, so he was startled and made a noise in greeting. The girl did not respond, only looked blankly at him. He saw himself briefly twin-mirrored in her sunglasses as he ran past. He wished he had not made the noise.

Seeing the insolent girl on the deserted corner, taking such a chance, hitchhiking, offering herself to the infrequent cars, made him remember. Yes, 1945 had also been the summer of the murder. Two girls, sisters maybe, he couldn't remember for sure, had been found in the forest preserve, naked, raped, and strangled. Fourteen and fifteen. Presumed to have been hitchhiking. Found by somebody walking a dog. It was like *déjà vu*, seeing the girl hitchhiker, as if he had seen her before, a long time before, in the dark. *Déjà vu.* Everybody knew what that meant now. It was like bartenders knowing that you put a celery stalk in a bloody mary.

Strange. It was this same forest preserve, several miles to the northwest, where they had been found. Fred remembered how the murders had crowded all the war news off the front page of the newspaper. He remembered how, back then, the war, the murders, the drinking, and the general fear of polio had all mixed together in his imagination. Horrified, fascinated, he followed the case in the papers. Once he dreamed that he had been the killer-rapist and felt absurdly guilty for a long time after, so vivid had the dream been. The feel of a slender throat in his hands....

He reached his house and jogged slowly up the drive to the kitchen door. Betty wasn't in the kitchen. Oh yes. She had planned to get up early and go to the scratch-and-dent sale at the mall. Last summer she had gone to the sale a bit late and swore never to go again. It had been primitive, she said. People had actually shoved and knocked each other down. Here it was a year later and she had forgotten her horror. They needed a new barbecue, Betty said, and it might be best to pick up a cheap one.

The children were all grown and gone, and it seemed to Fred that he and his contemporaries were out of the barbecuing phase of life. Perhaps you had to be younger and more hopeful to do it, like the euphoric families in TV ads. Even as Betty had these theories about his running, Fred saw a perverse symptom in Betty's determination to buy a new barbecue. Perhaps it was a final attempt to assert their own relevance. They weren't an over-the-hill couple.

Fred put the coffee on and showered. Alphonso, tell us. What were the captain and the crew doing, sitting around a campfire? Perhaps they had been shipwrecked.

The Forties. The war had always been there in those days, far away but close. Each block had a little raked sand or gravel plot set off with a flagpole set in the centre. At the base of the flagpole was a plaque with the names of the block's sons in the service on it. Gold stars were placed next to the names of the ones who were killed.

Almost every block had at least one gold star, matched by a gold star pennant hanging in a house's window. He remembered that old Mr. Crizek had been the speaker at his block's first gold star dedication. *They shall not grow old as we that are left grow old,* Mr. Crizek had said. Then something more, and finally, *At the going down of the sun and in the morning, we will remember them....*

When Fred finally did go into the service, the army, it was between wars, and he didn't want to go. He ended up a drafting technician, bored out of his mind. There were no hordes of screaming Japs to kill. There was nobody to kill. Just time. After he got out, he had a vague idea of using the drafting thing to become an architect. So he went to college. He wanted to be an architect who wouldn't sell out. *The Fountainhead* kind of architect.

After two years he quit college and got a job at Mason's. He was still there. So he had missed the wars and the killings and the dreaded sickness and hadn't murdered anyone and hadn't designed buildings. He *had* met a girl at the college. Her name was Nina and she was black. Back then of course she had not been "black." She had been a "Negro," or "coloured." At the denominational college they went to, the races did not mix. So they kept their affair discreet and quiet. They met in the city for dates or else they did a lot of agonized kissing in the back seat of his old car. They spent a lot of time in coffee shops, talking about their situation. There were long periods of silence in those coffee shops. Things were rather complicated by Nina's plans to become either a pianist or a missionary.

The situation reached a crescendo during Christmas break on a sofa in her parents' home on the far South Side. Her parents were not home. Even back then, the far South Side was a bad place to show a white face. Fred walked to the elevated train station from Nina's parents' house hunched in tense fear, as he had once walked down the polio streets of summer. After a week of winter-term classes, Fred withdrew from the college and wrote Nina a letter full of self-reproach.

Betty was a friend of Dick Mason's wife. Dick's first wife. Fred met Betty about a month after he started at Mason's. When Dick married his secretary, Betty stopped talking to him and naturally they didn't socialize. It made things at the office a bit tense.

Alphonso, tell us. Nina. What had become of her? Natural hair, probably. Radical stuff. Marches and battles he had not gone to. Sex. 1945. The summer air hung with the smell of lilacs. The sound of passing car wheels and sudden radios and voices coming from backyards. If he had met Nina back then....

Fred drank his coffee at the kitchen table. The refrigerator made its usual ship-in-a-storm moaning. It was a forty-minute drive to Mason's. Back in the nineteenth century, when old Mr. Mason, Dick's grandfather, started the business, it had been out in the country. Now it was surrounded by suburbs. Old Mr. Mason had been a master stone cutter. The business had been cemetery markers. His son had built up a sideline in lawn furniture and sod. By the time Dick took over, the headstones had become the smallest part of the business. Fred was in charge of the landscaping end of things, planning patios of reclaimed brick and doing stone archways and fountains.

Now trouble was coming. For the past week Dick Mason had been closeted with the emissary of a large conglomerate. The outfit was one of those exotic new names that appear in movie credits under the old familiar names of the studios. A Trans-Lux-Something Corporation. Just the other day, the emissary of the conglomerate and Dick had come out of the office and stood in the corridor, still deep in conversation, looking in Fred's direction.

Dick had the face of an old jockey. The rest of him, however, was not jockey-sized. He was taller than Fred, who was exactly six feet. Often Dick would squint into the distance, as he was at that moment in the corridor, standing next to the emissary, as if peering down some empty backstretch.

The emissary stood next to Dick looking absently in Fred's direction. The emissary, though manifestly younger than Fred, affected the tall, weary slouch of a middle-aged professor. As Fred stared back the words *redundant* and *terminal* thudded in his mind. He shall not grow old as we grow old. We will remember.

WISCONSIN, FRED THOUGHT, walking out to the car. His daughter Cindy lived there. She and her husband made safe wooden toys with nothing toxic in them which they sold at art and craft fairs in the summers. Cindy seldom wrote.

Wisconsin, where the two girls were presumed to be heading the night they were killed. On impulse, Fred turned north and down the road he ran on, instead of turning south to the expressway. The sun was full up now and there were more cars. The girl was gone from the corner. There was a small breeze. The trees in the forest shook their leaves in the early sun.

The girls had probably been done in, the police said, by a passing stranger. The girls themselves hadn't been from the neighbourhood. The murder was like the war. It came from far away.

The street curved along the edge of the woods, with places here and there cut in to get to picnic areas. On the other side of the street, a row of new cheap houses faced the trees. The raw fields beyond were already plotted and staked out to be more houses.

Fred thought of his office at Mason's. His desk with the framed family photo on it. Cindy was about six in it, Aileen thirteen. He saw himself putting the photo into a box of his things from the desk drawers. There wasn't much in the box. A picture of the first big patio job he had done, a coffee mug, a paper weight, a letter opener. Most everything in the office belonged to Mason's and would become part of the conglomerate's inventory, logged by some computer in Utah.

The woods looked pretty in the early sun. They were meant to look pretty, because of that old idea about nature as haven for city people. Soothing and recreating. But he had feared the woods. A terrifying place, haunt of pervert and maniac, a place for sordid trysts. At night, cars parked in there and a chorus of moans and gasps arose, as if from the damned.

So Fred never entered the forest preserve without a strong feeling of unease. It was a feeling he had known before, the dread he had felt walking down a street where he knew somebody had polio, as if the disease could penetrate walls and he might breathe in death.

The dream of killing the girls had been so strong. He, in the moonlight, breathing like an animal. The brutal scene went on in his mind, like a story told over and over. Crazy. But as a boy he had wondered: was it possible? Alphonso, tell us. *Could* he kill?

The case faded from the paper after a lot of false leads. Other crimes took its place, and the war ended. Now the two girls seemed almost like figures from a child's folk tale. Children lost in the forest, killed by a huntsman.

So. No murder for him, no war, no crippling disease. And the catastrophes of marriage had passed him by too. Many of their friends had had affairs, divorced and remarried, and gone through some ludicrous personality changes. He and Betty had discussed it and decided not to separate. She had all these habits, like making lists for him, the oh yes, the 'must do.' She wore her glasses on a chain around her neck and looked, at list-making time, like a woman executive in a Forties movie.

She didn't like to cook. She took any occasion to say that just for a change why didn't they try the new restaurant. There was always a new restaurant. When they quarrelled it was in the style of Fred's own parents, in lowered voices. Fred had got to the point where none of this annoyed him enough to make any drastic change.

He turned on Cermak and drove east. Usually when people went back to their old neighbourhoods they found shopping plazas or slums. A great satisfaction, finding such violent change. It made the present so much brighter. When Fred got to his old street, he found it quite unchanged. The same arching trees over the wide, clean street, the same well-kept, neat houses behind the careful lawns.

And there was his old house, now belonging to strangers who had bought it from strangers. He half expected to see himself come running out the front door, yelling something back to his mother. He circled the block looking down the alley where hollyhocks stood smugly inside the fences. Then he headed over to the Eisenhower Expressway. There, as he had before, he turned away from Mason's and headed instead toward downtown.

On the way through the West Side, in the early sun,

he felt as if he were in a boat on a broad river, his fellow sailors in the other cars, the sun glinting off glass and metal as if on whitecaps. Once he had seen a coffee-table book at a friend's about landmark buildings in Chicago which had vanished. Urban renewal. Over and over in the book it said "now a parking structure." He turned into one of these at the south edge of the loop.

"How long you going to be?"

Fred looked into the bloodshot eyes of a large black man. He realized with a start that this was the first human voice he had heard all day.

"Just an hour or so," Fred said.

He smiled as he spoke. The large black man made a noise like the one Fred had made to the hitchhiker. Fred parked and walked out under the old elevated structure, his parking stub still in his hand, the remains of a smile on his face, moving from the shadows of the pillars to shafts of dusty light. Overhead, a train came to a stop.

He passed a window full of expensive scissors and knives. In a coffee shop on the corner, people were standing at counters, intent on their newspapers. He was beginning to feel hungry. He crossed Wabash and walked toward Michigan.

There it was. The scene that had so excited him when he was seventeen and used to come here and watch the women from the offices going out to lunch. So much potential, the excitement of possible adventure. Now, today, he noticed several self-absorbed young couples. He moved among them. I am alone, he thought. I am invisible. I cannot touch. I am the centre of indifference.

He remembered a Saturday a week earlier when he took the second car in for front end alignment. They said it would take about an hour. All the magazines in the grubby little waiting space were about fishing and home improvement. He had gone out for a coffee he didn't really want. One storefront he passed was an ethnic bakery with a few shiny and knotted loaves on display in the window. The next store had a sign saying we supply drills, jigs, and fixtures, and in the window, drill bits were haloed around a large gear. The coffee shop was next. Although it was early in the morning, the coffee tasted old.

That's what life is, he thought. You wait for something you aren't really interested in in a place you don't like. And you are alone. You are nowhere. Between, like between planes. Nobody knows you.

Self-pity, he thought – a cheap escape. Even his pain was stereotyped, a TV sitcom. *Father Knows Nothing.* Was self-pity one of the deadly sins? There was envy, lust, gluttony. Had he ever committed any of them? It seemed somehow mean-spirited not to commit at least one deadly sin. Probably self-pity didn't count.

HE REMEMBERED a room in the library at the college. It was an old building with creaking floors and high ceilings. The room was intended for quiet study, with large, worn leather chairs. In the winter, the radiators clanked and the steam pipes shook on the walls. The ceiling was made of pressed tin, shaped into ornamental squares.

Out the tall window, you could see the snow-covered campus slope down to the train station. It was always too warm in the room and Fred spent a lot of time fighting sleep. He was fond of the place. It gave him a feeling of security. Everything – the uncertain future, the business with Nina – was outside the room. Inside, he lay in torpid snugness.

Here, now, in the late summer's heat, the dusty sun shafts coming down between tall buildings, there was no refuge. He was in the present moment, walking through the outside air, in light, then shade, then light, then shade again. He walked north. The street had a festive air. Coloured banners announcing some kind of exhibition hung from the light fixtures. The sun struck the mica dots in the sidewalk. Even through sunglasses, the light was brilliant.

"Hey man," said a young black kid, wearing yellow plastic curlers in his hair. The kid was carrying an open pop can. He didn't look like trouble. He seemed genuinely puzzled.

"Can you tell me what day it is?"

"Day?" said Fred. "It's the twenty-third, I think. No. Twenty-fourth –"

"No, no," said the kid. "I mean the *day*."

"It's Wednesday."

"Yeah. Wednesday. Thanks. Say, do you have the time?"

"Just past eleven," Fred said.

And the boy went on. How could you lose the day of the week? The kid hadn't seemed spaced out or anything. It was important to know when and where you were. Fred wondered if he should go into the Art Institute. When he was young, it had been a good place to meet girls. They trusted you more if they met you in a museum or at a concert.

Was it too early for a drink? He could have a few drinks and then a long lunch. Or else a quick lunch and then go do something. Maybe he should phone Dick Mason. Tell him to shove it. Or say he had the flu. Was the flu an old man's illness? Sick man. Resigned due to ill health.

He crossed Michigan at Ohio and walked toward the lake. Some artists had set up a display along the sidewalk. Perhaps that was what the banners were about. There was pottery and macramé and a young couple had a table of the same kind of wooden toys Cindy and her husband did. Everything down the sidewalk looked familiar. He had seen the same stuff at other fairs.

Everything, even art, was becoming standard, uniform. Not just art – authentic holy days were supplanted by cheap, consumer occasions like Mother's Day. Provoke guilt if you don't come across with the flowers and candy. Fred felt a slowly firming yet vague sense of malaise. Wasn't there a poet who said that when he was depressed he wanted nothing to be more than two feet tall?

It was television. Commercials promised ecstasy if

you tried the new chewing gum. Life was inevitably disappointing and you couldn't switch channels. He headed north again. The lake was nearer. The sounds of traffic on the Drive were louder.

Someone was running down along the water's edge. Across the Drive the row of familiar buildings had upcroppings here and there of new structures. Far down the beach, back where it curved eastward, the runner had stopped and seemed to be looking in Fred's direction. Fred turned and walked north again. Then he stopped and looked back. The beach was empty as far down as he could see. He started walking south, back toward the parking lot.

Now it was fully noon, and the streets were crowded with people on their way to lunch. They had earned it. Fred moved among them, feeling out of sync. He didn't seem to be going with the same dedication as the rest of them. He was a saunterer, ambling along.

Once in his car, with the air conditioner working to overcome the baking sun, he headed out on what used to be Congress, past the Auditorium and across Michigan toward the Drive. Then he turned north and went up past where he had walked. After a few miles, he turned off and went in a hesitant circle and found a parking space on a side street. Down the street he could see delivery trucks. Purposes. Packages were delivered. Barrels of beer were thundering down wooden skids into dark tavern cellars.

He walked back toward the lake and down into a pedestrian tunnel which led under the Drive and out to the beach. The walls were covered with spray-painted slogans. He could hear the traffic booming above him. Halfway through, he began to feel a rising tension. This was exactly the sort of place you weren't supposed to put yourself. The newspapers were always saying that the city was safe, but you had to take reasonable precautions. You couldn't even walk safely through a tunnel.

Well. The world hadn't changed all that much. Way back in the Forties, two little girls couldn't safely hitch-hike. He could see the light at both ends of the tunnel. He seemed to be only slightly more than halfway through. The air down here was damp, unpleasant, like the air in a public toilet. The walls seemed ancient. Lights hung behind metal grilles, all broken and half off the walls. For some reason he thought of old Mr. Mason's funereal statues. Sorrowing winged figures, cherubs, angels, doves. They shall not grow old.

He looked back. Nobody there. Then he turned and went back. He walked out into the innocent sunlight. It was time to go home or somewhere. He headed the car north again. The Drive looked strange yet familiar. He remembered coming down here with his parents to go to some beach. If he went far enough north, past Evanston, Wilmette, Winnetka.... He pictured the towns on the border of the lake, like beads on a string leading all the way up to Wisconsin. Clear lakes, green forests.

He remembered. His father whistling a tuneless tune in the Chevy on the way home from the box plant. Falling asleep to the sound of far-off trains, boxcars slamming together in the yards. That firm joining. The train whistles going away, going away. Voices on a summer night, and Nina's laugh.

He thought of Betty arriving home with a floor-model barbecue, all assembled. Dick Mason had been anxiously calling all morning. There was a new job for Fred, with a raise and stock options in the conglomerate. Cindy had called. He and Betty were grandparents. They had named the baby after him. Not that Fred had ever liked his name. You thought automatically of the Flintstones. Except that Fred was married to Wilma, not Betty. Nobody in a novel was named Fred.

He pictured the neighbours calling across their lawns. Figures in white against the lush green. The long light of a late summer afternoon. Sophisticated drinks being served. Would it be like this if he went home now?

Or would it be as usual: the silence of the empty street, houses all closed up, the deeper silence of his own house where Betty either was or was not, nursing grievances she dared not voice. The nearby forest standing close, in its own deep silence, holding its reproach of innocent bloodshed.

So here he was, in his car going nowhere or someplace. Who was he? Alphonso, tell us. One of the best things about the story was that it never ended. He wasn't the killer. He wasn't the victim. But here he was in any case, with maps in the glove compartment, clearly indicating the directions to places, sailing serenely among his fellow mariners in the other cars. The captain and the crew. Returning to the dark harbour or setting out for open water.

Freeze Frames

I WAS STANDING IN LINE IN THE SUPERMARKET reading the magazines for free. "Still happily married after two whole months," I read in one. "Sad," countered another, "a career conflict will lead to a breakup in the near future." And here is the lady who made a successful comeback at the age of thirty-one. Here she is in her beach house looking over possible new scripts. *Sorry,* it says on the rack next to the magazine I was reading, *Sold Out of Fifty Copies.* Raped by a UFO pilot. Plot to steal Elvis Corpse. Slain Man in Lingerie Eaten By Dog. Leon Westmore Dies.

"In a week that saw the deaths of David Niven and Raymond Massey, you might be forgiven for not noticing the demise of Leon Westmore. Leon *who?* Trivia buffs will remember his tough captain in that Sixties TV cop series *Front Line.* Late show insomniacs will have caught him in such forgettables as *Waterfront Tough.* His older, better known brother Wallace Westmore survives."

The piece didn't mention his daughter, Miriam, who also survives, who was standing in a supermarket reading magazines for free and discovered that her father had died.

I WENT OUT TO LUNCH with Liz. She is the closest person I have in my life. I was married once, when I was twenty-seven, and it lasted three years. He was nice to me. I liked him a lot. But that's not enough, you know? Anyhow, nowadays I try to keep most people at arm's-length. My mother died last year. Liz is okay. We work together in the same office at Craig & Peter which does market surveys. I detest the word *lifestyle*, but I cannot think of an appropriate synonym.

"The ironic thing was," I said at lunch, "that I called him last month. I hadn't spoken to him for over twenty – no *thirty* – years. In fact, I don't think I was even talking when he left. No, wait. He hadn't left. My mother walked out on *him* when I was about two. So I probably wasn't talking yet, right?"

"Anyhow," I said, "I found all these letters from my father to my mother after she died and I figured it out. She left *him*. All these years I pictured this playboy type father. So I called him up to say I wanted a reunion. You know, he cried? I was going out there on my vacation next month."

"It sounds like a movie," said Liz. "I am so sick of these cutesy salads. I'd like some real old-fashioned lettuce."

ROMOLA'S IMAGINATION had been shaped by sensational journalism. Girl hacked to pieces in love nest. Suicide pacts. Tycoons and chorines. Murder trials and what the defendant wore on the stand. Clandestine snapshots of hangings and electrocutions. Razzamuhtaz.

(I should explain that although I am calling my mother "Romola" in this story, our relationship in what I call "real" life – in our case it might be "reel" – never got to a point where I could call her anything but Mother.

In her heart, of course, she must have thought of herself as her name, so I now give it back to her. Which as I say, I could never do in waking daylight.)

Romola loved the peepholing columns. She loved the pettiness, the grudge-nursing that went on among the columnists. Daily she got her reports on the latest divorces, marriages, remarriages, infidelities, who was preggers, all about the latest public brouhahas, comebacks, failures, breakdowns, bankruptcies, suicides, gangster connections, drug busts.

MY FATHER had followed his older brother out to Hollywood in 1946. Wallace had by that time been in *Underworld, Dark Dragnet, Stone Streets,* and *No Exit Here.* Leon was a bit shorter than his brother. They both had the same regular features, blue eyes and square jaws: perfect for urban drama. Romola met my father in the all-nite supermarket she was clerking in. He was doing some stunt work at the time.

(Though I call my mother "Romola" here, I have some difficulty saying "Leon." Why is this?)

Romola dreamed of a sheikh's tent, silken divans, a draped room, brass gongs, Turkish carpets, a tiger's skin draped over a divan and she draped over the tiger's skin. What she got instead was working in the supermarket and my father.

She was prone to on-the-spot decisions. Those drapes are hideous, she would say. Or that woman is no better than she should be. This dress is glamorous. That man is debonair. The other man is a cad. She apparently made the same kind of decision about my father. She possibly thought that he had a future.

WHEN I WAS GROWING UP I often pondered the framed photographs in the living room. None were of my father.

"Your father was famous," Romola said defiantly. "He had *style*."

"How come I haven't seen any of his movies?" I asked. I was a very sarcastic kid. Defensive.

IT WASN'T UNTIL SOMETIME in the Sixties that I saw my father. Eleven-forty-five on Channel 2. He was the union boss in *Concrete Trap*. In a dockside office he ordered his thugs to maim a stoolie. He looked, I thought, unconvincing. There was something sort of yearning and soft in his eyes. It was sort of hopeful.

Style, a sentimental, semi-physical quality, is more superficial than the above characteristics (beauty, personality, charm, temperament). It depends not merely upon clothes, but upon an innate knowledge of how to walk, how to stand, how to conduct oneself generally.

– MARSHALL NEILAN, "ACTING FOR THE SCREEN: THE SIX GREAT ESSENTIALS," IN *Opportunities in the Motion Picture Industry*. BOOK FOUND ON ROMOLA'S SHELF.

ROMOLA HAD AN INORDINATE FEAR and adoration of her own mother. How do I know? It was the incessant quoting of her mother's shallow wisdom. And Romola never learned to cook. Leon (I learned from the letters) thought her bridal nervousness in the kitchen area was only a stage. The takeout food, the endless Chinese brown bags, the paper plates, the whole atmosphere of temporariness, all that would be a phase to outwait.

Four years later, when she left him, they were still eating medium pizzas on Wednesdays when you got a medium for the price of a small. And they were still eating off paper plates which she set out on the kitchen table each morning, a paper napkin folded beside each plate, ready for whatever the evening meal might be. It was as if she were always poised for flight, travelling light. When did TV dinners come in? I remember a lot of them.

DURING THE TWENTIES an entrepreneur bought a lot of land near the river and began to create a modern suburb. Trees were cut down and lots laid out. Sidewalks and lamp posts were installed. Work was begun on a sewer link-up. Some foundations were put in.

The Depression stopped all work. Weeds grew tall inside the low concrete walls of the foundations and along the sidewalks. Nobody ever to live in Belle View. The neighbourhood children took it for their own, bicycling and skating on the sidewalks, hide-and-seeking in the foundations. So it was when my mother brought me east and I grew up.

My first kiss was yielded up in Belle View, writhing against an unlit street lamp. I was twelve years old.

"If you're old enough to bleed," the boy who was kissing me said, "you're old enough to butcher."

It was two years before I realized what that meant. After Romola's death last year I drove past the place on my way to the funeral parlour. It was still there, weeds high, all surrounded by successful suburbs. It looked like ruins transported from postwar Europe.

I slowed, looking down the sunken, cracked sidewalks, a tourist of my own past, looking for a skinny girl being kissed and groped against a lamp post which would never give light. I am the child of two disappointed seekers of romance. Nowadays, if someone says *trust me*, I know I am being warned not to.

ROMOLA KEPT ALL HER HATS from the Forties

and Fifties. She had quite a collection. In the movies hats defined social class. Lower class men wore caps. When Cagney moved up from cap to hat in *The Roaring Twenties* we knew he was not just a minor thug anymore but a big shot. Often big shots wore white hats with a black band. Reporters wore snap-brim fedoras. Low on the forehead meant menace, so hotshot reporters pushed theirs back, pulled down their ties, overcoat collars up, all signalling a devil-may-care what-the-hell loose attitude towards life.

Hat removing in elevators a useful way to acknowledge presence of lady. In *The Damned Don't Cry* David Brian tried to make a lady out of tarty Joan Crawford and began with her hat. Then she got lessons in being a lady from Selena Royle. Spring Byington and Natalie Schafer bought expensive flighty-looking hats which came in opulent boxes. Diane Keaton tried to bring the woman's hat back in *Annie Hall.* Remember Ingrid Bergman's Casablanca hat? Marlon Brando and James Dean killed the man's hat in the Fifties.

Leon wore a hat in *Front Line.* He was the only one in the cast who did. The other cops, younger men, were New Frontier breezy, self-assured, hatless. Leon's hat rendered him obviously one of an earlier generation. Much humour was generated in this series on generational differences.

Leon stood for firm values, adherence to codes, World War Two stuff. He called himself a "book man." His young squad, however, believed in spontaneity, leaps of intuition, élan. Leon, the Captain, went by the book.

A history of my parents could be written as a catalogue of their hats.

Why is it that I could call my father by his name just now?

Cary Grant composed *Night and Day* at night with a stately clock standing against the wall, tick-tocking. Robert Alda composed *Rhapsody in Blue* for Paul Whiteman. Cornel Wilde coughed blood on the piano keys. He was in love with Merle Oberon who wrote novels. Dirk Bogarde and Henry Daniell were Liszt. Paul Henried, Katherine Hepburn and Robert Walker were Brahms, Robert Schumann and Clara Schumann: figure out who was which. Richard Chamberlain composed six symphonies and died of cholera.

I have, you see, learned much from the movies. How could it not be so, coming from a family in the business? I note that the agony of creation did not lead to happiness for these composers. I have a Sony Metal Capable Cassette Deck. I am not partial to classical music, despite my extensive knowledge of it. Classical music makes me nervous, except played softly in used bookstores. If classical music is being composed today, who will play the composers in future movies?

I listen to a lot of New Age. I like Kate Bush. Songs like *Lionheart*. Figure that out. Rob, my ex-husband, liked light classical and easy listening stations. I am not putting him down, but this divergence in taste should have been an early warning to both of us. Romola liked the old songs. I do not know what my father liked. How could I sing for him?

I remember the old Hollywood joke: An actor's career is summed up in five speeches by head of studio:

1. Who is Leon Westmore?
2. Get me Leon Westmore.
3. You know, we need someone like a Leon Westmore type.
4. Get me a young Leon Westmore.
5. Who is Leon Westmore?

My father's career was somewhere between one and two.

What was a slain man *doing* in lingerie?

LIZ WAS AN AMUSING WOMAN. She referred to Mr. Stanley, our superior, as "The Tool."

"Did you know," said Liz one day in the Xerox room, "that St. Thomas Aquinas passed his whole life in a kind of perpetual ecstasy? Once a *confrere* saw him at prayer before the altar, rising in the air about a cubit."

"No," I said, waiting for my turn at the machine. Light spilled from under the copy cover as the machine went on with the throughput.

"Also," said Liz, "after his death – seven months after – they exhumed his body and found it intact, exuding sweet odours. Same thing fourteen years later."

"Do you believe all that?" I asked.

"Of course," said Liz. "Or maybe not."

Mr. Stanley had a shock of white hair and piercing

blue eyes. He looked like a grandfather in a TV ad. Although he had four sons by two of his three wives, he had no grandchildren. The eldest son, also at Craig & Peter, claimed publicly to have undergone a vasectomy. The other sons were possibly merely careful.

Mr. Stanley shut his office door and commiserated with me. He said it was a sad thing when one lost his or her father. He said it was certainly very okay for me to go out to California to shape things up. He gave my elbow a small tremulous squeeze at the door.

How would my father's body be seven months from now? Had he ever risen in the air?

The movie they showed on the flight was called *ffolkes*. Roger Moore played a swashbuckling Navy type called in to take out some terrorists who had hijacked an oil rig in the North Sea. The leader of the terrorists was Anthony Perkins. Michael Parks played one of his hirelings in a vaguely sinister homosexual style. I remember having a crush on Michael Parks. Moore's character did not like women. Luncheon on the flight was sort of cordon bleu.

IN MANY SOCIETIES mourning rituals include purification ceremonies which often involve fire, laceration, cutting the hair, dietary restrictions (fasting as form of propitiation) and the erection of a hut on the grave. Oh, and avoidance of the deceased person's name. I did none of this.

PEOPLE TELL ME I look like Faye Dunaway in *The Eyes of Laura Mars*. I don't see it myself. I'm taller for one thing. Or maybe shorter.

I knew what to expect in Hollywood. William Holden face down in Norma Desmond's swimming pool. Tuesday Weld saying "Why not?" ironically. Donald Sutherland coming west for his health and going goo-goo over Karen Black. Jack Palance taking incredible bullying from studio boss Rod Steiger. All those beautiful doomed stars. Valentino, Frances Farmer. They had faces then. Fasten your seat belts, I said to myself as we deplaned, it's gonna be a bumpy day.

We talked to Wallace ("Wally") Westmore between takes on his new picture, *No Exit*.

"I am not temperamental," said Wally. "I have no swelled head. Why should I? I have done nothing. A thousand guys like me would love to be in my place. I just had good fortune."

A maid approached with a tray of sandwiches. Ham on rye, chicken salad on brown toast.

"My little brother Leon," said Wally with obvious pride, "he's working on a picture you know. First major role. And he's getting married! The kid's getting married!"

"The marriage contract," Wally went on seriously, "is the strongest bond in human history. It is the cornerstone of the temple of civilization. Free love is an alluring phantom. Ideally, a happy marriage should be founded on true love. When it isn't, the sanctity of the marriage contract must prevail over the errant heart. When my brother gets married, I know it will be for life. And when it's my turn –"

"What about the rumor of romance between you and Ann Savage?" we asked.

"You know how rumors start," Wally smiled with a wink. "There is absolutely nothing between Ann and I. We admire one another a lot and have doubled for tennis."

"But that's all?" we asked.

Wally only smiled. Ah, the sly sphinx.

– Excerpt from "Wonderful Wally," by "Cassandra," in *Photo-Fan*, Aug. 1946. Clipping found among Romola's papers.

WHAT I HADN'T TOLD LIZ at lunch was that I found all sorts of letters from Wally to my mother in a different bundle. There were all the letters from my father, all in chronological order, all tied together. And there was this bigger bundle from Wally, right next to my father's letters, both in a shoe box.

I am not a great writer of letters myself and I do not get many. Just the odd postcard. If I ever did get a lot of letters I think I would throw them out right after reading them. I do not like the idea of somebody else reading my mail. I did not like reading Romola's, except that I was involved after all.

I gathered that Wally's name was always linked romantically with some lady or other. Once it was Joan Crawford. When she won the Academy Award in 1945, the gossip tidbits in the columns stopped.

He never married. But he wasn't gay. He was secretly frying other fish. He must have gotten deeply involved with Romola right away. Even after she left my father their affair continued. Wally secretly paid the rent on her West Hollywood apartment until she left to go east.

Why hadn't they married? Was it Wally's reluctance to inflict more hurt on his brother? Was it the other fish he was frying on yet another back burner?

Miss Vera Tarleton was one of the last starlets. An over-the-hill cheerleader type, she missed the beach party bikini madness movies by about five years. She would have been perfect for them.

Romola's abrupt move east may have been triggered by her discovery of Vera's existence. Some of Wally's letters expressed maudlin resolve to end his midlife crisis with Vera. But he never attempted any reconciliation with Romola, never mentioned marriage, never asked her to return to him, and never came east to visit her. I carefully read all his letters searching for such attempts. I found none.

UNCLE WALLY LIVED in a bungalow about a block from the famous Farmer's Market. His street number was mounted on a piece of wood cut in the shape of a

Scotty dog. He was wearing a shirt with two crossed golf clubs over the pocket. His arms descended from the short sleeves shrunken, hanging down to end at his large hands folded on his lap. He looked like a giant caved in. His voice came out of a deep place.

"Leon was always a dreamer," he said. "Of course your mother was worse. I never did figure out what she wanted. Out of life I mean. Anyhow, he left his photo album for you. There wasn't any money you know. Funeral was paid out of a Guild policy."

"Keep in touch," he said, squinting out the opened screen door. "Watch yourself walking on this street. Looks safe, but no place is these days. I have my checks mailed directly to the bank."

MY FATHER'S APARTMENT building was a stucco ruin. It looked as if it had been designed by Raymond Chandler. But the landscaping around it was immaculate. There was even a little rock pool in the courtyard.

"Last of the real gentlemen," said the manager, a woman in her sixties with a determined tan. Her face looked like an Aztec mask. Her legs were superb.

"Some of your film types," she went on as we went up the stairs, "have only one thing on their small minds and you know what *that* is. Coke."

"The day it happened," she went on, "lordy, lordy, it must have been the *next* day. He was in there all night and all day before I went up to see. Different tenants have different cleaning days. Leon's was Tuesdays. So when he didn't answer I knew all was not copasetic."

Uncle Wally had said my father's pitiful residuals were just this side of shoplifting and dog food. There was nothing in the apartment but a few pieces of furnished furniture.

"I took the liberty of cleaning out the refrigerator," said the manager. "I gave the only personal thing – that album – to Mr. Westmore. I see he gave it to you."

"He showed me some of the pictures once," said the manager. "Your mother was certainly a looker. What's she doing now?"

"She died," I said. "Last year. She was in a facility."

"Ah," said the manager. "Say. You know who you look like?"

"Yes," I said.

In the photo album, all of my birthdays, graduations, First Communion, Confirmation, Prom, various Christmas scenes were documented. Romola had been faithful in this regard.

At Christmas I always watch *Miracle on 34th Street* and the Alistair Sim *Christmas Carol*. If Sim isn't available I'll watch the Gene Lockhart version. Last year neither was. All I could get was the musical *Scrooge* and, of all things, *Black Christmas*.

"I AM WRITING THIS DOWN because as I get older I forget things. I hope my daughter sees the scrapbook so she can remember that I loved her. I have all these pictures of her taken far away from me. I can't remember my own childhood too good. My brother says I was an impractical dreamer. I hero-worshipped him. As I look back over my career I don't think there is anything much to be too proud about, and nothing to be ashamed of either. I was in the Navy and served my country. I don't know why my wife left me. I wasn't a failure and I didn't drink a lot or cheat on her. I'm the one who feels cheated out of a real life."

WHEN I WAS ABOUT seventeen I read a novel about a famous painter (English. Author Arnold Bennett?) who is off in some remote place (on holiday?) and returns to find that he is thought dead. It is actually his butler (valet?) who died and now the butler is to be buried in Westminster with honour and the painter is thought to be the butler.

So the famous painter can lay down his burdensome reputation and take up a humble life. He has the chance to start all over again. Of course he still has his talent. Does he produce some "Lost" work to make a buck? (Few quid.) I don't remember. Of course he falls in love with some lower-class person. Was it called *Buried Alive*? Who was in the movie version? Was there a movie?

I was never told, but firmly believe that I know the story of my father's buried life, his fair seedtime. I could make a movie of it. If I did, it would be a kind of second chance at life for him, wouldn't it?

The Buried Life of Leon Westmore:
A Screen Treatment.

As a boy he took to wandering alone at dusk. He liked the word *dusk*. He liked the peripheral feel of being on the edge of many lives. People going home from work, carrying packages, grocery bags. What was in the bags, packages? Lights were going on in apartment windows. Women left rooms or entered them. Newspapers were unfolded.

Thus he went through neighbourhoods not his own, seeing yet himself unseen. One foggy night, walking near the park where the fog was thicker, a man came out of the dark saying *I need help. Sure,* said my father instantly. It was like one of those illustrations in the Sherlock Holmes stories.

Later on my father would discover that the Holmes illustrator was named Sidney Paget. But back then, it was as if the pictures were of an actual world. It was a world in the past, of course, and far away. But my father must have believed that Victorian London looked exactly like that, with words appearing under each scene: *He looked at him in surprise. Sir Henry suddenly drew Miss Stapleton to his side.*

On that night in the fog, perhaps the man seeking succour was going to lead him to a dock where they would board a rusty tramp steamer bound for Timbucktoo. (I know my father would prefer the spelling with the twin "o" at the end, like a pair of wire spectacles perched on an invisible nose.)

Or maybe they were bound for a railroad station and one of those mysterious trains that went to stranger places than Timbucktoo with furtive Hindoos on board. (Spelling of *Hindoo* for same reason mentioned.)

From its craggy summit I looked out myself across the melancholy downs. Perhaps my father's reckless assent in the fog led only to a stalled car and a request for a push.

Still he walked, searching for elegance, taste, romance, sureness. He wanted to stop at mysterious inns, meet strangers, exchange extraordinary stories, reunite long-separated families, find hidden treasure. He liked the neighbourhoods where the street lamps looked Olde English.

At his own home, among family and friends who had always known him, there was no room for surprise. He never confided his secret journeys to anybody.

Light filtered down through the Victorian iron of the elevated train structure. The air itself became dusty and old. He stared intently at the bolted and many times repainted iron pillars. Iron, iron. He listened to the groan and screech of the cars' wheels above him against the rails on their ceaseless round and shuttle. All around my father people arrived or departed. All were on their way. Only he was stopped, waiting, watching.

I am sure that waiting became a habit. In lunchrooms and coffee shops, on corners, in libraries, at bus stops he waited. *That is Baskerville Hall in the middle.*

Romola and I waited for him in the future. I am a great person for waiting myself.

TYRONE POWER, Clifton Webb and Rudolph Valentino are buried in Memorial Park. Marilyn Monroe is not. Her tomb is in Westwood Cemetery. Each day there are fresh roses in a vase on her vault. Tyrone Power's grave was in the path of an automatic sprinkler. Before I could read the epitaph, the sprinkler wrote a swift message across the back of my blouse. Was Tyrone Power gay? Who cared.

I found Clifton Webb's tomb in a mausoleum and gently touched the brass plaque with his name on it. The slab moved in about a quarter inch, making a grating hollow echo. I went out in the sunshine seeking shade.

MY FATHER IS NOT BURIED in either of these cemeteries. I thought of having him reburied in the east next to Romola but that would be useless for all concerned. I left my father where he was and my mother alone far away where she was.

Perhaps my decision not to reunite them is a kind of resolution, a firm decision not to decide. Inaction is as ephemeral a move as violent dramatic change.

Sometimes there are little fugitive moments in a movie – like the one where Marlon Brando absent-mindedly picks up Eva Marie Saint's glove in *On the*

Waterfront. Just as absent-mindedly, Brando puts the glove on his own hand as the conversation continues.

There it was, that little detail, like a little open window in Vermeer letting in a minor bar of sunlight, gone in a rush of other, more important details.

If anybody made a biopic of my life it would have to include these little moments, these freeze frames:

My first kiss pressed up against a dark lamppost in that city in which nobody lived in and nobody watered lawns or called children home for supper. It was a necropolis, except that no one was buried there.

A young woman in a supermarket waiting for destiny to walk in. A young woman in a supermarket reading the news. These frames could be segued.

Me dancing all alone in my room like Moira Shearer to a phonograph (gramophone).

My father in the air, leaping a horse off a cliff into a river.

My father, not dancing, not singing in one of those tap-dancing-on-the-battleship movies.

My father standing under elevated train tracks, waiting in hope.

Finally, me waiting. We all wait, sometimes in hope. I, the daughter, survive.

Falling In Place

THE CHINESE GIRL AWOKE IN THE EARLY morning, still dark out, and found her door unlocked. The corridor was empty, silent under humming lights. The ward door was ajar. She remembered the story of the prisoner who found his cell door open and went out into the palace garden. There the poor wretch met a kindly reassuring priest who was in fact the Inquisitor. Soon the man was back in chains with the added torment of illusory freedom and false sympathy to goad him. The deepened horror.

But outside the hospital no false priest waited for her. There was only the parking lot lying there like a silent bowl of arc light. And she walked beyond it into the deeper inverted bowl of night. A deep pool starred with white water lilies. She had dreamed of rain. A school of small fish scattering in the deep. She saw them through circles on the blistered surface, thought of rain falling in a farmer's yard. Would his barn doors blow away in the wind? The hospital drains sang with rain.

Now she went up the grade to the tracks silvered in the fading moon. And she lay down across the tracks, cushioned her head on the chill steel and looked up into the slowly waking sky. Waited. Oh my iron bridegroom, she said.

ON THE ROAD beside the embankment the apprentice machinist drove in early light. He had wakened to a charley horse, cursing, limping in his silent morning house. Now he drove, the night mists wipered away, the radio in cadence. His mind was already in the plant. So many there were missing fingers. The machines were hungry. He feared them. At the morning break the men will speak of women. They want full-bodied women. Somewhere else now women were breasting big waves on beaches the men will never see. The ditch beside the road was dry.

It had been a month of drought after a month of rain. He had dreamed of rain. He thought of keeping a rain journal. How many days, how many inches, what damage to property, how some drown in cars in viaducts. Good for the crops some will say. But someone else will answer no, the crop's in peril. Not enough and the lawn burns. Too much and the picnic's ruined.

Never just right, except in dreams where it falls like filmic mist in black and white movies of romance. Lovers dance in it.

Sudden there on the road in common light he heard the shudder of stopped steel on steel. Up ahead was the morning train shaking to a stop and someone there.

Oh God, he thought, and could only watch the meeting, see it happen.

EVERYTHING WAS FALLING IN PLACE as the passengers fell forward. The train had leaned into its curve, righted on the straightaway and settled down. Now, we thought. But instead we jolted from our seats in a hurtling protest of stopping. Then all was silent unmoving. We got off to see. There was blood on the sleepers. We turned to stare across the speechless fields at the still early sun. Tall weeds stood there helpless as any of us. Nothing could change now for her. The hard air stood still. It tasted like brass.

HE STOOD IN LINE at the supermarket, docile, thinking of nothing, and then sudden as the wreck remembered it all. His hand on the brake. Futile. Nothing doing. Throwing up afterwards into his useless hands. And now here in the supermarket line ahead of him a row of grocery carts like train cars derailed, askew. Someone back in aisle four had dropped a jar of beets. A mess for someone else to clean up. And now someone's meat on the conveyor belt red as a kiss moved on, added up, put into a bag. It cannot be called back. The young woman ahead of him tells her child again that they cannot buy the cookies, that they have plenty at home. Does the child know it's a lie?

No, he thought. I am unfair. She soothes the child at home, reads him stories. Her kitchen is orderly and everybody keeps his or her voice down. Wildly, he looked back down the checkout line. He was square in the middle of it, too late to give up or move, and more time to put in waiting. He thought, I'd like to be a private detective, save people from blackmailers, sit back in a creaking chair, stare at the smoked window, listen to the secretary type reports, wait for the phone to ring. The girl's silver voice calls to him out of the dark wire, calling for help. He could save her.

A POET ONCE SAID that her eyes were the colour of sherry in the glass the guest has left. My eyes are like that. But here in the false dawn my eyes keep in them the deep shadows of night. Pillowed on the polished iron, I could see the morning glory clambering on chain-link fences facing the embankment. Someone is hanging laundry on a line. White forms rising in the wind. I hear birdsong. A faint thrum in the rail. I lay down to sleep and I am certain to rise.

THE WEATHER CONDITIONS on that day: patchy morning fog thinning so that visibility was fair to good at the precise time of – and post-incident analysis indicated no mechanical fault in the braking system. From the initial locking of the brakes to the point of impact –

The provenance of the engine: Electro-Motive Division, General Motors Company, London, Ontario, 1958.

THERE ARE SEVERAL FACTORS involved in braking: torque, brake shoe function, condition of track and gradient. The brake shoe bears against the revolving wheel with a radial force called normal brake shoe pressure. The retarding force of the brake shoe cannot be increased or prolonged indefinitely as train wheels may slide as a result of excessive braking force. (See H.J. Schrader, "Friction of Railway Brake Shoes at High Speed and High Pressure," University of Illinois Engineering Experiment Station Bulletin 301, 1938, Urbana, Illinois.)

THERE ARE OTHER FACTORS involved in acceleration and deceleration of course: speed, velocity (speed in a given direction) mass, air resistance or drag, acceleration and the rate of change in acceleration. Mass. The gross weight of the engine. The gross weight of the engine. The weight of the engine.

WHEN I FINISHED hanging the laundry, I thought of cutting the roses back. They say to cut ruthlessly so they will grow more hardy. The cadence of my steps kept to the song we danced to last night. I was humming it and then I heard the chill cry and protest of the engine and then the day was nipped in the bud.

AFTER A LONG and aimless wait standing alongside the silent train, the passengers were put on buses. It was late morning. They were promised lunch in the next town. By now a kind of disaster-induced camaraderie had developed among them. A subdued cordiality ran through the buses.

I felt an odd lightheadedness, a feeling of post-excitement letdown. As the morning went on the things of our world slowly resumed their usual shapes. I smiled at my fellow voyagers. Everything seemed thick and alive and bright in the almost noon light. Just a little while ago it was all tenuous, fragile, brief and evanescent. I felt mildly hungry, on edge, jumpy, ready to burst into laughter or tears.

Then suddenly I thought of the first sight I had of the girl's foot next to the tracks as I stepped down from the car. Now all the air went just as suddenly out of the day.

ALREADY THE BLUE of the summer sky is turning harshly autumnal. The change has been both gradual and sudden. So also in a very brief time a man may be his actual age and simultaneously feel the swift errant emotions of childhood and youth. A man may feel grief over the loss of those periods of his life while at the same instant re-experience them. I did not know her name.

Thus I felt grief – not only for the wretched girl but for myself and my fellow passengers. Every previous experience of death came welling up. Pets, schoolmates, grandparents, friends, acquaintances, fellow workers. All crowded together in my memory in a hurly-burly of sorrow recaptured. The indifferent blue sky outside the bus window stretches on to everywhere anywhere and nowhere.

THE CHINESE GIRL had been studying music at the university. Her first piano recital had been enthusiastically received by the faculty. The recital by one of her fellow pupils, a young man from a farm in the southern part of the Province, was attended with less warmth. This did not lessen the young man's ardor. He found the girl endlessly fascinating. Her eyes were like quick fish in deep water.

SHE WAS SHY, elusive, reticent, dedicated and given to long hours of practice. There was not much time left over for romance. Still the young man persevered and a kind of wary relationship developed. She told him about her loneliness, her homesickness. He spoke with confidence of a piano career for both of them.

Then came her time of retrospection, introversion, fear and collapse. She went into the hospital. The prognosis was positive. Her period of treatment would be brief, followed by outpatient therapy and a lighter academic load.

There had been a long dry spell of weather. The young man sat one afternoon in a coffee shop near campus. Some people came in and were talking to the waitress about the news. Gradually the story filtered through the damp air and the young man became aware. Rain fell that night like a breaking mirror.

THE APPRENTICE MACHINIST dreams of counterboring holes. This procedure would be followed by milling a flat space at the bottom end of the holes. He squinted through a fine spray of coolant. Metal chips lay like sharp confetti on the grim concrete floor. Tolerances were tight – plus or minus one thousandth. Next to him an old timer ran a big Bridgeport. On the other side was another old timer running an obsolete Milwaukee V Mill. Its age was covered with many coats of grey paint.

The apprentice's hands flew from the ball crank to the reversing lever. His mind was busy with the examination he would soon take. Define running fit, push fit, force fit and shrink fit. Tables of stress conversion roll through his mind. His eyes are intent on the chips of metal curling and dropping to the floor.

And now without warning the accident flashes into his mind. Locked steel wheels grind and shear. In a grinding operation wheel and work must be kept in contact until sparks are no longer emitted. Define the function of a chucking grinder. Do not look into the shower of sparks. Do not look up into the morning sunlight. Do not look up at the tracks ahead of you.

THE RAIN FELL into the yard near the tracks. All the laundry is safely in, clean-smelling and folded. Lightning glints on the thorns of the cut-back rose bushes. The rain washes the tracks and sleepers, seeping into the roadbed gravel. Rivers flow into the lake.

THE RAIN FELL into the placid lake. The diesel horn mourned over the furrowed fields. Train going away someplace. Perhaps a bell on a wrecked ship far below is tolling. Caught in the currents off the Point, it might toll forever. Nobody there to listen. Bellsong sounds in ever-widening concentric circles.

I WENT BACK HOME. The apples were in. My father's orchard was full of pickers on ladders. Windfalls crushed underfoot. The air was thick and sweet. Bees hovered. We set up the old stand and sold jugs of cider to the tourists. I took my turns at the stand.

I tried not to think of her. But a glissando of notes fell in my mind, sharp as icicles breaking off a roof.

Su Lin at her recital. Thin, intent, as precise as the music. I saw her, not the tourists, not the bees slowly circling the cider jugs. Seeing her again was as tart as a bite into a green windfall.

The harvest is big this year. Truckload after truckload of tomatoes go past on the road to the canneries in Leamington. The subtle curve of the road at a point just past us causes the load to shift to the right. Then there is a four-way stop. The load shifts again and the intersection is soon awash with tomato juice and loud with bee clamour. At night I dream of drowning with her. I hear a bell deep under water. The harvest is heavy this year.

I LAY DOWN on the sleepers so that I could rise again. I heard a final word spoken clearly. I told the doctor not to judge me. Nobody can know my pain. My fingers made music come from struck strings. Who could tell my fingers not to strike the chords? My love told me of his apple trees. He wanted to climb and pick the sweetest for me from the top. Oh my love, I cannot wait. I must lie down and wait to rise.

THE MORNING TRAIN comes and goes many times. Things become usual. Journeys are undertaken. The rain sweeps the train windows, certain as the last things.

Look mommy, says a child as he points out the train window. There's the sea.

It's only a river, says the mother.

SHE DOES NOT LOOK out the window. The train goes on, resolute, implacable as a final judgment. Its horn announces us. The river rises in the rain and flows on its certain way. We are almost home or going far from home. Everything is falling in place.

The Dark Summer

T WO RABBIS DISCUSSED AND DISPUTED as they walked along a country road. Suddenly there was someone else with them, joining in the debate. Then the third person vanished as suddenly as he had appeared.

THE COLONY was awash with talent. There were drama students, visual artists, composers, photographers, video artists and the inevitable dancers in residence. Alan was the only writer in the Colony that summer. He was forty-two, a bit older than most of the other residents. He felt the air charged with ego. Drama students made entrances and exits. Sometimes they made an exeunt, severally. Their faces were eager, expressive, over-expressive. The dancers moved as if hovering an inch or so off the common earth with their little bun heads and their little buns.

Alan felt a mingle of feelings about his fellow colonists. There was so much damned youth and talent and determination. And they were so damned boorish. The dancers were the worst, cutting in the cafeteria line without apology. Once he was getting orange juice from a machine and a little dancer enjambed herself under his arm to get at the grapefruit juice spigot. Such self-centered egotism was awesome. Alan felt admiration, pity and distaste.

THE WILLIAM SURREY HALLECK COLONY for the Arts is near the Sangre de Cristo Mountains north of Santa Fe. The San Juan Mountains and the Rio Chama River are to the west of the Colony.

Edith Woodrow Halleck founded and endowed the Colony in 1906, two years after her husband, William, died of consumption. William had been a composer. Ill most of his life, he had not composed much. Edith had been studying painting in Boston when she met William. After their marriage she did not paint much. She devoted her life to caring for William. Money was no problem. Edith was the only child of Charles Haldan Woodrow, railroad baron.

Edith took William to the Southwest, hoping for succor from the salubrious climate. After William died in Santa Fe, Edith decided to found a colony as a memorial to him. She ran the place until her death in 1927.

When Edith's workers broke ground, the nearest

town was thirty miles to the south. As time passed, ,a little support community grew near the Colony, taking its name from it. Halleck now has a population of about three hundred, a post office, a gas station and a big log-cabin-style roadhouse where there is western music and dancing on the weekends. There is a footpath running downhill from the Colony into town. The path passes a small cemetery with a prominent mausoleum in the centre of it. William and Edith's.

ALAN'S STUDIO was in the woods behind the residence. The way to the studio lay between music practice huts. From one came the sound of a violin plucked, plucked. He glanced in the window. A young girl bent to her instrument. She looked oriental. She had not seen him looking in. From another hut came flute, from another, piano. The pianist was female, had short curly hair, thin semitic face. From further off came a cello. As he walked, the various musics impinged and his progress down the path made, he thought with pleasure, a kind of fantasia of his own.

A girl was coming up the path towards him. She had a pert chin and short hair. The chin was up, defiant, and her eyes brimmed with tears. He felt a Whitmanesque urge to enfold, comfort her. He did not, of course, do anything. The gesture would have been rebuffed, misunderstood, scorned and wasted. The girl passed him as if he were not there. His music fell behind him. He went on to his studio.

THERE WAS A PATCH of early morning sunlight on the carpet outside the dining room. He looked at it, his pen poised over the notebook. He wrote:

Two rabbis discussed and disputed as they walked down a country road. Suddenly there was someone else with them, joining in the discussion. Then the third person vanished...

A shadow fell across the light on the carpet. A woman appeared in the doorway. She had short curly hair and a thin clever face. Was it the pianist? She looked intently around the room, turned and went away. The patch of sunlight lay there.

HOW TO DESCRIBE the light here, he wrote. A kind of washed light, rinsed and young and new. As if it were the first light. Hurts the eyes. A good hurting....

THE RESIDENT MUSIC DIRECTOR, Caspar something-something, came in. He had been born in Austria some seventy years ago. He sounded and looked like the late Bela Lugosi. Alan smiled and inclined his head. Caspar did not notice the gesture.

For the past three days it had rained incessantly. But now the sun lay sprawled on the carpet. Perhaps better days lay ahead. Alan closed his notebook. Time to get back to the studio. On his way out of the dining room he stopped to look at the large portrait of Edith Woodrow hanging near the door. It had been painted about 1916. Edith was posed wearing Indian clothing, and a rug hung in back of her. Her hair was in braids. She had big naive eyes. She had a strong rather than a pretty face. Alan wondered what the local Indians had thought of her, dressing up and all.

There was an old story that the Colony had been built on sacred burial grounds. But other stories asserted that the Indians liked Edith, were grateful to her for all sorts of generosity.

Someone passed quickly behind him. He half turned. It was the thin-faced pianist.

"Hello," she said in a bright face, smiling.

She went into the dining room. Alan walked out of the building and down the path into his music.

JAMES BLASCO ENTERED the dining room the next morning. He entered the room as if he were an opera impresario and expected everyone to know who he was. He looked like the portrait of Fauré by Sargent. He was, in fact, an opera impresario. The opera currently in production at the Colony was based on the story of Harun ar Rashid, the caliph of Baghdad who put on beggars' rags and went into the streets to learn what his people's lives were really like.

The libretto included the kidnapping of a Princess, the entrance of banditti into a grotto, the march and chorus of the janissaries, and the rustic dance of maidens carrying baskets of fruit and flowers. Alan had gone to a few open rehearsals. He knew that the final act would include the denouncing of the Grand Vizier and the revelation of the caliph's true identity. There would be a duet with the caliph and the Princess.

Alan wondered how he could get out of attending the premiere. Colonists were expected to support one another. The opera, he thought, would be bearable. But there would be the afterglow party with Blasco hugging people, kissing cheeks, and swanning about. There would be curtsies and bunches of flowers. Squeals and bellows of self-congratulation. All that sort of swank.

And there was Blasco, in the dining room, large as life and twice as unnatural, approaching and then sitting with Caspar. Alan nodded to them as he left the room. They were intent in conversation and did not respond.

THE SUPPORT STAFF were all young, enthusiastic, athletic and tended to bustle a great deal. All wore pagers on their belts. The pagers beeped incessantly. The staff never got to finish a conversation. They were constantly rushing off to answer phone messages. They were all cheerful and over-helpful. Alan had, sometimes, the odd feeling that he was in that television series *The Prisoner* with its "village" full of orderly, smiling, placid guests and guards. If he made a run for the mountains a big balloon would bounce and roll after him. The place was too good to be true. Yet Alan moved through his days as if invisible. He was in a crowd, yet alone.

ALAN MET THE PIANIST with the thin face on the residence elevator one morning. Her name was Jessica. He ran into her again a day or so later at lunchtime. He was behind her in the line. She invited him to join her. Two of her friends were already at the table. Jackie and Jeanne. Three "J's." A frieze of young women. Jeanne was the girl with the pert chin he had seen on the path. She seemed over her sorrow.

Jessica with the thin face and curly hair was a pianist. Jackie was a sculptor. Jeanne was a video artist. Jackie looked impatient, ready to go even while she was sitting still. She got up for more coffee. Alan thought that her legs looked as if they wanted to play hopscotch. She was tall and her hair was dark and braided like Edith's. She had a kind of don't-mess-with-me air mingled with shy flirting. Jeanne seemed happy to have met Alan. For the first time in weeks Alan felt in communion with his fellow human beings. He was reluctant to leave the table and start the day's work. How lovely they were, his frieze of young women.

ONE OF THE PERKS of the place was free admission to any of the artists' showcase recitals. He was scheduled to give a reading of his work-in-progress in the final week of the residency. He felt uneasy about it and was reassured by going to the showcases. Audiences were mainly supportive. One afternoon he went to a performance of Messiaen's *Quartet For the End of Time*. He had been working all day and was half-asleep. Then there was a slow movement, a kind of dialogue between a wistful cello and a sedate piano. A man, he thought, walks with his young daughter. She speaks shyly, swiftly. The man's head is bent to the side to listen as they step along. Her words, sweetly shy, his steps grave, dignified and tender. I have, Alan thought, no daughter.

He woke up the next morning early to ungodly shrieking. Kids, maybe the young dancers. He looked at the digital alarm. Six bloody AM. Too early for kid's pranks. Some kind of animal. Wolf or coyote. It sounded like a child in pain or joy.

"Say," he said later at breakfast. "Did anybody hear that awful racket? Some kind of animal?"

"I heard nothing," said Caspar.

Jackie said she had heard nothing. Jeanne wasn't sure. The third "J" was not at breakfast. Alan checked later with some of the staff. Nobody had heard the animal. It might have been a coyote someone said.

HE WENT TO JESSICA'S RECITAL. It was Ravel's "Ondine" from *Gaspard de la nuit*. Jessica wore a dark dress and crystal earrings that glistened like small teardrops next to her ears. That proud profile. She played with restrained passion. Ondine, the water sprite who lures mortal men down to her chambers deep in the sea. To be drowned in love.

Alan remembered that someone once said to Ravel that she had been deeply moved by some piece of his.

Something about a child. She [Colette?] went on to Ravel about his daughter and Ravel replied with icy formality *But I have no daughter.*

No daughter, Alan thought. No daughter. The piano notes shimmered and fell like an avalanche in the sun. Chords of rapture and regret. The earrings winked and sparkled next to Jessica's face.

ALAN WALKED DOWN the path towards town. He felt an open road jocund feeling of hope. He passed the graveyard. Someone had vandalized a stone cross. Next to the broken cross was a small stone lamb. A child's grave. There were other stone lambs. Perhaps a turn-of-the-century epidemic. He felt a pang and paused on the sun-dappled path. Some local stone mason had done a brisk business with that lamb model. All the sickness that took children in those days. Infant mortality.

All the sunshine didn't help. Sun on dancing leaves. Someone on the path behind him was singing "Greensleeves" in a trained voice. He went on, quickening his pace. A shadow moved beside him like a small intent animal. He could hear the river, far off, incessantly falling. It sounded like an old man telling an interminable story while dozing off.

Alan's wife had left him in the autumn of 1988. She left him as one might leave a doctor's waiting room, with brisk preoccupation, thinking of where she was going next. She didn't blame him. It was just that he was suddenly irrelevant. Some men, Alan knew, coped with divorce by sitting in sweat lodges, hugging one another and chanting. He had avoided all that. He had survived the divorce on his own. But the other thing....

The summer of 1988 had been uneasy. There were record heat waves all over the country. There was drought and scanty crops. Miles of beaches on the East Coast had been closed after hazardous medical wastes washed up. Children had played with hypodermic needles. Fierce fires in the forests of the Pacific Northwest had been fought by armies of firefighters. The AIDS quilt grew. There was talk about the ozone layer or the lack of it. Black corrosive stuff bubbled up through cracks in a playground adjacent to an elementary school near Toronto. There had been skin disorders in the school's population.

Alan's daughter had not gone to this school. Her school was safely a mile away. That summer she drowned in the public swimming pool in plain sight of crowds of people. Two alert trained lifeguards had done everything they knew, all that they could.

The mountains from this distance looked like somnolent furry beasts. There were folds in their fur. Muscles were slack or bunched up under the fur. All around Alan was vigorous opulent nature-stern saguaro, the mountains and the far-off muttering river.

Yet even in this stunning sunlight Alan knew pernicious human evil lurked. He had heard stories of communes out in the desert. Survivalists, satanists, cultists of all kinds. Stories of people who disappeared while camping or just traveling through. Bodies were sometimes found. Children died....

He walked on down and went into the roadhouse. A big neon sign hung over the doorway: Q.T. The sign was, of course, not on. Inside was a big barny room with tables circled around a dance floor. There was a bandstand. Two men in bib overalls sat at one end of the bar. He sat about halfway down and ordered a beer. A big sign over the cash register said *Quittin Time*. That explained the place's name.

"Quiet today," he said.

The bartender, a young man who looked as if he worked out seriously, nodded slowly.

"Come back this weekend," said the bartender. "A whole different scene then."

"I just might do that," Alan said.

ONE MORNING Alan found a note that had been slipped under his door. *Why have you erected this wall between us? We must talk....*

The note was signed "J." Which one? What did it mean? All three were cordial with him but nothing more. Perhaps the note had been put under the wrong door. But it was Caspar on one side and two of the young bunheads on the other.

When he saw the three "J's" later, together or alone, everything seemed normal. Was it a joke? A put-on? He waited for some sign, a look, a word, another note.

THE FOLLOWING FRIDAY he went down to the Q.T.
As he came in a woman was on the bandstand singing
"You ain't woman enough to take my man." She wore
skin-tight jeans and boots and a T-shirt with someone's
face on it. From his distance Alan thought it looked like
Franz Kafka but that didn't seem to make sense. The
woman had a thin hardscrabble face like someone in a
Dorthea Lange photograph. Alan thought she looked
like a lesbian, but the way she was belting out the song
seemed to belie that notion.

Alan sat at the bar. The tables were crowded with
men wearing ten-gallon hats and women in a variety of
outfits. Some wore granny dresses, some were dressed
like the woman who was singing, and some wore buck-
skin skirts. One man had a sweeping piratical plume on
his hat. His belt was hung with silver conchos which
were the size of salad plates. Each concho must have
weighed ten pounds. He was not a big man.

When the singer finished, there was enthusiastic
applause. The band announced a new song: "Honkey
Tonk Heaven." With the opening chords the dance-
floor was full. There was a flourish of expertise, rhyth-
mic boot stomping, square-dance style ducking under
arms, promenading. Alan felt like a caliph in disguise.
He sipped his beer, looked around, absorbed the good
feeling. There was a confident, exuberant frontier air to
the place, the music, the people, the dancing. He felt
buoyed up. He stayed until closing. Then he went up
the dark path towards the Colony, humming "Your
Cheat'n Heart."

THE NEXT NIGHT he went back. The band was playing something slow. Couples hugged and swayed. He went to the washroom. On his way down the dark hallway someone brushed past him going the other way. Jeanne? The corridor was dark and narrow. He wasn't sure. There was dubious paper on the walls, stained, ripped, hanging. When he came out of the washroom the person who had passed him was deep in conversation with someone at the other end of the corridor. The couple looked, somehow, lewd, sinister. He couldn't tell if it were Jeanne or not.

The band was still playing the slow set. *Please don't tell me how the story ends* – and there, over there it might have been Jeanne dancing with someone dressed in black. And there, was it Jessica dancing too close with a man in a black T-shirt? The man had a tattoo. And there was Jackie at a table leaning across to kiss someone who looked like a biker. He wasn't sure. The uncertain light....

The band announced the final song, "Blue Eyes Cryin in the Rain," and everybody was out on the dance floor. Alan peeled at the label of his bottle. Then the lights went up. There was cheering and yip-yipping. He stood out in front while cars and pickup trucks revved and roared out of the gravel parking lot. The three girls did not come out. The neon sign went off. He started up the street and turned up the path back to the Colony. He was alone on the path. If it had been the girls they must have other plans. He had drunk a lot of beer. Halfway up he stopped to relieve himself. With the sound of urine splashing on the gravel came another sound, far-off. A cry, a howl. Perhaps a coyote.

THERE WAS A CONFUSION of birds' singing. Alan woke up too suddenly. He was cramped onto the couch in his studio, curled up, neck hurting. He got up and moved awkwardly around the studio. He had worked late and lay down for what he planned to be only a rest.

It was very early in the morning. They weren't serving breakfast yet. He plugged in the kettle and made a cup of instant coffee. Sunlight on the studio windows hurt his eyes. It looked like a promising day. He sipped the coffee, and looked over last night's work.

THE MEETING OF TWO SAINTS – an abbot and an abbess – who converse. As they are deep in their dialogue, astonished watchers saw that they were elevated several feet above the convent floor, continuing to talk, ecstatic and high in the air....

IT WAS CONFUSED. He would have to sort it out later, after it cooled off. He put the new pages on top of the almost finished draft and went off to breakfast. As he was locking the studio door he was conscious of someone standing behind him. He turned. It was Jeanne. She looked all washed out, eyes smudged, lips looked puffed.

"Alan?" she said. "Could I talk to you?"

They walked down the path. Jeanne began to tell him about her real life.

"The thing is that I married this guy – he was a slug – well, I was young. Young-young. And I wanted to get away from home – from my father – he's such a fascist. But you know all about that...."

Alan wondered who, what he was supposed to know. Why was she telling him all this....

"Anyway the thing – the marriage – lasted about thirty minutes – took a year to finish off legally I mean. But I kept his name. I didn't want to go back to my father's name. I always thought it sounded stagey anyhow, you know?"

Jessica was coming down the path towards them. She seemed in a hurry. She smiled a quick hello at Alan and said something in a low voice to Jeanne. The two set off back towards the studios, smiling goodbye at Alan. Both were wearing shorts and hiking boots. Jessica had better legs than Jeanne.

"Thanks for listening," Jeanne called back to him.

THERE WERE NO MORE NOTES under his door. His frieze of young women continued to be open and friendly. The note must have been meant for someone else. And the apparitions at the Q.T. must have been exactly that – projections of his own overheated imagination, phantasms caused by too much beer drunk to loud music in a dark room.

THE MONDAY of Alan's last week in residence, Jeanne turned up missing. She was supposed to go hiking with other people from the video program the previous Saturday. When she didn't show, they went on without her. But when she didn't make it to a Monday morning critique session they got worried. Security staff searched her room. Her wallet was in the dresser. It looked as if all her clothes and toiletries were there.

State police from Santa Fe came up. Alan saw Jessica and Jackie in troubled conversation in a lounge. He wondered if he should tell the police about the Q.T. About the dangerous-looking man. Maybe Jackie and Jessica knew something....

Maybe she was off on some innocent lark with someone innocent, someone from the Colony. But the wallet. Blasco walked around the place in a distraught daze. Jeanne was his daughter. Nobody had ever mentioned that to Alan. Everybody seemed to know it and probably assumed that he did too.

He walked out in the parking lot behind the residence and across towards the studios. Abstract oil stains were etched into the parking lot concrete. Like splashes of blood. Bushes at the border of the lot had sudden yellow blossoms on them. He looked up at the bland morning sky. A girl asleep in a meadow, tousled hair tangled in the grass and timothy. Oh child of the pure unclouded brow....

ALAN WONDERED if his reading should be cancelled. Good taste and all....

"No, no," said Alison, the resident counselor. "You must do the reading. The Colony's business must go on...."

She went on in her calm counselor's voice. Alan did his reading.

"This piece," he began, "is called 'The Marriage of Heaven and Hell.' Besides the obvious Blake thing, I wanted to work in nuances inspired by a piece by Ravel: *L'Enfant et les sortilages*. I must have listened to it a hundred times while I was working. I toyed with the idea of playing a tape as background music for this reading...."

Polite laughter. He began: "Two rabbis discussed and disputed as they walked...."

Caspar came up to the podium as the crowd was breaking up.

"Alan," Caspar said slowly. "What you have achieved – my young friend – extraordinary. The pain – so formal, restrained. What? Grief under pressure. Mystical. The rapture – the regret...."

"Caspar," Alan said, crouching down next to the podium, looking into Caspar's face. "I don't know what I did. I don't understand it."

Caspar shook his head slowly.

"But you don't need to," said Caspar. "It is not given to you. To understand. Yes?"

Blasco was standing out in the parking lot next to piles of luggage. He looked as if he did not know where he should be. He looked like a large hollow statue. Alan went up to him, tried to say daughter, your daughter, but could not. Blasco took his hand in both of his. Alan gripped Blasco's shoulder. It felt frail, breakable. Neither man spoke. Blasco looked deep into Alan's face as if he knew.

Alan sat in the back of the van. Jessica was in the seat ahead of him, wearing big sunglasses, looking subdued, pensive. No sign of Jackie. The van pulled out of the lot and onto the road. Alan looked back, but he could not see Blasco. Maybe Jeanne would show up, penitent, having been off someplace thoughtlessly. He thought of a dried-up river bed, fissured and cracked and a hurried grave dug in the river's bank. The van turned past the graveyard. There was the Halleck mausoleum. He could not see any of the small stone lambs.

The van turned on the road through town, passing the Q.T., which was silent and shut down looking, with its empty parking lot looking large. One of the van's tires struck a sewer manhole cover, which clanged like a sullen iron bell.

On the highway leading south past Chimayo was a small church where pilgrims came to pray and touch the sacred earth. Many had come there and been healed. A small room was filled with canes, supports and crutches. They would not, of course, stop at the church. Alan tried to form words in his mind. A prayer for all children lost in the dark. Oh Lord, he thought, Oh Lord. The van went on past Chimayo towards Santa Fe.

Terror Exile Or Despair

1980

CHARLES AND SHIRLEY O'NEILL HAVE just arrived at the Newbolts' after a six-hour drive. There is J.B., the eldest child, standing on the porch. He is wearing shorts that look like the Maine woods and Topsiders with no socks. Charles and Shirley are late. The house is crowded.

"Canada," says Carol Wakefield, a handsome black woman who has come down the walk to greet them. The Wakefields have lived next door to the Newbolts for twenty years.

"Canada," she says. "Now that's a long way."

"It's just across the river from Detroit," says Shirley.

It seems to Charles that they have had this conversation before, in fact many times over the years. They used to come every summer to visit Shirley's parents, who lived in Forest Park. After the parents died, Shirley and Charles continued to come for family reunions. Now

Shirley and Mary Ellen are the last of their family. The visits declined, and the only connection was the Newbolt Christmas letter.

But this summer the Newbolt children have planned an elaborate, surprise, twenty-fifth wedding anniversary celebration for their parents. So for the first time in five years Charles and Shirley have made the trip. Charles thinks of the drive to Chicago across Michigan and Indiana the second most boring auto route in North America. The way from Windsor to Toronto wins first prize. But family is family.

Jay Newbolt, Mary Ellen's husband, has always managed to make Charles feel tested, found wanting, second-rate. Charles feels that he is constantly explaining himself. Five summers ago he had a kind of argument with Ramona Chance (the Chances have lived on the other side of the Newbolts for twenty years) about Vietnam. Ramona's bosom was aggressive. It had pointed directly at him like twin cannon. It seemed that Canada was a haven for cowards and draft dodgers. Why didn't Canada have a draft?

"My father was gassed at Ypres," Charles said. "And my Uncle Louie was at Normandy."

None of this had cut any ice with Ramona. And now it is Ramona herself coming down the walk towards them.

"Well, if it isn't the Canadian cousins," she says.

"Sister," says Shirley who has never liked Ramona. Shirley dislikes all big bosomed women on principle.

The Newbolts were among the early settlers in

Brookhaven, which grew in the late fifties to rival the population of Winnetka, which lies to the east of it. Brookhaven has risen in status in the past twenty years. There are no sidewalks. Some people have horses. No lot is less than an acre. There are two or three conspicuously up-mobile black families. One of these families, the Wakefields, lives next door. He is a doctor who specializes in allergies.

"Hey there, Chuck," says Jack Chance, who comes off the porch and takes Charles by the hand and arm.

Jack is Athletics Director at St. Marcella's, a small nearby Catholic college. Nobody calls Charles "Chuck." Now Charles feels, as he is heartily walked up the porch steps, like the new ten-year-old kid on the block. He is being welcomed but also tested. Listen, Chuck, we're going to have a gang. What shall we call our gang? Can you play left field?

J.B. is the most elderly twenty-four-year-old Charles has ever met. He is named after his father, Jay Brendan. J.B. is the eldest of the five children. He is finishing law school at Northwestern. Three of the other children are at various universities. The two girls, Molly and Wendy, are at St. Marcella's. Jason has a football free ride at someplace like Kentucky. Philip, the baby, is still in grade school. Jay Senior personally had scouted universities and colleges (all in the Midwest) to find just the right places to fit each child's individual needs.

Charles has always found the Newbolt house aggressive. Like Ramona's bosom. The house seemed to make a statement about family and national virtues.

There are blown-up poster-sized photos from the wedding hung up. Mary Ellen looks pert, smiling shyly in a rain of flung rice. Jay has a Fifties crewcut. His smile looks too wide for his face. Shirley had been Maid of Honour. There she is, just behind Mary Ellen, seeing to the gown's train. Charles remembers with a pang how beautiful she had been. The wedding was the summer before they met.

Shirley and Mary Ellen grew up in a large West Side Irish family. Shirley once told Charles that all she remembers her relatives talking about was when and exactly where blacks would move in on their neighbourhood. They did not, of course, say "blacks."

Mary Ellen, a year older than Shirley, was "the pretty one." Charles wonders why the family made this decision. He has seen family pictures of the two girls at various ages, and at first they looked like twins. Only when they reached pubescence did a difference emerge: Mary Ellen was suddenly about two inches taller. But she still didn't seem to have a special edge on pretty.

Shirley said that she didn't remember much about their house on West Washington Boulevard. There was this vividly accurate rendering of the Sacred Heart in the hallway that she had been secretly afraid of. As soon as they could, her parents moved into the suburbs to the west.

Charles is only Irish on his father's side. His mother was French. She was the one who made sure that nobody called him anything but "Charles." His father was something of a bully. He wanted Charles to become a lawyer. When he went into Mechanical Engineering, his father talked seriously about disowning him. Perhaps this is why Charles has never pressured his own children. This is a sore subject between him and Shirley. She says he lacks gumption. Look at Jay, he will say. A martinet. A fascist.

"Hey," says Jay. He is wearing red trousers and a white T-shirt with some kind of tennis emblem on it.

"Where are your kids?" says Jay.

Jason, the second son, hands Charles a glass of draft beer. Shirley explains that Cynthia (the Newbolts' god-daughter) has this new job in Toronto and could not possibly take time off, and Steve was already on his way to climb mountains out West when the invitation came. Out West has to be explained to Jack Chance. Yes, Canada has a West too, and Rockies also.

Jay is a tall, plump man. He takes Charles by the arm and moves him towards a wall of family photographs. Jay regards the wall in the way he regards the world: he is superior to it and he has a deep conviction that it is his by right.

"It is just remarkable," says Mary Ellen, "how the kids pulled this off. It was really actually a surprise!"

"A real surprise," says Jack Chance.

"Uncle Charles," says Molly, "have you seen the sequel to *Star Wars* yet?"

Molly is Charles' favorite of the clan. She is a bouncy, unsophisticated girl majoring in something called Health Science.

"I don't think it's as good as the first one," Charles says.

"They never are," says Jason, bringing Charles another beer.

Jason is a second string linebacker. Charles is not quite sure where. Is it Kentucky? Charles feels that he is supposed to know and hence cannot ask. Jason's neck is as thick as Charles' thigh. Charles is fond of him.

"Hey there," says Nick Wakefield. "Did these kids do a real secret job or what?"

Now Ramona has cornered Charles again. More of the same. When, Charles thinks, will they get over their damned war? He thinks he would like to hurl Ramona into the pool.

"On the way here," Charles says to some people on the patio, "we saw this immense beer truck. I mean, it was big. And it had *Beer Brewed in God's Country* on it."

Nobody seems to find this as funny as Charles does.

Later on everybody is in the pool, playing a raucous game of water polo. Charles plays hard, but feels odd man out. New-kid-on-the-block business again. Mary Ellen is not in the pool. She is sitting at an umbrella table talking to Connie Quick, who has lived across the street for twenty years. Connie's husband, a big corporate lawyer, dropped dead about six years ago. Forty-seven and in hearty health.

Connie is an ample, slow-moving woman. Blonde, of course. From his angle at the pool's edge Charles can see her round thighs under the beige pleated skirt. She stretches her torso as she leans in to listen to Mary Ellen. Shirley is sitting with them. The Widder Quick, Charles had joked five years before. Shirley had not thought it was funny. The Widow Quick had seemed far too flirty and danced with too many men (including Charles) on that occasion.

BACK AT THE MOTEL, late, Charles feels keyed up. The motel is in Millrace Acres, a less fancy suburb to the south of Brookhaven. Charles watches cable TV with the sound down so Shirley can sleep.

They always stay at this motel when they visit. It is a strange sort of place. It never seems full. Nobody ever is in the pool. There is no coffee shop. Shirley calls it the Bates Motel. Charles says they probably do okay during the week with business travelers. There are religious and inspirational books on a rack near the front desk.

Charles is watching a Bruce Lee movie. The one set in Rome where gangsters are trying to take over Bruce's uncle's restaurant.

Just before they left the party, Charles had seen Jay talking to Connie near the poolhouse. Mary Ellen and Shirley were at the umbrella table, deep in a sisters' colloquy. There was something intent about Jay and Connie. Something, Charles thinks now as he watches Bruce Lee fight someone in the Coliseum, something private. Furtive.

Or was it all the booze and all the talking and horseplay that put him in this paranoid frame of mind? The Newbolts and Chances and all their crowd were vigorously straight-arrow. Why, young J.B. even defended Nixon, saying that all sorts of things would come out about the Kennedys. History would give Nixon justice in time.

Before he turns in, Charles lifts the curtain to look out at the open field which slopes down from the motel to a cinder block building. They drive past it on the way to and from the motel. It is a place where people board their dogs when they go on vacation. As one passes the place, one hears the incessant chorus of barking, howling and whimpering.

THERE IS A CELEBRATORY MASS at noon the next day. J.B. is asked by the priest to speak for the family after the homily. J.B. gives a rather moving and succinct tribute to his parents and also manages to say something nice about each of his siblings.

The church is much older than Brookhaven. It formerly served several generations of German farmers. After Mass, everyone mills around in front. Jack Chance is yelling over Charles' shoulder at someone. Something about who is riding with who. There will be a luncheon on the Newbolt patio. Charles and Shirley checked out earlier so they can start for home after lunch.

THE BENIGN SUN filters through the trees that flank the patio. It is sit-down and catered. Bottles of red and white wine are on each table. Shirley and Charles sit with Connie and Kelly, a school friend of Wendy's. Charles looks over at the bigger table where Jay and

Mary Ellen are bracketed by their children and the priest who is now wearing a golf T-shirt.

This whole thing, Charles thought, was one of those rites-of-passage moments in life. In two years it will be Charles and Shirley's twenty-fifth. He wonders if Steve and Cynthia will plan something.

They are the first to leave. Jay and Mary Ellen walk out to the car with them. Jay gives Charles directions that will save a lot of time getting to the interstate. Charles pretends to listen. He is going to go the way he always does. He is certain of that route and is reluctant to embark on the unknown.

Then they are on their way. Shirley says well, it was very nice. Yes, says Charles, it was a very nice occasion.

1990

CHARLES AND SHIRLEY are driving past the dog boarding place. The animals' hullabaloo rises and falls behind them. They have come back for the first time since the twenty-five-year party. This time it is for a sombre reason. Molly has died of leukemia. The Christmas letters stopped four years ago, when Jay told Mary Ellen that he wanted a divorce, that he had never loved her, and that he wanted a chance for both of them to have a new life.

Now Jay and Connie are married and live in Winnetka. Mary Ellen is still in the big house, but now that Philip has finished high school she will begin to look for something smaller and maybe not in Brookhaven.

J.B. is calling himself Brendan these days. He has accepted and embraced his ethnic roots. He and his wife, Candy, have a child, Deirdre, the first Newbolt grandchild. Wendy is married, but so far no children. All the children live in Brookhaven or close by. They seem to have coped with the breakup. They spend Christmas Eve with Mary Ellen and have dinner with their father the next day. They seem to have accepted Connie. Jack Chance died in 1983. Ramona has moved to Ohio to be near her daughter who lives in Shaker Heights.

Rumors had found their way to Charles and Shirley in the past decade. Wendy had an abortion and gave up her scholarship at Loyola to follow her lover to Alaska. Or was it Iowa? The lover was older and married. Or younger and black. Was any of this true? All they knew for sure was that Wendy is now married, is not at Loyola, and is living somewhere in or near Brookhaven.

Jason gave up his Big Eight football free ride to go into a seminary. He left that and finished his degree at a close-to-home college. Now he is in the quality control end of his father's plant.

With all this and the divorce, Charles and Shirley think their own family is dull normal. Steve is married and lives near Toronto. He phoned just before Charles and Shirley left for the trip to tell them that Michelle, his wife, is pregnant. Cynthia is not married. She teaches elementary school in Windsor. She was engaged but broke it off. She isn't seeing anybody seriously right now.

At the funeral parlor Jay stands near the foot of the casket. The coffin is closed. A framed photo of Molly is on the coffin. Brendan stands on one side of his father and Wendy on the other. Connie is sitting in the front row, talking to a young woman holding a child. Charles assumes that this is Brendan's wife and baby. Mary Ellen stands near the head of the casket. Philip stands next to her. She looks old and shrunken. Shirley embraces her, and they stand like that for a moment. Charles, standing behind Shirley, nods gravely to Brendan. Jay, who is talking to Nick Wakefield, has not seen them yet.

Now Charles puts his arms around Mary Ellen, says I'm so sorry, so sorry. She feels like a cage of spun glass in his arms. Then he stands next to her. Shirley stands next to Philip on the other side. Old friends approach, hesitate, then go to either Jay or Mary Ellen to express their condolences. There seems to be no pattern to the choosing of which parent will be solaced first.

So fragile a thing life is, Charles thinks. Fragile as love. Terror exile despair. Something he read in a literature course a long time ago. Something about our mortality. Something to say against the dark. Otherwise it would be like the helpless yowling of abandoned pets at the shelter.

Who has abandoned us? Left us here crying in the dark? The baby, now held on Connie's lap, begins to cry. Mary Ellen goes over to Connie, bends down. Connie holds up the child for her to take. Mary Ellen holds the baby up on her shoulder, crooning to it, making soft, soothing sounds. It is a posture Charles remembers, when Mary Ellen and Shirley held and comforted their babies. Something, he thinks, eternal in the act, timeless. It seems to him now that it transcends even the fury that must have existed between Mary Ellen and Connie.

The priest arrives. Everyone sits down. Mary Ellen, Shirley and Philip are on the left. Mary Ellen still holds the child. Jay and the other children are on the right. The priest reads the prayers. The responses are on laminated cards, like menus. Then the priest gives a brief homily. He says he only got to know Molly in these last weeks, but he had grown to admire her courage and deep faith which should be a powerful example to us who are left behind.

After the prayers, the funeral director asks the pallbearers to meet with him for a moment before leaving. On the way out Charles pauses to look at a collage of family snapshots on a bulletin board featuring Molly at various ages. There is one where she is about three and there is Shirley in the background talking to Steve who appears to be upset about something.

Charles realizes that he has not yet spoken to Jay nor to his new wife. Now he stands in the vestibule of the funeral parlor. It is raining. Charles wonders what would be the proper thing to do. Awkward to go back in. They are closing the place. Jay must be very tired. Charles holds the door for Shirley. They are going back to the big house for coffee or a drink with Mary Ellen.

"They should have asked you to be a pallbearer," says Shirley. "After all, I was Molly's godmother."

"Well," says Charles, adjusting the wiper speed, "remember that they didn't ask me to be godfather. Who was her godfather anyhow?"

"Jack Chance," says Shirley.

"Sure," says Charles. "Of course."

At the big house Shirley has coffee. Charles asks for scotch and soda. There isn't any soda. Plain water will be fine, Charles says.

They sit out next to the pool. The rain has let up.

"Phil cleans it every day," says Mary Ellen, "but nobody uses it anymore."

"It's something they outgrow," says Shirley.

Charles looks at the dark still water and thinks of the drunken, yelling crowd splashing and laughing. A maudlin memory. Jack Chance, big and alive. Ramona carrying her prejudices like a fierce banner. Molly on the diving board pretending to throw and then holding back the ball. Connie at the poolside table talking to the woman she was even then planning to betray.

Gone, all gone. He looks up at the dark and silent house. Soon strangers will live in it. Perhaps they will be younger and full of hope. Their children will love the pool. The water will be roiled and showers of flung water will be caught in sunlight.

Charles remembers Steve staying in too long at some motel pool, climbing out, shivering, his lips blue, to be covered with a towel by Shirley. Fun, taken to excess, like too much candy at a carnival. Too much to drink at a party. Young, old, we all crowd to the pleasure of the moment.

The rain stops early in the morning but the sky is still overcast. The ground in the cemetery is soggy. Carpets of artificial grass have been laid around the gravesite. By the time Charles and Shirley get out of their car and make it up a sloping hill, the priest is already starting the prayers. He sprinkles holy water on the coffin. Brendan steps forward and lays a single white rose on the coffin. Now the priest speaks quietly to Jay and Mary Ellen, who stand next to one another but apart.

People begin to drift back down the slope to the cars. Some have left their headlights on. Shirley and Charles are not going back to Jay and Connie's for the lunch. They are heading out for home right away. Shirley hugs Mary Ellen. Then they get in the car and head toward the cemetery gates.

After they get on the I-94 the clouds begin to break up. As they cross the Indiana line the sun comes full out. Shirley puts a K.T. Oslin tape on. They have become country and western fans. Shirley says something. Charles answers hmmm? He does this all the time now. Shirley says he sounds like Citizen Kane talking to his second wife. Charles is getting more and more hard of hearing but puts off going to be tested for a hearing aid.

The muffler falls down and bangs and thumps the concrete. They slow down and exit near Portage. They drive towards a tall Esso sign. When they get to it, the station is closed up. It looks as if it has been closed for a long time. Why don't they take the damn sign down says Charles. The muffler thumps and scrapes along. How can a road be so long without a single gas station.

Then they are suddenly in a small town and there is a garage with a big sign We Fix Mufflers. It is not a muffler chain. On the right of the garage is a pristine lake, sparkling in the sun.

The mechanic says their car is Canadian so he has no mufflers to fit. Something about emission laws. But he can weld a straight pipe on. It will get them home. It will cost fifteen dollars. Shirley walks down to look at the lake.

"Canada," says the mechanic as the car rises on the hoist. "That's real pretty up there. I've seen pictures."

On the way back to the interstate Charles feels an eye-smarting benevolence towards all of America. The small town, the pure and shining lake, the honest mechanic. He will tell people about it whenever there is anti-American talk.

It is dark when they stop to eat in Michigan. And there is a long lineup on the bridge. A lot of people have been over shopping and are making declarations. The customs inspector looks skeptical when Charles tells him that they have nothing to declare, that they have been at a funeral. The inspector sends them over to have the car searched. Charles feels justifiable outrage.

They have been on the road for a long time. The muffler thing and the customs hang-up have not helped. He brings the bags in, but they decide not to unpack until tomorrow. Charles brings two glasses of wine out to the screened-in porch. The summer is really over, Shirley says. Yes, Charles says, you can really feel a change in the air.

After awhile Charles goes in to catch the late news. Shirley stays out on the porch. A car drives past, slowly, as if searching for an address. She watches the tail lights go down the block. She remembers Cynthia and Molly as babies. Maybe Steve and Michelle's child will be a girl. She does not want to say this out loud. Something Irish keeps her from forming a final wish about the baby, keeps her from hoping too much. She will buy yellow baby clothes. She imagines a baby sleeping on her lap.

She remembers a time when she and Mary Ellen were little, about six and seven. They had been playing under the dining room table and their parents were sitting at the table, talking. Shirley remembers the feeling of peace and enclosure. The lace tablecloth hanging all around like a veil. Her father's voice, her mother's voice. Quiet, ordinary words. And being there, with her sister, feeling safe.

Maybe that was the very last time she ever felt that safe. Now she rises to go in to sit with her husband to see what the weather will be like tomorrow.

There has been another drive-by shooting across the river. Another child killed by mistake. Charles thinks about his grandchild-to-be. For some reason he pictures it as a girl. He will not say this out loud. The high pressure ridge that has been hanging around the Great

Lakes for so long is finally moving to the east. It looks pretty good for tomorrow. Heat wave in Arizona. Rain in Tennessee. Flooding in Calgary. Fire out of control in California. But finally it looks as if a better day is coming our way.

1956

CHARLES HAS HAD three interviews since graduation. One with Ford, one with GM, and one with the C.D. Bucke Company. Things look promising. The Bucke outfit is fairly new. They do parts for the big three. Bucke seems to Charles to offer the most challenge. He is off now to Chicago for a final interview at head office.

On the train he sits with two girls who are on their way home after visiting a school friend in Ann Arbor. One of the girls is pregnant. That's okay, because Charles fancies the other one, who looks like Leslie Caron in *An American in Paris*.

The train rolls across Michigan and Indiana. Charles is happy. The job seems to be a sure thing. This girl sitting across from him, smiling, is really first class. And then, finally, there are the towers of Chicago, shining in the late slant of sunlight. He has the girl's phone number in his wallet. Anything, everything, could happen.

Hubba-Hubba

Journeys

I AM IN SEDONA, ARIZONA, ON THE WAY TO visit my son in Calgary. He has genealogical questions to ask me: Why did my parents die so relatively young? I suspect that he fears that I too shall die young and also he fears for his own mortality.

I could tell him that it was the war, my father worn out by soldiering and my mother dragged down by the harshness of the home front. Or I could say she died of a broken heart. All of this could be true.

Or I could tell him the existential truth: my father died of cancer and my mother had a heart attack. So I watch my weight and do not smoke.

My son is about to become a father. I will become a grandfather. We will look into his child's face as if into a small mirror.

I am trying here to make sense of our blighted family history. I am writing this with a pen from Abilene Western Outfitters. They gave it to me when I bought a Stetson at their store in Cave City, Kentucky. I drove through there on my way here. I went far south to avoid a big storm in Manitoba.

There was freezing rain in Kentucky and Tennessee. I didn't hit okay weather until I was halfway through Texas. I lingered in New Mexico. Now I am here. I am reluctant to head north. There are tough questions waiting for me.

I like to use the free pens I acquire in places I've been. Twenty years ago my wife and I went to Palm Springs, California, and I got a pen from the Palm Springs Spa Hotel. That pen still works. I keep it next to the phone.

And I have a pen from the Motel Magic in Lethbridge, Alberta, where I stopped on my way to Calgary ten years ago. I was alone on that trip. My wife left me sometime between Palm Springs and Lethbridge. I also have a bar of soap from Motel Magic. It is still unwrapped.

These are not, strictly speaking, souvenirs. They are totems of journeys. I think of my travels as voyages of discovery. Hernando De Soto (1500?-1542) discovered the Mississippi River in 1541. They did not name the river after him. The Chrysler Corporation, however, did name a car the De Soto.

Abilene Western Outfitters also gave me a free bumper sticker: *Put Your Rear In Our Gear*. I have not attached it to my car's bumper. Abilene is a city in Texas. There is no city in Kentucky named Abilene. My father owned a blue 1940 De Soto. When he went into the army it was parked in the garage. I was too young to drive it.

SEEGAR

I NEVER CALLED my Uncle Louis (pronounced loo-eee) "Seegar" to his face. He was too imposing a figure to take a joke at his own expense. He loved cigars which he pronounced...well, you get the idea. There was always a cigar at hand, in hand, in his mouth, jutting out, jammed between teeth, stubbed out in regret when finished. Cigars were sniffed, rolled between his palms, held up next to his ear and caressed so they crackled. Cigars were offered, proffered from gaudy boxes with pictures of South American heroes on them.

Aunt Cora, Louis' wife, said she hated the filthy things. But she put up with them. The cigars came with Uncle Louis or vice versa and she sure didn't want to give him up. She was his second wife and about ten years younger. Uncle Louis was my father's older brother and sales manager of a big soap company. The time I am thinking about was during World War Two. My father, who called himself the oldest corporal in the infantry, was overseas. My mother was sad and anxious and preoccupied. I was in my teens and torn between my desire to be wounded heroically and my overwhelming sex drive.

Corner Time

My friend Vinnie was about a year older than me and therefore a source of wisdom and experience.

"I'm going with a nurse now," he said in a confiding voice, scratching his bicep, smoothing his hand down his crotch. "Nurses are smart. They're clean. They know all about it. They wash guys off in the hospital. They put it in for you."

We were standing on the corner, watching the traffic, hoping that beautiful girls would walk past us.

"Marrone," he muttered –smoothing his hair back as a young woman walked past.

"Hubba-hubba," I agreed.

Everybody had a corner to hang out on. If you were asked where you were from you would say the corner's name. Ours was Twelfth and Austin. There was a movie theatre there and a pool hall, a tavern and a drug store. Vinnie and I took up our post in front of the drug store every evening, watching, waiting. Vinnie had a syndrome of gestures: scratching his bicep, caressing his groin, smoothing down his hair as girls and women went past.

I somehow knew that Vinnie was lying and posing, but at the same time I wanted to believe it. About the nurses. All that. So I put in my corner time, learning things and watching and waiting.

Vinnie stared down the street as if he were expecting something wonderful to manifest.

"Nurses," he said. "Marrone."

I stood next to him, staring down the street. We waited.

Sex In The Forties

I PROWLED THE DIM WARTIME STREETS. Far off, down from my house, through a long dark tunnel of arcing tree branches, street lights shrouded by branches and leaves, was the big important street. Cars idled at the stoplight. Neon signs in tavern windows glowed red and blue. Back where I was, houses were dark, with a few windows here and there lit. In darkened windows hung gold stars. I walked past the dark houses and reached the corner lit by neon from the tavern. A juke-box song was loud when the tavern door opened. I imagined a war widow in there, drowning her sorrows, not wanting to go home to the dark house and the gold star. A war worker just off shift stops for a few on his way home and meets the widow. He is going to get lucky. Down the neon splashed sidewalk came the V-girls in tight sweaters and short skirts and no stockings and high heels. The V-girls were out looking for sailors. They were not interested in a part-time stock boy from the A & P.

A BEAUTIFUL GIRL in a sarong appeared on the screen and Bob Hope looked sideways, out from the screen right at me, rolled a roguish eye and said "hubba-hubba."

Sex in the Forties was a sarong, long shiny hair, wet lips. And more.

Sex in the Forties was a sepia-toned girlie book. A woman in black stockings with seams up the back, black lace panties, wearing boxing gloves, punches a bag with Hitler's face on it. A blonde woman in satin shorts and a soldier's cap is perched on a kind of pillar, bare legs crossed so there is a visible expanse of underthigh to be seen all the way up to the bottom of her shorts. She holds a war bond and smiles. Sex in the Forties was patriotic. The whole country had turned into some kind of sex monster. Everybody had the perpetual hots. There was screwing in the stockrooms of war plants, in telephone booths in train stations, in dark doorways, in parked cars. Everybody was getting some.

Except me.

AUNT CORA

She liked a good laugh. She really threw herself into laughing fits that ended with helpless choking. Her eyes would squint shut and her breasts shook. Hubba-hubba. It was difficult not to be seen looking. Aunt Cora had a habit of crossing her legs "carelessly," as a detective writer put it. It was difficult not to be noticed looking. She played the piano. I thought she had a good voice. I remember her singing "I'll Be Seeing You" with flourishes and intense feeling.

Her femaleness permeated their house like cigar smoke. Once I was sent down to their basement for something and there were her stockings and panties and a girdle hanging naked on the clothesline. I pressed my lips against the girdle's damp crotch.

Exciting Words

IT WASN'T JUST AUNT CORA or the V-girls or the women in the sepia girlie book. It wasn't just native women in sarongs or Veronica Lake with grenades clutched between her breasts walking towards the leering, drooling Japs. It wasn't just Ann Sheridan getting raped by the Nazis and Erroll Flynn getting so angry that he almost screws up the whole Norwegian resistance.

Or the Nazis in *Batman* who are interrupted in a rape's progress by the caped hero. Batman arrives in time to save the girl, but cannot stop her skirt from flying up. Not just these images but words. It was words like "carelessly." I read Maupassant and came across *frou-frou*. I did not know for a long time what it meant, but the word excited me. I said it to myself in bed in the hot panting dark. Years later I learned that *frou-frou* meant a rustling sound, especially of skirts. Or the slow rasp of silk on silk as stockinged legs were slowly, carelessly crossed. The susurrous whisper of silk, the feel of silk rubbed until it murmured. The sweep of long gowns across rich foyers, the swell of *décolletage*, the heave of *embonpoint*. The French were our gallant allies.

In The Park

WE WERE INVITED to Uncle Louis' company picnic, which was held every summer in the big field on the river-bank near the amusement park. After eating, all went into the park. Aunt Cora went on lots of rides. She went on the parachute jump, on the giant swing and into the fun-house where she knew air jets would blow up her skirt.

I tried not to be seen noticing. Was it all for me?

I have a photograph of my Uncle Louis at that picnic. I found it in a box of family photos in my mother's clos-et after she died. I could not identify many of the people in the pictures. But I remember my uncle and that day. In the photo he sits on the running board of his Packard, staring thoughtfully at the ground between his knees, his cigar gone dead between his fingers. The whitewalled spare tire mounted next to him is a large letter "O."

What was he thinking about? Aunt Cora and her flighty, flirty ways? I remember that they had "words" on that picnic summer day. Was he thinking about tires and gasoline, ration stamps, meat and cigarettes?

You see, besides working for the big soap company, he had other work. It was work that began late at night. Often he would appear in our alley, cut the headlights and unload cartons next to father's car. Then there would be an intense conversation in hushed voices between my uncle and mother. She did not approve.

Uncle Louis had a meat locker in Joliet. He had an arrangement with some downstate farmer. All through the war our family had an embarrassment of meat. My mother could not enjoy it. She kept on saying how could you with your father in some foxhole eating Spam? I lied to my friends and joined them in grousing about shortages. But everyone seemed to know that my uncle was in the black market. He could get you what you needed. Cigarettes, tires, ration stamps. Things talked about out the side of the mouth, in whispers, in the dark. He received and made strange terse phone calls. Once in the alley behind our house, I saw him pull a wad of money out of his pocket and give it to a man I had never seen before.

THE DREAM

IN THE LAST YEAR of the war I had a strange dream:

The lecture hall was unheated, and I along with everyone else kept my coat on. The chairs were spindly, small and set close together. Our bulked coats kept us in uncomfortable proximity. The hall was as large as an airship hangar. Tall windows were coated with frost. The lecturer was at the far end. His amplified voice went on and on. The subject was technical, difficult, subtle, tiresome. I shifted in discomfort, and my chair's legs grated against the concrete floor. Because of being so muffled up and crowded, I felt sleepy. The unheated air became more and more stuffy. I felt a surge of oppression. I shifted in my seat again. Down the row, a woman leaned forward and looked at me. She had a stately, gracious poise. She whispered something in a language I did not understand. But the tone of her voice was deep and thrilling. I felt a stab of arousal. Then I became aware that silence had fallen. The lecturer had stopped. Perhaps he was impatient and annoyed. I felt the crowd shift uneasily. I felt the weight of their disapproval. I leaned forward and looked down the row. The woman was gone.

Last week I had this dream again. What can it mean?

The End Of Something

ON V-J NIGHT an impromptu celebration began in the alley behind our house. A keg of beer was suddenly foaming away (courtesy of Uncle Louis) and Mr. Stastney played the accordion. He sat near the beer, in the doorway of our garage. Everybody on the block was out there, dancing, singing. A few sailors passing through were welcomed. One of the sailors danced with Aunt Cora. Her skirt whirled up in a wild jitterbug. Nobody noticed me watching and nobody noticed me getting beers. Soon I had to pee and weaved into our dark backyard.

There was a couple back there kissing. It wasn't like kissing in the movies or the brief fumbling experience I had with Jane Cusack in Phil's dad's car. This kissing was deep and adult and desperate. In a brief moment of moonlight I saw that it was my Uncle Louis and it was my mother. I went back out in the alley, down into the dark away from our garage. I urinated against a telephone pole. I did not know what to do. Nothing made sense. The war was over. It was too late for me to be wounded heroically. I could hear Aunt Cora laughing as she twirled and whirled, showing off her legs carelessly.

Mr. Stastney was playing a polka. I walked back slowly. There was my garage, our house, the alley, my neighbours and friends. There was my father's blue De Soto. Everything was where it should be. I had drunk too much beer. I went back down the alley to throw up. The war was over and I had not been in it and my father would be coming home. He would tell war stories and we would tell him about life on the home front and how tough it had been. He would give me driving lessons in the blue De Soto. Things would be all right again.

STICKNEY

STICKNEY LAY just to the north of the Sanitary District. It was a sad blight of land where raw open fields of weeds and scrub brush met the canal. Junked stripped cars lay in a small stream that moved like oil, choked with condoms, towards the canal. There were a few hopeful Victory Gardens. On the horizon, smoke stacks let off a slow, insistent knot of white. From the far off bulking factories came the slam of drop hammers.

It was Victory gardeners who found my Uncle

Louis in his Packard far off the road, shot in the forehead. People said it was the Syndicate. Aunt Cora almost went crazy. For a time there were leads reported in the paper, but then interest died. Nobody was ever caught.

Somehow in my mind I see my uncle's death scene all mixed up with a picture I once saw of the capture of Buck Barrow. He was Clyde's brother. A car is in the middle of a field. Buck, wounded, sits on the running board. His wife sits in grief and despair on the ground a bit away from her captured and dying husband. I see my Aunt Cora in that same pose of grief out in a field in Stickney. But of course all this is wrong. She was at home when the news came on the telephone. There were no pictures in the paper of the death scene. My uncle died alone.

AUNT CORA seemed to hurtle into old age after Uncle Louis died. She got very religious. She sent money away for masses in remote places in Quebec and then began to make pilgrimages there. I pictured armies of French priests saying masses around the clock. After my father died, my mother began to join Aunt Cora in those journeys to Quebec. My mother and Aunt Cora became two frail old ladies. Our house was filled with rosaries and holy pictures and crucifixes. Priests all over the world incessantly said masses for my father and uncle.

Stickney began a postwar housing boom. All those blighted fields filled in with tract houses. I began to date a girl from out there. The buses were still not dependable.

The Island

A CRONY OF MY UNCLE'S got me a job in the soap company after I graduated from high school. I remember it as a sprawl of decay and obsolescence. The soap company was on an island in the middle of the river. When I say "river" one might picture beaches and blue waters. There were no trees or beaches on this island. It was jammed to the shore with factories, railroad spurs, and warehouses.

I remember one early evening, working overtime in the tall, tabescent warehouse. I stood at an open receiving door on the top floor looking out over the city's rooftops, wet from a rainshower which had just ceased. I could see the taller buildings at the city's centre. The amusement park was next to the river's curve far off there, like an abandoned toy. I imagined the sound of carousel music, the screams, half in delight, half in fear, from the rollercoaster. Behind me I heard the freight elevator gate slam down and the whine of the motor, the shudder of metal ropes on pulleys. The elevator descended, leaving me alone, looking out. The lights went on at the amusement park. The ferris wheel was a circle of turning lights. I leaned out and looked to the side. I could see the words Frigid Fluid on the red brick building next door. The air smelled of wet ashes.

Sex And Death

ONE NIGHT I had a dream about being in an auditorium and there was a woman who said something to me that I did not understand. Could the woman have been my Aunt Cora? When I think back to the war and my youth, it seems now to me that I was merely waiting to live. It was like looking down my street through the tunnel of tree branches, looking far off down to light and life. That time seems at once irrevocably lost and so close I can almost put out my hand and touch it. My father's car was named after a Spanish explorer who discovered the Mississippi River. There is a legend that he is buried in that river but nobody knows exactly where. I mean the explorer. I know where my father is buried.

My father came home to the postwar peace to find his brother murdered and his son almost grown-up. Time seemed to speed up after that like a fast-forwarded movie. The De Soto is put back on the road and zip, is traded in on a new green Chevy; cars grow tailfins and lose them. I go off to college and stay up late talking intensely about social justice and what is Art. I am zip in love and blooie my heart is broken. My father, once a full-faced strong picture in uniform on the piano shrinks into a brown cardigan sweater and zap dies in the veterans' hospital and is buried next to his brother. My mother decides to sell the house but dies before it is on the market. I am left to tidy things up.

EVERYTHING blurs together, running like water over drowned bones.

CAVE CITY is the nearest town to Mammoth Cave. It is also near the cave where Floyd Collins, the spelunker, was trapped and died. That was in the Twenties and was one of the first media events. Hordes of reporters and gawkers waited for the rescue or death. Death won.

I DID NOT VISIT either cave. I only stopped for a hat. I am writing this in a motel room in Sedona, Arizona. It is early morning and already too hot. Outside the window is the formation they call "Snoopy." With a generous stretch of imagination one can see that, yes, the rock does resemble the cartoon dog lying on his back on top of a cartoon doghouse. But why call a natural wonder by a cartoon name? Perhaps it is the human attempt to cope with the awareness of brute nature. To trivialize. Sedona is full of New Agers who believe that the rocks here are a vortex of spiritual forces. Perhaps they are right.

Now I get up and put on my hat from Cave City and set it at a jaunty angle. I look in the mirror, wink at my image, and nod to a ghostly Vinnie who stands on the eternal corner. I look like a cowpoke, a trail-boss, an explorer. I tip my hat to myself, roll a theatrical eye and say it under my breath –

hubba
hubba

The Island Of Sponges

THE FERRY TO KALYMNOS LEFT IN THE morning and returned in the late afternoon. She would have to spend a whole day on the island, and during the hottest part of the day, when shops and tavernas would be closed. Perhaps she could take a lunch.

There always seemed to be crowds waiting for the ferry, crowds getting off – tourists and tradesmen. And big bundles of large sponges coming back from the island – the chief export for thousands of years. It would be awkward to scatter the ashes from the boat without being seen. There was a night crossing. But it too seemed always to be bustling.

Last night's sunset had been dramatic. But they all were. The sun's disc dropped like a coin into a slot, the afterglow suffused the sky and an ocarina-shaped cloud hung just over the place on the horizon where the sun had slipped down. Then it was suddenly full night and the taverna lights came on.

She had awakened this morning to what sounded like words, tumbling and incessant. Someone with a wet mouth saying *there is something I think you ought to know....*

Victoria thought *I wish you hadn't told me.* But of course she did not know what it was.

She could see the beach from her balcony. It was still quite early. Not many people were down there. A rooster was crowing. In the field behind her *pension* goats and cows were tethered. A child in white, wearing a red sun hat, was patiently going back and forth from the water's edge carrying a green pail. He was building something in the sand. From this distance the child was a white dot surmounted by a red dot on a beige canvas. The green pail. The Aegean was blue. The island of Kalymnos was a dark frame for the picture. A single white sail was motionless out there.

Now beach umbrellas were being set up, adding more colours. Two young tall girls walked out to an umbrella, brushed off their feet, stood there, and began to brush their hair thoughtfully.

The beaches at home on Lake Huron would be similar. Beaches were universal. Umbrellas, girls brushing hair, children with pails, inflatable rafts. But at home there was always, even in severest heat, a sense of after, when leaves would turn; and then, in winter, snow on the sand, the waves slate grey. All the human restlessness and activity gone.

Here on the island of Kos, the seasons were seamless. There was no sense of after. Only a before and a now.

Victoria had been a professor in the art history department at Tecumseh University for thirty years. She had retired two years ago. A buy out. To look after Harold. Her book on medieval iconography had been the definitive text on the subject for fifteen years. She seldom thought about any of that now.

Harold had often quoted Wolfe's *You Can't Go Home Again* to her. But where *was* their home? Harold had come from Illinois to teach English at Tecumseh and met Victoria who had come from Oakville. Now there was nobody in Illinois or Oakville that she knew.

She and Harold had been coming to one or another Greek island each spring for the past ten years. This was her first time alone. Harold had died the previous summer, just after their return from Kos. In those last days he made her promise to come back to Kos one last time. He wanted his ashes scattered in the sea between Kos and Kalymnos. *Cremains* the helpful woman at the crematorium had called them. Now in a small metal cylinder on the dresser in the *pension*.

Mastihari had been a small fishing village on that last trip. It was still relatively small, though there were ominous signs of change. Several large hotels had sprung up, catering mainly to well off German tourists. There were more tavernas and souvenir shops.

Still, one could look down a narrow side street and see old women in black mending a fishing net or an old moustached man in a black cap sitting on a chair. She was conscious, always, of the past persisting to exist with the present, like an all but inaudible murmur under the noise of the day-to-day.

On her small radio in the morning one could hear Moorish sounding music coming across the strait from Turkey, wailing, intense, which seemed to say something to her about white buildings against the hot sky.

Now bouzouki music was crowding out the Turkish station, and then some inexplicable classical music came on. Mahler, perhaps. A slow, stately, sedate melody, resigned, wise. It said that one had to accept what must be: nightfall, illness, the seasons' change, age, absence, death.

But there was also joy in the sure grasp of what remained, what was still there. Like being in a café at closing time, as the tables were being cleared. We are reluctant to leave – we want to hold on to those last moments.

I want to tell you – the music said to her. *How much* – A final looking back, a fond gaze at the fading beloved. All the ache of temporariness. An opening of arms – a gesture of acceptance.

Then bouzouki music shouldered its way in, rude as life. The Turkish station was apparently gone for the day.

"PARKINSON'S," she had said to the woman seated next to her on the tour bus yesterday. "Last summer. A year ago when we came here he was in a wheelchair."

At the plane tree of Hippocrates he had reached up to touch a low hung leaf. *Heal me*, he had joked. Not a joking matter.

"He was so stubborn," she said. "So *determined*. He made me promise to come back here to...."

"God," sighed her seatmate, "What can you *do* with a man like that?"

Victoria remembered the look of compassion on the statue of Hippocrates in the local museum. A severe and useless compassion. He wore a toga and was missing an arm. In a field near the museum there were broken columns lying in tall weeds. An indifferent arch stood over nothing.

Now more people were arriving on the beach. The small boy with the green pail was still going to the water's edge and back. The waves were coming further in. His fort must be in peril. She looked again at the small map, not to scale, provided by the tour company. A spot marked *Byzantine ruins* was not too far from the *pension*.

"An old church," the tour courier had said. "Thirteenth century."

"Or Sixteenth," she said. "Anyhow. A short walk."

It was nine in the morning by the time Victoria set out down the main road away from town. In the distance she could see a new hotel. She was sure she'd heard it called either the Hercules or Agamemnon. She turned off the main road and down a hill. Then up a hill. The hotel seemed no closer. It hung in the air, a white marble mirage.

The sun was almost directly overhead and the air was very still. Even the insects in the roadside weeds were moving slowly. The hotel hung and floated between earth and sky. There had to be a path off to the right. Something moved in the bushes and a horned face peered out at her.

Several baby goats jumped out and ran across in front of her to their mother, tethered in a clearing. And now she was almost at the wall that surrounded the hotel's parking lot. No path off to the right. Only impenetrable scrub.

She walked slowly along the side of the wall to the hotel's forecourt. There was a small fountain in front of the entrance. It was a copy of something—the Garden of Love? Where young people conversed, feasted, played musical instruments. The fountain was surmounted by a cupid and a satyr holding a fish whose open mouth spouted water. The satyr looked like one of the baby goats.

The lobby was spacious and almost cool.

"I wonder if you can help me," she said to the desk clerk. After some smiles, shrugs and gestures, the clerk went into an office behind the bank of key and message slots. Victoria heard subdued Greek and German words. An older woman came out of the office, smiling.

"May I assist you?"

"Yes," said Victoria. She pressed the small map out on the counter.

"There are supposed to be ruins near here – an old church…."

"Ah, the church," said the woman. "You must go back to the main road into Mastihari…."

"No no," said Victoria, pointing at the map. "Not the *real* church. This one is very old. Ruins."

"Perhaps Stavros can help," said the woman. "He is the barman. At the pool? He knows much about the area."

Victoria walked out to the pool patio, which was shaded by a trellis overhung with vines. The sun splashed through the vines and onto the tiles. Stavros was a dignified man in his fifties.

"The ruins of the church." He nodded, gesturing off to the left. "All but inaccessible. Over that way. But there is no real path. There is not much there. Some stone blocks."

Victoria ordered a soft drink and sat at a table under the vines. Some children jumped into the pool. She could make her way down the shoreline back to town. The path led to the beach outside her *pension*. And perhaps there would be a way in from the beach to the ruins. Why did they put them on the map if one could not reach them?

She remembered that in Kos Town, near the old fortress where she had caught the bus to the Asclepieion, was a bas-relief of a man wearing a modern-looking military helmet. There were crossed palm fronds under the profile. The man had a firm jaw. Could it be Mussolini? The waiter in a nearby cafe had shrugged. He didn't know.

Asclepius, god of healing, to whom the Asclepieion had been erected, had been orphaned in infancy and suckled by a goat. Like the goats near the hotel parking lot.

She got up, took her glass back to the bar, smiled at Stavros, who was cutting limes into wedges. He smiled back.

Beyond the patio was a concrete path leading to the back of the hotel and the beach. She walked down it and out onto the boardwalk. She could see the white buildings of Mastihari far down there. Children playing on the water's edge near her called out. Voices irresistible and insistent. Victoria felt a surge of painful joy. It was, she knew, a maudlin feeling, self-indulgent.

There was no path off the boardwalk away from the beach. She stepped off the walk and went in about a yard or so and sat down on the ground. She opened her bag and dug around for the spoon she had taken from the *pension*. The ground was iron hard and cracked. The spoon scraped and slid and then bent in half. Useless, useless she almost said out loud.

"You are all right?"

A man stood on the walk. He wore one of those Greek fishermen's caps.

"Oh yes," she said, putting the bent spoon back in the bag. It clanked against the cylinder.

"I just stopped to rest."

"Is not wise," said the man. "To be out in the sun."

His English was good but obviously a second language.

"You are staying at the Hercules?" he said. "I could accompany you.…"

"No no," she said, struggling to get up. "I'm in Mastihari...."

He walked over and held out his hand. She stood up, brushing sand off her slacks. She said *thank you, thanks* a number of times, said there was no need to accompany her. All that way to Mastihari. She was perfectly fine. Thank you again and she was off down the walk. She turned to look back. The man stood there in a posture of concern and the hotel was floating above the island and the sky behind it was all open.

Despite the breeze coming off the water it was now very hot. Everything would be closed by the time she got back. A fool's errand. The man must have thought she was deranged or sunstruck.

She kept on walking, slowly, the heat all around her like a blanket of light. Finally she was on the outskirts of the village. She passed a place on the beach which rented surfboards with sails on them. There was a name for them, but she could not think of it. Music came from a nearby boom box. And up ahead there was a place to shower off seawater and sand. The beach in back of her *pension* was almost as empty as it had been early this morning. There was no sign of the two young women who were so preoccupied with their hair, and none of the small boy in white with the green pail.

SHE WENT UP the steps to her room. One flight, another, and there was the door. Inside was relatively cool. The maid had closed the jalousies, but a few shafts of light came through. A kind of Vermeer light, full of smug, cozy domesticity. She thought of the swings in the playground attached to the *real* church. They would be empty now and still. That child in white, building so patiently this morning. She and Harold never had children. Now she was so tired but too keyed up to sleep. She lay on one of the beds, arms crossed like a stone Crusader on a tomb.

Harold in his childhood, somewhere in Illinois where he had lived for half his life, before coming to Canada. Where they had met and married and lived.

Harold's father had worked for the railroad. That was the way Harold put it: *The Railroad.* As if there were only one. She imagined Harold the boy listening to trains in the night, thinking perhaps of his father swinging a lantern as freight cars were shunted. Great dark engines splitting the prairie silence with light and iron clanking. A far travelled father who had died before she could meet him.

After her, there would be nothing of Harold. Or of her.

She awoke in the dark. How long had she slept? She opened the shutters. The sky was still full of light. She must have just missed the sunset. Her watch was on the dresser next to the bag. She could not make out the time but did not want to put the lights on. She opened the fridge and poured herself a glass of wine.

Out on the balcony the air was turning fresh. A breeze was coming across onto the beach, blowing sand across the road. Two waiters were unfurling a plastic sheet on that side of the taverna. The sheet bellied in like a sail.

It was still early but full dark when she stepped out on the street. The souvenir shop across from the taverna had foreign newspapers – English, German, American. There were small figurines on a table. Ugly copies of famous statues. Priapus incredibly erect. Who would buy one of *those*? Pan seated on a rock playing his pipes. There were small triptych icons on a shelf. St. Michael easily subdued a large snake with a lance.

She went out of the shop and across to the taverna. George, her usual waiter, wasn't around. She sat at a table near the front and away from the plastic sheet, which was making crackling sounds as it swelled and fell.

"Madame is feeling better now?"

It was the concerned man from the boardwalk. He was smiling and wearing a T-shirt that said *Florida* on it. A woman in pink jeans stood unsmiling next to him.

"Oh yes," Victoria said. "It was just the sun. I'm from Canada, but we get plenty of sunshine. I *should* be used to it...."

"We have relatives in Toronto," said the woman.

After a futile effort to decide just where in Toronto, the couple left to join other people at a table near the back.

Victoria ordered Dutch beer and the catch of the day, an unfamiliar fish whose name in Greek did not help to identify it.

"Excuse me," said her waiter. "I could not help but overhear. I lived in Toronto for six years. My son was born there. But my wife was homesick. So we came back. Home."

Victoria began suddenly, helplessly, to cry. The waiter sat next to her and took her hand.

"You are homesick?" he asked softly. "Canada is a wonderful place."

"I'm all right now," Victoria smiled. "I don't know what...."

"Allow me to buy you an ouzo," said the waiter, waving off her protest as he stood.

"My son has forgotten his English," he said. "He was so young."

She sipped her beer. The fish was tasteless. The inevitable french fries were limp. Why did she always come to this taverna? There were many others.

A small glass was set before her. The waiter raised another glass.

"To Canada," he said.

"To Greece," she said.

As they sipped there was a shout of approval from the German table.

"Toronto!" someone called out.

SHE WENT DOWN to the ferry dock early the next morning. It was her last chance. Tomorrow she was going back to England and then home. There was already a lineup.

"Hello," said a voice behind her. It was Faith, who had sat beside her on the tour bus.

"You didn't get to the Greek Festival last night," said Faith. "I sort of looked for you."

"Oh," said Victoria, trying to hold her bag behind her leg. "I didn't sign up right away. And it was sold out when I remembered. How was it?"

"A bit touristic," Faith sighed. "But quite nice. I drank *too* much wine...."

Faith was a faded pretty woman in her early sixties. She was wearing shorts, hiking boots and a khaki shirt. She had a nice smile which gave her an abstracted air.

"I don't know where my friends are," Faith said, peering up and down the line. "We aren't all at the same hotel."

"You know," Victoria said. "I do think I'm going to pass on this trip. I leave tomorrow and really can't spare the time...."

"Too bad," said Faith. "But let's keep in touch. Let me give you my address."

She dug in her purse and wrote on the back of a hotel receipt.

"I live in Asheville," she said as she wrote. "Not *Nash*ville. Thomas Wolfe country? So you stop and see me sometime? I have my own ceramics shop. Asheville, North Carolina, *Look Homeward Angel?*"

"Yes," said Victoria. "I think that was one of my husband's favourite books."

"I bet he read it when he was a teenager," Faith laughed. "It's sort of a young man's book...."

"Well, I will certainly try to come your way," said Victoria, edging out of the line. "And you have my address now. Let's keep in touch...."

The line was beginning to move, slowly, towards the boat. Victoria waved and turned the other way. It was no good. Too many people. Faith was the sort of person, she had learned, who did a lot of fussing around other people. On the bus tour she had been constantly helpful, holding her arm coming down the bus steps, making sure she had all her packages after a stop.

She walked back to the small restaurant behind her pension. She sat on the patio and ordered an omelette. It came with fries. The beach was beginning to fill up. North Carolina. That's where the Outer Banks were. Once she and Harold had gone to Washington, where she gave a paper. They had done the Smithsonian buildings and visited the White House. They had talked about going on to the Outer Banks but there had been no time.

Now there was lots of time. To go there or somewhere. Or perhaps there wasn't much time.

So she had not gone to the island of sponges. And she would never come back to Kos. Maybe not Greece either. There was just so much time left. There were so many places she had never gone to: Cape Breton, Vancouver, the Outer Banks of North Carolina, and Taos, New Mexico, where D.H. Lawrence's ashes were cemented in a wall.

Oh my dearest, she thought with a pang. For nearly forty years I have loved you. Now the sun was climbing and the sky was a startling blue. She thought of the sky seen through the olive trees on the tour. Like shards of broken glass.

She remembered going down the streets of the Near North Side in Chicago when she had been in graduate school. Skies of summer blue. She had been in her twenties, overburdened, anxious, prowling the library. But full of small town awe for the mysterious life in the elegant brownstones. She yearned for sophistication. She had learned to live with mysteries, never going into any of those buildings. Even now, years later, she imagined high ceilings, classical music, antiques, clever conversation....

Once, somewhere in Southern Ontario, she and Harold stopped for dinner after a matinee in Stratford. The inn was on a river, and on the opposite bank an immense water wheel turned and turned. It was as large as a carnival ferris wheel. But this wheel had some serious purpose. Their waitress confessed that she did not know what the wheel actually *did*.

After dinner they walked down to the river's edge in the twilight. There were swans. The wheel turned and turned endlessly. That had been two summers ago. The summer before the wheelchair.

As imperceptibly as grief, the Dickinson poem went. *Our summer slipped away....*

THERE WAS NO FUSS about the cylinder in her luggage going through customs in Toronto. The whole trip had been surprisingly swift. The flight from Toronto to Windsor, by contrast, was turbulent. Windsor was in early summer doldrums. Thunderstorms were followed by heat waves and bouts of chill. Last summer had been a smoggy ordeal. What lay ahead?

IN PENNSYLVANIA she stopped at a Wal-Mart and bought a styrofoam cooler and some beer, ice and orange juice. She walked in the silent streets near her motel. There was a memorial to Civil War dead in a small square. A stone Union soldier stood on top of a plinth. A bronze plaque said that the monument had been purchased by the donations of school children. It took thirty years to complete.

It was a long drive the next day. She reached Nags Head in late afternoon and was at her motel at Buxton before dark. She stood on her balcony, which overlooked the pool and beyond it the beach and beyond that the Atlantic.

Children were still in the pool, and some fishermen were working the surf with long poles they anchored in the sand. She sat on the porch and ate the remains of a sandwich she had bought at Norfolk and opened a beer. The sun set on the other side of the complex. All she could see were long lines of last light on the water. It took a long time to be fully dark.

She went down the stairs and out onto the beach. The surf was slow and mild. Near the lighthouse, she stopped at the water's edge and opened the cylinder. It did not take long.

She left the cylinder in a trash can near the motel pool. The woman who had said *cremains* had spoken of the possibility of *urnment*. It had seemed an impossible alternative.

Tomorrow, Victoria thought, she would take the ferry to Ocracoke Island and another ferry back to the mainland. She could drive to Asheville, visit Faith, see Thomas Wolfe's grave. Something scuttled across the sand near the path to the stairway. She hunched down. The beach must be crowded with creatures frantic to live.

MORNING CAME THROUGH her windows like the first light of creation. She made a cup of instant coffee and went out on the balcony. It was impossible to stay there. The light surged and dazzled. The beach was on fire with morning.

Maybe she would change her mind and stay here for awhile. Perhaps go on a fishing boat. Or just walk on the beach and talk to the fishermen at the surf line. They would tell her that this season was not as good as the last. Or the recent hurricane had driven the fish elsewhere. Nothing was ever as good as last year.

She walked out on the beach. The sand blazed white. "How's the fishing?" she asked a man who had three long poles held in pipes sunk in the sand.

"Pretty good." He smiled. "This is a good spot."

She walked towards the lighthouse. Then she realized that the air was filled with kites. The beach was crowded with children holding the strings. There were so many kites and of such varied sizes and shapes. There they all were, flying in place in the wind, straining to break free, held by taut lines and filling the sky with joyous colours.

She wanted to turn to someone and say, *There are so many of them! Look, aren't they beautiful?*

The kites seemed close but far away, hovering and dipping and rising. She wanted to reach up and touch one. It would be fragile and tough. To hold one in her arms. She stood there looking up into the sky which seemed to shout in all those young colours, and she was in the centre of it.

Travelling Through The Dark

THE BUS, AN IMPRESSIVE BLUE AND black presence, pulled into the gallery parking lot at 7:45 AM. Over the top of the bus windshield a banner proclaimed *Art For All.* The lineup waiting was mostly women with a small number of husbands. Clare knew most of the women from the Gallery volunteers. Many of them had been friends of her mother's. One of the women in line, Agnes Thorpe, touched her on the arm.

"I was so sorry about Lila, dear," she said. "We were friends for almost fifty years."

Clare smiled. She had been accepting condolences for a month now and still had not come up with the right response. When someone in her eighties dies it really isn't an immense surprise. Most of her mother's friends were in their seventies and eighties. Maybe that was part of all this concern: the guilty relief of the survivor.

Clare was the daughter who stayed home to look

after mother. Since she was an only child, there wasn't much of a choice to be made. If someone had to stay home, she was it.

"What are you going to do now?" Agnes asked.

"Oh, I might go back to teaching," Clare said.

This was not true. She hadn't been in a classroom in ten years. She was in her fifties, a nuisance and threat to any pension plan. Her degree seemed distant and her experience obsolete. Besides, the market was glutted with fresh new teachers hungry for jobs.

She really did not know what she could do. It seemed too late in life to start something. Pottery lessons. Sell real estate.

"So how is Tommy?" she said.

"He's fine," Agnes smiled. "About to become a grandfather. Which will make me a great-grandmother. I'm not too sure how I feel about *that*."

"Give Tommy my best," Clare said as she stepped up into the bus.

The bus was not full. There were seats for the choosing.

"I wonder which side the sun will be on," a man said, smiling at her.

"Let's see," she said. "We'll be going north and then west?"

He made a comical oh-what-the-hell gesture and sat down in a seat on the right, halfway back.

"Over here," the man called to an anxious looking woman who carried a canvas bag with the gallery logo on it.

"Hello, Clare," the woman said. "I was so sorry to

hear about Lila. We were in Arizona."

There was a surge of last-minute arrivals and some sorting out of seats. As it turned out, Clare ended up sitting alone.

"May I have your attention?" a woman holding a clipboard spoke into a microphone. "We will leave in a few minutes. I see many, many familiar faces here. We've had a few cancellations...."

The doors swung closed and the bus began to move.

"We'll stop for coffee and a stretch at about ten," the woman went on. "And then lunch at noon. We have to be at the museum by one-thirty. We will have a private viewing of the exhibit and the lecture. So sit back and relax and enjoy your day!"

There was scattered applause. Clare had brought along a cassette player and some Glenn Gould tapes. But it might seem anti-social. She opened the morning paper, which had arrived just as she set out for the gallery.

All the news was bad. Home and abroad. The Arts section wasn't much better. Another publishing house closes. A controversial art opening in Alberta causes questions in the legislature.

Clare was an intense woman with grey-streaked hair and young blue eyes. Her mother's eyes, everyone said. Her father had died when she was a child and Lila went back to work to raise her. Lila was a living saint. All Lila's friends said so.

Now the bus was in the midst of cars intent on getting to where they were going. Jobs to be done, children delivered to day care centres. There was a lot of waiting at traffic lights. And then they were on the highway heading out of the city past open bare fields. The rising sun cast a pale light on the fields. The day began to unfold before Clare, as if stretching and rising from sleep.

Clare and Tommy had been high school sweethearts. They were serious about one another in teachers' college. Then he got a job out west, and then mother fell for the first time. Tommy came home on holidays a few times. He wrote to her a few times. Then he got married. And then he had children. Now one of his children was about to have a child.

It occurred to Clare that he probably wasn't "Tommy" anymore. He was probably "Tom" the husband, father and soon to be grandfather.

He had held his children when they were babies, seen them grow to adulthood. She found it hard to picture him as he was now. Grey hair? No hair? He had been tall and gangly. Was he fat now? A bent-over geezer? All that she was reasonably sure of was that he probably wasn't "Tommy" anymore.

Maybe he was still "Tommy" to his wife in a tender moment. He was a faded blur in Clare's memory. She could not recall what his voice sounded like. She could half remember the songs they had danced to, listened to on his father's car radio.

Fragments of melody and words rose and sank in her memory. Trying and failing to remember those songs seemed to her more important than remembering Tommy.

She tried to recall old friends. Other boyfriends.

Movies they had gone to. All merged in her mind as a fleeting mélange of almost-grasped objects.

THE RESTAURANT was in a truck stop area, but clean, the driver said into the microphone. Please be back on the bus by 10:30. We're on schedule so far.

Clare stopped in the ladies room first. When she came out, most everyone else had gotten their coffee and were seated here and there. Men who looked like truck drivers wearing big buckled belts were talking into cell phones.

She got a small coffee, which was too large and too hot. She took it outside and stood next to a raked gravel area surrounded by a rustic wood fence. Large stones had been set in the gravel. A sturdy wind blew from across the highway. It smelled of spring, loam, quickening.

The coffee was still too hot. She spilled some of it out on the gravel. People were coming back. She put the half empty cup in a garbage can. The morning sun was hot on her back.

A few of the group had headphones on. She got out her player and a tape.

THE BUS CAME into the city over a bridge which traversed railroad yards, a small sullen river, and more railroad yards. They went past old begrimed warehouses, red brick factories and stately church steeples which stood almost as tall as the smokestacks.

The lakefront had been given a strong dose of revitalization. Where there were once closed up businesses and homeless people sleeping under cardboard, now there were shops, restaurants and a brisk tourist trade.

Lunch would be in a galleria complex. Three floors of boutiques surrounded an open court under a giant vaulted glass and iron ceiling. The whole ground floor was given over to a food court grouped around an immense fountain which pulsed to recorded amplified music.

One had many choices: Chinese, Mexican, Creole, Tex-Mex and the usual fast food franchises. Some of the crowd were obviously on their lunch hour from nearby offices. Women in business suits, men in dress shirts and ties pulled down, women with babies in strollers, young girls in school uniforms and the elderly. And the old.

Some were sitting at the tables scattered among the food kiosks, others were sitting on the edge of the fountain, eating their lunches or reading paperbacks. Some, like Clare, were obvious tourists, between events, to whom all this was foreign exotic, a place to be savoured and passed through.

Clare did not see anyone from the bus. Possibly many were shopping. She made her choice alone.

"I'll have the chicken caesar salad," she said, "and a glass of your dry white house wine."

"That'd be the Chablis?" asked the young girl behind the counter.

"I suppose so," said Clare.

She took her tray to a table near the windows overlooking the street. Somewhere out there was the lake. Under the building subway trains arrived or left, making an intermittent tremor under her feet. The fountain water arced and fell.

THE CURATOR gathered them in a circle in the hall just outside the exhibit. This was the only major exhibition of Jessie Obregon's work to be seen this year in North America. The exhibit, *The Apotheosis of Semele*, would leave this museum and travel to Europe in the fall.

Semele, the curator said, was a mortal who asked Zeus (her lover in some form or other) to reveal himself to her in his full, terrible, divine glory. He did so, and she was destroyed.

Finally they moved into the main gallery. The paintings were huge, displaying hovering figures that could have been men or women or angels or demons. Their skin had a kind of corpse-like lividity. Clare wondered what all this meat had to do with Semele.

After they had finished viewing the work, they went into an auditorium and heard a lecture on the artist. She was, of course, the wife of the famous South American muralist who had been more famous than she during her life. Now, after her death, her own work had been discovered, curated, archived, the subject of symposia and, of course, this major exhibition.

And a number of caustic journals kept by Jessie had

been found, edited and published. These books were available in the museum shop. Jessie had meticulously observed her husband's self-promotion, infidelities and pomposities. She had also documented their friends' sycophantic efforts to influence important critics.

These critics had not escaped her keen eye. They had ballooned their own reputations by promoting the "Obregon Circle." Which did not include Jessie. How clearly she had seen them all. And now she had the last word.

After the lecture they were on their own for an hour. They had to be back on the bus promptly at four. The gift shop was on the main floor, near the entrance.

Clare wandered from one room to another. Then she went downstairs to the washroom. Down there was a "Yesterday's Main Street" construct, with cobblestone streets and gas lamps and store fronts. There was a hardware store window full of old tools surrounding a keg of nails, a dress shop displaying mannequins wearing authentic and fragile fashions from the past, a drug store with giant glass urns filled with red and green water, a barber shop complete with striped pole and a penny arcade.

The penny machines actually worked. Clare bent to a machine with a placard on it. "Caught in the Act!" As her penny dropped a light bulb inside the machine came on and photographs flipped as the crank was turned. A woman came into a room and began to pull her clothes off. First her dress, then a slip, and then she sat down on a chair to unroll her stockings. Finally she was down to a black chemise. As she pulled the shoulder straps down the light went off.

The turning crank made the woman's motions jerky, uneven, not attractive. Clare suspected that another penny would result in the same unfolding of events leading up to the abrupt halt before a final disrobing.

Another penny machine had a placard on it saying "Deed Ah Do!" Her penny dropped, the light bulb came on and a man in blackface wearing a black suit and white gloves climbed out of a coffin, did a brief jerky tap dance and got back in the coffin as the light went out.

Clare felt uneasy. The woman in the "Caught in the Act" pictures looked like her mother – her mother when she had been younger, about the age of the eternally undressing woman and probably at about the same period in the past.

There were photographs of her mother from that time in a shoebox. There were many other photographs in the shoebox, none labelled, all mysterious. A family picnic with people sitting at a long table placed out on the grass in a farm's front yard.

Who were these people? Men in shirtsleeves and suspenders holding up bottles of what might be pop or beer. A man in a straw boater stands next to the table holding a child in his arms. The man looks uneasy. He is not smiling. He looks stern or impatient, waiting for the shutter to click so he can hand the child to someone else.

There was a formal studio photograph of her mother in a dark lacy dress, like the one worn by the woman caught in the act. Her mother holds Clare on her lap, a little bundle of white lace. Perhaps it is her christening day. Her father stands behind them. He looks slightly bloated, as if the photographer had gently inflated him for the pose. He looks dazed, standing behind his fate. Mother looks neither pleased nor displeased. She is merely there. Mother had promised to sort out all these pictures someday but she never did get around to it.

DINNER WAS AT Country Fare, a good, basic, wholesome place that catered to families and bus groups. One entered through an immense gift shop. The smell of bayberry was prominent. There was no waiting for tables. The bus group separated into fours, sixes and twos.

The walls were weathered barn wood. Everywhere there were metal signs hung advertising obsolete brands of motor oil, baking powders, cigarettes, bicycles and patent medicines. There was a framed picture of a guardian angel hovering over two small children next to Clare's table. The children were about to cross a very unstable bridge. There were planks missing. The river looked lively. The angel looked serene and confident.

The menu announced an awesome array of choice: comfort foods, meat loaf, stews, cornbread. The dessert menu was even more extensive.

Clare looked around. Everywhere there were families, babies in high chairs, young parents coaxing mashed potatoes into small reluctant mouths. Dessert was certainly a serious thing here. Men with thick strong necks were bent to custards, sundaes, pies and cakes. There were mason jars with spears of wheat in them on each table.

Mary Alice Benson, a tall patrician woman with uncompromising white hair and a narrow face, stood uncertainly next to her table.

"Won't you join me?" Clare said.

"Well, my dear," Mary Alice said as she sat down. "I hope you are coping."

"Oh, well," Clare said. "Everyone has been so kind."

"Yes," Mary Alice said, looking vaguely off to the side. "Lila had many friends."

"May I take your order, ladies?" said a harassed-looking young woman.

"I will have the salmon patties," Mary Alice said. "And a glass of water."

"I'll have the same," Clare said. "But with root beer. Diet root beer."

"I guess you and mother were friends for a long time?"

"Since high school," Mary Alice said, looking down at her knife and fork. "You know, your father was my boyfriend. Until Lila came along."

"Oh," said Clare.

"It turned out for the best," Mary Alice sighed. "Your father was a man with a restless heart. He *did* run off when you were a baby. I married a dear man who never did that."

"Ran off?" said Clare. "But he died...."

"Years later," Mary Alice said.

The water and root beer arrived and a basket of cornbread. A nearby child was screaming in his high chair.

"Lila should have written novels," Mary Alice said, smiling. "You'd be rich."

When they were finished there was still time to look around the gift shop. But there was nothing there she really wanted. They walked out on the porch to go back to the bus. A row of rocking chairs was lined up on the porch as if waiting for aged aunts to come out and sit in them, drink lemonade and wait for evening to become night. The chairs were all for sale.

The bus turned out of the restaurant lot and onto the highway. She didn't know where Mary Alice was sitting. There were questions to ask. Clare was not sure she wanted answers. It was full dark now. Clare looked out at the lights of cars coming at them in the other lane. Beyond were fields and isolated houses set in a lonely immense space. The lights in those houses seemed brave. The bus tires thrummed and hit some sort of structural bump in the road at regular intervals. Into the dark. Into the dark.

She remembered trying to teach the poem "Travelling Through the Dark" to a class of sixteen and seventeen-year-olds. The poem was about a man who stops his car on a country road because there is a dead deer in his way. He is about to pull the carcass to the side when he discovers that there is a live fawn in her belly, ready to be born.

What can he do? He is alone, far from help. He hesitates, then pushes the body to the side.

Clare thought that the poem was about those tough choices in life. Sometimes there isn't a good one, the right decision. The dead animal in the road, a hazard, dangerous to traffic. But there is life there waiting to be delivered.

Her students disagreed with her. They held a range of opinion: Who killed the deer? People should drive more carefully. Why didn't he deliver the fawn? Why are animals treated so badly?

Clare remembered her frustration. Why couldn't they comprehend the inconclusive toughness of life-choices? Perhaps they had to live more life, experience some hard lessons. Maybe they were not ready for that poem.

Travelling through the dark – several kinds of darkness. Optical, moral, mortal. At least she had not faced those pull-the-plug decisions. Mother had died in her sleep. No pain. For her. Now only this aftertime. Her father was bent over in the dark, dragging a dead deer to the edge....

She began to sink into a pleasant doze. The bus seemed to be accelerating, almost to lift up off the highway and hurtle into the encompassing night.

Everything she had seen during the day was unspooling in her mind. Like the faded photographs in the penny machines, cranked and flipped, a woman speedily undressing, a man doing a frenetic dance and leaping back into his coffin. A man in blackface wearing a straw boater dances and waves goodbye. And the hovering shapes of angels or demons under immense iron branches. The woman briskly dresses and backs out through the door. The door shuts and is firmly locked.

A dull light came through the heavy glass dome. Fountain waters were flung high, high in the domed light. A hurly-burly of music rose and fell as the light dimmed.

The waters fell to stillness. Under her a constant train arrived and arrived. Forever, the train muttered, forever. None of this will stop. This is the way it is, always the way it is. The woman undresses and dances with the man in blackface. Always, always, forever, arriving, arriving always.

AND THEN she was suddenly aware. All motion had ceased. The engine was off. The ceiling lights had come on and the driver said:

"We're back home folks. Please be sure you have all your belongings. It's been a pleasure being your escort."

There was a flurry of applause and people began to move into the aisle. At the door the driver offered Clare a gallant hand to help her step down. The woman with the clipboard stood next to the driver, smiling bravely. Tall arc lights surrounded the gallery parking lot, casting an unnatural chill light on the people hurrying and bending to their car doors. As she opened hers some of the women called to her. She waved in response.

Home wasn't all hers yet. Her mother's room still

glimmered at night with glow-in-the-dark crucifixes and rosaries draped over religious pictures. But she had made some territorial inroads in the rest of the house. The coffee table in the living room was heaped with her half-read books. Mother would not have approved. The calendar in the kitchen advertising a funeral parlour with a different saint for each month had been replaced with one featuring twelve Monet gardens.

It had been a long day and she felt the full overstimulation and fatigue of it. Sleep would be difficult. She pulled into the driveway and sat for a moment with the engine off. Nobody was waiting up for her. That was at once a relief and a sad fact.

So often she had been wakened by her mother's frail voice, calling out in pain or loneliness. She had not, in that final time, had one full night's sleep. She had come to know those small hours of the night when most everyone else in the world was asleep. Two, three, four in the morning, pulled abruptly awake, and then later a fretful lying back down, in a fevered frenzied half-sleep, expecting another tremulous call.

Now there would be nobody to call out to her. The house was silent tonight.

Tomorrow, she thought to herself, tomorrow. She went up the steps to her door. In the dark.

Waterfalls

A BOY STANDS BETWEEN HIS PARENTS ON the sidewalk. They have just gotten off the street-car, which groans and clangs away. The sidewalk is crowded, and they move to a better spot on the corner.

"There it is," says his father, pointing up at the spotlit falling water.

Later on the boy will remember music playing as the lights moved over the lichened rocks and the water, the always falling water. Later on the boy will wonder: Had there been music? He was not sure. Had there been a statue of an Indian maiden?

But a waterfall in the middle of the city! It is more wonderful than an ordinary waterfall like Niagara or something in Africa. Two streetcars going in opposite directions clang and grind their iron wheels against the shining tracks. The sounds fade in both directions.

The corner is crowded with families jostling to find the best vantage point. All their faces are lifted and lit by refracted light streaming and bouncing off the spray from the falls.

SUNDAY AMONG THE INSANE

MY LIBRARY CARREL began to shake. It was someone on the other side of the partition vigorously erasing something. It must have been a vast passage. It was in the fall, just before mid-terms. There was all this anxiety, penitence, salvage efforts. A female voice said *no*. The voice was too loud for the library.

I was there, trying to find a quiet place to finish my paper. *Whitman and Richard Bucke.* I was going to deliver it in Chicago in two weeks. My attention was obviously wandering. I had not been to Chicago in some twenty-five years. I was born there, met my wife there. Nobody we knew was alive there anymore. We would not see much of the city. I was chair of a division of the Modern Languages Association and we would meet a lot to discuss what we would do about the challenge of multiculturalism.

No. *They* would face the challenge. I was to retire at the end of this year. This would be my last paper. It was becoming obsolete as I wrote it. Two old white men. One Canadian, one American. Two Eurocentric guys.

But I *would* finish the paper and I *would* deliver it. What with the paper and the division meetings I doubted we would get out of the Palmer House or beyond the shadow of the Loop's elevated tracks.

That city I lived in, I suspected, was long gone. Once I saw this map which showed geological faults. There were bright bunches and blobs of folds and substrata and plates. I stared closely and figured that my mother must have been born at the edge of something called the Illinois Basin. This was a useless discovery. The earth which I love is not a firm reality, but is instead a trembling complex of conflicting forces. There is nothing I can do about it. On the other side of the carrel, the unseen person began to tap a nervous foot. The foot tapping stopped and was replaced by more erasing.

THE CHICAGO of my youth was a place where you could walk for miles without fear. I remember walking when I was sixteen or seventeen from a pizza place on the West Side, almost at the city limits, all the long way to downtown. There, we – I was with a friend on many of these excursions – went down to South State Street, past the tattoo parlors and penny arcades and then over to the lake and Grant Park and Buckingham Fountain, which was lit with different colours and spouted up in endless strength. Then we walked back to Michigan Avenue and somehow on Maxwell Street, and it was two in the morning and a gypsy woman tried to sell us sex with her daughter.

Now I think of those journeys as magical. We were privileged to see everything, and we walked through it with no harm. We had anywhere to go and we went there. I loved the feeling of anonymity, moving through crowds like a private eye on a case.

Now my wife and I live in this small city in Southern Ontario, near the river, across from Detroit. Chicago is the place to the west where we sometimes pass around on our way somewhere. I suspect that those streets I walked on are dangerous now, as dangerous as Detroit's. The city, like many others, has grown grim, gritty, tough.

When I step out of our house I can look to the west and see the bridge that can take me to the highway to Chicago. I look in the opposite direction and imagine the hundred miles to the east. To London, where Walt Whitman visited Dr. Bucke in the summer of 1880. I stand between. I can go either way.

To The Waterfall

I MUST HAVE been nine or ten years old when I was first taken to see the Olson Rug Company Waterfall. This was Chicago in about 1939. The company was somewhere on the northwest side of the city. It was a building that took up a whole block. A factory and showroom. At one side of the building an artificial waterfall had been constructed three or four stories high. There were plants and rocks and perpetually falling water. It was lit up at night. I remember holding my father's hand and staring up at the falling water. I fell asleep on the streetcar on the way home. We had to transfer, and my father woke me up.

When I grew older I heard the jokes about the waterfall. I was working on the shipping dock of a factory and someone asked someone else where he was going on his vacation. "The Olson Waterfall," was the wry answer. I remember seeing a postcard of the waterfall on the shipping room bulletin board right next to the cards from Wisconsin and California. A rueful joke, on the same level as a "honey-do" holiday.

But was it a joke? A commercial gimmick? It must have cost a lot to erect and maintain. There was no charge. You didn't have to buy a rug. Pristine water falling among green rocks and the sound of car tires and horns and streetcars. Inside the big red brick building, men and women wove rugs and could not see the waterfall which their labour helped to make. Maybe on their lunch hour.

My wife says there was a statue of an Indian maiden, kneeling next to the pool at the base of the falls. I think she is confusing it with the maiden on the box of Wisconsin butter. I do not remember a statue.

Sunday Among The Insane: Notes for a paper on Walt's visit to London, Ontario in July 1880

"Did you ever hear of a man called Walt Whitman?"

Hunt asked the question as he prodded the wood in the fireplace. It was the winter of 1867. Dr. Hunt was visiting his good friend Dr. Richard Maurice

Bucke in Sarnia, where Bucke practiced.

"No," said Bucke. "Who is he?"

"An American poet," said Hunt, thoughtfully poking at the fire. "He writes in a very peculiar style...."

Hunt went on to quote what he could remember from *Leaves of Grass*.

> I celebrate myself, and sing myself,
> And what I assume you shall assume

Bucke felt an involuntary psychic assent stir deep inside him. He knew that he must find out more about Whitman and his writings. He *knew* that Whitman was going to become very important in his life.

Outside, the voices of children on sledges rose in chill joy. One of the logs in the fireplace fell and cracked in a shower of sparks.

After this visit Bucke searched in vain for a copy of *Leaves*. He was able to find only the Rossetti edition of selected poems. He did not see a copy of the complete book until 1870 when he went to visit Hunt in Montreal. He finally got his own complete edition in 1872.

In 1877 Bucke wrote to Whitman and stopped in Camden to visit him on the way to Philadelphia, where the Centennial Exposition was still on.

Bucke afterwards said that he experienced a "spiritual intoxication" when he first met Whitman. It was not unlike a previous mystical experience Bucke had in London (England) in 1872, when he felt an "intense joyousness" and intuited that the cosmos was a living presence.

Bucke went on to Philadelphia and stood before the Corliss engine which ran all the smaller machines at the Exposition. It was the largest steam engine in the world. Whitman and the giant engine. Two kinds of force.

Bucke went to Camden again in the summer of 1880 and travelled with Whitman back to London, where Bucke was now the director of the Asylum For The Insane. Bucke was one of the foremost alienists of the day. On the journey from Camden to London, the two men stopped at Niagara Falls. They walked out on the suspension bridge, their white beards streaming in the wind. Whitman had to hold onto his slouch hat. His eyes were full of awe. He looked at the tumult of falling water with the rapture of a newlywed. They stood there for a long time.

On their way back off the bridge, Whitman noticed for the first time that his friend walked with a limp. Bucke later told him that he had lost a foot to frostbite while trying to cross the Sierra Nevadas in 1836. Whitman detested poor health and infirmity.

Whitman stayed all summer with the Buckes, whose comfortable house was on the grounds of the Asylum For The Insane. On the first Sunday of his visit, there was a church service on the lawn for the inmates. Whitman sat where he could study the faces of the patients. Later he would write about this experience in an essay titled "Sunday Among the Insane." Bucke later took Whitman on side trips to Lake Huron, Lake Erie and up into Quebec.

In September Whitman came back from this trip to Canada convinced that the country would one day peacefully become part of the United States. Thus travel may broaden but does not always deepen. Bucke travelled with Whitman as far as the falls, where they went out on the suspension bridge one last time.

Bucke wrote the first biography of Whitman. It was published in 1883. It can be shelved under *hagiography*. The book is embarrassingly ardent. *What happened out on the suspension bridge the second time?*

While he was in London, Whitman had several photographs taken by the Edy brothers. Whitman once said that he had been photographed so often that all the cameras must be tired of him. This did not stop him from having more taken.

Bucke was devastated by Whitman's death in 1892. Only a firm mystical belief that he and his friend would be reunited in an afterlife kept him from complete collapse.

THE 1992 FILM *Beautiful Dreamers* was a fictional account of Whitman's 1880 visit to Bucke. Colm Feore played Bucke and Rip Torn portrayed Whitman. The producers tried to do location shots around London, but had a hard time finding places where there were not things like telephone wires. The woman who played Mrs. Bucke (look this up later) was a lot prettier than the real-life person. Art and life.

IN JANUARY, 1880, Whitman had a dream. A ghost ship was floundering in a fierce storm. Standing on the deck was a slender, dim man who was enjoying the terror and the murk. He was at the centre of it all. He was the victim, but he was at the centre of it.

"That figure of my lurid dream," Whitman said, "was Edgar Poe."

The dream was some five months before Whitman's trip to stay with Bucke.

IN ONE OF HIS landscape studies, "The Domain of Arnheim," Poe describes a dream journey down a winding river. The trip ends with a drop into a gorge and onto a lake. There is a dreamlike descent, but it is by no means a drop over a waterfall. There are no waterfalls in the works of Poe.

NONE OF THE ABOVE made it to the final paper. We went to Chicago and I delivered a pale, inoffensive, witty, knowledgeable talk at the conference. Nobody could think of a sensible question to ask.

Oh, they *did* ask questions. But I made it through the pass without an ambush.

I wanted to call my paper *Sunday Among the Insane*, but wisely did not. After the division meeting, in which we considered the decanonization of Emerson, Hemingway, Mailer and Whitman (!), and tabled the problem for the following year, we elected my young colleague Adams as incoming chair.

"You did all that so adroitly," said Adams as we

walked out of the meeting room. "I mean postponing all that nastiness. Leaving it all to me."

"If you ever see me wearing a woman's dress and getting into a lifeboat," I said, "go there also."

I remembered that Adams grew up in Chicago.

"Listen," I said. "Do you remember—maybe your parents might have told you—the Olson Rug Waterfall? Someplace on the Northwest Side?"

"The what?" Adams said with a wary look in his eye.

"I grew up on the South side," he said. "A *water*fall?"

"Oh it was there," I said. "It was there."

In my mind I could see Bucke and Whitman suspended high in the air above the falls, staring at the always falling water.

People in barrels going over the falls, people on tightropes walking across the falls. Gawkers crowding to see the daredevils. People wearing slickers on a boat going under the falls. And from the suspension bridge, all, all stare in rapture at the falls.

"Do you remember the little waterfall at that castle restaurant?" my wife asked. "It was The Cave? Maybe The Castle?"

We were driving out to the West Side on the morning after the conference ended. Neither of us could remember exactly where the Olson Rug Waterfall was. Or had been. We had never gone to it together.

"I remember the restaurant," I said. "But it wasn't The Castle."

When we were young, before we were married, we used to drive out to the suburbs to that restaurant on the river. The place looked like a castle or a fort in a movie. The walls inside were all rough plaster and lights hung in iron sconces.

Outside was a small waterfall and a mill wheel. The water at the base of the falls was a brown froth of bubbles and used condoms. We had been embarrassed by the condoms. We were young and innocent. We never mentioned them.

We had never gone to the Olson Rug Waterfall together. We had been taken, separately, by our parents. When you were a child you went places with your parents on a bus or streetcar or you were in the back seat of a car and did not know exactly where you were. You travelled in trust.

On this day after the conference ended, we could not find the waterfall. So we started the long drive home. All in all it had not been too rough a weekend. My wife made it to the big department stores and bought things for our grandchildren. I got through my paper safely and off-loaded myself from the division chair. We could take a deep breath. It had not been like whitewater rafting.

LATE THAT NIGHT, safe home, I lay awake listening to my wife's quiet breathing. The trees outside began to sough in a quickening wind. Rain and wind have been forecast. More wet leaves to rake. Why are people so romantic about this necrology of leaves?

So we could not find the waterfall and could not remember the name of the castle restaurant with its mill wheel. I remember that storm scene in *Jean-Christophe*. It was a book I bought when I was seventeen. That big tempest takes the hero up and infuses him with creative force. I wanted something like that to happen to me.

I could not sleep. I got up quietly and went into the TV room. I looked up *Beautiful Dreamers* in Leonard Maltin's book. Jessie Bucke had been played by Wendel Meldrum. I turned on the TV without the sound. Randolph Scott and Joel McCrea are pinned down in a gully. Bruce Dern and his bullies are directing a murderous fire at the old gunfighters. Scott and McCrea look at one another. There is no need for words here. They climb out of the ditch and tall walk towards Dern and his men. Bullets whip past them and through their coats.

Two old cowboys. The movie was *Ride the High Country*. It was about integrity, age and dignity. Scott was the rascal in this film. McCrea was the stern upholder of a code. But for this magnificent moment they were together. Leonard Maltin gave this movie four stars.

I went to the corner bookcase and looked for my old copy of *Jean-Christophe*. There was one summer when I carried it to the beach every day. Towel, lotion and book. The book got sand and lotion on it. I remembered the sun making the page too bright and the wind flapping the pages.

I could not find the book. Maybe I sold it at a garage sale when we moved to the smaller house or gave it to one of our children. To be taken by a tempest. To think *let's do it* and rise from a ditch to face danger.

In *Wild Strawberries* the old professor tries to soothe himself to sleep with happy sunlit memories of childhood. I try that too. It sometimes works.

I went back to bed. My wife made half-awake noises as I carefully lay down. It was still raining. The wind had died down.

Bring me home, I said to myself as the rain continued to fall. Bring me home.

I STAND ouside the Palmer House under the iron webwork of the elevated train tracks. It is night. My companion on my magical journeys is gone. I do not know where. I have not seen him in thirty years. A grey figure stands next to me, wearing a slouch hat. Could I take his arm and walk to the Olson Rug Waterfall?

I want to show him the waterfall. Together we will stand, our white hair tousled by the wind thrown off the falling water. Inside the big red brick building rugs are spinning off the looms. Outside, streetcars come and go. We stand on the corner, watching the wonderful magical waters fall.

Home in the Dark

Home is so far from Home since my Father died.
–EMILY DICKINSON

I don't want to go home in the dark.
–LAST WORDS OF WILLIAM SIDNEY PORTER (O. HENRY)

one

The Trembling of a Leaf

VIVIAN ARRIVED AT TECUMSEH College in the autumn of 1951. Her reputation had arrived well before she did. Father Lally, the Dean, had a confrere at Toronto who told him that everybody on campus had gone gaga over this girl. She had all this promise. But some of the faculty had made fools of themselves. There had been a scene in a faculty club dining room. A professor's wife screamed and broke dishes. There had been a lot of hushing up. But somebody with all that promise could not simply be expelled. Phone calls were made. Favours were traded.

Tecumseh did not at the time have a full degree program in music. All it had was Trevor Herrick who taught Music Appreciation, Speech and Introduction to Literature. He had a few students in composition tutorials. How could Vivian's promise be nurtured in such almost barren ground? But there was at this time no place else she could go. And Herrick had a reputation as a comer, almost a Boy Wonder.

THERE IS A PASSAGE in Maugham about the trembling of a leaf. A still landscape is disturbed by a faint breeze. Everything changes. So also a minor gesture, an offhand remark, a sideways glance of the eye can have enormous consequences. Kingdoms are lost, fortunes squandered, marriages are broken up, lives are given over to obsessive pursuits.

TREVOR CAME INTO Tecumseh's coffee shop one morning between classes. The coffee shop was a low, dismal room under the gym. The ceiling reverberated with the sound of bounced basketballs. Trevor had an hour between Introduction to Literature and Music Appreciation. There was not enough time to do anything useful like going back to his office. So he had taken to dropping in for a coffee and casual talk with some of his serious music students. On that morning, only one of them was around. He was sitting at a table with Vivian. Trevor looked like the French writer André Malraux, except that he, Trevor, did not smoke. Trevor wore tweeds that looked European. They were. He was in his early twenties but already had a stoop-shouldered, academic, world-weary air. He had, also, a kind of reputation. Virgil Thompson came through Windsor on his way to Toronto and stayed with him. The tweeds were too heavy for the humid early fall weather. Vivian decided that Trevor was definitely heterosexual.

"Hello, Danny," Trevor said. "May I join you?"

Danny made noises of yes, yes, certainly and Trevor sat down across the unsteady table from Vivian. Danny reluctantly introduced them.

Vivian was wearing a silky light green blouse. A few buttons were opened. A thin gold chain with a small cross on it lay against her skin. A pulse moved faintly beneath the chain. The sound of a dribbled basketball thudded across the ceiling above them.

She took the cross in her hand, delicately turned, twisted it, slowly. Her eyes looked off just to the side of Trevor's gaze. A hint of a smile played at the corners of her mouth as if she were remembering a secret. The trembling of a leaf.

Whether Vivian stage-managed her posture on that afternoon, or improvised her bit of business with the gold cross, the moment would have far-reaching consequences. It became one of Trevor's most treasured memories. For him it summed up female allure and mystery.

"I think I'm supposed to come to see you," she said. "The Dean said that maybe we could work out something for me. The piano?"

"Ah yes," Trevor said, trying not to keep staring at her hand trembling on the chain.

"Well, I have office hours every Tuesday and Thursday morning," he said. "Or right now I have about a half hour."

As usual it was too hot for September. Trevor felt damp

and troubled as they walked back toward his office. He felt over-large and shambling walking next to this slim girl. He had heard all the gossip, all the forewarnings, and thought he was safe. He had, after all, spent years in sophisticated countries and had, yes, his share of carnal experience.

But nothing had prepared him for the physical shock of the girl's presence, her mystery. And underneath it all was a disturbing awareness that something invisible and electric was arcing between them. Was he fooling himself or was that shy sideways smile just now special, just for him? A secret promise.

He found himself talking too much and not saying anything. Pointing out buildings and giving her their history. Was he committing the sin of boredom?

"I don't know if I'm good enough to keep on with the piano," she said in a voice that sounded distant, not really involved with the question.

"I have other options," she went on. "So why don't we make an appointment and I'll strut my stuff?"

He smiled and leaned back in his chair.

"Sure," he said. "How's your calendar tomorrow?"

"Perfectly white," she said.

When she smiled, as she did right now, an amazing complex of laugh wrinkles appeared around her eyes. He had a sudden thought: she would age well or gracefully. She probably did not laugh or smile too much.

HER TECHNIQUE WAS SUPERB. She had perfect pitch. Her approach was direct, forceful and mature.

The sound was flawless. But it was dead. There was no spirit, no electric spark. What was missing?

He sat motionless after she finished. She did not look up from the keyboard, kept her hands folded in her lap. Then she looked at him. She had the most amazing eyes. Like a cat's, changing size and colour in different circumstances.

He stared up at the ceiling. The practice room was a makeshift corner of the main building's basement. Old green carpeting had been nailed up for soundproofing. Someone had put up a cartoon of a long-haired pianist playing histrionically.

"Let's talk back at my office," he said. "Gets too hot in here."

"I don't want to sound sententious," he said. "But you know there is something to say for – dedication? Passion? Technique, oh yes, technique. But without the other thing, what does it come to? Mere competence. Think of all those oh-so-accomplished nineteenth century academic painters."

He was staring off and away from her as he spoke. He spoke slowly, choosing the words carefully. He did not want to lie to her. But he wanted to be honest without being harsh. He looked at her.

Her eyes were immense in a face that looked too fragile to contain them. And there at the base of her throat, her fingers were on the gold chain, trembling.

He stood up and she rose as suddenly to meet him. He kissed her mouth, hair, throat, all over her face. He was afraid that she might say something to stop it. He kissed her mouth to hold off words of caution. There would be none. Her whole body was straining against him.

She moaned as he leaned into her. He felt a giddy sense of the room circling them. They sank to the carpet. He pulled at her dress. She hiked it up. He looked down, saw the tops of her stockings, a chaste white garter button and her fingers tearing at his fly.

Nothing in his life prepared him for the shock of that first time. Impetuous, eager, both of them hungry and intent, almost furious. What if someone had come to the door? A janitor with a pass key.

After that first time, they found discreet places to meet. But in public she oscillated alarmingly between shy prudence and open wantonness. She groped him under the coffee shop table. Her eyes fondled him. He looked around the crowded coffee shop wondering if anybody noticed the professor with the younger student. He thought of himself as a controlled, restrained person, a man with a classical bent. But Vivian had reached easily right through his defences and found somebody else – someone all hot breath and grasping hands.

THEY WERE MARRIED in the summer of 1952. Their son Ned was born in 1953. Their daughter April was born in 1954. Things went wrong in the Sixties, and then there was the bad summer of 1970.

YEARS LATER, Trevor's memories of the years when

his children were young turned like a rack of kodachrome postcards. Neddy, aged two, sitting in a sandbox. There is a pail and shovel next to him. He is clutching a popsicle stick. Nobody can take it from him. There is April in her mother's arms. They are posed in front of a Christmas tree. There is Trevor in a rowboat. April, aged three, is sitting next to him. Ned is holding one of the oars and is trying to look capable.

April on an amusement park pony frowns into sunlight. Trevor stands next to the pony with his arm around April. Trevor looks uncertain about the pony.

Vivian in a white sundress sits in a lawn chair. Her legs are crossed. She holds an opened book on her lap. She wears sunglasses. It is not possible to see the book's title or her eyes. She tries not to smile. She looks wearily chic, like one of those French film actresses from that period. She is a shimmering presence. The weather is paradisal.

Trevor thought that someone not involved, like a tourist in a souvenir shop turning a rack of those postcards with the deep aching colours flickering past, might think, *this world is so much more beautiful than my own. These people are more favoured and happy than I am.*

The tourist might turn the rack as the sun slanted lower and lower until it became too dark to make out the figures in the pictures. The tourist would stop turning the rack. He would leave. The sun would set on the mundane world outside the souvenir shop.

WHEN TREVOR thought about the summer of 1970

years afterwards, it seemed to him that things had been sliding sideways, out of control, for a long time. Vivian had been in a constant state of distraction, hurtling from one heady and momentary enthusiasm to another. He feared that she was heading for a breakdown. And the children were at an especially vulnerable stage. Ned had a freakish early media success that he, Trevor, knew would not last and would ultimately cause pain. But he could not quite say so, because Ned would not believe it, might even think it was sour grapes, an over-the-hill Boy Wonder jealous of the new kid on the block.

April had become a furious ball of pubescence. All the doors in the house and in the cottage had been slammed in the fights between her and her mother. All Trevor could do was watch in anguish.

Once in the late Sixties, Trevor was on a train coming back from a conference in New York. He was somewhere in Ontario and it was the middle of the night. He woke up in his roomette to silence and no motion. He raised the shade. They were at a siding. A single light under a metal shade lit up an empty platform. There was an iron-wheeled cart standing on the platform. A box, perhaps a coffin, was on the cart. The light fell on the cart. Beyond the circle of light was the dark and empty station platform.

He lowered the shade and lay back in his berth. At home his children were safe and asleep. Was his wife awake and thinking of him? He felt a chill loneliness. The empty platform, the silence and that box on the iron-wheeled cart.

Later he would remember that night on the train between cities, between countries, far from home. It was like a forecasting of the bad time to come. The bad summer.

DURING THAT SUMMER, he had a lot of commuting to do. The family was in residence at the cottage, but he had lumbered himself with special tutoring. The highway was jammed with vacation-bound families or families coming home. And the season's corn was in, so there were lots of trucks and cars turning too suddenly into the roadside stands.

That day he was later than usual getting to the cottage. Ned, Vivian said in a remote voice, was not back from sailing yet. April had gone for a walk. She didn't know where Gil, his student, was.

Trevor had seen Gil walking along the edge of the road as he had turned onto it. Gil was walking towards the highway, head sunk down in thought, and had not seen him.

He had to hurry, Vivian said, so they could make the first act curtain. Trevor remembered hurrying and the frantic drive to the theatre and Vivian's more than usual silence. And he remembered that things went awry. He had breathed shocked dusty air and there was pain in his leg and he could not find the strength to push a large plank off his leg and he remembered trying to call out for Vivian.

two

Homecoming

THE TRANQUIL LOOK OF THE RICH FLAT fields along the shoreline is deceptive. Point Pelee juts out of the northern side of Lake Erie like a finger pointing towards Ohio. Strong currents build around this playful finger. Signs are posted about the dangerous undertow, but there are always the brave or foolish who ignore the warnings and drown themselves.

They join all the other drowned swimmers and sunken ships. *The Phillip Minch* rammed her prow into the *Frank E. Vigor* near here. That was in 1944. The *Frank E. Vigor* sank in scant minutes. The wrecks of the *Clarion*, the *Lexington*, *New Brunswick*, *Cleveco* and *The Kelley Island* lie near the *Frank E. Vigor*. The big storms of 1869 and 1913 took many ships and men.

The Herrick cottage stands on the top of a bluff about ten miles to the east of the Point. It was built by Trevor's grandfather in the latter part of the nineteenth century. The cottage retains, despite all the subsequent renovating and improvements, a slightly raffish seashore air. A veranda once ran all around two sides and a remnant of this porch still faces the lake. The bluff is steep. A wooden stairway zigs and zags down to a boathouse and a concrete-buttressed shore. A fanciful person might imagine men in straw skimmers and ladies in muslin on the veranda.

There is, in fact, in the Herrick Archives at Tecumseh University, a photo, circa 1912, of Trevor's mother at age two on that veranda. Aunts in big brimmed hats stand next to his mother.

A history of the Herrick family could be written based on evidence marked on the house's screens and storm windows. *Ned's Room, Sun Room, April's Room* and *Kitchen* were written with marking pen or scratched on the frames. Ned's room became, in time, Miriam's sewing room and then studio. The Sun Room became the variously named TV Room, Other Room, Guest Room, Conservatory and New Room before it vanished in a final remodeling.

April's room was for a time the library and Trevor's study after she moved out. But the aluminum frames still wore either the scratched-in or inked name of their original occupant and use. Only Trevor and Miriam – his second wife – and possibly Ned and April knew what went where. Anyone else would have a tough time sorting it all out.

When Trevor retired from Tecumseh in 1990, he had the cottage winterized and sold the house in Windsor.

A sound move. He had few friends left alive. Many of his contemporaries lived elsewhere if they were among the living. His younger colleagues in the School of Music either envied his reputation or looked on him as an embarrassing fossil. They left him pretty much alone. And so he had come back to the old summer place. At eighteen Trevor had his Carnegie Hall debut behind him. He was singular in his generation for *not* having studied with Nadia Boulanger. Throughout his teens, his summers were spent at Tanglewood, Eastman, Julliard and Banff. When he was nineteen, he came in first in the prestigious Pressler Awards. His career as a composer began in 1950 with his *Fantasia on a Theme of Corelli's*, which commentators said was thoroughly musical, had spontaneity, was full of life and ended in a brilliantly executed recapitulative repose. Later they would say that his 1951 *Children's Games* for solo piano had flowing melodic lines and severe harmony. "Summer Lawns," from that same year (the second of *Three Miniatures* for piano), became the most frequently played work from his repertoire. It was light without becoming insubstantial. It had severe harmony.

Adagio For a Daughter (1956), with its sustained lyrical poise, was genuinely touching. It was wonderfully affectionate and warm and richly reverberant.

The 1958 *Piano Concerto in D Minor*, on the other hand, possessed leonine power. It was bold, passionate and scintillating, with its hair-raising allegro. The hard diamond precision of the second movement was matched only by the impetuosity of the third.

The concerto exhibited virtuosity without flamboyance. The massed horns, the plucked basses and the rapid, impassioned piano sounded like an importunate debate. Finally the mood sank into serenity and became lyrical, strong, confident. The whole air of the concerto was large and expansive, with broad gestures.

Some of the critics raised questions. Did Herrick's concerto sound dangerously close to music written for a Forties movie? It veered close to the corny. There was a disturbing air to it that reminded one of late nineteenth century American music, written under European influence. Some of the commentators found this reassuring. It was like the big architectural gaffes of that period: imitation Romanesque department stores, Greco-Roman banks, all that blatant ebullient spending of lots of money. It was somehow so *American*.

Except that Trevor was a Canadian. Oh well, his next composition gave no trouble. The *Andante and Variations* for flute and piano (1963) was charming and brisk. It was eloquent. It was disarmingly simple. It possessed natural sensibility.

And then came the *Symphony in F Minor* (1964). It was simply enchanting, full of warmth, colour and sparkling *zest*. Its surging lyricism, its volatile, vivid and robust rhythms in the first movement gave way to the genially resilient chording of the second. The third and final movement was alert, intelligent and wonderfully precise. This symphony had panache. It had insight.

But *The Light That Puts Out Our Eyes* (c. 1972), based on passages from Thoreau, evoked only puzzlement.

What *was* it? A sort of sloppy cantata, an almost orato-rio? A blighted choral symphony? It was big, lumbering, ungainly, full of pain.

Herrick might still have been in grief over his wife while composing it. But was the suffering in the work *honest?* Was it *noble?* Was it *exultant?* Or merely self-indulgent whining?

Following this disturbing perplexing work, Trevor Herrick fell into silence. He sank into teaching until his retirement. He became a footnote in histories.

GILBERT WELLES was the oldest young composer on the circuit. He had a much-used routine, mixing his own work with a sampling of what had been avant-garde twenty years earlier. As he walked into the recital hall at Tecumseh, his face had the foolish, hopeful look of youth. He was fifty-two and was, in a sense, coming home. He had studied at Tecumseh under Trevor Herrick. He had showed promise.

Now here he was, walking behind John Audel, Director of the School, with the half smile of the anxious to please on his face. He had the "please don't hurt me" air of a tourist in a bad neighbourhood. And Audel walked like an aristocrat being led to the scaffold.

The recital hall was the Law School's moot court during the day. It was grand piano and wheelchair accessible. It had mildly okay acoustics. Audel presented a hurried summation of Welles's past accomplishments. Welles sat at the piano, head bent modestly, rubbing his palms with a handkerchief. The first row of seats seemed hardly a yard from him. Then tier after tier of seats rose at a steep angle.

Welles was conscious of a face in the front row staring intently at him. He tried not to look in return. Instead, he glanced up and over the first row. In the third row a woman's immense, fleshy thighs were spread as if for his inspection. The succession of banked faces and knees gave him a sense not of audience but of a panel of judges gravely considering his case. That Bergman film. An anatomy lesson. Audel was finished and now Gil had to begin performing.

When Gil finished, he stood, bowing to the applause. He finally looked at the face he had been avoiding. For a moment he did not recognize her, and then it rushed in on him. It was April Herrick. He hadn't seen her for over twenty years, not since the day she had seen him and her mother in the boathouse.

"I THOUGHT MR. HERRICK might be here," Gilbert said to Audel as they walked across campus towards the reception.

"He never comes into town anymore," Audel said, stepping nimbly past a small banked pile of late snow.

"I haven't seen him for, oh, two years," said Audel. "When he came to the dedication. You know. The Archives."

Audel's voice held a nuance of scorn. Obviously he did not think much of Trevor's bequest of manuscripts.

"Ah yes, the Archives," said Gilbert. "I forgot about that. Say, you know, I think I saw his daughter – April? in the audience."

"Don't know her," said Audel. He was walking faster than Welles and talking back over his shoulder, like the president of an automobile firm in a TV commercial.

They walked into the building where people were already attacking the buffet and standing around with glasses in their hands.

"Be sure to leave me your traveling receipts," said Audel. "I have to have all that for Accounting."

He hadn't said anything about the recital. It was almost as if he had not been at it. He was acting more like a harried functionary in a state hospital than the director of a music faculty.

Seen them, caught them in the boathouse. It had been hot and stuffy in there, smelling of canvas. He had been awkward. It had been impetuous and sweet. And then he heard April's gasp, turned to see her shocked face. And Vivian must have seen her looking in and said nothing.

Audel got him a drink and then excused himself to catch, as he put it, someone he had to have a word with. Gilbert stood in the midst of the crowd, his half smile still inviting abuse, wondering how long he should stay until it would be proper to leave. Tecumseh, where he showed promise.

Yes, he had showed promise back in the Seventies. Now he merely persevered, teaching, getting the odd grant, winning prizes (usually second or third) and the occasional Artist in Residence post at a university – usually mediocre places.

And there was April, standing a few yards away from him, alone as he was. She seemed to be staring at nothing in particular. He moved slowly towards her. What the hell could he say? The blonde hair had grey in it. Or maybe it was the light. Fine wrinkles around the eyes. Same startling green eyes. But there was a new petulant set to her mouth. And a slight thickening at the waist and hips. Well, hell, she wasn't fifteen anymore.

It was the look around the mouth. She was beginning to resemble her mother. Champion grudge holder. A look of impatience at some task done for her or not done well enough. Charges against life or fate.

"Hello Gil," she said. "I liked your music. But then, I always have."

She wore an insistently cheerful public smile.

"I thought – oh, yes, thanks – are you living here now? I thought you were living in Chicago."

"Visiting Trevor. He hasn't been too well."

She wasn't looking directly at him. She glanced swiftly around the room, down at the floor, briefly at him, then around again.

"Actually, Miriam asked me to see if you could come out. For the weekend."

"Why, sure," said Gilbert. His voice sounded fake-hearty. "It's been so damn long...."

"Ned's coming down," said April. "From Toronto. Sound like Agatha Christie? All the guilty parties at the scene of the crime."

Now she looked directly at him.

"Do you have a bag somewhere?"

"It's in Audel's office. They were going to put me up in a residence."

"The thing of it is," April said. "Trevor died yesterday."

APRIL DROVE HELTER-SKELTER head-on and Gil's right foot pressed down on his invisible brake.

"Relax," she said. "After Chicago, this is nothing traffic."

"Nice car," said Gil. He didn't know what to say. Trevor dead.

"It gets me, as they say, where I never want to go. Say, you seem sort of uptight. Afraid to see us after all those years?"

"No, no," Gil laughed lightly. "It's just the whole thing – Trevor – you…."

"Still carrying that cross?" April kept her face firmly forward. "Listen, I don't blame you for anything. Whatever I made of my life, it's my fault."

"But, oh boy," she said. "Did I ever. Blame you, I mean. Back then."

Back then.

GIL LEARNED EARLY in life all the fat kid's ploys: Buy everybody candy. Toadie, good guy, faithful pal. Second best. Always second. George Brent as child.

Second banana, callow spear carrier. Gil learned the cringe and hunch of the incessantly bullied. He learned it daily at recess. And, hoping to escape pain, he practiced anonymity. If seen, he resorted to the placating smile, to pleading and fawning. He bought and gave away candy.

Later in life, losing the fat, he kept the devices and learned new ones. Masks: the immature and passionate child (little boy lost). The con man (Harold Hill comes to River City). Lovable dolt (veteran of one broken marriage and three messed up emotional relationships – not counting Vivian – and, oh yes, April).

He thought of all the aspects of his life: his youth, work, hard times, pain and betrayal. The accidents, illnesses, violence (either done to or by him), and now his entrance into old age.

He had known fear, sadness, regret, shame, despair, greed, egotism and anxiety. He felt both powerful and petty lust. He fussed, practiced antsiness, over-busyness, sloth and some rare moments of pure joy. Above all, he had this fatal tendency to believe the worst about himself and to think the best of people who were in reality perfect swine.

And now April was cutting right through all his defences as she had in the summer of 1970. He snuck a quick look at her profile as she drove. A bit of softness under the chin. Back in 1970, April's tanned face under a cap of close-cropped blonde hair, all tight curls, her startling green eyes, the faint down of hair bleached by the sun on her arms and legs (he knew that to touch it would be electric and dangerous), her movements quick as a startled fish all drove him out of his mind. Here, years later, driving with April the mature woman, his remembered excitement mingled with new interest.

"There I was," April said, turning onto the expressway. "In what mother called her study being lectured on responsible behaviour, and I bet your come was running down her leg."

"Of course," April said to Gil more than twenty years after that moment, "I got over it. Resiliency of youth and all. But *she* must have had big hopes for you. Final autumnal fling or something?"

Gil wished they could go on driving in the dark forever. The headlights made a moving space ahead of the car, steadily traversed it and put it behind. He had an ongoing sense of presentation, revelation, things shown and rapidly lost. There were swiftly seen parcels of road, roadside and intersecting road, trees, fields, other cars. He felt comfortably disconnected, free. He had left the place where he had once again trotted out a puny talent, left a masked personality back there. He felt a vague shame. But he wasn't yet at the place he didn't want to be at. The place where Trevor was dead. With the ghostly light from the dashboard revealing a speed somewhat above the limit and the radio set on a station thirty miles behind them, Gil slumped, trying to resign himself to whatever lay in wait for him.

BACK IN THE SUMMER OF 1970, Trevor took pains with his most promising pupil, Gilbert Welles.

"It's nice, very nice," Trevor said, looking intently at Gil's score. They were in a university practice room, seated at the piano. Gil stared blankly at the score. What did Herrick *really* think?

"But here –" Trevor placed his fingers on the keys and played a chord. Then, nodding, he moved an octave higher and played it a bit uptempo.

"See?"

Gil saw. It sounded like Stephen Foster muzaked. "Whenever I get the urge to show off," Trevor smiled, "I go for parody. I imagine it played in a dentist's office. Welles, you can either decide to do the real thing or try to become a household word."

"You're – what? thirty – late bloomer. Inelegant word. Anyhow, stop the showboating. I mean don't settle for less. Chopin once said he didn't want his pants to be admired in a museum."

TREVOR INVITED GIL to spend the summer with him and the family. By now, Gil's hero worship of Trevor had reached a high, fervent level. When he met the family, he transferred some of the heat to them. Trevor's wife, Vivian, was a faded blonde who had to avoid the summer sun. She moved from room to shuttered room in the cottage, dressed in cool-looking white. She had a rather thin face with a set slightly reproachful look. *Patrician* was the word that Gil settled on. She was probably a killer in bed.

He immediately loved the children. April was a happy,

uncomplicated fifteen-year-old, all bouncy enthusiasm and hearty athleticism. No dark neuroses, as Gil imagined his own teen years had held. Gil felt large and slow and old sitting next to her. Ned, April's brother, about two years older, was a sullen, sulky copy of his father.

Gil tried to picture life in the house when there wasn't a guest. Probably a hurly-burly of creativity. Ned wrote poetry, published some of it in little magazines, and was perhaps going to be the next Leonard Cohen. One of the big publishers was interested. So Gil pictured Ned gnawing a pencil, sitting on the veranda, squinting out at the lake while Trevor composed and April arrived or departed and Vivian floated serenely about doing haute cuisine or reading Proust.

Gil was wrong about the haute cuisine. Vivian hated cooking. No Proust either. She was a firm postmodernist. The cottage was crowded with op art and pop art. A pink neon *EAT* sign from a defunct diner buzzed softly on the dining room wall. Vivian was a disappointed woman. Once she realized that Trevor's talent surpassed her own, she turned from the piano to art, to the dance, and even did pottery for a time. Then she turned to artists, decorators, hangers-on, actors, and set designers. She thought of herself as a free spirit.

"I think sometimes I'm the last romantic," Trevor said. "Why not? We live in such resolute ugliness. Everything debases. Take the university. The new buildings. No windows. You might as well try to teach in a submarine."

Now Vivian's slender knee pressed firmly into Gil's thigh, insistently asking a question.

VIVIAN HAD MANY CHOICES to make when it was time to consider a career. She had perfect pitch. She played piano, cello and flute, all fairly well. She was a whiz at math. She won a prize for a science project in her last year of high school. Something to do with genetics and mice. She started out in science at university. In her second year, she switched to business. Then she went into music.

Vivian was one of those blondes who look washed out in certain lights, fatigued, interestingly pale. She drove men crazy. In high school, she was much fantasized about. She seemed unapproachable. At university, her classmates kept a wary distance, but all of her professors fussed over her. Much was made of her future. There was a constant, hectic, brink of hysterics about her. She worked to the edge, and when conferring with a teacher, seemed about to collapse. There was about her the appeal of danger, like the pit of the stomach queasiness when one is near a precipice or on a tall building's observation platform.

Her hands seemed to tremble a bit. Her eyes seemed over-large and feverish. A quality of febrile moistness hung about her. Men wanted to comfort her, hold her close and soothe the frantic beating of her heart. There was a sense of something momentous about to happen when one talked to her, got up close to those immense, desperate green eyes with the blonde lashes, the delicate spray of freckles across her nose and cheeks, and the equally delicate pulse throbbing slowly in her throat.

Cocteau once said that the privileges of beauty were

enormous. He would have been pleased and satisfied with his prescience had he met Vivian.

Marriage and childbirth did not fulfill her. She lunched a lot. Not many of these lunches were with women. Sometimes these chic encounters stretched on into the boring zone of mid-afternoon. Post-prandial flirting moved on to couplings in various awkward places: loft studios, parked cars, motels.

Did Trevor know? His silence, which was either indifference or naive ignorance, annoyed her. And now he brought his prize pupil home for the summer.

Entering Vivian, Gil thought, was like going into silk. She gasped, moaned, clutched his back, clutched the sheets, tossed her head back, moaned, shuddered. She was a complicated, cunning confusion of soft, smooth, wet and warm. But she was ultimately elusive. Gil felt sad after their lovemaking. And, still working with Trevor, he carried a lot of guilt. Vivian liked to take chances. That summer, they made love in Gil's room in the very early morning. Later on, about five or six o'clock, in early light, she would sneak back into bed with Trevor. They made love in that bed when Trevor was off at the university and might return at any moment. Or Ned was off sailing and what if the wind died and he motored back? What if April, off with some girlfriends, remembered something forgotten and came back for it?

They made love in the boathouse in the afternoons.

It was an uncomfortable place. Vivian liked the messy tawdriness of it, the dust, the musty smell, the spiders in the corners. She knelt and undid his belt. Then she pulled his shorts down and wantonly took him in her mouth, looking up, her eyes managing to be both docile and fierce. Groaning, Gil would bend to her, lay her back on the old beach chair cushions.

It was a hot day in August, just before April's sixteenth birthday. Trevor and Vivian had gone into Windsor. Something about an experimental play that Vivian was involved in. Ned was in Toronto seeing about a possible scholarship. Gil spent the morning working. He was hyperexhausted. Vivian had wakened him about five AM and he hadn't gone back to sleep until about eight. Then he got up at nine. Maybe he'd go for a swim or a walk after lunch. April was off someplace. The house was very still. He was starting into the kitchen when April ran smack into him. They both laughed awkwardly and Gil found himself staring down into eyes as big and green as Vivian's. They kissed ferociously, sinking back against the counter. They moved into the living room and continued on the sofa. April was on his lap, her bathing suit still damp. They were hurried and frantic, hearts pounding.

Gil felt a muddle of emotions. He was almost twice her age, she was just a kid, below the age of consent, he was involved with her mother, her father was his father figure who might return at any moment and find them all twisted up and kissing. April's bathing suit straps were down, her breasts were out and she was trying to lift herself up enough to pull the suit off completely. And then they heard the car crunch on the driveway's gravel.

It was farcical, April frantically pulling up her suit, and hustling out the back door to get down to the dock, Gil stuffing his pulsing erection down. They made it. Trevor and Vivian came into an empty room. Gil hunched innocent as all hell at the piano.

The next day April took his hand as he walked out on the veranda.

"I know it's crazy," she said. Her eyes were big and serious. "But I love you."

"Hey," she said as she went down the steps. "Smile. It's my birthday."

What the hell was he going to do? Just a kid. And Vivian. Mingled with his fear and guilt was a strong sense of smugly selfish pride. What a cock man he was becoming in later life.

EARLY THAT AFTERNOON, Gil was restless. He walked through the empty house and out on the veranda. Down there April was sitting on the dock. She had been swimming, but the waves had turned rough. Now a great calm descended. She sat, one leg under her, the other dawdling in the water. She stared out at the horizon, not seeing. Gil had acted so damn strange. This morning, meeting by chance, and he seemed about to say something and didn't. He had looked so strained, face all flushed.

It was a still, hot and cloudless day. The sky hurt to look at. Ned was still in Toronto. Trevor had gone in to his office at the university. Vivian was in Windsor, shopping for the birthday dinner.

Gil was on the veranda, moodily sitting in a wicker rocker and staring out at the same horizon that April was studying. She was sitting in her usual pose, one leg dangling in the water, the other either under her or hugged to her chest. It was a fetching pose. And it was not calculated. Damp blonde curls lay on her tanned neck. Her body, Gil knew, was hard as a trout.

His observation of her at this moment was in keeping with the normal heterosexual regard of any nearby female. And when a girl child crosses over that delicate borderline into womanhood, men of any age take notice. Thus he comforted himself. For Gil up on the veranda on this first day of April's sixteenth year, she was just part of a lovely summer landscape. There was nothing personal. Thus he lied to himself.

When he began the descent of the long slope that led to the wooden stairs, it was perhaps still an impersonal feeling. Perhaps he still felt guilt. A sixteen-year-old girl! And just last night he had fucked her mother! Now, perhaps he meant only to express some kind of meaningless guest-phrases, set the whole thing in order, make some decent human noises, make amends for the kissing session, communicate, mend fences, attempt to get her out of her adolescent funk, play the kindly uncle. But somewhere on the way down there it came to him that he desired her, more than desired her, and simultaneously with this awareness came the certitude that she could be had for the asking.

And then Vivian was on top of the slope calling down to him. He stopped, halfway down or up. April was looking up, drawn by her mother's voice. Gil looked up, then down, then back up again. He started back up. And that afternoon he and Vivian would be in the boathouse and April would look in and nothing would ever be the same again.

TREVOR WOULD NOT have been in the theatre that night by his own choice. But Vivian was on the Board. She attended all their damn meetings and openings. The trouble with a theatre converted from an old church is that all the sightlines are wrong. And pews were never designed for aesthetic comfort. A series of platforms had been erected at the back to squeeze in more seating.

To make matters worse on this particular night, they were to experience Theatre Beyond Cruelty. George Mitchum, the playwright, promised fear and loathing. Bruce Leonard, the director, promised to deliver.

The set was a tacky living room, such as might be shared by several impecunious students: third-hand furniture, a large old round-shouldered refrigerator which dominated the stage, and people sprawled about. The overall effect was of a back alley abortionist's waiting room.

The curtain was already up. Gradually it dawned on the audience that the play was in progress. The action consisted of low conversations which nobody could hear, of getting up and going over to the refrigerator. When it was open, one could see that all the shelves had been removed and that it was stacked with beer cans. After about an hour of people getting up, opening beer, going back to sit down, the voice levels from stage began to rise. Laughter was raucous. The individual actors went to the edge of the stage and berated people in the first few rows.

Trevor and Vivian were on one of the platforms. It was warm in the theatre and getting warmer. Smoke from cigarettes lit and puffed on stage made the warm air sting and smart the eyes. No programs had been handed out. There was no hint of an intermission or scene change. After about another forty minutes or so, a low murmur began in the audience. Then someone shouted.

Other voices took it up. *This is a lot of crap!* someone yelled. Some people headed for the doors. They were locked. A mild panic began down there as the actors stood in a group on stage, jeering and laughing. They were beginning to act drunk. They *were* drunk. Somebody behind Trevor got up and tried to swing down from the platform. Somebody had taken the ladder away. The platform swayed and then it yawed sideways, collapsing in a screech of splintering wood. Fifteen people were injured. Trevor's right leg was broken and Vivian was killed instantly.

* * *

NED WAS ON THE TRAIN and remembering the time he had come down to Chatham to read poetry at one of the high schools. His father's wife had insisted on meeting him afterwards and bringing him home for dinner. He didn't want to go. The place was too full of memories. It was haunted. And Miriam, cow-faced bland thing, reminded him just by her presence that his mother was gone and would never brighten the world again.

The reading had not gone well from the start. Nobody was at the station to meet him and there were no cabs. He called the school and eventually somebody came to pick him up. Half the students he read to seemed stoned and the others perhaps merely did not give a shit.

And now he was coming back for a different reason. April was going to meet him. It was his father, silently summoning from his deep final sleep. April would be meeting him. And probably the swine Welles, with his hungry waif look, nose pressed forever against his family's window like some damn Dickens character. That summer Welles had sucked and mooched around, kissing Trevor's ass and then making out with April. Lousy perverted jumped-up manipulator. Ned had always despised him. In the fading afternoon light, Ned felt outrage, frustration, grief. Yes, grief.

HE WAS ALSO SLIGHTLY DRUNK and hungry. The train was stopping. He swung his bag down from the rack, bumped his knee with it, muttered *shit*, and the woman across the aisle looked up with disapproval. Ned gave her his wolf smile, leaned down and said:

"I was just in the can. Somebody on this train

has been eating asparagus."

His face had the arrogant self-complacency of a Regency rake. His eyes were cold, flat, full of contempt for whatever they regarded. He did not seem to acknowledge the right to exist of any person or thing that fell under his gaze. There was a heavy, petulant set to his mouth. He seemed perpetually on the brink of violent rage. The disapproving woman wisely kept silent.

April and Welles were standing on the platform. He could see them through the window. Both of them had aged. He hadn't seen Welles since that summer of 1970. When he thought of Welles, he pictured him as he had been then: a clone of the actor Montgomery Clift. Now Welles was balding, had a slight paunch and looked like a furtive accountant.

Ned awkwardly put his arms around April. Generous tears of self-pity ran down his cheeks. April's face was dry. Faint lines around her eyes. His baby sister was getting on.

"God," he said. "I thought he was immortal."

"I knew he wasn't," said April. "Look. Miriam is waiting dinner for us."

"Oh we must not keep Miriam waiting," said Ned. "Welles, you old devil. How have you been keeping?"

As they walked off the platform toward April's car, Gil tried to answer Ned's question with too much detail. Ned was not listening, but was muttering *must not keep Miriam waiting* under his breath.

"I saw you have a new book out?" Gil said. "How's it going?"

"Four years ago – the usual small press bullshit," said Ned. "Like dropping a fucking feather down the Grand Canyon. A fart in a windstorm. Who reads anyway?"

"Well," said April as she opened the door, "I for one was glad to hear about it. Daddy wrote to me…."

"Oh?" said Ned, as he flopped into the front seat. "So you kept in touch? And here I was living just a couple hours away and I haven't – did not – see him since…."

He began to cry, huge racking sobs that shook his whole body.

"I feel this fucking guilt," he gasped.

"So do I," said Gil in a soothing tone.

"You should," said Ned. "All the hurt you gave him. And this whole family."

"Let's not throw glass houses," said April. She was putting on glasses before she bent to put in the ignition key. Gil thought the glasses made her look older and sexy – schoolmarmish. Like the girl in the bookshop in *The Big Sleep*.

"You should talk," said Ned. "Letting this sneak get into your pants. You broke Mother's heart…."

April peered over her glasses at him. Her mouth was set in a firm pout. Gil felt a numb coldness seep into his groin.

"As usual, Neddy, you've got everything all bassack-wards," said April in a neutral voice.

Ned retreated into a mumbling silence as they drove away from the station and was asleep by the time they arrived at the cottage. Gil and April said nothing during the drive.

"I've ordered a pizza," said Miriam as they came in. "No anchovies."

Miriam looked like a late-sixties earth mother. She gave off an aura of health foods, natural childbirth and granny gowns. In fact she hated cooking, like the previous Mrs. Herrick, and had never given birth. It had been okay with Trevor. He, like Thoreau, had been indifferent to food. And he maintained that fatherhood obviously was not one of his strong suits.

"Let's not get all maudlin," said Miriam. "Trevor would not want that. He was really lucid this past month and made all the plans."

"What are the arrangements?" said April.

"There aren't any," said Miriam. "Not in the ordinary sort of way. Trevor wanted cremation. No wake or visitation. No flowers or prayers. And especially no music."

"How about sorrow?" said Ned. "Would that be all right with you?"

"Yes, Ned," said Miriam looking directly into his reddened eyes. "We can all do that on our own."

"Ah," said Gil, clearing his throat. "When will the cremation – I mean, when will –"

"Already has," said Miriam. "We're supposed to scatter the ashes into the lake. We can do that tomorrow, if that's okay with everybody. Look, sit down and I'll get some wine. Pizza should be here soon."

There were big comfortable chairs grouped in a square around a low table in what had once been Ned's room and was now remodeled so that one wall had been taken out and replaced with glass. It was too dark to see the lake, which rolled in sounding deep and serious far down the slope beyond the glass.

Ned was sinking into a mean sobering-up pout. Gil listening to the pounding waves, felt a thalassic, elegiac sadness. He looked over at April, who was sitting in the half light of a green glass library lamp on a desk behind her. A woman. Disturbingly like her mother. Yet the young girl she had been – vestiges, hints, remained. *Remains.*

The word jolted him back to the real thing of the moment. Trevor Herrick. Giant of his youth.

"Local," said Miriam, carrying a tray with a bottle and glasses on it. "We liked it. Trevor said too much for our health."

"What are you going to *do* Miriam?" said April. "I mean are you going to stay here or what?"

"Best not to make any rash decisions," said Gil. "I mean that's what they say – for a year at least –"

"Trevor planned all that too," said Miriam. "There's a will. But there's no need for melodrama. No secrets. I'm going to move back into Windsor. Least for now, I'll stay around here. This place has been left to you two."

"Ned and April, I mean," she said. "Jointly."

"Just as well," she said. "I never liked living out here anyhow. I put up with it for Trevor's sake. I am not your country house mouse."

The doorbell rang.

"That'll be dinner," said Miriam, getting up. "Help yourselves to more wine. How *do* you like our plonk?"

Gil followed her, tried to help and tried to make

himself useful, got in the way. April and Ned sat in stunned silence.

"And you, oh former golden boy," said Miriam, "Trevor made some plans for you. If you have time. If you're willing. He wanted you to be Executor of his estate."

"Not the house and all," she said. "Only the Archives. OK if we eat out here?" she said, carrying the pizza in its box out and putting it down on the table.

"I didn't mean to lay all this on you right away," she said. "But when would be the right, good time anyway?"

NED WAS IN what he suspected had been his mother's studio. Now it was a kind of library with a sewing machine. The couch unfolded into a damned futon. With great difficulty, he lowered himself onto it, lay looking up at the bookcases and the window. Clouds racing. No stars. A cold, unforgiving blackness.

He felt a slight fuzziness. Not a complete whirling pit-drunk dizziness, but on the edge of it. So odd to be in his parents' home, the summer cottage of his childhood when he had been heedless and happy. Now both parents were gone. And the place was to be his. Half his.

What the hell would he do with it? What had his father been thinking of? April lived too far away to make any sensible use of it. So did he. Was it some sort of symbolic gesture, this curious bequest?

Our summer place, he soothed himself. *Winterized.* A chilling word. *But still our summer place.* He fell asleep remembering white sails.

APRIL LAY in dry-mouthed silence, staring up into the dark. The house seemed to sway in the wind off the lake like a sailboat, outward bound or coming to harbor. She lay as if in a bunk, below decks, listening to the creak of taut lines, the sounding keel.

My father, she thought. *I am home and far from home.*

GIL WAS ON THE FOLD-OUT BED in the glassed living room. Scuds of clouds moved swiftly above him. Storm seemed possible. How could they scatter the ashes if it rained and there was wind?

Scatter. Like *archive* the word hung in the air like a sharply struck note.

MIRIAM STAYED UP for awhile. She sat in bed trying to read an Iris Murdoch novel. She kept forgetting who the characters were, despite the uniqueness of their names. The empty space beside her on the bed reminded her of empty time that lay ahead. First things first. These people, children and the favored pupil he had loved so stubbornly for so long with nothing in return. She wanted to pray but did not remember how.

THE HOUSE gathered them all in, living and dead in a shroud of sleep. Tomorrow would come and take care of itself.

three
April in Chicago

URING APRIL'S FIRST YEAR AT ST. EDMUND'S College, she and the girls on her floor used to play strip poker, forfeiting articles of clothing. The one who lost most had to call a boy she knew and, naturally, not saying who she was, try to turn him on. Once April was the loser and called a boy she had known back in the swimming club. She hadn't known him well. Whispering, trying to make her voice sound older and husky, she told him she was wearing nothing but a black lace garter belt. The other girls could hardly contain themselves, giggling convulsively, rolling on the bed, stopping their mouths with their hands.

Years later April had an erotic dream and that boy's face was on the body of her lover. Gil was never in her dreams or fantasies. She wondered about it. Did the skin remember the press of all its lovers? Names and faces were lost in time, but the faint down on a pale arm or the press of a thigh across a leg, the cooling damp of afterlove on skin had a biography of their own. Take Nicky. April knew the geography of his back better than she knew her neighbourhood. Yet sometimes she had the disturbing feeling of his wife's presence, like an invisible tattoo or a cologne that clung to clothing.

It was winter when April moved to Chicago. From her apartment, which never seemed to get quite warm enough, she should have been able to see the lake, but the windows were all coated with frost. They rattled in the wind which came in from the lake. The radiators thudded with pent steam. She went out in the mornings through mounds of snow plowed to the curbsides and getting higher as the season dug itself in for a long stay. Day by day, successive snowfalls made the mounds higher and higher until she felt she walked through an arctic valley. Cars unlucky enough to be parked during an earlier storm were now buried for the duration of winter. At the el station, the platform shook in the wind.

At the office some of the women had small electric heaters under their desks. Everyone wore sweaters. The building was ultramodern with lots of glass and open space. Like her apartment, it never quite got warm enough. Next door, in an older building, there was a cafeteria in the basement. A covered walkway connected the two buildings. One could go from one to the other without putting boots on. There was also an outside entrance. The revolving door emitted people from outside, red-faced, stamping snow off their overshoes, making histrionic gestures of chill. Pools of brown water lay on the floor in front of the elevator bank in the older building. Outside, the wind bellowed between the two structures. April had found her nothing nowhere job through an agency. She was not qualified for much, having dropped out of college after two years of an arts course. She took typing at night school. And here she was at the bottom of the job ladder in Browne's Travel Agency. Dorothy Browne, a chain-smoking woman in her sixties, had taken the agency over when her husband died. She doted on her forty-year-old son Ross. He came in and went out a lot, but didn't seem to have much to do.

Ross ("Nicky") Browne was a big, confident looking man with dark blond hair and superhonest blue eyes. He radiated sincerity. His wife, Catherine, was a fragile looking lady with terrific fashion sense. April saw her only once, arriving at the office in a silver-grey Continental which matched her hair. The Brownes had one child, a girl majoring in Speech Therapy at Northwestern. Ross tended to be very sentimental about his daughter. He was sentimental about holidays and family, both of which together made him moist-eyed.

When his mother died, he became morose. He often spent hours alone in her old office, door closed, not to be disturbed. The staff began calling it the necrophilia room.

"I DON'T WANT anybody to get hurt," he said to April.

They were lying in bed in April's apartment. The radiator shuddered. April stared up at the walls rising tall in the cold. Susan, his daughter, was getting in with a bad crowd at Northwestern. Peaceniks, who detested the military, yet wore army surplus jackets and talked strategy. Nicky was very considerate. He made time and room for April in his life. Take today for instance. Catherine was at some luncheon and he had made up a business appointment. Why, thought April, do I always feel guilty when I can't make time for a quickie?

Nicky claimed that Bobby Goldsboro's song *Honey* was Their Song. She did not know why. She did not like the song, found it too cute for words. Right now Willie Nelson singing Kristofferson songs was on her cassette player. She was developing a fondness for country and western. She knew all the words to "Your Cheatin Heart." She liked the image of honky-tonk adultery.

On the way to her el stop was a place, Billie's Tap, all no-nonsense cinder blocks, door painted black, a pickup truck or two in the lot. She imagined sullen men in baseball caps listening to Bob Seger and tensely waiting for quick hard sex or quick hard violence. She had never gone in. Music throbbed as she walked past in the early evening. If the door opened, she could hear the music on the jukebox. Momma and leaving home, prison and unfaithfulness. Attractive danger. Cruel-eyed men with taut biceps and tattoos drank with thin sluttish women who had pale skin and ate only fast food.

Browne's was more than a simple travel agency. In the late Sixties, Dorothy Browne had booked a series of flights for a rock group. The group, impressed by her efficiency, gave her all their business. As they became more successful, they recommended her agency to other groups. Soon the rock scene belonged almost exclusively to Browne's.

Dorothy began even further expansion. She conceived, planned and launched a massive rock concert in a little-used minor league baseball stadium downstate. The event spawned other, larger efforts. By the time April got her job, Browne's was into community festivals. Hardly an annual cherry harvest day or a pumpkin week, grape crushing week or Oktoberfest came about without Dorothy's input. Only with her death did the agency's fervid growth begin to slacken. Nicky was a sweet man, but no businessman.

HE WAS AN IMPULSIVE and dramatic lover. He often burst into tears, knelt and clasped April's thighs, buried his flushed wet face in her lap. He proclaimed the depth of his devotion, mourned the predicament, said he did not want anyone involved to be hurt.

After April calmed him down with soothing words that convinced him of his worthiness, he could set out for home, preparing an excuse for his tardiness.

Aside from Bobby Goldsboro, Nicky loved Tchaikovsky. She could not listen to Tchaikovsky. She said his music was full of self-indulgence and self-pity. It was not simply that she was a modern composer's daughter.

"It's dangerous," she said to Nicky. "His music is too

cozy? Too much like a lot of rich dessert."

April feared self-love. She thought that self-love could too readily turn into self-loathing. Looking back at her life, she felt that she had spent too much time putting on and pulling off emotional band-aids. Now she had, finally, a grip on it. With great care, she had constructed a kind of life. The grip was precarious, yes, but she felt in temporary control.

TAKE HER APARTMENT as evidence: there was a white pitcher bought at a garage sale with dried flowers in it and a wicker table (another garage sale) spray-painted white. The pitcher and table announced *April is in residence here.* Yet she simultaneously prepared a fall-back position. Deep down, perhaps, she was not convinced that she really belonged in this scene which she had constructed. She kept on buying instant coffee.

HER PLACE was on the North Side. Once it had been crowded with Swedish immigrants. The area to the west was semi-upperclass Jewish. There were some pretty good delis there.

But her neighborhood was now non-ethnic and impersonal. Moving up from the south side was a new arty crowd. Folk clubs became coffee houses or fringe theatres. Momentarily "in" restaurants were born and died like mayflies. Warehouses became discos, or later on, punk clubs. The discos became restaurants, boutiques bloomed and then became left wing bookstores. They crept closer to April's area. When they came, she knew, her rent would go up.

Nicky left early in the evening. A sad time of the day in any circumstance. It was too early to start dinner, too cold to go out and too early to watch TV. Somehow she got through these mean hours and set herself down to watch the premiere of a new series about a dedicated high school teacher.

A girl was supposed to be working hard to get a prime scholarship. She was obviously on the verge of emotional collapse. The strain of it all. Finally, she broke during a class discussion on The Bill of Rights and ran out of the room. The teacher and the camera pursued her through the halls up to a chemistry lab where she swallowed poison. The principal entered right after the teacher, having run out of his office to chase the teacher and the girl and the camera; and a doctor was called, and the girl's parents arrived just after the teacher made an impassioned speech to the principal about the intolerable pressures put on students nowadays – the pressure to succeed, to enter the college of their choice, to have sex or not have sex, and the principal answered that we maybe don't have the best educational system in the world, but this is a democracy and do you know of a better way to do so much for so many?

The girl's parents arrive in time to say that she means everything to them and the principal says then why put all this burden on her. The camera zeroes in on their guilt-ridden faces, stricken with realization. The show ends with the teacher and the principal going off for a coffee. Job done for one more day. Just another day in the educational system. April switched channels to a cop show. She doubted that the high school series would make it through the thirteen week season. Not enough jiggle. Maybe they would introduce some cheerleaders.

APRIL LOVED to read old-fashioned mystery and detective novels. Stories set in exotic locales with punkah-wallahs and overt anti-Semitism. There was such superbly arrogant class consciousness in them. And the mystery was always solved to everyone's satisfaction. Unlike life. People on trains and steamships sized up their fellow passengers swiftly. They knew who would funk and who would turn caddish or be a rotter. They knew as well which chaps would be sound and dependable in a crisis.

The world moved to the tick of a slower clock in those books. Ellery Queen batched with his father and a houseboy (brown-skinned and not uppity) and no reader suspected Ellery of pederastic yearnings towards the houseboy. Ellery smoked a lot, swanked around, interfered with official police business, drove a rare auto and solved crimes. Philo Vance dropped the *g* from his adjectives. Bespoke tailors must have been rolling in money.

April remembered going to an old-fashioned haberdasher's with her father when she had been about nine or ten. The place had obviously been obsolete even at that time. The wooden floor creaked in a pious hush. Shirts were laid out in glass cases. Clerks who knew her father personally were of assistance. The word *trendy* had not been coined. April remembered feeling, even then, the alienation of her gender, and feeling envy. The foreign country of maleness.

In this decade there was nothing magical about men's clothing. It was hung omnivorously on androgynous racks. The severe and reverential clerks had been replaced by insolent thin youths. The men's and women's departments blurred into one another. April thought with mild regret that some mystery had been lost. She yearned to buy a shirt for Nicky. She knew she could not.

Waking during the night, she saw the figures on her digital alarm blinking. The radio was on, low and buzzing. There must have been a power failure while she slept and service restored now to wake her. She readjusted it by her wristwatch and turned off the light.

Out of her apartment window, April could see a horizontal slice of lake, a hard blue knife. It was becoming familiar, but it never became friendly. Still, she consoled herself, it was all the same shared water in the Great Lakes. When she looked into her bathroom mirror, she saw the girl she had been just under the thin, pale, intense surface. A tanned girl who had lived in a bathing suit all summer long.

PEYTON, her friend from Browne's, had won a trip for two and was trying to talk her into it. Peyton hunched to the table, arms crossed under her breasts so they bunched up. The posture gave her a down-home confidential air, like an aproned neighbourly gossip.

"You seem to have this self-destructive urge," Peyton said. "I mean in men."

She had noticed Peyton at Browne's right away. April later learned that Peyton had been christened Deborah but had her name changed legally after reading a William Styron novel and deciding that she resembled the heroine in both body and soul.

Peyton had mixed dark and grey hair, cut short. At the time, when it was fashionable for women to have long slender limbs, Peyton's had a rounded Percheron look. She had the kind of legs that would look good in old-fashioned nylon stockings. The kind that went with black garter belts. Peyton's hips were not wide, but her bottom seemed rounder than what was thought to be fashionable at the time. She filled her skirts to the brink of tautness.

THE SMELL of hibiscus mingled with something citron hung on the warm air.

Already April felt in a hurry to get out of her northern clothes, which felt bulky, inhibiting. Customs was a waved-through bit of theatrics. A mix of music came from the radios in cabs parked in a rank. Songs sung in Spanish, reggae and calypso. A bus waited for them to clear customs. Their hotel was the second stop. When she and Peyton had looked over the brochure and made their choice, Peyton warned her:

"Whatever hotel we pick, once we get there you can

go out of your mind wondering if you should have picked another one. There's *always* a better one you didn't choose. Let's make up our minds right now not to waste our time there moaning about how much nicer it is down the beach."

The bus passed vacant lots between the hotels, where sparse weeds competed with signs announcing yet more hotels to come. If it all came true, then the view of the beach and the water would be blocked out. April had foolishly read *Jaws* on the way down and now feared the ocean.

Welcome punch was served in the hotel lobby. When April registered and received her key, she was given a folded-up pink phone message. *Call me office. Nicky.* Getting through was not easy. The call had to be routed through Aruba and Florida. She sat in the airless phone booth listening to the disembodied voices of the operators. Finally Nicky's voice came through a chorus of static. *I miss you* was the message. *And when you get back we've got to get things straightened out. I mean it.*

APRIL NOTICED the girl who was at the bar every evening, sitting alone and drinking until the bar closed. She always arrived after Happy Hour, as if deliberately setting herself apart from guests who had to budget. She always came in from the cabana side, so her quarters were evidently more posh and private. She dressed in long flowing beach cover-ups. April suspected that the style was designed to distract attention from an overly plump behind or thunder thighs.

But the girl's upper body was exquisite, and her bare arms were elegant. She had large haughty eyes and hair cut in a curiously dated Forties debutante style.

After about an hour alone, she was joined by a man in his sixties dressed in flowered shirts which hung outside his trousers. He was usually half-drunk before arriving and didn't last long at the bar. One night two waiters had to help him back to his cabana. The young girl stayed on alone, indifferent.

"I don't care how much money he has," Peyton said. "How can she stand him? I'd have more pride…."

"Maybe she just closes her eyes and thinks about the charge accounts," April said.

The local young men in tight white trousers and equally tight shirts arrived each evening halfway through Happy Hour. Gold chains tangled under their opened shirts and hung around their wrists. They carried Continental-style bags for their money and cigarettes: a practical even necessary device, given the tautness of their trousers.

The local young men were adept at sizing up the place, lighting cigarettes, sipping drinks; swift glances seeking the lonely, the desperate, making equally swift judgments on who had the most money.

None of them approached the girl in the kaftan at the bar. Perhaps they had already been rebuffed. But none of the male tourists made any overtures either. She definitely gave off a *don't touch me* message.

"Maybe the old guy's a Mafia don," said Peyton.

April went to the bar one afternoon when Peyton had gone for a walk down the beach. April thought and said that it was crazy. *Nobody* went out in the sun at this time of day. All the shops in town closed up. The local young men were taking post-prandial naps, gathering strength for the evening's preening. Even this shaded poolside bar was empty. Nobody was in the pool. There was one customer besides April. The girl in the kaftan was sitting in her usual spot, drinking something tall and staring out at the achingly blue water.

This evening was to be the hotel manager's cocktail party. Trays of free hors d'oeuvres would be attacked and everyone would drink and talk too much. April felt an ambivalent mix of feelings. She anticipated the evening, thought about what she would wear, half hoped to meet someone. At the same time she knew that it would be loud husbands or men too young for her. She was thirty-three. A *young* thirty-three, as Peyton put it. Peyton lied about her own age. Seemed somehow not modern, not-up-to-date, not post-liberation correct. But Peyton harboured some old-fashioned ideas. She thought men in general were wonderful. Right now she was risking sunstroke in her big straw hat, hoping that Mister Wonderful would be out there searching for conch shells.

"What can I do for you, mam?" said the bartender.

April wondered if this were a code phrase for a siesta time quickie. No, probably just routine politeness.

"I was hoping to get some lunch," said April. "But I suspect the kitchen's closed?"

"'Fraid so, miss," said the bartender, his face set in rueful sympathy. "But I can get you a cold sandwich."

"Chicken please, and some coffee?"

"Too hot for coffee," said the girl in the kaftan. "Why don't you have one of these? Mostly iced tea."

"Why not make one of these for the lady, Albert?" said the girl in the kaftan. "It's called a Nooner. Wonder why."

April smiled tentatively. Then she and her fellow passenger sipped their Nooners and stared out at the empty beach and the empty sea and sky.

"Why not join me over here," the girl in the kaftan said. "So I can confide all my girlish secrets without yelling."

After yet another Nooner, April thought the girl was one of the finest people she had ever met in her whole life.

"Will your husband be joining you?" she asked.

"Husband," said the girl. "Oh, you mean *Daddy*."

She gave the word a derisive ironic twist. "He's my father. He's still sleeping off the morning drinks. Getting strong for the Happy Hour. So he can collapse early in the evening."

The girl, Kathy with a K, and her father spent the whole winter on the island. They went to New Mexico for the summer. Home was, however, in upstate New York, where they never ever lived.

A man in his late forties, possibly early fifties, sat down a few stools away from them. He ordered a local beer. His name, he told them later, was Clausen. Bruce

Clausen. He was Assistant Director of Corporate and Foundation Relations at Saguaro College in Arizona. He knew the area in New Mexico where Kathy and her father summered! He knew April's area of Chicago!

Formerly, before Arizona, he had been VP Marketing at Super Software Associates, the Wong Laboratory in Minnesota. St. Paul Minnesota, across the river from Minneapolis. He had lived in Minnetonka, a suburb. April did not know of which city. She wondered which of the two women he planned to hit on. Possibly he had not yet made up his mind.

"Miss Herrick?" the desk clerk was at her side. "A phone call for you. Long distance."

"Oh," she said. "Where can I take it?"

"In the lobby?" said the clerk. "How are you today, Miss Holst?"

"Peachy," said Kathy. "Peachy-keen. Let me introduce you to Mr. Clausen, who is from across the river."

It was Nicky. Another nightmare connection, with what seemed to be astronaut-style hesitations and pauses between patches of dialogue. *Love* and *miss* were words she got out of the squalls of transoceanic static. *Come back to me*, he said, suddenly clear as if from across the room.

Back at the bar, Bruce was leaning in towards Kathy in a posture of frankness.

"I was a widower for five years before I remarried," he said. "Now I'm divorced."

"Isn't everybody," mourned Kathy. "Or else they're married."

April was sleeping off the Nooners when Peyton came back. The noise of the opening door woke her up.

"There's a message for you," said Peyton. "To phone Nicky. You have to do it from the booth."

"I got that call already," April said. "Couple hours ago."

"This, I think, is a new message," said Peyton. "Whoever heard of a grown man whose name ends in 'ee'? A real clue to his character."

"Nobody on the beach? Nobody nice?" said April, yawning and sitting up. "How would you like to go through life and be my age and have this girlish name?"

"You could always change it," Peyton said brightly. "Now hurry up and get dressed. I don't want to miss a minute of Happy Hour."

"I met these nice people at the bar," April said. "The mystery lady? And a nice man."

"*Will* you hurry?" said Peyton.

April decided not to return the second message. What was the point? There did not seem to be the possibility of a good connection, and what could she say in answer to Nicky's words? They were full of urgent hope, but nothing specific.

There was a telegram for her at the front desk. *I am waiting in love for your return....*

The band had finished "Little Yellow Bird" and began to play the song that was so popular on the island that season – "I've Said Goodbye to You Before." The late afternoon light slanted in an acute angle. Sunsets were swift and operatic down here. They gave the time a special poignance, always brief and final as the return flight's number on the tickets in the desk drawers in all the hotel rooms.

The slanting last light sheened over everyone in the bar, tourist and native. April felt a post-afternoon drinking maudlin affection for all of them. They looked golden and momentary in the brief light.

I've said goodbye to you before, the lead singer breathed into the mike. *And I'll be sayin' it again....*

"Hello," said a voice at her side. It was Bruce, wearing a shirt that looked as if it had been washed in the surf and pounded on a rock. Still, he looked healthy and glowing and youthful in the aching, lowering light.

They began to dance. She looked down at his hand holding hers.

In the times when I'll be lonely I'll hear your voice again....

Bruce was saying something in her ear which she could not quite make out.

Down all the streets of night time....

Bruce kept her in his arms for a moment after the song ended. Then they went to the bar where Peyton had found a seat. It was getting more and more crowded. A young waiter came through the bar with a tray of cheese and fruit. He was instantly surrounded and the tray was savaged. Kathy and her father were in their usual position on the other side of the bar. Kathy raised her glass and an ironic eyebrow at April. Bruce and

Peyton were trying to keep up a shouted conversation. Peyton loved the Southwest. Bruce told her that Saguaro was the name of an indigenous cactus down there.

April and Bruce danced to "Help Me Make It Through the Night." April noticed with surprise that it was full dark and the hanging Japanese lanterns were lit. Peyton and Kathy were being chatted to by two of the slim locals. The band was doing something local and reggae. The small dance floor was jammed with jumping, jolting bodies.

Bruce suggested a walk on the beach. It was suddenly another world, with the music and voices coming from receding distance. The surf rolled in placidly, with a white froth on the sand as it slipped back. A lunar light shimmered. It seemed very natural to have stopped and to have Bruce's arms around her and to be kissing fervently. It was somehow so adolescent and heady and so what-the-hell.

When they came back to the bar, Happy Hour was, alas, over and people were drifting off to their separate dinner plans. Bruce asked her if she and Peyton had planned to go to the barbecue at the neighbouring hotel. A full native feast was to be laid on, including a goat stew.

"We bought tickets the day we arrived," said April. "Are you going?"

"Yes," said Bruce. His face shone youthfully. He looked hopeful and ardent. "I'm sure glad I got a ticket. They're sold out by now."

Kathy and Peyton were not at the bar. Hardly anybody was. The keyboard player covered his instrument with a plastic cloth. Kathy's father was half asleep in his usual place.

When it was time to meet Bruce in the lobby, Peyton had still not returned. April wondered if this were the night for the long native-styled dress she had bought in the hotel's boutique. She put it on, took it off, settled for a plain white skirt and knit top.

A courtesy bus picked them up and a courier told bad jokes during the drive. Each night, a different hotel provided some kind of special function to which guests of the other hotels were invited. A limbo contest, drink-mixing demonstration, special meals, a cabaret. Nobody could ever complain about not having enough to do.

April and Bruce sat at a table with two couples who were traveling together. The wives looked as if they had just completed a day of too much shopping and the men seemed to have little to say to one another. They seemed about ready to go home. Bruce tried a few lines of conversation, got nowhere, and finally he and April spoke only to one another.

Peyton arrived just after the soup (turtle) and crouched down next to April, in a very un-Peytonesque posture.

"Sorry I'm late, but I got hung up," said Peyton, out of breath, face flushed. "We had an incredible time...."

"We can squeeze another chair in here, can't we?" said Bruce.

"S'okay, I'll find a spot," said Peyton. "I'll see you after."

She swayed off a bit unsteadily and found a seat at a table with only three people at it. Three men of a certain age. She was probably safe with them, April thought.

On the bus going back, songs were sung, voices were raised and even a feeble joke was received with exuberant laughter. April and Bruce stood out in the hallway after Peyton went in, whispering urgently. Bruce wanted her to come to his room. No hanky-panky intended. Just whatever they both wanted. April demurred. It would not be, somehow, fair to Peyton. They settled for deep, standing-up kissing. April's legs felt weak, she wanted to yield, to lie down right there.

Finally, all mussed up, confused and aroused, she went into her room. Peyton was already asleep, on her back, mouth open, breathing with resonant sonority. Obviously she would not know or care where April slept.

April lay awake, listening to Peyton snoring. Moonlight lit up a gap between the drapes, lighting up the low coffee table where a white flower floated in a black bowl of water.

There was only one more day before the vacation would end. What was she going to do about Bruce? What about Nicky? On their way in from the airport, their bus had passed another bus coming into the airport parking lot. A load of people ending their holiday, reluctantly returning to the cold and snow of Chicago or Toronto, sunburned or tanned, envious of the ones arriving and all of it still ahead of them. April had felt a premonitory sadness, as if her two weeks were ending rather than just beginning. She was in a similar mood right now.

"You know why the Miami luggage tags are MIA?" said Bruce after they finally cleared customs. "Stands for Missing in Action."

"I can't imagine that customs in Russia would be any worse," said Peyton. "Do I *look* like I'm smuggling drugs in?"

Bruce bought them drinks at a little stand-up bar. His connecting flight was about an hour before theirs.

"I'm going to call you," he said to April. "Tomorrow night. And either I'm coming to Chicago or you're coming West, right?"

A snowstorm in Chicago backed everything up and delayed their takeoff. April and Peyton roamed through the souvenir shops, which Peyton called the airport *guilt* shops. Businessmen away on ostensibly legitimate trips bought overpriced gifts for the little women and the kiddies waiting innocently for them. Waiting for the men, Peyton said. Not for the guilt gifts.

They arrived at O'Hare in a shambles. Only one runway was open. Baggage area a jumble. Someone dropped a bottle of duty free liquor. Tempers were lost. Cabs? Forget it. The whole return trip from the island took twelve hours. The tour company had promised an easy four.

"I don't think I ever thanked you for the trip," said April. "I really did enjoy it. Is the fun part over now? Is God trying to tell us something?"

NICKY WAS NOT at the office when April came in the next morning. Something about this family emergency. Catherine's mother. The emergency was over, but Nicky and Catherine were snow-stranded in Boston.

April learned all this from Nicky's new secretary, a young thing who had lots of hair. Maybe, April thought, there was affirmative action for airheads.

The drab day went on. April thought about Nicky. All those frantic phone calls and now nothing. Of course, it would be difficult with Catherine on the scene. Still, he had managed last week. She thought about Bruce. The possibility of Bruce. The week went on, slowly. Snow made commuting hazardous, weary-making. Nicky wasn't in town and was not calling her all the time. Bruce kept on calling. April felt that she had to do something decisive about Bruce.

"I should have told you," she said. "I should have been more honest. I'm involved."

"Well," he said. "How involved? I mean, how serious? I mean there are degrees of involvement, right?"

His voice sounded anxious, but still oddly youthful. April pictured him in an ochre-colored room, a cloudless aching blue sky outside his opened window, tall cacti standing like old grandees in the distance.

"I'm afraid that it's serious," April sighed. "I'm sorry."

"So am I," Bruce said, his voice taut.

IT WAS EARLY in what the calendar said was spring, but there were still patches of snow under bushes, gathered in dirty clumps at corners and on the shady sides of buildings. April was supposed to meet her father for lunch. He had called (after eleven) the previous Sunday.

"Trevor," April said. "What a nice surprise."

She had stopped calling him dad when she graduated from St. Edmund's. But she still felt a faint, residual self-consciousness about using his given name. It seemed falsely sophisticated to her. But it also served quite well to keep him at a distance.

"I'm coming to Chicago next week," he said. "I'm going to be on a panel. De Paul's School of Music. Thought we could get together for lunch one day. What's good for you?"

They settled on Wednesday and she suggested The Lime Tree, the latest wine bar.

"Okay, I'll meet you there at noon. Do we need reservations?" he said.

"I'll make them," said April. "It will be so nice to see you again."

"Yes," he said. "Lots has happened. To me, I mean. What about you? *Your* life...."

"Oh," she said, "nothing much. I'll tell you whatever at lunch. Long distance always makes me nervous. Sorry."

After they hung up, April thought about it. What news was he bringing. Good or bad? If he were ill, he wouldn't have sounded so eager and happy.

TREVOR DECIDED to drive to Chicago for the conference. He was in a jaunty mood. He remembered auto trips with his father all over Ontario and once into New

York State and across to Boston. Several times into Michigan and to Chicago. Had it been a different country back then? He remembered it in gold-brown hues: Rivers flowed past sturdy red brick factories, creameries, breweries. One factory boasted an immense clock in its tower that worked and tolled the hours and could be read across the river in another state. The brown river flowed gravely, broad, and stately past.

Where was that river, that town and the clock? He could not remember. It would not be there anyway. Or if it were, the place would be shabby and empty and the clock would not work.

Had his father been trying to tell him something? Not geography lessons. Something else, unstated, implicit. He suddenly remembered coming home when his father died. When his ship entered New York harbour, it seemed to him that the skyline fairly swaggered, bold as Gershwin. A silver twin-engined plane had swooped low over the ship. Looking up into the cloudless sky, he felt his grief lift. Coming home.

"DON'T WALK in this neighborhood," the bell captain warned. "Not at night. Nosiree."

The trip had been long, placid, flat and boring. He had looked forward to walking in Chicago. Years ago he had gone all over. He remembered being tempted by a gypsy on Maxwell Street at three AM. Now he was a prisoner in his hotel. He stood at the window looking down at the street. There *were* some people out there. A man and woman were walking past the hotel. Cars went around the corner. A cab pulled up and stopped. He could not see who got in or out.

He stared at the Piranesi print framed and bolted to the wall above his bed. The grandeur of ruins, the romance of the antique and melancholy. One has to be very young to truly appreciate it.

That night he dreamed of April as a child. In the dream, he saw her turning slowly, beckoning, calling to him. It was his remembered vision of her when he wrote *Adagio For a Daughter*. He woke in the dark. He had been dreaming so much lately. Would there be a final dream?

One night he had dreamed that he was in an immense hotel in an unnamed Mediterranean country. He was alone. Although the weather was benign and the sunlight threw shadows of blooming flowers and trees against the sand-colored walls, the surf pounded heavily on a sullen, empty beach. He walked down silent empty corridors. In the huge lobby there was no desk clerk. There were no porters, no cooks, no maids.

Even while dreaming, he knew that it was a dream and thus the absurd was plausible. Time slowed and slipped and jumped. It seemed to him that he had been there for a very long time. Then the silence in the dream was broken by a ringing telephone. He picked up the phone and listened to static. Through the storm of noise came a small voice. It was a child's voice and he answered it with love. The child, he knew, was his grandchild.

When are you coming home? his grandchild said. He

did not know if it were a boy or girl. *Soon,* he answered. *Soon.* As he said the word, he knew he could leave the place and cross the ocean. His grandchild's voice had freed him, released him from this strange empty place. He could come home.

And then, in the strange logic of the dream, he became the child. And he was running headlong towards his father, who would, he knew, take him up in his strong sure hands and lift him up forever in his joy and freedom and certain strong love.

THE NEXT MORNING the spring sun was aching and clear. The dangerous night street had been replaced by calm innocence. Men without topcoats, women in sweaters, moved briskly or slowly as the mood suited them. He craned his neck at the window to look up at the buildings across the street, a frieze of white clouds and eye-hurting blue above them.

Trevor felt as if he were sloughing off more than winter clothing or time. Or age. He felt an inner quickening, a sense of hope growing in a dark place where he had not let light in for a long time. And today he was going to see his daughter. What more could a man ask for?

OHMIGOD, she thought when she saw him come in. He had gotten so old. And just since Christmas. No, it had been the Christmas before. She hadn't made it home for the last holiday. What had been her excuse, her lie? Pressures at work, the flu? The Christmas before had been a horror show, with Ned drinking too much, bullying his wife, sniping at Trevor; snide asides to April about her married boyfriend. She didn't think she had the strength to face another sick-making holiday without making a scene with her brother.

"April, honey," he said, putting his arms around her in a clumsy hug. "You're just as pretty as ever...."

"Oh, Daddy," she laughed. "You always say that. I think you need glasses."

They had to wait a few minutes at the bar. Trevor ordered two glasses of house wine. It wasn't chilled enough.

"Here's to – what? Us? Spring? To Life?" he said, clinking his glass against hers.

"Whatever," she said. "There's something they say in the islands, but I can't remember."

"That's right," said Trevor. "You were down there this winter. Did you enjoy it? Swim a lot?"

"My swimming days are over," said April. "Did some paddling in the pool though."

"So," he said after they had been seated and had ordered. Tuna salad for her, a roast beef sandwich for him.

"So tell me all about your life," he said. "Just as you used to when you were little. Don't leave anything out."

"It's too complicated," April said. "I'm in love with someone. Thing of it is is that he's involved. I mean he still isn't quite divorced. He's going to – the marriage is all over. But still...."

"It's complicated," she shrugged. "But what about you…."

"I'm looking forward to retirement," Trevor said. "I still love teaching, but the politics, the budget pinching, the careerism wears me down. I am counting the days."

"You'll have time for your own work," April said. "Will they give you a party? A gold watch?"

"The party, maybe," Trevor smiled. "You'll get an invitation. I've been putting an archive together. I'll donate it to the library and get a tax break."

"Selling the family secrets?" April sipped her wine. "How is Miriam?"

"She keeps well," said Trevor. "Secrets. I didn't know we had any."

April felt a rush of mixed-up emotion. For a long time she had harboured a kind of remote almost contempt for her father. It was as if he were to blame for everything – for the accident, for her mother's unfaithfulness, for her own messy love life. Logically she knew that it was not true. Her mother had been the instigator, the mechanic of her own doom. But the resentment she grudged against Trevor, childish as she knew it to be, hung on tenaciously.

"You know," he said, "I've always felt I could talk to you. That's a great blessing. My own father – bless him – well, it was partly because he was getting on when I came along. He didn't know how to treat me. So it was awkward and arm's-length. You and Ned, though. You taught me to play, to relax and love. I'll always be thankful to you for that. And that's what I tried to put in the music I wrote for you. That kind of wonderful, open running headlong – what? Leaping, I don't know how to put it in words…."

"I'll never know what was driving your mother those last years," he said, frowning down at the table. "Nothing I did could make her happy."

"There," he said. "*Make* her happy. Impossible thing. To force another human being to feel happy."

"April my dear," he said looking directly at her. "I hope, though, that you will find your happiness. You deserve it."

Out on the street in the chill sunshine, Trevor's thin hair blew awkwardly. He should wear a hat, she thought.

"Let me know when the retirement party is," said April. She was jostled one way and another. They tried to stand out of the way, nearer to the building.

Then her father hugged her again, looked into her face and kissed her on both cheeks. He muttered something that she could not quite make out and then set off to find a taxi. April watched him go. He looked smaller, slower. Older. There were tears blurring her vision.

She walked back to the office down Wabash. Light, sparse and dusty, fell through the iron girders of the elevated station. She stopped in front of Rose Records. They might have it. She went in.

"Yes," said the impatient young man in the classical section. "Marriner. We don't have it in stock. There's an arrangement on Peregrine. We only have that on cassette."

"That would be fine," said April.

"*Adagio for Strings* is on it too. That's Barber."

"Ah," said April. "Fine."

She listened to it that night, her father's gift to her, tears running down her face.

A simple eight-note phrase repeated in several modes with variation, urgent, intent as a father's gaze into a crib. The music had a joyous impetuosity, like a child rushing in trust into her father's arms after school. Urgent like a river that falls down a slope, surges around rocks and fallen trees, goes on, goes down to reach the flat land, slows its pace, still moves on, determined to reach the sea.

Then it became a stately turning dance. Under the dance someone seemed to speak directly and simply about a love he had to express. It said *forever* and *now*. There was an edge of poignancy in the joy. A father holds his child in his hands for such a little while. A daughter grows up and moves away. The love remains. She had slipped, called him *Daddy*. A grief swelled in her. All that time wasted licking old wounds. The music ended, the tape clicked off and she was left in the sudden silence.

four
Lives of the Poet

NED CAME TO TEACH AT NITH IN 1980, the year after his father remarried. Ned lived about five miles from campus in a high-rise similar in style to Gil's. The two men lived about a mile from one another. They might just as well have been living in different countries. Downtown Toronto was twenty-five miles away.

Each morning Ned fought the traffic, cursing, muttering. He was almost late every morning. There was always the problem of finding a spot in the overbooked faculty lot. Time was eaten up as he circled further and further out and found a spot far away from the building. Then he ran for the door and down the corridor, coat half off and flapping. No time to check in at the office. A few straggling students went into classrooms and the hall lay before him, empty and accusing.

HE HAD BEEN HIRED at Nith during boom times. Nothing was too good for the new, daring, innovative college. All the President of the Board had to do was hold a hand out to the government and money was swiftly given. Nothing at Nith was traditional. "English" and "Theatre Arts" were not taught. Instead there were "Modules" grouped around "Concepts." Ned, for instance, was hired because of his poetry. He was to teach media, communications, creative writing.

But now the flood of dollars was slowing down. What was society to do with all these half-baked ill-prepared graduates in a shrinking job market? Back to basics, the government said sternly. And so Ned was hurrying down the hall to teach Business Report Writing.

He had only one course in creative writing each term and fewer and fewer students in it. In another year it might very well dwindle away completely and Ned would be nothing but a functionary, teaching useful skills.

When he had first begun teaching at Nith, the counter-offers from more prestigious institutions came in dramatic profusion. Letters, phone calls, telegrams, all-expense-paid flights to be wooed, taken up to mountain tops to be shown the glittering cities laid out at his feet. But Nith always matched the offers, gave him early tenure, and promises were made.

The promises were broken, times got tough, the outside offers ceased, and it became more and more evident to him that this was it: Teaching at Nith was all there was going to be. And then they farmed him out to the satellite campus, a piece of government surplus which was mainly given over to night school classes or remedial upgrading. The staff out there was made up of burnouts, of young fresh graduates willing to be exploited so they could pay the bills, and terminal cases like Ned. Ineptitude, alcoholism and marital discord ran rampant through the staff.

NED THOUGHT of this time (c.1982-1989) as the Bad Time. His second book (*What I Want*) came out in 1980. He went off on a flurry of readings, lusted after poetry groupies, got some very positive reviews, was short-listed for a prize and then it all dribbled away. And he began the slide into the Bad Time.

He did get *some* readings, sat on committees, reviewed other people's work, swanned and strutted and had affairs.

But it was a slide. He felt himself going into it. Sometimes he sat at home in the room he called the library and his wife, Heather, called the TV room. He would sit there, drink in hand, staring at some dumb show, his mind surging. He wanted to fling the glass at the screen, yell and kick something. It was all so unjust. No prize. No more mention in the critical journals. Nothing but this apartment, the dreary job at Nith, the reproach-filled air between him and his wife.

HEATHER HAD COME to Nith at the same time Ned did. She had her brand new M.A. under her arm and a thesis *(Patterns of Animal Metaphor in the Poetry of Sylvia Plath)* which her advisor told her was publishable if reworked. Heather was confident that her teaching duties would leave lots of time for the rewriting. Then she married Ned and got a better job offer as a research analyst at a large private consultancy. When she finally went back to her thesis, a whole new feminist approach to Plath made her work hopelessly obsolete.

EACH MORNING was a hazard of instant coffee, murmured words and a hurrying to go. She had a long drive downtown and he had as far to go in the other direction. Sometimes they had dinner together. Sometimes Ned simply sank into the TV room.

Sometimes he stopped for a drink with a few colleagues and students on a Friday afternoon, right? Sometimes this went on until nine or ten at night or later. So fucking what. Sometimes they closed the bar, went on to somebody's apartment for a nightcap.

Once he went for lunch with a few friends and did not make it back for an afternoon class. People at nearby tables came and went and on he stayed. That was the time Heather accused him of hankypank with Kelly. The fucking injustice of it. Ned threw a righteous tantrum. It was simply not true and so damn unfair. But Ned did not disclose that a week earlier, it had been true. Kelly had decided after that to break off. It was wrong, she said. She owed something to the boy waiting patiently back in her home town for her to finish her nursing courses.

Now Ned was semi-involved or between involvements or on the brink. But the injustice of Heather's accusation stung him. He raged and sulked for a long time.

He sat in the library/TV room contemplating his lovelies. He summoned them up: Karen and Joy, Natalie, Nadine, Marie-Thérèse, Renée, Pamela and Kelly. Ah Kelly, Kelly. Yes. Her hair had that sun-tipped look one associates with beaches, surfing, diet pop commercials, money, mindless harmless movies about high school.

But there was sure nothing mindless about Kelly. Her eyes. That was it. Her eyes were so clear that you were tempted to think *childish*, *naive*, and *nobody's home*. The clarity was deceptive. It was a clarity resulting from Kelly's certain grasp of the world and her rightful place in it. Kelly was no victim. She was no pushover. And now it was over. *Her* decision. A first for Ned.

Well, now there was the possibility of Brenda. Brenda's handwriting. She did not dot her "i." Instead she made a perfect tiny circle in place of the dot. This same tiny "o" appeared at the end of each sentence. Her mind, Ned reflected as he sipped his scotch, must be a robin's-egg-blue room filled with stuffed animals. Pink animals. What was it that drew him to her? It had to be something depraved deep down in him. She was so free of guile. Everything about her was up front. Including those perfect breasts, startling and pert. Ned read her poems, imagined turning each tiny "o" into an idiot, smiling happy face.

Kelly's eyes. He remembered seeing the same look in

a collection of Dodgson's photographs of young girls. The look said *I know who I am.* Cheeky. The original Alice. Ah, the insolence of beauty.

"Your father called," Heather said. "It's on the machine."

Ned stooped, put his briefcase down in the hallway, sighed and slowly stood up.

"He was wondering if we might come down for Thanksgiving," Heather said.

Ned pressed his forehead as if it ached.

"Do *you* feel up to another gathering of my family?" he said.

"It *was* a lot like Christmas in *Portrait of the Artist,*" Heather smiled. "But your father is getting on…."

Ned waved a weary hand. The last family fiasco ended with a shouting scene in the kitchen. April and Ned. The April and Ned Show. And then a month later Heather miscarried.

"Let's think about it," Ned said. "Slowly. Carefully."

Brenda was late for her conference with Ned. That was okay. Ned was late too and he needed those extra minutes in the office by himself to establish his dominance over the space. If he and the lovely arrived at the same time, the necessary moments alone were lost and then everything would go badly. He'd be preoccupied, anxious, self-conscious.

Brenda arrived all out of breath. The little dear. Her eyes seemed to look directly into and through him as if she knew, *really* knew, what was there inside: all the muck and mush and desire and passion and kinky dirty thoughts. It was as if she knew and yet accepted all that and could still sit in the chair across from him and talk, not needing to run screaming out of the office.

Could she? Really see? He frowned in deliberation, staring down at the desk, hand across his mouth, propping his chin, thought fiercely: *Brenda, I want you. I want to to fuckfuckfuckyou.* There. He almost said it aloud, a rune, a charm. Did she hear it, see it deep in him? Did she know all? What would she say if he did indeed say it aloud? Would she say *sure, come on*, and lift her skirt?

She spoke, instead, of her poem.

"So, Mr. Herrick, I mean, what you said Williams said? About no ideas but *in* things?"

"Yeeeeesss," said Ned, leaning back so that his chair creaked dangerously. "Yes, yes, yes. The words must seem to live and breathe. Anything else is tap dancing. Eliot – no, it was Frost – said we should leave the *grievances* alone so we can concentrate on the *grief*. Something there all right. Share it. None of this damn stamping a small foot against fate. No heigh-de-ho. I, personally, think a poem should be as nervous and keyed up as a horse before a race…."

Ned believed, sort of, in what he was saying. But at the same time he was using, shamelessly, the things which once had meant so much to him. At one time they were all he really believed in besides, of course, himself.

Yet here he was using them to allure and attract and seduce a girl he actually was not interested in. Was he trying to see if it would work, if the words would charm, words spoken aloud work like an incantation? The words so strongly thought had not charmed her into lifting her skirt saying, *sure, come on* – Ned felt furtively cheap, tawdry, tired suddenly.

Lately he had fallen into a habit of double thinking. He saw every action as it might appear in some future literary history. Everything around him thus was ironic, seen from a detached perspective, as if the parentheses behind his name had been filled in with a final date. Edward ("Ned") Herrick (1953 – something).

Yet at the same time he was intensely *in* his present moment. Brenda's eyes, for instance. Like a twin-barreled shotgun leveled at him. And her quirky, off-to-the-side private smile. Only for him?

How cheap and low he was. Yet Brenda's eyes seemed, so direct and honest as they were, to see into the slippery labyrinth of his soul and still look and not turn away in revulsion. How generous she was. Too bad her poetry was so awkward and trivial and hopeless. Yet he treated it as if he were reading *Paradise Lost*, with a frown of concentration, saying *hmmmm*, and praying that there would be please, please, a word or line or image he could seize on, single out, say *that's good, that's good* – Fucking phony that he was. "That's good, Brenda, *really* fine…."

He pointed to a line in the poem. They smiled at one another across the poem which lay on the desk between them. To her it was a carved jewel. To Ned it was something he could use. Part of the strategy. Joan Fink, who was well named, was coming out of her office and looked down the hall as he was ushering Brenda out of the door. Fink saw him gallantly hold the door open so that Brenda had to squeeze past him, and saw Brenda's breasts brush against his arm or perhaps not brush against him, nothing touched, but Fink probably thought that contact had been achieved, dried-up old bitch that she was, and he was so preoccupied in wondering what Fink saw or thought she saw that he wasn't even sure if Brenda's breast *had* brushed against him. He had hoped for that.

Fink. And here he was only doing his job for godsake. Fucking damn Fink. He needed, suddenly, a drink and some masculine companionship. He slammed his office door and went off to the pub. Ms. Fink had gone back into her office without acknowledging his presence. He felt a small smarting of resentment. It was about a two-block walk to the bar. Autumnal chill in the air. Should have worn a coat. He hunched his hands into his jacket pockets. The pub was crowded, but there wasn't anybody there he knew. Everyone looked very young. He stood at the bar. The TV was on. Some soccer game in Europe. Prufrock, he thought. Prufrock in the pub in his new clothes. Today's Prufrock, with an inflatable woman from Hong Kong in his room. Complete in every anatomical detail. Yes sir, Prufrock has a honeymoon in the hand. Prufrock's hand never turns him down or says it has a headache. Prufrock's inflatable woman doesn't get pregnant or get out of sorts.

He went home and had a large scotch in the kitchen.

He listened to Mahler's *Song of the Earth* and felt a maudlin sense of peace. Then he switched to FM and found a station which had people phone in and give their opinions on the subject of the day. This day it was about orgasms. My, my, the things people were willing to talk about in public. Of course, he, as a poet, or former poet, or poetaster, should know that.

NED PROWLED the library, looking at the current periodicals. The poems and short stories did not interest him. Then he wandered down stacks in areas foreign to him. He took a book off the shelf which was about corset and binding fetishism. Seemed to be all the rage in Victorian times. Both men and women lacing themselves into unconsciousness. Ned did not find the fetish attractive. But he felt himself slightly stirred by it. Thing was that he wanted to give himself over to *something*. Women in stiletto heels, feet, *something*. He tried homoerotic fantasies, imagined himself degraded, pissed on, committing fellatio.

Nothing doing. He had a semi-erection while looking at the corset study, but it waned. He was becoming like the corset study himself: somber, learned, detached. He read case histories in *Psychopathia Sexualis*. The medical student at Greifswald who exhibited his genitals in public, and always to girls of virtuous family. Sometimes he went so far as to defile them with urine.

Then there was the case of Mr. Z who began masturbating at age seven and by age nine was inattentive and forgetful. As an adult, Mr. Z had a malformed head, large prominent ears and deficient innervation of the right facial muscle and neuropathic expression of the eye. All this added up to a typical degenerate, neuropathic fellow.

Take Mr. X who was excited by the odour of leather. Whenever he saw a woman in laced high boots, he experienced pollution. There were cases of hair fetishism, hair despoliation, theft of women's handkerchiefs. There were men who loved velvet, who wanted to be flogged, who sought humiliation, who loved fur or feathers. There were cases of coprolagnia, hysteria, necrophilia. What a busy, busy place Germany must have been back then. A sassy girl went past the carrel Ned was reading in.

She was incredibly lean in her faded jeans and yet, paradoxically, soft and curvy looking. Ned thought *I am unseen*. If she had seen him, she probably would have thought automatically *old guy*. He felt a hollow coldness.

The day went on. It was slowly deflating. What happened to lost hours when the clocks changed? Lost in one season, get it back in another. Balance, fairness, give and take.

Just a week ago, he had been driving down an unfamiliar street. There, in front of a small house, a young girl was watering a very unpromising patch of lawn. An old woman stood next to the girl, overseeing the task. The old woman had a stern, ethnic look, all in black and wary of anybody approaching the girl. Ned had slowed down, pretended to be scanning the house numbers. The girl was taller than the old woman and had long, supple legs. She wore cut-off denim shorts which appeared to be painted on, they were so tight. The word *nubile* came into his mind and at that moment she looked up, locked into his gaze and he could see *old guy* in her eyes.

AFTER THE MISCARRIAGE, Ned brooded, avoided Heather and went into a sulk. During that time he went back to writing poems. He did not show them to anybody. At first, he did not send them out to magazines. He kept them in a folder in his desk. The poems were, he thought, much more mature and sure than his early work. He alternated between enraged drunkenness and calm creativity.

These poems, he thought, were evidence of a major phase. Mature, wise, autumnal. He was trying for honesty. He had given up the priapic strutting. Many of the new poems were about his father. And slowly, hesitantly, he began some love poems for Heather. In periods of calm, he made awkward gestures of rapprochement. They were welcomed.

Many of the little magazines which had been so receptive in his youth had disappeared. He made the rounds of the new ones. A few said yes. He was back in the game.

WHEN HEATHER announced that she was pregnant again, Ned's reaction was a mix of fear and hope. Was he too old for fatherhood? Hell, he wasn't over the hill. He felt, inside, that he was still a child himself. The enormous importance of a child, his child, a slender chance to get a fingergrip on fate and time, in a way to cheat death....

Feb. 12, 1989
Dear April:

I know I have not been in touch for a long time. I could plead busy-busy but you know that's a lie. Everybody in the world is busy. Well. You are about to become an aunt. Yes. Heather and I are expecting. I phoned Dad to tell him that he is about to become a grandfather. He seemed pleased.

And I'm writing again. Hope springs. How trite I am. But happy.

yer brudder,
Ned.

He had a lot of new ground to break. Now editors were younger than he was. When he had enough new poems to make a book, he wrote to his old editor at Zebu and Python.

The editor was no longer there or in this world. The Editorial Assistant who answered his query was a woman. He suspected that she was younger than he was. She was afraid that Zebu and Python's plans for poetry had all been made for the near and distant future. Had he considered any of the fine small presses?

Ned's new collection of poems, *A Hard Rain*, made the weary, futile rounds of the small houses. He imagined it forgotten under a desk among the dust bunnies, coffee-stained, dog-eared. Or worse, poems from it read out loud in the publishing office by some recent journalism school graduate. Sniggering laughter, jeers, contempt.

Finally a new midget press took it. Seemed they had to use up a government grant before the end of the year.

The book came out. Ned wrote to old friends and former admirers and drummed up a sort of reading tour. One of his hosts in a very small community phoned to make final arrangements.

"We are really looking forward to your reading." The man had a deep, cultured voice.

"My lady – the lady I live with – really, really admires your work," he went on. "And bring copies to sell!"

Ned felt encouraged. Odd term. My *lady*. Sounded like someone in *Ivanhoe*. Lately Ned noticed certain terms, certain words used by people just a decade younger than he which must have, he surmised, a special meaning for the people using the words. A meaning he did not – could not – catch. It was like being invited to a big family dinner and having the in-jokes and lore pass him by. But maybe he had something to say to this new crop of readers. Maybe this tour would be the start of a new career.

THE CAMPUS RADIO STATION was in a gentrified Victorian house, all tarted up with San Francisco-hued paint. The gingerbread was too intact to be original.

Promotional posters from record companies covered the walls. A girl who was smoking ostentatiously looked at, considered swiftly and dismissed him. She wore an outsized black sweater, short black skirt over black dancers' tights. Her tousled hair gave her the look of an intelligent rag doll.

"Studio B is upstairs," she said and gestured in the direction of the hallway. "To your right."

Ned gave her his kindly avuncular smile. As he went up the narrow stairs, people kept on coming continually down saying excuse, sorry, as he pressed against the wall. He held a copy of his new book.

He remembered the first tour, back in the early Seventies. Everything had been smoothly arranged. The publishers, Zebu and Python, had contact people in every city. Good hotels. Even a fruit and cheese tray sent up to that top floor in Calgary. Lunches with aggressive media women who had, back then, all been older than he. Now he took buses holding copies of the new book on his lap.

People who were supposed to meet him did not show. He was put up in suspect places. A student dorm during Christmas recess. The only occupant on the cold, hollow floor full of night echoes. Useless thermostat there. Somebody's rec room that still retained a basement odour. A child's room, complete with gerbils in a cage, their small gnawing incessant all night.

Buses. Occupied mostly by old women and students in down-filled parkas. The buses took forever and kept stopping to take on strange-shaped parcels or offload them.

Old ladies and students boarded or got off. He always seemed to have a ticket for the ultimate destination, looking out at wintry fields and dreading the reading.

The readings were fiascos. At a co-operative art gallery in a medium sized city, nobody showed up, not even the charlatan who arranged the affair. Ned stood out on the street staring at the locked door on which a hand-lettered poster announced his presence. At other places he read to audiences of three or four.

Now here he was doing the only interview on the tour. Back in the days of so-easy success he had been on prime time TV panels and network radio. Lunches paid for by the ambitious aggressive media women. Why *were* so many of them women? Didn't any young men want a media career?

Studio B was cunningly crammed with turntables and a reel-to-reel tape recorder. He could see someone in the midst of all the machines talking into a microphone. Ned was welcomed by a young man (at last! a young man in media!) who wore National Health-style glasses. A style which was coming back. He looked like a photo of a young Soviet composer in the Thirties, holding a cigarette in sensitive white fingers, hair close cropped and ascetic.

"Sonia is just finishing a tape," said the young man. "Can I get you a coffee?"

"No, thanks," said Ned with his open, comradely smile. "All coffeed out this morning."

Indeed he was. The loud-mouthed, foul-mouthed *lady* his host shared his place with had not gotten up to fix any breakfast and the damn cat had mewled and scratched at his door all night trying to get into its litter box. Sharing a room with a box full of cat turds.

In the too early morning, Ned had gotten into yesterday's clothes and snuck downstairs to stand in the kitchen wondering if he dared fool with the coffee maker, decided not to, stared out at the back yard and then sneaked back up for his bag, which was full of unsold copies of his book. He went down the empty street and found a coffee shop where he had too many coffees and a day-old doughnut.

"Ah, the green light," said the young man, pulling at the heavy door. "Sonia, this is Edward Herrick? The poet? The All about Arts interview?"

"Call me Ned," said Ned.

Sonia was one of those small intense girls one might be tempted to term, too swiftly, *boyish*. She was definitely a girl. You might be tempted also to say *skinny*. Paradoxically so curvy. Ned felt that even her bones would be soft to the touch. She had confident, self-possessed eyes.

The interview was conducted with boom mikes dangling between them, requiring much adjusting for balance. Ned felt himself swell, become bulky and clumsy. His knees, dangerously close to hers, looked thick and threatening.

"Actually I don't know much about your work," was the opener. "Would you read a poem for us?"

Ned had to reach down past her disturbing knees to get at his book bag; his head bumped the mike. She rewound the tape and after he had his glasses on she began again with the same opener.

"What do you think about the poetry scene today?" was the next question, with no comment or follow up after his poem had been read. Then she asked if he knew, *actually*, Margaret Atwood.

NED HAD AN OVERPRICED and fatty corned beef sandwich and an overpriced beer for lunch. Alone. He paid for it. He had two hours to kill before the bus. Sonia had the eyes of a turn-of-the-century tragedienne. Have to remember that metaphor. Good seduction line. Not with Sonia. Ned had the absolute and sure sense that nothing he could ever say would work on Sonia. Or the sassy girl in the library, or the nubile girl watering the lawn. World full of thin girls with hopscotch legs.

Ned munched slowly, fingered out an obdurate wad of fat under cover of his napkin. And the previous night's farce. He had been picked up *finally* at a bar near the bus station. Then too many glasses of native red wine in a too hot room and a too hyperactive dog kept insinuating its snout into his crotch. The dinner was late because his host's lady was late coming home from some damn conference or other.

All the damn dinner took was some thawing out. And all through dinner the *lady* kept on pushing absolutely honest questions at him. The questions were calculated to find out if he were imperialist, right wing, militarist, philistine, antifeminist or shocked by coarse language.

Ned thought he had held his end up fairly well, resolutely polite and not yielding an inch. Then there was a helter-skelter rush to the library where the reading was to start in ten minutes and the *lady* did not even for chrissake have the grace to come to it. She stayed home to await some mysterious emissaries they had forgotten were to arrive that very evening. After he had expended all that fucking charm and forbearance, Ned felt cheated.

He had kept a copy of his book to give them and now, as the evening went on its inexorable and dismal way, wondered if it should be squandered. There had, of course, been nobody awake to receive it that morning.

Last night he had lain on the hard futon, staring at the small bookcase next to the litter box. A hodgepodge of pop sociology, Sixties revolution and lots of contemporary writing by women.

HE MADE THE ROUNDS of Toronto bookstores, obsessively checking to see if they stocked his book.

"Have you got *A Hard Rain*?" he asked. "It's poetry. Just been published."

"All the poetry is over there on that wall," said the clerk. Who was a woman.

As young as the Editorial Assistant at Zebu and Python.

"I don't see it," Ned called to the clerk. "Is it alphabetical? By author?"

The clerk came over briskly, efficiently, reluctantly, perhaps even impatiently.

"Now who's the author? *Early Morning Rain*?"

"It's *Hard Rain*. Edward Herrick."

The clerk crouched down, pulled a book or two out, replaced some out of order, straightened up.

"No, I don't see it."

"Well," said Ned, "is it on order?"

"We could order it for you," said the clerk, looking alertly across the store at a derelict who was pawing the current periodicals.

"No," said Ned. "I mean is the book on order already? Can you check?"

"The owner does all the ordering," she said. "Thing of it is, he's not in today."

"No way for you to check? Records?" said Ned.

"Not really," said the clerk. "Maybe you could call back later on."

"You mean like tomorrow?" said Ned.

"I guess so," she said.

They stood there for a moment. Ned stared at the racks of other people's books, across the room at the other customers, out at the street where it was beginning to rain, back at the clerk who stood there looking potentially sympathetic and helpful with a bright little smile.

"Maybe you could try the Book Bag," she said. "Over on Queen Street? They have a lot of small press stuff."

"Ah, the Book Bag," said Ned. "Thanks. I just may do that."

He walked out of the store with his empty hands at his side, out into the rain, where he stood wondering which way to go.

As he walked towards their apartment building, he felt a weariness that was not because of any labour. It was a fatigue of the spirit. He had been so careless with his talent, so heedless. And with his life. So much time given to feeling grief for his mother, resentment toward his father. So much time given to futile affairs, tawdry gropings in a loveless dark, passion spilled on loveless sheets. And not much left over for the one woman he truly loved. The rain had stopped and a weak sun shone on wet streets and bushes. It was a sad-making time of the afternoon. He hurried his tired feet towards home.

What an awesome thing the ego was. The great and incessant demands it made.

The toll it took. Pain. Gnawing envy. Rage.

Heather survived it too. How brave she seemed to him. How noble she had been through all of it. And now she was an even more precious vessel. He wrote a poem about it called "Safe Harbour." It began with a quote from Melville: "Through storms you reach them and from storms are free."

Ned, after Heather became pregnant, seemed to be getting a grip on his life. So much time had been wasted. Thrown away. As if he had an endless supply of time. As if he could live forever.

But now he knew his remaining time was precious and not to be wasted. He was getting a grip on it. He did his work. He gave his students a fair and equitable share of his creative energy. He worked at his poems steadily and in a mature manner. He sent his poems out and tried not to be discouraged by rejection. He thought of the fiasco of *A Hard Rain*'s launching (sinking, scuttling, foundering) as something to be put behind him. A new book, comprised of better, more mature work, would come out in due time.

He drank very little. No more boozy lunches. No more end-of-the-week farragoes. No more hankypank. He was tenderly attentive to Heather. They waited in excited serenity for their child.

But the ego is a gnawing worm which dieth not. Nor is it ever sated. It lies in wait. It keeps its own counsel. It will have its day again.

SOMEONE CLIPPED a review of *Hard Rain* from the Winter issue of *FemePoem* and taped it to Ned's office door. He looked at the end of the review. Friend or enemy. Natalie Cushner. One of his past lovelies who was now doing fine in the network.

> The poems in *Hard Rain* (Rodent Press) are simply not relevant to any of today's concerns. They are merely male menopausal postures of self-pity, thinly disguised as poems.
>
> Herrick's first book, *Sitting Up Erect* (1972) had the panache and élan of youth. But read today, from the perspective of a more enlightened time, the poems in *Sitting Up Erect* are hopelessly dated, steeped in jejune male chau-

vinism. They are the vain posturings of a priapic and callow person in perpetual heat.

His second book, *What I Want* (1980) was more of the same. Penis-waving. A bit pathetic, as the boy wonder was no longer a boy. A one trick pony and dog show.

The poems in *Hard Rain* are, by contrast, post-coital (sic) and limp. There is nothing worth reading, thinking about or even writing about. This reviewer will stop now and not waste any more of her time. Or yours, dear reader.

All the air went out of the room. Ned felt sick, beaten up and betrayed. What had he ever done to her? She had been one of his star creative writing students. He had encouraged her, helped her get through a self-centered confessional phase quickly. He wrote letters of reference for her, helped her get grants.

Oh, yes, there had been some dalliance, but nothing too heavy. That was one of her phrases: *nothing too heavy*. A slim almost skinny girl with big, thoughtful eyes and hair cut cruelly short. She wore boys' clothing. Big workshirts, faded jeans and clunky hiking boots. She looked perpetually ready for rock climbing or gun running.

The clothes could not conceal her curviness, the supple softness of her bud breasts, the elegant curve of waist, the downy firm heft of her buns (those buns he had kissed and, yes, licked.)

But nothing too heavy. Her choice. He was married.

And she obviously had her thoughtful eyes on something far beyond him.

She married some boob, of course. They all did. She and the boob went off someplace west to teach and get higher degrees. They divorced, of course. Ned learned that from the boob who came back to visit his parents and dropped in to say hello to Ned.

Natalie had gone far and fast since the boob-dumping. She wrote articles, gave readings, sat on important committees, went abroad to give lectures on the New Feminist Canadian Poetry. Ned saw a photograph of her in a literary magazine. She was posed with some visiting European woman poets. No more boy's clothes for Natalie. She was dressed for success. But the style still looked utilitarian, as if she were denying something that her body wanted to say. In the photograph her smile looked sly.

And now Ned held the review and wondered what he could do about it. This sneaking, snide attack. Why? He had not hurt her, ever. And he wasn't (this smarted) a big figure to bring down.

Ned went that afternoon to bars where he was not known. By evening he was sodden. When the bars closed, he was in a fine drunken rage. He was ready to take it out on somebody. "The barometer of my emotional something is set for a spell of riot," he quoted to someone who was helping him to the door. The last bar was now closed and there was nowhere for him to go but home, where he knew that they always have to take you in.

five

Fandango

GIL'S FATHER WAS KILLED IN A FACTORY accident in 1950. Gil was ten years old. An overhead crane operator, perhaps benumbed by too much double-shift work, hit the wrong button and unloaded half a ton of angle iron. His mother never got over it. She mourned for years. She spent a lot of time in bars. When he was old enough, bartenders called to get him to take his mother home.

In his teens Gil led a double life. Late at night he read the poetry of Kahlil Gibran and *The Portable Oscar Wilde*. During the day he was silent and sullen. After he graduated from high school, he went to work in the same factory in which his father had been killed.

He worked a six-day week. On Sunday he went out alone, wandering all over Toronto, searching, yearning for love and beauty. One summer Sunday he went down to the lake.

The air was awash in simple sunlight. Sullen dockside water slapped the rocks and the tar-smelling piles. It was an oily, skunky water, green and heavy with algae. It was a primordial water. To see and smell it incited unease and fear and disgust in him. Its stink reminded him of his own mortality, of the awful grossness of his flesh.

He walked on the pier, feeling the sun on his back. The sun could not quite warm him. He heard the sluice and ooze of the water underneath, felt the rough planking sway under his feet, heard the voices and coarse laughter of the crowd around him. Every place he looked, there was something else to revulse him. He left the pier and started for home. The journey only increased his despair. The bus was hot, slow, filled with sweating passengers. Crying children were punished by tired parents. And he had to transfer. He stood for a long time on a sun-baked corner in a miasmal stew of exhaust fumes, overheated and spouting auto radiators and cooking smells. He did not want to go home. His mother might still be there and not drunk enough and she would play the guilt game. Or else she would be gone and he would sit alone in the reproachful silence of the house.

Where was there someplace he could go? He looked up at the pale, blazing sky. It told him nothing. Finally the bus came, crowded, no seats, standees hunched and jammed together. He slumped forward and entered the bus.

GIL'S MOTHER DIED IN 1965. In the fall of 1966

he signed up for two night school courses. Introduction to Literature and Music Appreciation. He went to symphony concerts. He was alone. He discovered the secret, musty joy of second-hand book stores. He prowled the downtown streets, hollow-eyed, hungry for love.

He began piano lessons. His teacher said he had a natural talent which should have been nurtured years earlier. She sent him to Windsor to see Trevor Herrick, who took him on as a pupil. It looked as if, finally, his life was going to change.

GIL'S APARTMENT was in a brand new high-rise about six miles north of campus. Zwingli College had been in existence since 1880. Back then, it had been a fiercely independent denominational institution which forbade smoking, drinking, card-playing and dancing. In the mid-twentieth century it began a music program which steadily became more serious. But now, in 1976, when he came to teach, Zwingli was in the throes of expansion, having been swallowed by a provincial university. Zwingli's original building, a severe Greek Revival, was surrounded by the concrete facades of new, bland, fascistic concrete. They were far from downtown Toronto, far from the Great Good place.

By the time he arrived, students could and did dance and drink all they wanted. There were condom machines in the residence washrooms.

He had the usual first job jitters. His M.A. (1974) from Tecumseh was marginal, a scraped through patched up mess resulting from his abrupt dropping of individual compositional study with Herrick. And then there was a period of missed classes, a botched senior recital and erratic moodiness. But somehow he had gotten through and now he had this precarious position, filling in for two half-sabbaticals.

He taught Music One, a fundamental which dipped into notation and harmony (MWF 8:30 AM) Music Two: The Great Composers (WED 7-9:30 PM) and a humanities course, The Enjoyment and Understanding of Music (THURS. 7-10 PM). He was also part of a team teaching Basic Skills.

Ever since the horror of Vivian's death and the thing with April, Gil had tried not to get involved. However, he did have a romance with Sheryl Brand, who was a cellist in the Dillon Quartet. She dumped him and went off with David Howdowan, who had himself dumped a mate of seven years. Gil rebounded with Anne Hitzman, who was with the CBC and got off more on career than human beings.

Everything Gil attempted seemed cursed, tainted. But, he consoled himself, even the times he was living in seemed askew. Magazine feature writers were having a hard time finding a suitable label for the age. In the late Seventies and into the Eighties, selfishness and greed and insensitivity were rampant.

In the Zwingli College library, students moved about with elaborate courtesy. If someone coughed, he apologized fervently, in a discreet whisper. Drama students bent over copy machines, intent on the pages with their roles on them. Gil distrusted all of them. If push came to shove, he knew they would sell him out, give false evidence, rend their garments, band together in a cabal against him.

MARIE GRAY, one of his Basic Skills colleagues, was a pasty-faced red-haired woman who seemed perpetually on the go. She was a single mother of two small children who were always being delivered to or picked up from a nursery school. Ex-husband was supposed to provide some child support, but who knew where he was? She was working on a doctorate in music history (The Twentieth Century) and had picked up somebody's prejudices.

"So you worked under Herrick," she said one late afternoon while they had a coffee in the local restaurant. Everyone on campus called it The Sad Cafe. The formica counter and tables could have been lifted from a Hopper painting.

"Warmed-over Howard Hanson," said Marie, with the patronizing, superior smile Gil was beginning to see over and over on his colleague's faces.

"Well, now," said Gil in a mild, no-sweat voice, "I think I see what you mean."

"But," he added out of guilt and loyalty, "there are some fine works there. Take *Adagio for a Daughter* –"

"Wet dream music," said Marie.

She looked defiant and determined. Her fingernails were gnawed and inky.

Did women have wet dreams? Gil looked at her neck

and the opened buttons of her blouse. He pictured her home life: a few free moments after working, teaching, getting dinner for the kids, plastic bags of frozen stuff dropped in boiling water, baths for the kids, toys all over the place, maybe a little TV before she caved in. Pity strong as lust welled up in him. Hey now, he thought at the same moment. Don't get involved.

HE TOLD MARIE too much about himself.

"I was your classic late bloomer," he told her. "Until I was in my twenties, I thought classical music was *The Warsaw Concerto*. Know what that is? It's movie music. While you were a child prodigy practicing all day, I was going to the movies and working in a grocery store. I had a lot of catching up to do."

When Marie dumped him she spent a good hour reminding him of his culturally deprived youth. She sat at her kitchen table, leaned her chin on folded hands, quite as if talking about groceries or sharing departmental gossip, and gave him back the confided secrets, putting the knife in as only an ex-lover knows how and just where to put it.

"So you were a fat child and an orphan and your mother was a drunk," she said in a reasonable, measured social worker voice. "And here you are. You have survived. It's time to stop playing the orphan card."

He silently thanked himself for not telling her about Vivian and April. What Marie would have done with *that*.

MARIE QUIT ZWINGLI after the kitchen analysis. She had begun to develop some new avenues of criticism. She began to get around. He sometimes ran into her name in literary and art magazines. Then she was in a Sunday newspaper feature article. She was out of the mouse race and now moved with confidence in the big world. She was an important critic.

IF HE HOPED to get off the mouse track and out of this career prison, he had to establish some credentials. It was late, almost grotesquely late, but he had to win a prize. To win a prize, he had to apply and be accepted in a competition. Winners of prizes got grants. Grant-winners got artist-in-residence posts, concert tours, recording contracts. They did not have to teach at Zwingli. He decided to break the long silence and write to Trevor.

> *August 15, 1979*
> *Dear Gil:*
>
> I have tried to keep up with your career but to no avail. I'm glad we are back in touch. There *are* worse places than Zwingli. Tecumseh is sinking slowly.
>
> I will do all I can, of course, to support your application for the Goldenweiser. Competition will be stiff. I think Aranov's star pupil, Hildy Cohen, will be entering. Remember what I always harped on: no stiff wrist, flexible fingers always!
>
> Win or lose, Gil, finally it makes no differ-

ence as long as you do your utmost. My own career, as it is, is quiescent. I have only a few students in composition and a couple of those large bastardizations – half "appreciation" and half pop history.

I was in Chicago recently and met April for lunch. She seems to keep well. In my real life I am making plans. Miriam, a woman (girl, I admit with rue!) was my student last year. There was, despite the age difference, a mutual attraction. I kept my distance while she was under my tutelage. What a stiff-necked pedant I seem to be! We plan to get married.

At my age I should be deep in disillusion – the recent shame in Washington is a symptom of a deep, cynical world sickness. A more minor though closer to home symptom: a new metal "sculpture" in the city hall square here. Everytime I go downtown I have to pass it. Resolutely ugly, it seems to be trying to offend and depress. But the human spirit is tough. Look at me, an old duffer about to embark on matrimony again!

Good luck in the Goldenweiser and in your life!

As ever,
Trevor

THE ONLY TIME Gil's doorbell rang it was somebody with a commercial proposal: did he want the newspaper delivered, did he want distilled water in a cooler, did he want to join the free pizza a month for every four bought? When the phone rang it was somebody who mispronounced his name to offer carpet cleaning or a free diamond (hidden in a cluster of diamonds one had to purchase in order to get the free one).

He felt that his loneliness was only skin deep. There were always flies in the apartment corridor near the trash chute door. A constant procession of studious looking Asians kept moving in and out of the building. A confused odour of curry and soy sauce and cabbage hung in the corridors. He tried to spend as little time in his apartment as possible. He spent long hours in the practice room at the college. Maybe he had a decent shot at the Goldenweiser. And he had picked up where he had abandoned his senior composition project. *Stephen Foster Muzaked.* Trevor would not like it, but John Cage certainly would. Gil thought of scoring for squeezed balloons (dry-finger rubbed, recorded and taped and played back) but shelved the idea for the time being. If he didn't want to fall flat on his face in the competition, he had his work cut out for him.

THE AIR WAS DRY and thin and full of flowers. Gil was so used to Ontario flatness and damp heat and sinus trouble that his imagination could not quite comprehend the possibility of anything else. As a result he moved in the California landscape spiritually hunched over, ready to flee if it were all suddenly yanked away by a giant hand, revealing the only real world (flat fields, rain, cornfields standing in dank air, summer heat that hurt, winters which bent the spirit.

IN THE FOLLOWING DAYS, he spent long hours in the practice room. You have to get inside him. Whoever you want to play. That's what Herrick had said. Inside, so his skin doesn't feel loose on you. Then what you do will be natural. It will seem effortless. The key word, Trevor had said, is *seem*.

Satie. A man who wrote a spoof biography that ended, *I have always smoked. My doctor says to me Smoke my friend! for if you do not, someone else will.*

A man who took an armadillo for a walk on a leash in a Paris park. Who was the man hiding behind the joking? There was a strain of seriousness, of dignity in the face of adversity, despair kept at arm's-length. A brave smile in the face of carnage, determined jocosity as survival procedure.

THE GOLDENWEISER COMPETITION that year was held in a heavily endowed artist's colony near Los Angeles. Built in the Santa Monica mountains in 1907 by the widow of a minor composer who died young (consumption), the place was a wild mélange of styles: early Frank Lloyd Wright, Spanish Mission, Norman Cottage, Art Nouveau and Big Cottage. A swimming pool had been added in the Twenties and an outdoor amphitheatre in the Thirties.

The contestants (six men and six women) were housed in individual "cabanas" (modeled on Thoreau's cabin at Walden Pond, a calculated piece of environmental-artistic inspiration) but meals were communal, in the Long House (Beowulf Style).

"I'm Hildy Cohen," said the girl across the table from him.

She had the kind of red hair one associates with the Irish, and the kind of skin that goes with it. Her eyes were a startling green. Gil's first reaction was a jumping urge of attraction, sexual and romantic. His second was a coldly critical warning, like a sobering hand pressing down an erection: *This girl could be trouble. She could psych you out.*

"You used to study with Herrick, didn't you," she said. "Anton – my teacher – is a good friend of his."

Her smile could melt steel. To hell with prudence. Gil smiled back.

"What are you planning?" she asked.

Bad form or disingenuous? This was Gil's first competition, but he knew a few of the unwritten rules. You weren't supposed to ask an opponent for advance information. Gave too much opportunity to play program games. Offset a romantic piece with strict classicism – that is, if one were at all certain about the judge's taste.

"I'm still deciding," he said. "Got it narrowed down to a few –"

"I'm doing Bach," she said. "*Two and Three Part Inventions.*"

"Oh," he said. "Fine."

It was an audacious choice. The comparison with Gould would be inescapable. Could work against her. Or for her.

She smiled. Gil felt that he could dive right into her eyes, dive in and sink down. Down and down.

THE JUDGES: Thomas Inch, (1930-) legendary martinet, one of the first of his generation to concertize in China, now browbeating students at a conservatory in Pennsylvania. Steven Berova (1918-) fled from his native Hungary in the Fifties, long a pet of the New York scene, a flamboyant performer, who once premiered a new work in the sewers of that city. And Karen Swede (various dates given) thin of chest, tall and imperial in bearing, could have been a great dominatrix if her musical career waned. None of them took bullshit, none was approachable.

Gil decided on Satie's *Nocturnes* and *Gnossiennes*. A calculated choice. Modern, but early modern. Might appeal to Berova. Inch was reputed to be anti-modern, but perhaps it was really anti-postmodern. About Swede's personal penchant he could find nothing.

THE CONTESTANTS met in a common room to meet the judges. There was a little bit of in-gossip exchanged, some name-dropping, and then they got down to the real thing. First matter to settle was the order in which they would perform. A very crucial process. It was bad to be first, because you could be forgotten as others played, and each new splendid display put your own worth further and further out of consideration.

But it was equally unlucky to be last, because by the time the judges listened to you they were probably overloaded with listening and jaded. Where was the best place to be?

It was hot. Gil suspected that it was warmer than usual here, high in the mountains. Everywhere else in the civilized world it was winter. Old men suffered heart attacks, fell on the sidewalks in front of their houses trying to shovel snow. Here palm trees spread green fronds carelessly, bushes bloomed, flowers were heedless and shamelessly in bloom.

There was air conditioning in the main dining hall and in the practice rooms, but none in the cabins. Gil gulped the thin air as he walked out of the dining hall haven and across the long lawn to this room. The swimming pool glistened in refracted light, blue, innocent and unused. It was skimmed and vacuumed daily.

He felt a furtive, skipping school excitement as he stepped into the shallow end. Did he imagine it, or could he actually hear the faint sounds of many pianos being played? The practice rooms, of course, were soundproofed. Was there any pleasure to match being the first to break the calm surface of a swimming pool? The sunlight broke into wavy lines on the bottom. Then someone bright and flamelike plunged across his path in a shower of froth.

Hildy surfaced right in his path. She wore no bathing cap. Her hair seemed to be on fire.

"You're escaping too," she laughed.

Gil realized that her eyes were the same brilliant color as Vivian's. As April's. Hildy turned and began a swift crawl to the deep end. He wallowed in her wake, a what-the-hell impetuous spring of something inside him. It was like some tautly wound-up thing expanding or breaking. Let it happen, he thought.

"You've been working too hard," she said. "You're too pale."

"I tend to get burned," he said. "Should live in a cave, I guess."

"So do I," she laughed. "Get sunburned I mean."

They said nothing for a few uncomfortable moments. The sunlight was at a painful, eye-aching angle. Gil squinted at the horizon and turned to look at Hildy. She was awash in light.

Gil was right square in the middle of the order, right before Aaron Klein. Hildy was to be last. Poor dear, Gil thought. It was safest in the middle.

The first three – all from Julliard, all disgustingly young – put on a collective blast of pyrotechnics, big, bold, full of bravura. Gil's performance was a study in contrast. He worked the Satie for all its hidden irony, brought out the shy and haunting poignance. His approach was deliberate, controlled, giving the impression of more, oh, much more, leashed in, pent up, aching to be released. What he strove for was mature. He achieved it.

As Hildy walked to the piano, Gil felt a wild leap of his heart. She was breathtaking, fragile, fleeting. Her bow to the audience (they, he thought, gasped simultaneously with him) was graceful and swift as birdflight.

She sat poised on the bench for a caughtbreath moment and began. From the first note Gil felt wonder and terror. There was a firmness, a rigorous control which betokened an inescapable and evident genius. There was nothing to hide behind. Her choice, he realized, or Aranov's, was perfect. The starkness, the sturdy bone-hard simplicity, was set out for all to appreciate for its own bare beauty.

Gil saw his own efforts as cheap and tawdry in contrast. He felt as if the floor under his seat were giving way to drop him out of the hall, out of the competition where he had no business being, out of Hildy's life and great career which loomed ahead.

Mingled with a growing sense of shame and self-pity was an even deeper sense of loss. Hildy was, note by note, putting herself further and further out of his reach. Her world was going to be the big world, the important place, where important people moved secure in their right to be there. Hildy belonged there. Each certain breathtakingly right note was proving it.

Each note moving her steadily and inexorably away from him. Gil, too late and not enough again. He glanced furtively down the row at the rapt faces. They all knew it too. He sank deeper in his seat and in his misery.

NOTES TAKEN BY THOMAS INCH:
Cohen: impeccable balance internal choirs. instrumental fabric transparent rich tones – phrasing: subtle yet dynamic-scale is broad. *superb.*

Welles: clear, logical, forceful restrained bravado no warmth Where is pathos? Little tension. No illumination.

HILDY WON. Gil, to his surprise, came in third. O'Neil was second. That was okay for O'Neil. She was just starting her career. Second in the Goldenweiser was respectable. She had lots of time for the first place in other venues. But Gil knew that third place at his age was not good enough. This competition had been an almost last chance to break out of his world of also-rans. Break out or in. To move on. To move up.

Oh, there would be other competitions, but none quite as prestigious as the Goldenweiser. If he were younger, third place would be satisfactory. For him, here and now, it was like a prison sentence.

And then there was the dour thought that Hildy had won first prize. If only *she* had not been the one to beat him – it was a mean-spirited thought, but icily realistic.

SOME NINE YEARS AFTER the Goldenweiser, Gil ran into Aaron Klein at a conference. Klein had done well. He was in residence at the George Institute in upstate New York and had won a Grammy. Klein still retained his brash air of arrogant self-confidence.

"Welles," he said. "Let's have a drink."

A temporary bar had been set up in the foyer of the school's auditorium. They carried their plastic glasses over to a leather-covered bench. Klein had been on a panel and carried a briefcase full of papers. He looked as if he needed an early afternoon shave.

"How has life been?" said Klein. "Since the competition I mean –"

"Oh, okay," Gil said vaguely. "To tell the truth, that was about the most important competition I was ever in. I know how well you've done since."

"Yeah, well," said Klein, frowning at his drink. "It took me a long time to get over that fiasco. Sort of an initiation thing."

"Well, you were pretty young," said Gil.

"I resented you for a long time," said Klein.

"Me?" said Gil. "But all I got was…."

"Was I naive," Klein sighed. "Inch invited me to dinner. I thought that was strange. Judges weren't supposed to consort with the contestants. Anyhow, he came on to me…."

"Inch?" said Gil.

"Was I *dumb*," said Klein. "I didn't react – I didn't know what the hell was going on. He got angry and called me a little flirt. He'd make sure I got bubkes, *nothing*, in the competition. He personally would see me humiliated…."

"But I thought maybe the other judges would outvote him, that I'd get at least the silver or bronze," he went on. "That's when I got all paranoid about you. Why did he pick you for the third? What was the secret message?"

"Maybe it simply meant I won the third," said Gil. But the sour question stirred in him like a bad meal. Even this pitiful third-place prize was questionable, tainted. He and Klein talked a bit more, exchanged anecdotes about the other contestants.

"What about Hildy Cohen?" Gil asked casually. "Never hear anything about her."

"I think she died in a plane crash," said Klein. "About two, three years ago. Or maybe it was some disease," he went on. "Maybe MS. Something like that."

Or maybe, Gil thought as they made the ritual insincere gestures of camaraderie that two people who have nothing or little in common make, maybe all this information is wrong. Hildy was alive and well somewhere in the world.

A comforting thought, grasped at and held.

GIL HAD KEPT UP with Hildy's career for a few years after the competition. Spoleto, the Berkshire, won (twice) the Aspen, studied at the prestigious *Hochschule für Muzik und Darstelle Kunst*. Then her name sank in the wave of newer names. There was, for instance, the brash duo piano team that everyone knew as the "Julliard Brats." And O'Neil came into her own, with a strong showing in the Tchaikovsky. What had happened to Hildy?

"ARANOV," said the voice. Gil paused, expecting an answering machine message. But no, it was the man himself.

"Professor Aranov, my name is Welles. Gilbert Welles?" said Gil. "I'm calling about one of your former pupils. Hildy Cohen? I met her in a competition…."

"Yes, yes," came the voice, deep, histrionic, with Slavic flourishes.

"I know of you Mr. Wales. You were once with Trevor Herrick, yes? But what do you want to know of Hildy?"

"Well we haven't been in touch for years," said Gil. "And someone told me that she had been ill…."

"Ill? Hildy? How can this be? Who is this person who tells you –"

"Well, that's not important," Gil said in a hurry. "What I wondered is, do you have a current address for her…."

"She is in Switzerland," said Aranov. "She has lived there for some time now. With her husband. She has two children. The boy is named after me."

"Ah, then she is not ill," said Gil. "I am happy to hear that."

"Where did you hear such things?" Aranov said.

"Someone with a lot of misinformation," said Gil. "I am happy to hear that she is well and not sick and she's happy. That is the main thing. She is happy. She deserves to be happy."

"Yes," said Aranov. "She does."

After he hung up, Gil sat staring at the phone in its

cradle. So she had not died in a plane crash. And she did not have a terminal illness. If she did have one, it was kept a secret from Aranov. Gil was glad and relieved and disappointed. She was further away now than ever.

six

Home from the Hill

THEY WOKE UP TO RAIN IN THE MORNING. It looked like an important storm, a major storm. Long sheets of blown rain came from several directions at once. A dirty greenish light permeated everywhere. It was impossible to see the lake. Water ran down the glassed-in area. A leak sprung and Miriam put a wastebasket under it. A trap drum rat-tat of water sounded frantic in the wastebasket. Gil looked up through the glass roof at a rain gutter which was full and overflowing. He looked down at water foaming out of the downspout.

Wind pulled at the house, trying to wrench the roof off, tear and hurl the house itself down the slope and into the lake. It was ten in the morning and they had all the lights on. The bulbs flickered. Power lines were evidently in peril.

By noon the wind died down but the rain fell just as

hard. Every time the lights flickered Gil thought uh oh. He feared the loss of light. Clocks would stop, no cooking could be done, radios would not work.

They all sat under the glass roof, which was crazed with falling water. Ned glowered sourly at April and Miriam, who were sitting across from him.

"Rain, rain, go away," he said in a low voice. "Well, sweetie. What's happening in Chicago lately? See a man there dance with his wife? On State Street, that great street?"

Ned's eyes hurt. He was in the midst of a hangover. Christ, he thought, what I wouldn't give for a Bloody Mary. But he would not demean himself and ask Miriam. No siree.

"Nobody dances in Chicago," April said. "Only happens in songs."

"How about the boyfriend? Does he dance with his wife?" said Ned. He felt mean-spirited.

"He's divorced," said April. "Maybe he dances with his new wife. I wouldn't know."

"Aha," said Ned, wagging a triumphant finger. "I knew there was another wife in the wings. Not you. Younger woman, right? You are a born victim."

"I suppose that's why I like country music," said April. "It's all about second chances."

"Born fucking loser," mumbled Ned. "First with the simp here…."

"Why not lighten up, Ned?" said Miriam.

"Why not mind your own business?" said Ned. "This is a family discussion."

"You're the expert on family," said April. "Aren't you?"

Ned did not answer, stared straight ahead into the glass wall, which blurred the trees and bushes into masses of undefined shape.

"Aren't you?" said April.

"You too, April," said Miriam. "God save me from happy families."

"This used to be a happy family," said Ned. "Until the outsiders invaded…."

"I'm glad of one thing," said Miriam, lighting a cigarette. "Damn. Will you look at this? I haven't smoked in five years. Maybe now I can lose weight. I'm glad I never had any children. If I'd had any like you two, I would have strangled them at birth."

"Think I'll see what we might have for lunch," she said, getting up. "I think there's some leftover roast."

After she went into the kitchen, nobody said anything for a minute or two. There was no sound but the insistent rain on the roof, the now slower drip of the leak in the wastebasket and a gurgling from the downspout near the door.

"So Mr. Wonderful dumped you," said Ned. "Would it help at all for me to tell you I knew he would? *Any*body would have known. Somebody who won't leave his wife for – what – ten, fifteen years? Isn't going to suddenly make it all up to the little bit of fluff he's kept on the side. Because she's suddenly ten or fifteen years older than she was when he first noticed her," said Ned.

"Why not let her alone?" said Gil.

Ned swung his head around to face Gil, as if he had just now realized that Gil was in the room, in the world.

"Well, well," said Ned. "The voice of chivalry. Where were you, oh, shining cavalier, back when she needed you? When she was in grief and had her innocence ripped off by you and you dropped her like a good habit?"

"Maybe I can help Miriam," said Gil, getting up. He felt hemmed in, cooped up, threatened. Ned's anguish was being flung in all directions, hitting April, then Gil.

The lights flickered and went out.

"Great," Miriam said. "No electricity and little Ned carrying on."

"People grieve in different ways," Gil said, making futile gestures towards the counters. "Anything I can do to help?"

"Not really," said Miriam. "Unless you can make Bloody Marys. I think we all could use one."

"Right on," said Gil, opening the freezer compartment. "Won't everything in here spoil?"

"There isn't much in there," said Miriam. "Except ice. Last few weeks it's been takeout and delivered. Ned always did stuff to extremes. It was tough enough marrying into this family. All that sad history. And then Ned acting like Hamlet's brother…."

"Did Trevor ever say much about the past?" said Gil. "I mean about when Vivian died."

He kept his head bent over the drinks, measuring out the vodka.

"No," said Miriam. "I didn't want to know all that much anyhow. But from what he *did* say, I got the impression she was not a serene person."

"Not hardly," said Gil. "Say, did I just quote John Wayne?"

He laughed.

"I suppose she had these intense love affairs," said Miriam.

"I suppose you were one of them," she said and quickly went on. "Don't worry. I'm not asking. I don't want to know."

"Did Trevor..." Gil began.

"He didn't," said Miriam. "It wasn't in his nature to suspect people. Especially the ones he loved. He had this immense blind spot for his children, for instance. Unless he was lying to himself all the time. Which I don't think he was."

"April," she called to the other room. "There are some candles in that washstand. The one with the marble top?"

She turned back to Gil.

"Now you carry the drinks and I'll bring the sandwiches, okay?"

"Ah, the funeral-baked meats," said Ned as they carried the trays out to the porch.

"And drinks," said Miriam. "I don't think it's too early."

"It's almost too damned late," said Ned, raising a theatrically shaky hand out to take his drink, waving the sandwich away.

"What kind of Jap wheels have you got?" Ned said to April.

"It's a Ford Tempo," said April. "Probably made right here."

"Ah, patriotism," said Ned, making a snorting noise as he bent to his drink. "The last refuge of something."

"Trevor loved to sit out here," Miriam sighed. "He liked to watch the lake. It keeps changing. The light, the weather, and the boats. He'd sit out here for hours, listening to music. Mostly string quartets. The late Beethoven. Dvořák. Nothing too modern. He said his happiest memories were all mixed up with this place. Summers when he was a child. Then his own children and then with me…."

"Oh," sneered Ned. "Happy, *happy* families are all…."

"He regretted not having grandchildren," said Miriam.

Ned said nothing more.

April thought, *will this day ever end?* Would the roads wash out? Ned lurched to his feet and went out to the kitchen to make another drink.

"Jesus," said Miriam in a low voice. "I've got plenty of booze on hand. I hope the ice holds out. Maybe he'll pass out."

"I doubt it," said April. "He's developed a big capacity."

"Gil took the L.A.-S.F. test once," said Ned, weaving his way back to his seat. "And you know what his answer was? *San Pedro.*"

"I gave a recital there once," said Gil. "Nice place, really. Surprising place."

"What's the L.A.-S.F. test?" said Miriam.

"It's your personal choice of the two cities," said

April. "It's supposed to typecast you right away. But I think all it proves is that there are Northerners and Southerners everywhere."

"And what do you do with yourself," said Ned to April. "Now that your gentleman caller has left?"

"I have a VCR," said April quietly. "I've got a pretty good library of old movies. *It's a Wonderful Life, Casablanca, Algiers* – that sort of thing."

"Romance," said Ned. "Romance. A black-and-white world and what is your opinion of colourization," he said, swinging to Gil. "Candidly, I mean. Aesthetically."

"I don't think about it," said Gil. Was there no escape from this man?

"Remember Jack Benny's routine on *Algiers?*" said Ned. "No, no, not you girls. You're too young. But Welles here, he'd remember...."

"I remember," Gil smiled. "Puppy le Moko. He's dead, isn't he?"

"Dead? Pepi le Moko?" said Ned.

"No, no, Jack Benny," said Gil.

"I hope so," said Ned. "They buried him. When I go, I want to be buried in some place. I don't know about this scattering business...some definite place."

"Why?" said April. "So people can visit your grave? Who would do that? *I* wouldn't. Do you visit graves? Vivian's?"

"Don't," said Ned in a warning tone. "Don't push your luck, kiddo."

"I wonder if your father had some kind of joke in mind when he left this place to you two," said Miriam.

"Thing is that the way it's set up, you can't sell it. Until one of you dies."

"All these treasures," Ned gestured vaguely.

After Trevor married Miriam, he discovered a pack-rat hitherto unexpressed in his being. They spent most Saturday mornings out at garage and yard sales, estate auctions and junk shops. Trevor had sold Vivian's modern art after her death. Later, when he retired, he sold most of the furniture in the Windsor house.

Refurnishing the cottage became a symbolic act for him and Miriam. They found the entrance hall bench in a country school about to be torn down. A commercial butcher's block from a demolished hotel stood in the center of the kitchen. Bits of architectural detail from wrecked buildings were here and there. There was no sense of calculation, of a decorator working with a theme in mind. The place was a happy clutter, a carefree helter-skelter mess.

"All of mother's art," said Ned. "Gone with the fucking wind."

"He didn't much like – trust – modern art," said Miriam. "He used to say that there was probably one man, a critic in New York who was saying what was in, what was out, and making a fortune."

"Same with the stock market," she went on. "He said there was somebody in Hong Kong pulling strings and all the stock market puppets danced. Most of the family business money went into real estate."

"Funny for a modern composer to be so down on modernism," said Ned.

"I guess he was a classical modernist," said Gil. "Not a postmodernist."

"He used to sit out here," said Miriam. "And read. He liked to sink into a big work. Proust. Then all of Thoreau. In between the really big projects, he'd read a smaller big book – Mann. *Magic Mountain*. Like that."

April, sitting next to Miriam, could see the tears on her cheeks.

The lights and radio went on. April and Gil made noises of relief. The radio was playing some contemporary piece. A big chorus sang exultantly. A wordless chant rose above triumphant horns, a pulsing rhythm behind and under the voices carried the music up and up. Then the voices ebbed down, down to a chorus of whispers, soothing and reassuring.

The rain had stopped. Lightning flashed out on the horizon across the lake. Gil could see a large toad sitting on the grass just outside the back door. He was as impassive and green as the grass. He looked disinclined to move.

"And the afternoon, the evening," Ned mumbled, his eyes shut. "Sleeps so peacefully...."

"I have this great idea," said April. "Why don't I fix dinner? A special dinner. I'll do it all. I think maybe we deserve it...."

"I'll help," said Gil eagerly. "I'll be the *sous-chef*. I'm not too bad in the kitchen."

"Gilbert Welles in the life of Uriah Heep," said Ned in a loud voice. "Best biopic of the year. Always a bridesmaid. Left at the altar. The joys of coming in always second. Or last. Assistant to the chief chef. Second banana."

"Listen," said Miriam to April. "What I said to you earlier. About strangling you in the crib. I didn't mean it."

"I know," said April in a quiet tone. "I know."

"Let's all get down and hug the *shit* out of each other," said Ned. "Look at em. Niobe all in tears…."

"I think," said April, getting up slowly and deliberately, "that I am going to go into town for a few groceries. I will not be long."

"I'm going with you," Gil said firmly. "If I don't, somebody is going to be killed."

Miriam followed them to the door.

"Don't hurry," she said in a low voice. "He might pass out – which would be a good thing for all of us."

"My god," said April as they walked across the soggy gravel in the driveway. "Doesn't the air smell fresh? It's so good to get outside."

Her hand shook as she unlocked the car door. Gil felt a maudlin surge of pity for her.

"It's a nice car," he said as he buckled his seat belt. "My first car was a Ford. Best car I ever had."

"What are you driving now?" said April.

"I had a K Car until last winter. It died on me. Cost more than it was worth to fix."

"I trust this car," said April. "More than I trust most people. If I take care of my car – the routine check ups and all – it doesn't let me down."

Nobody said anything for a while. April switched

the headlights on. The roadside ditches were swollen full of water.

"I don't know how to say this," said Gil. "But I didn't know about your – about the man you were…."

"Yeah," said April, staring straight ahead. "Well, nobody's to blame. Except me. I should have known better. Anybody with any sense could see the situation was deadend. But when did I ever have any sense? But I'm not writing myself off. I still have hope for myself."

"What is it you do now?" said Gil. "I suppose I should know, but lately my memory is a sieve."

"I left Browne's two years ago," said April. "Went into business for myself. With a friend. We have our own travel agency. Doing okay."

In the half-empty supermarket, April moved slowly, as if half asleep. Gil moved awkwardly next to her, bumping into the shelves or the cart, fell behind, made helpless gestures of assistance.

"I do this pretty fair dish," said April, "with chicken and tarragon and rice. I wonder if they have wild rice. "Or we could do beef braciole. I don't have much of a chance to do gourmet cooking."

"I know," said Gil. "Cooking for one. I eat out a lot or do frozen dinners. Some of them are not bad at all."

"No deboned chicken," said April, peering down at the packages. "Life is hard."

"I wonder if Miriam needs anything else," said April as they unloaded the cart at the checkout. "I forgot to ask."

After they put the bags in the trunk, April sat at the

wheel for a moment without turning the ignition key. Then she began to cry. She shook with sobs, put her head against the wheel. Gil patted her shoulder, tried to put his arm around her, said there, there.

"I'm sorry," she said, turning to him, her face swollen with tears. "I haven't been able to cry. I don't know why."

"It's not just for my father," she went on. "It's my brother. He's become such an asshole. He used to be such a sweet boy. You didn't know him then."

"Well," said Gil grimly. "I never saw that side of him."

"He was jealous of you," said April. "Because Daddy thought of you as a kind of son or crown prince. And then Ned thought you were messing around with me."

She stopped, stared out at the almost empty parking lot. "How wrong he was," she said. "And it's something I can never tell him."

"I wish we didn't have to go back there," said Gil. "That place is full of ghosts. I wish we could drive away from here and go someplace else."

"Hope springs eternal in your peterpan breast," sighed April. "We'd better get back. Before Miriam kills Ned."

The wind was rising and shaking water off the over-hung trees and onto the road. The sky was ominously heavy.

"It could rain some more," April said, fiddling with the radio dial.

"Lucky there isn't a basement to flood," she said. "Look, I'm sorry about what just happened. Delayed grief, I guess. Suppose there'll be more."

"God.'" she said with a shaky laugh. "What a family scene. I keep wondering: are other families different? I used to daydream when I was in boarding school that one of my friend's parents would adopt me and everything would be so damned *perfect*."

After a moment she asked. "Did you have a happy childhood?"

"I don't know," Gil said. "I have these specific happy memories. Going out with my parents to bring home chop suey. Every Friday. Waiting for it and me holding the brown bag on my lap in the car. The smell of hot brown paper and soy sauce. Some vacations. Sunday drives in the country. Some specific moments from vacations. There was a lot of unhappy stuff too. My father died when I was young. My mother was an alcoholic. If only we could have been ethnicky or rich. Either extreme."

"My father was Welsh," he went on. "But he didn't work in a coal mine and I don't remember him singing. You know why I'm named Gilbert? It's not a family name or anything. There was this cute kid down the block named Gilbert. So my mother named me after a cute kid I've never even met."

He shook his head.

"Named for a kid I never met," he said. "Middle class. What inventiveness. The thing about being born early in the year – at least for me – is that I always begin to think I'm that age right after New Year's Day. So I've got an extra three months when I feel a year older. It always comes to me on my birthday that, hey, I really haven't been that age. *Somebody* owes me a lot of time to pay back."

They turned into the road leading to the lake. There was no moon. The headlights lit up the edges of the road. Dark wet fields spread out beyond the light.

"I hope your brother has passed out by now," Gil said.

"He has these enormous recuperative powers," April said. "He'll go from complete falling-down drunk to mean sober – just like that."

She cut the engine and turned off the lights. They could hear voices coming from the house. The kitchen windows were open. The voices sounded normal and everyday. They went in, set the bags down on the counter. April said, *well,* to announce a task completed. Gil began to unpack the bags.

Ned and Miriam were sitting at the kitchen table. Ned was drinking coffee. But there was a brandy bottle standing near his cup.

"The eternal return," he said. "Say, sis, do you believe that rock and roll is here to stay? It will never fade away? Buddy Holly and all that? Or is that country music? Isn't there something called cow punk? Please, oh please, define your tastes for me."

"Eclectic," said April, taking off her raincoat. "I forgot to ask you if you needed anything. So I got some coffee and bread."

"Yes," April said, "I've found Roy Orbison. I know he was around when I was young. But back then it was just the Beach Boys for me."

"Not the Iron Butterfly?" said Ned, an ironical eyebrow raised.

"Doesn't he do great eyebrow?" said Miriam.

"It's *give* great eyebrow," said Ned.

He looked terrible. His face was puffy, his eyes sunk in, dead, red-rimmed. His mouth drooped.

"I decided on the beef," said April. "No deboned chicken."

"Hell," said Gil. "I didn't know that's why you didn't get the chicken. I could have done the deboning."

"The beef will be fine," said Miriam. "What can I do to help?"

Miriam got up from the table. The necessary motions of getting dinner lifted their spirits. Gil began slicing shallots. Then he peeled and minced four garlic buds. He began to whistle softly. He enjoyed performing these simple menial tasks. Maybe he should have stayed at the factory. He'd be retired by now. Thirty and out. Living in a trailer park in Florida. Wearing a cap with the name of a team on it.

April took his choppings and mixed them with sausage. "Do you brown the sausage?" Miriam asked.

"Some recipes call for it," said April. "But the one that I follow doesn't."

There was something so normal, so mundane and everyday, about the sound of women's voices in the kitchen that Gil found it comforting. It was reassuring, like a mother crooning to a child. He felt a contentment welling up in him. It was something he could not voice. They would perhaps resent it, call it chauvinism.

Woman's place in kitchen. Except that he wanted to be there too, in perpetual reassurance. He wanted to be forever in the country of everyday.

"There," April said, shutting the oven door. "It bakes in the wine sauce for an hour. Or until tender. I never could figure out how you'd find out if it's tender without screwing the whole thing up."

"So we put the rice on in about forty minutes?" said Miriam. "Gil, would you uncork the wine? I always seem to break up the cork. That's why I try to buy wine with screw caps."

Gil bent to his task, holding the bottle between his knees, wrenching away as if strangling a chicken.

Ned waved the wine away. He was sticking with the brandy for the time being.

"Anybody want to watch the news?" Miriam gestured at the TV.

"The news is always bad," said Ned. "And it's always the same. Isn't there a game show on? Something where people get lucky and jump up and down?"

"It's a bit too early for the game shows," Miriam said.

"Look," she said to Gil, "I don't know how soon you have to leave. But I could stick around for a few days to help you get started on the archives. The correspondence alone is kind of overwhelming. There are about six big cardboard boxes. Letters from everybody who was anybody in music. Roger Sessions, Copland, Glass. And then there's other stuff – all the music – the scores...."

"Scores?" said Gil. "You mean new work? I thought

he stopped a long time ago."

"No," said Miriam. "He never stopped composing. He just gave up trying to get anybody to hear it. There's a concerto. Complete. Finished. And part of a symphony. Lots of work for solo piano."

Gil felt a surge of excitement. Instead of a dull, meaningless, routine task, something major and exciting might lie ahead. A retrospective. Articles. Maybe a biography.

April and Ned sat in silence. Ned felt a dull resentment. Why hadn't his father told him he was still working, still creating?

April felt happy. So he hadn't spent all that time brooding, sunk in despair. He had gotten through his grief and gone on with his life. *There is work*, he had once quoted to her, *and there is love.*

"I have to go back to finish the term," said Gil. "And then I better see about finding an apartment in Windsor. I can probably get out of my lease. Toronto real estate is hard to find and really easy to turn over."

"My neighbourhood is in the process of being gentrified," said Ned. "Armies of rubbies and bums being turned out so the yuppies can renovate the rooming houses. No wonder there are so many homeless people. They've made room for the young professionals. More fern bars. More futon shops. More frozen yogurt."

"I better put the rice on," said Miriam. "Help yourselves to more wine."

Gil turned to look at April. There was a half smile on her face.

"Say," Ned said to Gil. "Weren't you involved with a woman, Marie something? I met her at this arts conference. Strange lady. *Strange.* Said she used to teach at Zwingli. So I asked in my discreet way if she knew you in all senses. And she let on in a coy, girlish way that you two had been an item."

"How could you?" he went on. "She looked like a Czech female athlete. All stringy muscles in her neck. She looked *mean.* Like a cheap motel towel."

"It was a long time ago," Gil said. "I hear she's changed a lot."

His voice sounded apologetic. Damn it, he thought. Why do I feel I have to justify myself to this ass? Or perhaps to April, whom he carefully was not looking at. Or, indeed, to anybody at all.

"It was a dumb thing, a fiasco," he went on. His voice still sounded apologetic.

"You like that word, fiasco," said April. "Funny. Ned uses it a lot too. So you have at least one thing in common."

She laughed. She laughed so hard that she doubled over in her chair. Ned stared angrily at nothing in particular.

"Who has what in common?" said Miriam, coming into the room with a bowl of peanuts. "They're dry-roasted."

April could not answer. She was still laughing too hard. Ned and Gil said nothing.

"Well," Miriam sighed. "I wish you'd let me in on the joke. I could use a laugh about this time of my life."

The dinner was excellent. Gil realized how hungry he was and how frazzled. They all must be, he thought. Miriam's skin looked like stretched thin paper that had suddenly sagged. There were dark bruise-like hollows under April's eyes. Even Ned had shut up and was eating.

"What part of Chicago do you live in?" Gil asked. His voice sounded too loud in his ears. Why had he broken the blessed silence? There was a minute pause.

"Oh," said April. "the North Side. What they call Near North."

"I know that area," said Gil eagerly. "It's up off Sheridan Road. Right near a big cemetery."

"It's a big arty cemetery area," said Ned. "That right?"

"Close," said April without looking up. "You're close."

"This is very good," Miriam said. "I haven't done any serious cooking for a long time. Since Trevor began to...."

"Anyhow," she said firmly, prodding at the plate with her fork, "this was a good idea. I think we all needed it."

"Yes," Gil said. "Yes."

"Would a toast be in order?" said Ned. "No. Not really. Not good form. Some other time. Maybe when I come back down here. Maybe this summer. It *is* about halfway between Chicago and Toronto."

He looked across at April. She looked up.

"Yes," she said. "It is that. About halfway for both of us."

"Let me help you clear," Gil said to Miriam.

"Well kiddie," said Ned. "You do know how to cook. First rate."

"Thank you," said April with a slight and modest incline of the head.

"You'd make some man a good wifey," said Ned. "Too bad. *Too* bad. All that goodhousekeeping talent down the drain."

"Maybe it was that play nurse's kit you gave me when I was little," said April. "Stereotyped me forever. Now I'll never be a neurosurgeon."

"Do you think it's true what they say about nurses?" said Ned, "No. If you had become a nurse, at least you'd be contributing something useful to society. *Something.* To society, I mean. I mean, who *needs* another travel agency? By the way *is* your partner a lez? Are you so to speak changing your luck in your mature years?"

"Peyton is heterosexual," said April in a tight voice.

"Why not lighten up?" said Gil in a low voice.

"Welles," Ned sighed. "Please, *please* fuck off? It's my duty as the older sibling to watch out for my sister's welfare. To warn her about pricks like her old lover. And you."

"Gil hasn't killed anybody," said Miriam in a quiet tone. "How does it feel to have murdered your unborn child? How did you do it, anyhow? Kick Heather in the belly?"

Ned's face was stiff and pale.

"You can dish it out okay," said Miriam. "But can you take it?"

"It's something I have to live with," said Ned. "All the time."

"Do you ever see Heather?" said April.

"Oh she's alive and well and living in Toronto. About two subway stops away from me. She won't talk to me. She said if I kept bothering her she'd get a court order."

"Well," said Miriam, getting up, gathering and stacking plates. "The end of the Herrick line, eh?"

"How come you didn't have a baby?" said Ned. "You have – well, *had*, a kind of child-bearing look. I tell you I feared some snotty half-brothers."

"Trevor didn't want any," said Miriam in a flat tone. "Said it wouldn't be fair to leave children fatherless."

"I sometimes wonder how it feels to have children," said Gil, He was hoping to divert the conversation into more general and safe waters.

"I think I have a child somewhere," said Ned. "One of those things that happened. A girl – woman – anyway, we were involved and she got pregnant."

"I think she did it on purpose," he said, drawing faint designs in the tablecloth with his fork. "This was one independent woman. Said she did not believe in killing babies."

"The kid would be about sixteen now," he said softly. "Out there in the world some place."

In Ned's imagination, his child was a daughter who looked like his sister. Quite often he was overcome with the certitude that he saw her. This or that stranger was his daughter.

The firm belief came on him in the most accidental of ways. He might, for instance, be walking on an ordinary day, perhaps a March Saturday in Toronto, on his way to the record stores on Yonge Street. The air is still chill, but everything glistens with spring promise. And there in the anonymous crowd ahead of him is a girl – the right age – and he will be certain that she is in fact his daughter.

Why is she here? She is with friends, laughing, wearing jeans and a sky blue jacket. He hurries to catch up, tries to pass them so he can get a better look at her face. She and her friends are spread out across the sidewalk. She half turns to say something to a friend and they are convulsed in repulsive giggle fits.

It must not, should not, be her. How does he know that his child is a girl anyway? As illogical as it is, his sense of conviction has a steel grip on him. The girl on the street ahead of him is chattering in an overly animated manner, as if the public street were her private stage.

She and her friends have learned their style from television. Their swift, snappy, bright-eyed interchanges are modeled on sitcom repartee. The lines are delivered in an insincere, perky, pert way. It is a style of putting off, putting down, putting in place. Would any daughter of his be such an airhead?

Yes, is the dour truth he acknowledges. The girl and her friends are getting further and further ahead of him. No matter. In other places, at other times, he will have this same haunting experience.

"My God," said Gil after Ned described his hauntings, "That must be terrible."

"Yes," said Ned. "So I've lost two children. Funny, I'm just as sure that the other one would have been a boy."

He smiled bitterly down at the tablecloth.

"Say," said Gil, getting up. "you were going to show me Trevor's collection. I have quite a few myself. Nothing really valuable."

Miriam had mentioned that Trevor had managed to gather a rather awesome number of old books, some rare, some odd, some curious.

"I have a whole line of the old Boni and Liverwright Modern Library classics. Remember those? Uh, well, limp leather, titles stamped in gold."

"When I was a kid, I used to take them off the shelves in the second-hand shops just to feel them in my hand," he went on. "You could have worse vices."

He stopped and the last words hung with more importance than he had meant.

"Trevor has forty-two copies of *The Rubáiyát*," said Miriam. "Different ones, I mean. All sizes, different illustrations. Maybe it's forty-three."

"I have a few myself," said Gil. "The one that's boxed? With the Dulac illustrations? There must be five million different editions of it, eh? Could we see them?"

"Sure," said Miriam. "They're in the library." She gestured off to the left.

"In the glassed-in bookcase," she said. "Look, I'll show you...."

She led him into the library. Gil remembered Trevor's office at Tecumseh. The same incredible sense of too much going on. Books opened, face down, some journals holding down a sheaf of papers. Books crowded on the shelves, other books slotted in on top of them, piles of books here and there.

"I gave him that library lamp a couple of Christmases ago," Miriam said. "He said it made him feel academic."

"And those over there," she gestured. "Those are my beach books. Popcorn books. I recycle them at a store in Leamington. I just devour them. Trevor liked the odd mystery. The kind with a swastika on the cover? After the war, a CIA cover-up."

"I like those too," Gil said. "*The Schweinhund Conspiracy*. Titles like that? I've read so many that I sometimes buy the same one again."

"The treasures are in here," said Miriam, lifting a glass front on a bookshelf. "Not real treasures. He used to say he would like to own a second-hand bookshop. Except that he would never sell anything. Only buy."

"Me too!" Gil cried. "I always had this secret hankering. Only I'd go bankrupt in a week."

He touched the backs of the books. The two-volume Random House Proust. A dark green *Walden*. And a whole shelf of the *Rubáiyát*. Gil touched the spines of the books. He started to take out the Thoreau and stopped, gently shut the glass door.

"Okay," he said, "okay, I'll look later on. Later on."

Miriam turned off the library lamp. They went back to the porch.

"A lot of tears have been spilled in this place," said Ned. "Generous tears, helpless, gushing, outpouring tears. Oh, all the weeping. So much water spilled and gone and under the bridge."

"Remember the story of Aunt Harriet?" said April. "Daddy told it and he thought it was a tragedy, and it was, only you and I could hardly keep a straight face."

"She the one who ran off to get married in Indiana?" said Miriam.

"No," said April. "Harriet was the one who was driving and went into a ditch during a storm and drowned."

"I thought she died of diphtheria," said Ned. "Or something like that. One of those nineteenth century diseases. Cholera?"

"It was definitely the car," said April firmly. "Don't you remember? It must have been an open car, like a Model T with brass lamps. And when she went into the ditch it turned over. It was morning before they found her. Now that I think of it, I wonder why we ever did think it was comical. It's a very sad story."

"Trevor was the only one of his family that survived," said Miriam. "I mean aside from the one who ran off to get married. Why did she have to run away?"

"Married a bad sort," said Ned. "What they called a drummer in those days. Travelling salesman. He abandoned her someplace. Toledo or somewhere. She got married again. Died young. That was Aunt Julia."

"There's something so comforting about family history," said Miriam. "I remember being all confused about how this or that cousin was related to me. I could never figure out 'once removed' and why certain relatives were forever out of favor."

"Yes," said Gil. "I think that's why some of the families on TV shows are so popular. You know when Lucy – *I Love Lucy?* – anyway when she had a baby the studio got all sorts of baby gifts. Like the audience loved her and the baby more than maybe their own."

"Babies on TV never need to be changed," said Ned. "You know," he turned to April. "The thing about Welles is that he justifies watching TV by in tel ect u liz ing it."

"Right?" He turned to Gil. "Because you preferred Kate Jackson to the other Angels, that made you special? She was *so* intelligent."

"Tell me, really," he said, leaning forward to look seriously into Gil's face. "Didn't you think things began going to pot when Farrah joined the team? Fess up. All that sensual *hair*. Of course, you could always intellectualize the hard-ons you got watching her."

"Ned," Gil said. "If you don't get off my back, I swear I'm going to beat the shit out of you."

Gil stood up. He stood in front of Ned, who peered up at him with a quizzical expression.

"Maybe you can beat me. You're bigger. But I'm not going to take any more shit from you."

"OK," said Ned in a mild voice. "I was just making noises. If you want to fight later on, we can go out on the lawn."

"Stop it, you two," said Miriam. "This is tough enough to get through without people fighting on the grass."

"You're right, Miriam," Gil stuttered. "I'm sorry,"

"So you *do* have a temper," April said. "Good. It's a

good thing to lose it once in a while."

"Oh, sit down," said Miriam.

"I for one," Ned said, getting up with a grunt, "am going to have a drink. Not a nightcap. Not a digestif. Not a little drinkee. A drink. okay? We'll tussle later, pal. This town ain't big enough for the two of us."

He paused at the door.

"'Of all the gin joints and all the towns of the world,'" he recited in a burlesque Bogart accent. "Is that the line? It was Mother's favourite movie."

"Yes," said April. "Of course it was."

GIL WOKE UP SUDDENLY. For a moment he didn't know where he was. Then he remembered. He was on the sofa bed in the glassed-in room. He looked up through the glass roof at the clear sky. Tomorrow would be a clear day. Maybe a day without wind or rain. So the ashes could be finally scattered. And that would be the end of something. And then something else could begin. Gilbert Welles, archivist, curator of someone else's work. Always a bridesmaid. Ned, that swine bastard.

But it was true. And now perhaps it was time to get off the circuit. Stop what he secretly thought of as the Welles Mouse Race Circus. Give a recital in a third-rate venue so he could claim that he gave recitals when he applied for a grant. So he could wave the grant, offer it as evidence that he deserved a short-term artist-in-residence post which would give him entree to other third-rate recitals.

And always back there waiting was Zwingli. Each

year a cliffhanger at contract time. Poor pitifully meagre tenure-less Instructor Welles, scrambling, running in circles in the Mouse Race Circus.

Time to get off, get out, settle back with a sigh of relief into mediocrity, the sham over at last. With this soothing thought, Gil was sinking back to sleep when he heard a stealthy sound. He got up and crouched toward the kitchen. The light from the opened refrigerator door lit up the figure bent to peer in. It was April. He made a throat-clearing noise.

"I didn't mean to wake anybody up," she said. "I'm looking for a pop or beer or *something*."

Gil bent next to her. They found two cans of diet root beer on the bottom shelf behind a tired and rusty head of lettuce.

"I don't want to keep you up," April said. "I can take this back to my room."

"No, listen. I don't seem to be sleepy at all. God! I think I *should* be."

He sat on the edge of the opened bed and April sat in a chair.

"I used to remember this house," April said. "When I was feeling lonely at boarding school. I'd shut my eyes and remember summers here and peanut butter sandwiches in the kitchen. My mother fed us peanut butter all summer. It's a wonder we didn't get scurvy. I felt like such an orphan in that school. My mother dies and I'm packed off to school. Lose all my friends. That's when I quit speed swimming. St. Edmund's didn't have a pool."

"Well," said Gil. "Think of it from your father's point.

Suddenly he's got to be father and mother and maybe he thinks it would be better for you with the nuns...."

"Daddy was an agnostic," said April. "Just like his father, he used to say. Of course his mother was Catholic. So maybe he did think the nuns would be a good influence on me. If they were, it sure hasn't shown up yet. Of course, I've got lots of time to develop a strong character."

"I'm a Catholic," Gil said. "I mean I'm supposed to be one. It's what I put down in census forms. I keep meaning to think about it. The Church I mean. Read up on it. Aquinas. All that."

"I don't suppose he had any last-minute doubts, do you think?" said April. "Like *Brideshead*. One of those deathbed things. But Miriam would have known."

In the light from the one lamp they had lit, April looked young. Or maybe it wasn't so much young as vulnerable. She was looking thoughtfully into a dark corner of the room, away from Gil, as she spoke. Then she looked directly at him.

At him and into him. Or so it seemed to him. Suddenly he was overcome with a pang of desire he had not felt in years. And he could tell that she knew and, yes, accepted. He knew that. He stood up and moved towards her, knelt clumsily, put his arms around her. She twisted around in the chair to receive him. They stood, and both of them pulled at her robe. His erection was painful. It leapt in his pyjamas like a hooked trout.

Then they were on the bed and he hovered over her, her hand was guiding him in and he came. All over her thighs, hand and the bed he would have to sleep in later. "I'm sorry," he started to say, but she shushed him, held him, cradled him, and they almost went to sleep.

Then she shifted out from under him and began to pull her nightgown on. He had another erection, not as Wagnerian as the first, but a perfectly useful one. He reached out for her.

She went back to her bed in the false dawn and he lay in a half sleep. What was going to happen now?

April lay awake thinking of what she could say in the morning. Don't worry, she would say. I mean whatever is going to happen will....

Silly. Vapid. No. She would begin: I've learned not to trust happiness. Not to hope for too much.

No. Better to begin: I'm going back to Chicago and you are going back to Toronto....

Suddenly she had a picture of Gil and Ned on the same train going back to Toronto and fighting in the aisles, a conductor trying to pull them apart. She had to smother a giggle fit.

But I'm going to come back, she would say. And you'll be at the Tecumseh library, won't you?

What would he say? Would he say that he loved her? Or say look, this was all a mistake. Grief-induced irrational behavior. In cold light of day, it will not work at all.

Or would he say, his face all loving foolish as it had been a little while ago, I love you and always have.

She fell asleep with the comforting words in her mind, almost as if they had been spoken and were true.

NED WOKE UP to what he imagined were the damp sounds of lovemaking. Odd. Perhaps a dream. There was only the steady sound of the lake waves on the rocks at the shore. His mouth was very dry. The bathroom was so very far away and the way was dark. He might bang into some damn thing and wake everybody up. He wanted a drink of water. Did he need to piss? Could he go back to sleep without satisfying either need? The problem loomed large in the dark.

He tried to remember Heather's face. Her Rachmaninoff eyes. The eyes of a Russian tragedienne. Another word he seemed to be fond of. Ever since Heather had left him – no, *fled* was the word, as if from a burning building, she appeared more and more beautiful in his memory. Absence makes the heart more stupid, maudlin, wet.

There was something essential and tough in Heather. Tough as a Russian winter. Images from *Dr. Zhivago:* Vast open space. Fields of snow that went on forever. Leathery faces of enduring peasants. Fields again, this time in bloom.

But she would not let him in. A quote from a poet. No. She was through with him. Irrevocably. Pity welled in him. He caught his breath as he almost sobbed aloud. Nothing to be done about it. He thought he already had accepted it, but there were times like this, in the night, when he was vulnerable, when an impossible hope –

He had kicked the life out of her. Not only the child she had been carrying, but any hope of any other. The crude and brutal truth. He was lucky he wasn't in prison. What cons did to baby killers. She had lied so nobly at the hospital. They were not convinced, he knew. A gallant lie. Her final gift to him.

He still had the immediate problem of a full bladder and fierce thirst. Fuck everybody. If he woke them up, so what. He groped his way down the hall. He could hear rain sluicing through the downspouts. Another postponement? Oh father, he thought, when can I finally say goodbye to you?

GIL WOKE UP. It was light out, but it felt very early. A day to walk out on the promenade and to the café for early coffee. The beach empty at this hour except for one swimmer out bravely in the waves. Then the swimmer comes out of the surf and comes up towards the promenade, towelling her hair.

She sees him and waves. He waves back and watches her walk toward him. Today they will leave the hotel and motor further down the coast. There is a little village where they will have *demi-pension*. In the afternoons they will nap and wake to the sound of metal shutters being raised. From somewhere nearby a piano is being played. Someone is playing Ravel. Here, under the glass roof, he catches himself beginning to whistle along with the piano.

He looked up at the sky through the glass roof. It was overcast. Droplets of rain were running down the glass. Maybe the scattering would have to be postponed again. Whatever was going to happen, he could handle it. He turned on his side and closed his eyes.

Ravel. Urgent, importunate like a lover's fevered protestations. Triumphant, passionate, intense and open as a lover's foolish loving face. Someone is wetting down the dust in the *pension*'s courtyard. Their room is waiting for them.

Gil was awake before anybody else. He closed the folding bed. Rain, not as hard as yesterday's, was falling. In the pale light, the lawn was an eye-aching green. It looked like an all-day rain.

In the kitchen he opened and closed cupboard doors. Where did she keep the instant coffee? He tried not to make any noise.

"Morning."

April's voice was close to his ear. She gave him a swift brush-of-the-cheek kiss.

"Don't say anything," she said. "We're past promise making and all aren't we?"

Her smile was brave and perky. She looked sweet standing there in her bunny-soft robe. He felt thick and old. He always did before the first and second coffee in the mornings.

He started to say something and Ned came lurching into the kitchen groaning *morning, morning*. April thought she heard Gil say, "and always have."

"MIRIAM," said April, frowning over her coffee cup. "This is probably a dumb thing to ask and you can just tell me it's none of my business –"

"God," said Miriam. "Say it, just *say* it."

"Well I was wondering if, near the end, did my father ever express any doubts about, what I mean is, his religion…."

"He told me he was baptized," Miriam said. "His mother was Irish and all. But he said he was an optimistic agnostic. Like his father."

"I have all sorts of negative feelings about church," said Miriam. "My parents were evangelicals. I was what they call shunned years ago. It's like disowning. They didn't come to our wedding. Funny, Trevor said when he met me he thought that I was a nun. Or an ex-nun."

"It's that serene look you have," said Ned. "Is there any tomato juice? Just tomato juice, I swear."

"Anyhow," Miriam said, "he once quoted Thoreau's last words to me. About how he and God had never quarreled."

Gil was wondering if the Catholic Church had changed its stand on divorced people getting married. How could he ask?

"I was wondering…" he said.

"If it rains again," said Ned, "we have a real problem. I mean, it's not as if I'm trying to hustle things along, but it's like pulling off a band-aid very slowly. Is this a crisis? Should we be boiling water, lots of water?"

"The women could be tearing their slips for bandages," Gil said.

"I think you just made a real joke," Ned smiled. "There may be hope for all of us."

"It's going to clear," said Miriam.

Later on April found Gil in the library holding one of the books.

"Look at this one," he smiled. "The Gilbert James illustrations. 'And in the fire of spring the winter garment of repentance fling.'"

He looked at her.

"I don't want to muck things up. Help me not to screw up again."

Miriam had once been a small intense woman. Now she had put on a bit of weight. Her face was naturally round and looked a little moonish.

Still, Ned thought, she had nice brown eyes. It was very difficult for him to look directly at her. A woman his father had loved and lived with.

"I think I should apologize to you," he said. They were still in the kitchen. April and Gil were talking in the library. The rain had stopped, but it was grey and overcast.

"Oh," she sighed, "maybe you should tell your sister that you're sorry. Anyway, I think I know what you're going through. I've already gone through it. I'm a bit burned out now. You know, your father kept on thinking of reasons why we shouldn't get married. He kept up this 'when I'm seventy you'll be' routine. I told him I was never too good at math. Besides, a few years of happiness is maybe all anybody can expect in one life. It's better than nothing."

Ned stared out at the sky over the lake.

"Yes," he said. "Anything is better than nothing."

A coffin slid into fierce brilliant fire. Was that how it was done? Cemeteries were comforting in a way. Statues of mourning angels, draped urns and flowers growing. They shall not grow old as we who are left grow old. Soothing funereal words. Oh, but the harsh final fact of burning. The clouds were slowly, slowly lifting.

CREMATION. The residue of an average-sized person comprises from five to seven pounds of ash and bone fragments. Some crematoriums will reduce large bone fragments to pebble size. Crematoriums usually regard certain types of caskets as unacceptable because they cause excessive smoke in the combustion chamber. Plastic or fiberglass for instance. Representatives of the crematorium are careful in their choice of words when dealing with the bereaved. They speak of "preparation for inurnment or interment" and "cremated remains" or "human remains" because the word "ashes" suggests, almost automatically, the act of scattering. Nobody makes any money out of scattering.

At the crematorium, if there is a service (there was none for Trevor), following it the casket is removed to the committal chamber. In some cases the catafalque is mechanically equipped to lower the casket through the floor, or to slide the casket through a door, or a curtain is drawn.

Sometimes a witness is designated by the family to be present at the beginning of the process in order that they may be assured that cremation has actually taken place. Flowers usually are not put into the furnace because often floral arrangements contain non-combustible wires.

Once the casket is in the cremation chamber, intense heat is applied by a series of oil or gas flames. The process requires about one and a half hours to complete.

The water content of the body is evaporated by the intense heat. The carbon-containing portions of the body are incinerated and the inorganic ash of the bone structure is all that remains. And the grief.

THE LAKE WATER had a slate-grey look under the oppressive sky. By afternoon the cloud cover rolled back towards the Ohio side and the water took on a stiff blue hue.

Miriam carried the box of ashes. It was square and about the size, Gil thought, to contain a softball. The four of them went down the slope and down the steps. It was just past four and the wind was picking up. The waves sluiced up and over the lichened rocks, sucking back and up again, throwing a spray over the dock. The boathouse, April thought, certainly needed some attention. The paint was chipped and peeling and the windows were grimed.

"I'll do this, if nobody minds," Miriam said. She had to raise her voice over the sound of the waves.

None of the others objected. Miriam opened the box and spilled the ashes down on the rocks. Some wafted off in the wind, but most hit the rocks and were swiftly washed away.

Gil thought, *somebody should say something. Some final word.* But he himself could think of nothing appropriate. They turned in silence and went back up. Halfway up, the angle of the slope cut the wind. Gil turned to look back. The long slanted light of afternoon made his eyes hurt.

They went on up the stairs. They came up. Far off, against the high pack of clouds, a ferry went resolutely on towards the island. Two sailboats lay over on a reach towards the Point. Tomorrow would be a fine day. At the crest, they looked back down the slope at the water shimmering innocently in the sun. Then they turned to start up the lawn towards the house. They went on up to it.

Acknowledgements

GRATEFUL ACKNOWLEDGMENT IS DUE TO THE editors and publishers of the magazines, books and anthologies in which some of the stories collected here earlier appeared:

"Fathers and Daughters," *Denver Quarterly* (Spring, 1972)
"The May Irwin-John C. Rice Kiss," *Malahat Review* (1975)
"The Search for Sarah Grace," *Canadian Fiction Magazine* (Spring, 1976)
"Midwinter," *Ontario Review* (Spring-Summer, 1978)
"At the Going Down of the Sun and in the Morning," *Saturday Night* (March, 1981)
"Freeze Frames," *Canadian Fiction Magazine* (Summer, 1985)
"Falling in Place," *Ontario Review* (Fall-Winter, 1988)
"Terror Exile or Despair," *Antigonish Review* (Summer, 1993)
"Hubba-Hubba," *Quarry* (Vol. 44:3, 1995)
"Waterfalls," *Ontario Review* (Spring-Summer, 1996)

"The Island of Sponges," *Queens Quarterly* (Summer, 1998)

Salt, Sono Nis Press (1975)

The Search for Sarah Grace, Black Moss Press (1977)

Spectral Evidence, Black Moss Press (1985)

Fox Trot, Black Moss Press (1994)

"Freeze Frames" was also in *Moving off the Map* an anthology edited by Geoff Hancock, Black Moss Press, (1986)

"Terror Exile or Despair" was selected for *94: Best Canadian Stories,* Oberon Press (1944)

"Midwinter" was broadcast on *CBC's Anthology* on Feb. 10, 1979.

I also thank Geoffrey Ursell and Barbara Sapergia, who had faith in this book, and Dave Margoshes, my editor, who made me look closely at the details, which, he said, have God in them. If my collection is better than its parts, it is due to him.

And, as I do each day, I thank my wife Margaret for loving me and believing in me. Without her, all this would be straw.

EUGENE MCNAMARA has published over a dozen volumes of poetry, including 1998's *Keeping in Touch: New and Selected Poems,* and four previous short story collections as well as two books of literary criticism. He is Professor Emeritus at the University of Windsor, where he was an English professor and, for many years, editor of *The Windsor Review.* McNamara has published stories in dozens of magazines in Canada and the US, and has had work in many anthologies, including *Best American Short Stories* and *Best Canadian Stories.* A native of Chicago, Eugene McNamara has lived with his wife in Windsor for over thirty years.